Praise for Ken Scholes and *Lamentation*

"This is the golden age of fantasy, with a dozen masters doing their best work. Then along comes Ken Scholes, with his amazing clarity, power, and invention, and shows us all how it's done. No more ponderous plotting—Scholes barely gives us time to breathe. Yet he creates vivid characters, a world thick with detail, and wonders we've never seen before. I wish my first novel had been this good. I wish all five volumes of this series were already published so I could read them now."

—Orson Scott Card

"This is fantasy as it should be. Scholes's subtle and complex plotting are the breadwinners here, but his world-building and political scheming bring home the bacon, as well. This reader has never read a freshman novel this good."

—*Romantic Times BOOKreviews*
(Top Pick, 4½ stars)

"As intricate as a Whymer maze, Ken Scholes's *Lamentation* will keep the reader up until the wee hours, winding through this splendid labyrinth. Bravo!"

—Dennis L. McKiernan, bestselling author
of the Mithgar series

"Ken Scholes is a hot new voice to watch for on the interesting frontier between science fiction and fantasy. He has a keen eye for action and a keen ear for the sounds of the human heart. Grab on now, because he's going places."

—Harry Turtledove

"Ken Scholes's *Lamentation* is an iconic SF story cloaked in fantasy, drawing raw material from classics such as *A Canticle for Leibowitz* and *Earth Abides*, but forging something new, with colorful characters, compelling scenes, and unfolding miracles." —Kevin J. Anderson, bestselling
coauthor of *Sandworms of Dune*

"Ken Scholes's *Lamentation* is a whale of a first novel, set in a world where technological magic has come and gone, and come again, where organized religion has attempted to recover and restore lost knowledge, if with a certain amount of censorship, where no one is quite what they seem, and where parental ambitions for offspring are filled with deep love and sacrifices, along with double double-crosses, conflicting motives, and tragedy."
—L. E. Modesitt, Jr.

"Ken Scholes is one of the better writers you've never heard of. . . . [*Last Flight of the Goddess*] is warm and loving and a very enticing invitation to look at any future item with the Scholes name on it."
—*Analog*

"*Lamentation* is literally a lament; the lament for the city of Windwir, a seat of ancient learning that is suddenly and terribly destroyed. Characters emerge—a boy leaving the city who witnessed the carnage, an old man who is closely linked to the city, a ruler of a nearby kingdom looking to rise to the challenge of the situation, and a mysterious figure and his daughter who seem to have been involved in events for a very long time indeed. The tone of the book is precise and just about exactly right: I was engaged from the opening page, stayed up late looking to finish it, and then begged Scholes to let me see the next book as soon as possible. If I had to give you shorthand for what the book is like I'd describe it as intelligent epic fantasy done right and written with all of the flab removed. It's nothing like George Martin's first Song of Ice and Fire novel, except, like that book, it has the chance of standing as an important book in the evolution of the epic fantasy form, is a delight, and is a book that readers are very likely to take to heart. It's one of the best first fantasies I've read in some time."
—Jonathan Strahan

Lamentation

KEN SCHOLES

TOR®
fantasy

A TOM DOHERTY ASSOCIATES BOOK
NEW YORK

This is a work of fiction. All of the characters, organizations, and events portrayed in this novel are either products of the author's imagination or are used fictitiously.

Portions of this novel originally appeared in the short story "Of Metal Men, Scarlet Thread and Dancing with the Sunrise," published in *Realms of Fantasy*, August 2006.

LAMENTATION

Copyright © 2009 by Kenneth G. Scholes

All rights reserved.

Map by David Cain

A Tor Book
Published by Tom Doherty Associates, LLC
175 Fifth Avenue
New York, NY 10010

www.tor-forge.com

Tor® is a registered trademark of Tom Doherty Associates, LLC.

ISBN 978-0-7653-6091-5

First Edition: February 2009
First Mass Market Edition: September 2009

Printed in the United States of America

0 9 8 7 6 5 4 3 2 1

This book is brought to you by the letter J:
For Jen, Jay, John and Jerry.
Thanks for helping me roll the rock.

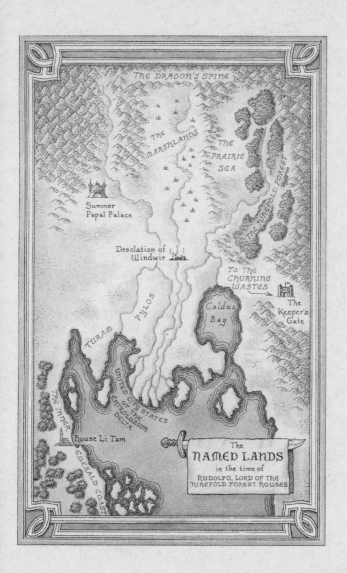

THE DRAGON'S SPINE

THE MARSHLANDS

THE PRAIRIE SEA

THE NINEFOLD FOREST

Summer Papal Palace

Desolation of Windwir

TO THE CHURNING WASTES

Caldus Bay

The Keeper's Gate

TURAM

PYLOS

UNITED CITY STATES OF THE ENTROLUSIAN DELTA

THE INNER EMERALD COAST

House Li Tam

The
NAMED LANDS
in the time of
RUDOLFO, LORD OF THE
NINEFOLD FOREST HOUSES

Prelude

Windwir is a city of paper and robes and stone.

It crouches near a wide and slow-moving river at the edge of the Named Lands. Named for a poet turned Pope—the first Pope in the New World. A village in the forest that became the center of the world. Home of the Androfrancine Order and their Great Library. Home of many wonders both scientific and magickal.

One such wonder watches from high above.

It is a bird made of metal, a gold spark against the blue expanse that catches the afternoon sun. The bird circles and waits.

When the song begins below, the golden bird watches the melody unfold. A shadow falls across the city and the air becomes still. Tiny figures stop moving and look up. A flock of birds lifts and scatters. The sky is torn and fire rains down until only utter darkness remains. Darkness and heat.

The heat catches the bird and tosses it farther into the sky. A gear slips; the bird's wings compensate, but a billowing, black cloud takes an eye as it passes.

The city screams and then sighs seven times, and after the seventh sigh, sunlight returns briefly to the scorched land. The plain is blackened, the spires and walls and towers all brought down into craters where basements collapsed beneath the footprint of Desolation. A forest of bones, left whole by ancient blood magick, stands on the smoking, pockmarked plain.

Darkness swallows the light again as a pillar of smoke

and ash blots out the sun. Finally, the golden bird flees south-west.

It easily overtakes the other birds, their wings smoking and beating furiously against the hot winds, messages tied to their feet with threads of white or red or black.

Sparking and popping, the golden bird speeds low across the landscape and dreams of its waiting cage.

Chapter

1

Rudolfo

Wind swept the Prairie Sea and Rudolfo chased after it, laughing and riding low in the saddle as he raced his Gypsy Scouts. The afternoon sun glinted gold on the bending grass and the horses pounded out their song.

Rudolfo savored the wide yellow ocean of grass that separated the Ninefold Forest Houses from one another and from the rest of the Named Lands—it was his freedom in the midst of duty, much as the oceans must have been for the seagoing lords of the Elder Days. He smiled and spurred his stallion.

It had been a fine time in Glimmerglam, his first Forest House. Rudolfo had arrived before dawn. He'd taken his breakfast of goat cheese, whole grain bread and chilled pear wine beneath a purple canopy that signified justice. While he ate, he heard petitions quietly as Glimmerglam's steward brought the month's criminals forward. Because he felt particularly benevolent, he sent two thieves into a year's servitude to the shopkeepers they'd defiled, while sending the single murderer to his Physicians of Penitent Torture on Tormentor's Row. He dismissed three cases of prostitution and then afterward, hired two of them onto his monthly rotation.

By lunchtime, Rudolfo had proven Aetero's Theory of Compensatory Seduction decidedly false and he celebrated with creamed pheasant served over brown rice and wild mushrooms.

Then with his belly full, he'd ridden out with a shout, his Gypsy Scouts racing to keep up with him.

A good day indeed.

"What now," the Captain of his Gypsy Scouts asked him, shouting above the pounding hooves.

Rudolfo grinned. "What say you, Gregoric?"

Gregoric returned the smile and it made his scar all the more ruthless. His black scarf of rank trailed out behind him, ribboning on the wind. "We've seen to Glimmerglam, Rudoheim and Friendslip. I think Paramo is the closest."

"Then Paramo it is." That would be fitting, Rudolfo thought. It couldn't come close to Glimmerglam's delights, but it had held on to its quaint, logging village atmosphere for at least a thousand years and that was an accomplishment. They floated their timber down the Rajblood River just as they had in the first days, retaining what they needed to build some of the world's most intricately crafted woodwork. The lumber for Rudolfo's manors came from the trees of Paramo. The furniture they made rolled out by the wagonload and the very best found its way into the homes of kings and priests and nobility from all over the Named Lands.

He would dine on roast boar tonight, listen to the boasting and flatulence of his best men, and sleep on the ground with a saddle beneath his head—the life of a Gypsy King. And tomorrow, he'd sip chilled wine from the navel of a log camp dancer, listen to the frogs in the river shallows mingled with her sighs, and then sleep in the softest of beds on the summer balcony of his third forest manor.

Rudolfo smiled.

But as he rounded to the south, his smile faded. He reined in and squinted against the sunlight. The Gypsy Scouts followed his lead, whistling to their horses as they slowed, stopped and then pranced.

"Gods," Gregoric said. "What could cause such a thing?"

Southwest of them, billowing up above the horizon of forest-line that marked Rudolfo's farthest border, a distant pillar of black smoke rose like a fist in the sky.

Rudolfo stared and his stomach lurched. The size of the smoke cloud daunted him; it was impossible. He blinked as his mind unlocked enough for him to do the math, quickly calculating the distance and direction based on the sun and the few stars strong enough to shine by day.

"Windwir," he said, not even aware that he was speaking.

Gregoric nodded. "Aye, General. But what could do such a thing?"

Rudolfo looked away from the cloud to study his captain. He'd known Gregoric since they were boys, and had made him the youngest captain of the Gypsy Scouts at fifteen when Rudolfo himself was just twelve. They'd seen a lot together, but Rudolfo had never seen him pale before now.

"We'll know soon enough," Rudolfo said. Then he whistled his men in closer. "I want riders back to each of the houses to gather the Wandering Army. We have kin-clave with Windwir; their birds will be flying. We'll meet on the Western Steppes in one day; we'll be to Windwir's aid in three."

"Are we to magick the scouts, General?"

Rudolfo stroked his beard. "I think not." He thought for a moment. "But we should be ready," he added.

Gregoric nodded and barked out the orders.

As the nine Gypsy Scouts rode off, Rudolfo slipped from the saddle, watching the dark pillar. The column of smoke, as wide as a city, disappeared into the sky.

Rudolfo, Lord of the Ninefold Forest Houses, General of the Wandering Army, felt curiosity and fear dance a shiver along his spine.

"What if it's not there when we arrive?" he asked himself.

And he knew—but did not want to—that it wouldn't be, and that because of this, the world had changed.

Petronus

Petronus mended the last of the net and tucked it away in the prow of his boat. Another quiet day on the water, another day of little to show for it, but he was happy with that.

Tonight, he'd dine at the inn with the others, eating and drinking too much and finally breaking down into the raunchy limericks that made him famous up and down the coast of Caldus Bay. Petronus didn't mind being famous for that at all. Outside of his small village, most had no idea that more fame than that lay just beneath the surface.

Petronus the Fisherman had lived another life before returning to his nets and his boat. Prior to the day he chose to end that life, Petronus had lived a lie that, at times, felt more true than a child's love. Nonetheless, it was a lie that ate away at him until he stood up to it and laid it out thirty-three years ago.

Next week, he realized with a smile. He could go months without thinking about it now. When he was younger, it wasn't so. But each year, about a month before the anniversary of his rather sudden and creative departure, memories of Windwir, of its Great Library, of its robed Order, flooded him and he found himself tangled up in his past like a gull in a net.

The sun danced on the water, and he watched the silver waves flash against the hulls of ships both small and large. Overhead, a clear blue sky stretched as far as he could see and seabirds darted, shrieking their hunger as they dove for the small fish that dared swim near the surface.

One particular bird—a kingfisher—caught his eye and he followed it as it dipped and weaved. He turned with it, watching as it flexed its wings and glided, pushed back by a high wind that Petronus couldn't see or feel.

I've been pushed by such a wind, he thought, and with that thought, the bird suddenly shuddered in the air as the wind overcame it and pushed it farther back.

Then Petronus saw the cloud piling up on the horizon to the northwest.

He needed no mathematics to calculate the distance. He needed no time at all to know exactly what it was and what it meant.

Windwir.

Stunned, he slid to his knees, his eyes never leaving the tower of smoke that rose westward and north of Caldus Bay. It was close enough that he could see the flecks of fire in it as it roiled and twisted its way into the sky.

"'Oh my children,'" Petronus whispered, quoting the First Gospel of P'Andro Whym, "'what have you done to earn the wrath of heaven?'"

Jin Li Tam

Jin Li Tam bit back her laughter and let the fat Overseer try to reason with her.

"It's not seemly," Sethbert said, "for the consort of a king to ride sidesaddle."

She did not bother to remind him of the subtle differences between an Overseer and a king. Instead, she stayed with her point. "I do not intend to ride sidesaddle, either, my lord."

Jin Li Tam had spent most of the day cramped into the back of a carriage with the Overseer's entourage and she'd had enough of it. There was an army of horses to be had—saddles, too—and she meant to feel the wind on her face. Besides, she could see little from the inside of a carriage and she knew her father would want a full report.

A captain interrupted, pulling Sethbert aside and whispering urgently. Jin Li Tam took it as her cue to slip away in search of just the right horse—and to get a better idea of what was afoot.

She'd seen the signs for over a week. Messenger birds coming and going, cloaked couriers galloping to and fro at all hours of the night. Long meetings between old men in uniforms, hushed voices and then loud voices, and hushed voices again. And the army had come together quickly, brigades from each of the City States united under a common flag. Now, they stretched ahead and behind on the Whymer Highway, overflowing the narrow road to trample the fields and forests in their forced march north.

Try as she might, she had no idea why. But she knew the

scouts were magicked, and according to the Rites of Kin-Clave, that meant Sethbert and the Entrolusian City States were marching to war. And she also knew that very little lay north apart from Windwir—the great seat of the An-drofrancine Order—and farther north and east, Rudolfo's Ninefold Forest Houses. But both of those neighbors were Kin-Clave with the Entrolusians, and she'd not heard of any trouble they might be in that merited Entrolusian intervention.

Of course, Sethbert had not been altogether rational of late.

Though she cringed at the thought of it, she'd shared his bed enough to know that he was talking in his sleep and restless, unable to rise to the challenge of his young redheaded consort. He was also smoking more of the dried kallaber-ries, intermittently raging and rambling with his officers. Yet they followed him, so there had to be something. He didn't possess the charm or charisma to move an army on his own and he was too lazy to move them by ruthlessness, while lacking in the more favorable motivational skills.

"What are you up to?" she wondered out loud.

"Milady?" A young cavalry lieutenant towered over her on a white mare. He had another horse in tow behind him.

She smiled, careful to turn in such a way that he could see down her top just far enough to be rewarded, but not so far as to be improper. "Yes, Lieutenant?"

"Overseer Sethbert sends his compliments and requests that you join him forward." The young man pulled the horse around, offering her the reins.

She accepted and nodded. "I trust you will ride with me?"

He nodded. "He asked me to do so."

Climbing into the saddle, she adjusted her riding skirts and stretched up in the stirrups. Twisting, she could make out the end of the long line of soldiers behind and before her. She nudged the horse forward. "Then let's not keep the Overseer waiting."

Sethbert waited at a place where the highway crested a

rise. She saw the servants setting up his scarlet canopy at the road's highest point and wondered why they were stopping here, in the middle of nowhere.

He waved to her as she rode up. He looked flushed, even excited. His jowls shook and sweat beaded on his forehead. "It's nearly time," he said. "Nearly time."

Jin looked at the sky. The sun was at least four hours from setting. She looked back at him, then slid from the saddle. "Nearly time for what, my lord?"

They were setting up chairs now for them, pouring wine, preparing platters. "Oh you'll see," Sethbert said, placing his fat behind into a chair that groaned beneath him.

Jin Li Tam sat, accepted wine and sipped.

"This," Sethbert said, "is my finest hour." He looked over to her and winked. His eyes had that glazed over, far-away look they sometimes had during their more intimate moments. A look she wished she could afford the luxury of having during those moments as well and still be her father's spy.

"What—" But she stopped herself. Far off, beyond the forests and past the glint of the Third River as it wound its way northward, light flashed in the sky and a small crest of smoke began to lift itself on the horizon. The small crest expanded upward and outward, a column of black against the blue sky that kept growing and growing.

Sethbert chuckled and reached over to squeeze her knee. "Oh. It's better than I thought." She forced her eyes away for long enough to see his wide smile. "Look at that."

And now, there were gasps and whispers that grew to a buzz around them. There were arms lifted, fingers pointing north. Jin Li Tam looked away again to take in the pale faces of Sethbert's generals and captains and lieutenants, and she knew that if she could see all the way back to the line upon line of soldiers and scouts behind her, she'd see the same fear and awe upon their faces, too. Perhaps, she thought, turning her eyes back onto that awful cloud as it lifted higher and higher into the sky, that fear and awe painted every face that could see it for miles and miles around. Perhaps everyone knew what it meant.

"Behold," Sethbert said in a quiet voice, "the end of the Androfrancine tyranny. Windwir is fallen." He chuckled. "Tell that to your father."

And when his chuckle turned into a laugh, Jin Li Tam heard the madness in him for the first time.

Neb

Neb stood in the wagon and watched Windwir stretch out before him. It had taken them five hours to climb the low hills that hemmed the great city in, and now that he could see it he wanted to take it all in, to somehow imprint it on his brain. He was leaving that city for the first time and it would be months before he saw it again.

His father, Brother Hebda, stood as well, stretching in the morning sun. "And you have the bishop's letters of introduction and credit?" Brother Hebda asked.

Neb wasn't paying attention. Instead, the massive city filled his view—the cathedrals, the towers, the shops and houses pressed in close against the walls. The colors of kin-clave flew over her, mingled with the royal blue colors of the Androfrancine Order, and even from this vantage, he could see the robed figures bustling about.

His father spoke again and Neb started. "Brother Hebda?"

"I asked after the letters of introduction and credit. You were reading them this morning before we left and I told you to make sure you put them back in their pouch."

Neb tried to remember. He remembered seeing them on his father's desk and asking if he could look at them. He remembered reading them, being fascinated with the font and script of them. But he couldn't remember putting them back. "I think I did," he said.

They climbed into the back of the wagon and went through

each pouch, pack and sack. When they didn't find them, his father sighed.

"I'll have to go back for them," he said.

Neb looked away. "I'll come with you, Brother Hebda."

His father shook his head. "No. Wait here for me."

Neb felt his face burn hot, felt a lump in his throat. The bulky scholar reached out and squeezed Neb's shoulder. "Don't fret over it. I should've checked it myself." He squinted, looking for the right words. "I'm just . . . not used to having anyone else about."

Neb nodded. "Can I do anything while you're gone?"

Brother Hebda had smiled. "Read. Meditate. Watch the cart. I'll be back soon."

$\sim$

Neb drew Whymer Mazes in the dirt and tried to concentrate on his meditation. But everything called him away. First the sounds of the birds, the wind, the champing of the horse. And the smell of evergreen and dust and horse-sweat. And *his* sweat, too, now dried after five long hours in the shade.

He'd waited for years. Every year he'd petitioned the headmaster for a grant, and now, just one year shy of manhood and the ability to captain his own destiny without the approval of the Franci Orphanage, he'd finally been released to study with his father. The Androfrancines could not prove their vow of chastity if they had children on their arms, so the Franci Orphanage looked after them all. None knew their birth-mothers and only a few knew their fathers.

Neb's father had actually come to see him at least twice a year and had sent him gifts and books from far off places while he dug in Churning Wastes, studying times before the Age of Laughing Madness. And one time, years ago, he'd even told Neb that someday he'd bring the boy along so that he could see what the love of P'Andro Whym was truly about, a love so strong that it would cause a man to sacrifice his only begotten son.

Finally, Neb received his grant.

And here at the beginning of his trip to the Wastes, he'd already disappointed the man he most wanted to make proud.

⟋⟍

Five hours had passed, and even though there was no way to pick him out from such a distance, Neb stood every so often and looked down toward the city, watching the gate near the river docks.

He'd just sat down from checking yet again when the hair on his arms stood up and the world went completely silent but for a solitary, tinny voice far away. He leaped to his feet. Then, a heavy buzzing grew in his ears and his skin tingled from a sudden wind that seemed to bend the sky. The buzzing grew to a shriek and his eyes went wide as they filled with both light and darkness, and he stood transfixed, arms stretched wide, standing at his full height, mouth hanging open.

The ground shook and he watched the city wobble as the shrieking grew. Birds scattered out from the city, specks of brown and white and black that he could barely see in the ash and debris that the sudden, hot wind stirred.

Spires tumbled and rooftops collapsed. The walls trembled and gave up, breaking apart as they fell inward. Fires sprang up—a rainbow kaleidoscope of colors—licking at first and then devouring. Neb watched the tiny robed forms of bustling life burst into flame. He watched lumbering dark shadows move through the roiling ash, laying waste to anything that dared to stand. He watched flaming sailors leap from burning bows as the ships cast off and begged the current save them. But ships and sailors alike kept burning, green and white, as they sank beneath the waters. There was the sound of cracking stone and boiling water, the smell of heated rock and charred meat. And the pain of the Desolation of Windwir racked his own body. Neb shrieked when he felt this heart burst or that body bloat and explode.

The world roared at him, fire and lightning leaping up and down the sky as the city of Windwir screamed and burned.

All the while, an invisible force held Neb in place and he screamed with his city, eyes wide open, mouth wide open, lungs pumping furiously against the burning air.

A single bird flew out from the dark cloud, hurtling past Neb's head and into the forest behind him. For the briefest moment he thought it was made of gold.

Hours later, when nothing was left but the raging fire, Neb fell to his knees and sobbed into the dirt. The tower of ash and smoke blotted out the sun. The smell of death choked his nostrils. He sobbed there until he had no more tears and then he lay shaking and twitching, his eyes opening and closing on the desolation below.

Finally, Neb sat up and closed his eyes. Mouthing the Gospel Precepts of P'Andro Whym, Founder of the Androfrancines, he meditated upon the folly in his heart.

The folly that had caused his father's death.

Chapter

2

Jin Li Tam

Jin Li Tam watched the grass and ferns bend as Sethbert's magicked scouts slipped to and from their hidden camp. Because her father had trained her well, she could just make out the outline of them when they passed beneath the rays of sunlight that pierced the canopy of forest. But in shadows, they were ghosts—silent and transparent. She waited to the side of the trail just outside of camp, watching.

Sethbert had pulled them up short, several leagues outside of Windwir. He'd ridden ahead with his scouts and generals, twitching and short-tempered upon leaving but grinning and

chortling upon his return. Jin Li Tam noted that he was the
only one who looked pleased. The others looked pale, shaken,
perhaps even mortified. Then she caught a bit of their conversation.

"I'd have never agreed to this if I'd known it could do
that," one of the generals was saying.

Sethbert shrugged. "You knew it was a possibility. You've
sucked the same tit the rest of us have—P'Andro Whym and
Xhum Y'Zir and the Age of the Laughing Madness and all
that other sour Androfrancine milk. You know the stories,
Wardyn. It was always a possibility."

"The library is *gone*, Sethbert."

"Not necessarily," another voice piped up. This was the Androfrancine that had met them on the road the day before—an
apprentice to someone who worked in the library. Of course,
Jin Li Tam had also seen him around the palace; he had
brought Sethbert the metal man last year and had visited from
time to time in order to teach it new tricks. He continued
speaking. "The mechoservitors have long memories. Once
we've gathered them up, they could help restore some of the
library."

"Possibly," Sethbert said in an uninterested voice. "Though
I think ultimately they may have more strategic purposes."

The general gasped. "You can't mean—"

Sethbert raised a hand as he caught sight of Jin Li Tam to
the side of the trail. "Ah, my lovely consort awaiting my return, all aflutter, no doubt."

She slipped from the shadows and curtsied. "My lord."

"You should've seen it, love," Sethbert said, his eyes wide
like a child's. "It was simply stunning."

She felt her stomach lurch. "I'm sure it was a sight to behold."

Sethbert smiled. "It was everything I hoped for. And more."
He looked around, as if suddenly remembering his men.
"We'll talk later," he told them. He watched them ride on,
then turned back to Jin. "We're expecting a state banquet tomorrow," he told her in a low voice. "I'm told Rudolfo and

his Wandering Army will be arriving sometime before noon."
His eyes narrowed. "I will expect you to shine for me."

She'd not met the Gypsy King before, though her father
had and had spoken of him as formidable and ruthless, if
slightly foppish. The Ninefold Forest Houses kept largely to
themselves, far out on the edge of the New World away from
the sleeping cities of the Three Rivers Delta and the Emerald
Coasts.

Jin Li Tam bowed. "Don't I always shine for you, my lord?"

Sethbert laughed. "I think you only shine for your father,
Jin Li Tam. I think I'm just a whore's tired work." He leaned
in and grinned. "But Windwir changes that, doesn't it?"

Sethbert calling her a whore did not surprise her, and it
did not bristle her, either. Sethbert truly *was* her tired work.
But the fact that he'd openly spoken of her father twice now
in so many days gave Jin pause. She wondered how long
he'd known. Not too long, she hoped.

Jin swallowed. "What do you mean?"

His face went dark. "We both know that your father has
also played the whore, dancing for coins in the lap of the Androfrancines, whispering tidbits of street gossip into their
hairy ears. His time is past. You and your brothers and sisters
will soon be orphans. You should start to think about what
might be best for you before you run out of choices." Then
the light returned to him and his voice became almost cheer-
ful. "Dine with me tonight," he said, before standing up on
his tiptoes to kiss her cheek. "We'll celebrate the beginning
of new things."

Jin shuddered and hoped he didn't notice.

She was still standing in the same place, shaking with rage
and fear, long after Sethbert had returned whistling to camp.

Petronus

Petronus couldn't sleep. He couldn't fish or eat, either. For
two days, he sat on his porch and watched the smoke of Windwir gradually dissipate to the northwest. Few birds came to

Caldus Bay, but ships passed through daily on their way to the Emerald Coasts. Still, he knew it was too early for any word. And he knew from the smoke that there could be no good news, regardless.

Hyram, the old Mayor and Petronus's closest friend from boyhood, stopped by each afternoon to check on him. "Still no word," he told Petronus on the third afternoon. "A few City Staters said Sethbert marched north with his army to honor Entrolusia's kin-clave. Though some are saying he started riding a full day before the cloud appeared. And the Gypsy King rallied his Wandering Army on the Western Steppes. Their quartermasters were in town buying up food-stuffs."

Petronus nodded, eyes never leaving the sky. "They're the closest of Windwir's kin-clave. They're probably there now."

"Aye." Hyram shifted uncomfortably on the bench. "So what will you do?"

"Do?" Petronus blinked. "I won't do anything. It's not my place."

Hyram snorted. "It's more your place than anyone else's."

Petronus looked away from the sky now, his eyes narrowing as he took in his friend. "Not anymore," he said. "I left that life." He swallowed. "Besides, we don't know how bad things are."

"Two days of smoke," Hyram said. "We *know* how bad things are. And how many Androfrancines would be outside the city during the Week of Knowledgeable Conference?"

Petronus thought for a moment. "A thousand, maybe two."

"Out of a hundred thousand?" Hyram asked.

Petronus nodded. "And that's just the Order. Windwir was twice that easily." Then he repeated himself. "But we don't know how bad things are."

"You could send a bird," Hyram offered.

Petronus shook his head. "It's not my place. I left the Order behind. You of all people know why."

Hyram and Petronus had both left for Windwir together when they were young men. Tired of the smell of fish on their hands, eager for knowledge and adventure, they'd both become acolytes. A few years later, Hyram had returned home for a simpler life while Petronus had gone on to climb the ecclesiastical ranks and make his mark upon that world.

Hyram nodded. "I do know why. I don't know how you stomached it for as long as you did. But you loved it at one point."

"I still love it," Petronus said. "I just love what it was . . . love how it started and what it stood for. Not what it became. P'Andro Whym would weep to see what we've done with it. He never meant for us to grow rich upon the spoils of knowledge, for us to make or break kings with a word." Petronus's words became heavy with feeling as he quoted a man whose every written word he had at one point memorized: "Behold, I set you as a tower of reason against this Age of Laughing Madness, and knowledge shall be thy light and the darkness shall flee from it."

Hyram was quiet for a minute. Then he repeated his question. "So what will you do?"

Petronus rubbed his face. "If they ask me, I will help. But I won't give them the help they want. I'll give them the help they need."

"And until then?"

"I'll try to sleep. I'll go back to fishing."

Hyram nodded and stood. "So you're not curious at all?"

But Petronus didn't answer. He was back to watching the northwestern sky and didn't even notice when his friend quietly slipped away.

Eventually, when the light gave out, he went inside and tried to take some soup. His stomach resisted it, and he lay in bed for hours while images of his past rode parade before his closed eyes. He remembered the heaviness of the ring on his finger, the crown on his brow, the purple robes and royal blue scarves. He remembered the books and the magicks and the machines. He remembered the statues and the tombs, the cathedrals and the catacombs.

He remembered a life that seemed simpler now because

in those days he'd loved the answers more than the questions.

After another night of tossing and sweating in his sheets, Petronus rose before the earliest fishermen, packed lightly, and slipped into the crisp morning. He left a note for Hyram on the door, saying he would be back when he'd seen it for himself.

By the time the sun rose, he was six leagues closer to knowing what had happened to the city and way of life that had once been his first love, his most beautiful, backward dream.

Neb

Neb couldn't remember most of the last two days. He knew he'd spent it meditating and poring over his tattered copy of the Whymer Bible and its companion, the Compendium of Historic Remembrance. His father had given them to him.

Of course, he knew there were other books in the cart. There was also food there and clothing and new tools wrapped in oilcloth. But he couldn't bring himself to touch it. He couldn't bring himself to move much at all.

So instead, he sat in the dry heat of the day and the crisp chill of the night, rocking himself and muttering the words of his reflection, the lines of his gospel, the quatrains of his lament.

Movement in the river valley below brought him out of it. Men on horseback rode to the blackened edge of the smoldering city, disappearing into smoke that twisted and hung like souls of the damned. Neb lay flat on his stomach and crept to the edge of the ridge. A bird whistled, low and behind him.

No, he thought, not a bird. He pushed himself up to all fours and slowly turned.

There was no wind. Yet he felt it brushing him as ghosts slipped in from the forest to surround him.

Standing quickly, Neb staggered into a run.

An invisible arm grabbed him and held him fast. "Hold, boy." The whispered voice sounded like it was spoken into a room lined with cotton bales.

There, up close, he could see the dark silk sleeve, the braided beard and broad shoulder of a man. He struggled and more arms appeared, holding him and forcing him to the ground.

"We'll not harm you," the voice said again. "We're Scouts of the Delta." The scout paused to let the words take root. "Are you from Windwir?"

Neb nodded.

"If I let you go, will you stay put? It's been a long day in the woods and I'm not wanting to chase you."

Neb nodded again.

The scout released him and backed away. Neb sat up slowly and studied the clearing around him. Crouched around him, barely shimmering in the late morning light, were at least a half dozen men.

"Do you have a name?"

He opened his mouth to speak, but the only words that came out were a rush of scripture, bits of the Gospels of P'Andro Whym all jumbled together into run-on sentences that were nonsensical. He closed his mouth and shook his head.

"Bring me a bird," the scout captain said. A small bird appeared, cupped in transparent hands. The scout captain pulled a thread from his scarf and tied a knot-message into it, looping it around the bird's foot. He hefted the bird into the sky.

They sat in silence for an hour, waiting for the bird to return. Once it was folded safely back into its pouch cage, the scout captain pulled Neb to his feet. "I am to inform you that you are to be the guest of Lord Sethbert, Overseer of the Entrolusian City States and the Delta of the Three Rivers. He is having quarters erected for you in his camp. He eagerly awaits your arrival and wishes to know in great detail all you know of the Fall of Windwir."

When they nudged him toward the forest, he resisted and turned toward the cart.

"We'll send men back for it," the scout captain said. "The Overseer is anxious to meet you."

Neb wanted to open his mouth and protest, but he didn't. Something told him that even if he could, these men were not going to let him come between them and their orders.

Instead, he followed them in silence. They followed no trails, left no trace and made very little sound, yet he knew they were all around him. And whenever he strayed, they nudged him back on course. They walked for two hours before breaking into a concealed camp. A short, obese man in bright colors stood next to a tall, redheaded woman with a strange look on her face.

The obese man smiled broadly, stretching out his arms, and Neb thought that he seemed like that kindly father in the Tale of the Runaway Prince, running toward his long lost son with open arms.

But the look on the woman's face told Neb that it was not so.

Rudolfo

Rudolfo let his Wandering Army choose their campsite because he knew they would fight harder to keep what they had chosen themselves. They set up their tents and kitchens upwind of the smoldering ruins in the low hills just west, while Rudolfo's Gypsy Scouts searched the outlying areas cool enough for them to walk. So far, they'd found no survivors.

Rudolfo ventured close enough to see the charred bones and smell the marrow cooking on the hot wind. From there, he directed his men.

"Search in shifts as it cools," Rudolfo said. "Send a bird if you find anything."

Gregoric nodded. "I will, General."

Rudolfo shook his head. When he'd first crested the rise

and seen the Desolation of Windwir, he ripped his scarf and cried loudly so his men could see his grief. Now, he cried openly and so did Gregoric. The tears cut through the grime on his face. "I don't think you'll find anyone," Rudolfo said.

"I know, General."

While they searched, Rudolfo reclined in his silk tent and sipped plum wine and nibbled at fresh cantaloupe and sharp cheddar cheese. Memories of the world's greatest city flashed across his mind, juxtaposing themselves against images of it now, burning outside. "Gods," he whispered.

His first memory was the Pope's funeral. The one who had been poisoned. Rudolfo's father, Jakob, had brought him to the City for the Funereal Honors of Kin-Clave. Rudolfo had even ridden with his father, hanging tightly to his father's back as they rode beside the Papal casket down the crowded street. Even though the Great Library was closed for the week of mourning, Jakob had arranged a brief visit with a bishop his Gypsy Scouts had once saved from a bandit attack on their way to the Churning Wastes.

The books—Gods, the books, he thought. Since the Age of Laughing Madness, P'Andro Whym's followers had gathered what knowledge they could of the Before Times. The magicks, the sciences, the arts and histories, maps and songs. They'd collected them in the library of Windwir, and the sleeping mountain village grew over time into the most powerful city in the New World.

He'd been six. He and his father had walked into the first chamber, and Rudolfo watched the books spread out as far as he could see above and beyond him. It was the first time he experienced wonder, and it frightened him.

Now the idea of that lost knowledge frightened him even more. This was a kind of wonder no one should ever feel, and he tossed back the last of the wine and clapped for more.

"What could do such a thing?" he asked quietly.

A captain coughed politely at the flap of the tent.

Rudolfo looked up. "Yes?"

"The camp is set, General."

"Excellent news, Captain. I will walk it with you momentarily." Rudolfo trusted his men implicitly, but also knew that all men rose or fell to the expectations of their leader. And a good leader made those expectations clear.

As the captain waited outside, Rudolfo stood and strapped on his sword. He used a small mirror to adjust his turban and his sash before slipping out into the late morning sun.

⌒

After walking the camp, encouraging his men and listening to them speculate on the demise of Windwir, Rudolfo tried to nap in his tent. He'd not slept for any measurable amount of time in nearly three days now but even with exhaustion riding him, he couldn't turn his mind away from the ruined city.

It had been magick of some kind, he knew. Certainly the Order had its share of enemies—but none with the kind of power to lay waste so utterly, so completely. An accident, then, he thought. Possibly something the Androfrancines had found in their digging about, something from the Age of Laughing Madness.

That made sense to him. An entire civilization burned out by magick in an age of Wizard Kings and war machines. The Churning Wastes were all the evidence one could need, and for thousands of years, the Androfrancines had mined those Elder Lands, bringing the magicks and machines into their walled city for examination. The harmless tidbits were sold or traded to keep Windwir the wealthiest city in the world. The others were studied to keep it the most powerful.

The bird arrived as the afternoon wore down. Rudolfo read the note and pondered. *We've found a talking metal man,* in Gregoric's small, pinched script.

Bring him to me, Rudolfo replied and tossed the bird back into the sky.

Then he waited in his tents to see what his Gypsy Scouts had found.

Chapter

3

Jin Li Tam

Jin Li Tam watched the commotion and wondered about the boy. He'd opened his mouth to speak after Sethbert's embrace, but all that had come out of him was a rush of words. Muttered lines of what sounded like Whymer text. And though he couldn't have been older than fifteen or sixteen, his tangled hair was white and his eyes were wide and wild. Of course, when Sethbert realized he couldn't speak, he'd dismissed him to the care of one of his servants. His only interest in the boy was to hear something firsthand of his handiwork.

It turned Jin's stomach.

Now, as the day wound down, Jin stood in the shadows and watched the scouts return dragging their nets behind them like proud fishermen. The magicks had burned out and she could see them clearly now, their dark silk clothing gray with ash, their faces and hands covered in soot. Metal twitched and gleamed in the nets they dragged.

She counted thirteen metal men in all, and the Androfrancine apprentice was with them, crouching next to them, poking and prodding them through the mesh of the nets. "We're missing one," he said.

"He's down there babbling," the scout said. "He won't get far; I took his leg off. We'll go back for him as soon as we've dropped this lot off."

"If the Gypsies don't get him first," their captain said as he approached from the direction of Sethbert's tent, his eyebrows furrowed. "They're in the city now. Re-magick and shadow them."

"And if they see us?"

"We're not at war with them." He paused and shot a worried glance back in the direction he'd come from. "Not yet anyway."

The apprentice was untangling one of the metal men from the net. The mechoservitor clicked and shot steam out of its exhaust grate, its glassy eyes fluttering open and then closing. "Are you functional?" the apprentice asked.

"I am functional," the metal man said.

The apprentice pointed to a nearby tent. "Go into the tent and wait there. Do not speak to anyone but me. Do you understand?"

"I understand." The mechoservitor, tall and slender, shining in the afternoon sun despite the coating of grime and the dents and scratches along its chassis, walked to the tent.

The apprentice turned to the next, and Jin Li Tam slipped away.

༄

She found the boy in the servants' tents. He sat silently at a table, a plate of food growing cold in front of him. He was still dressed in the filthy robes they'd found him in, still covered with dirt and ash.

She sat across from him, and he glanced up at her.

"You should eat," she told him. "How long has it been since you've eaten?"

He opened his mouth to speak, but then closed it. He shook his head, his eyes filling with tears.

She leaned in. "Can you understand me?"

He nodded.

"I can't imagine what you've seen," she said. Of course, she *could* imagine it. Last night, it had filled her dreams, just that briefest look at the wasted remains of Windwir. In those nightmares, Sethbert laughed with glee while dead wizards wandered the streets of that teeming city, calling down death by fire, death by lightning, death by plague. A dozen deaths or more, raining down on a city of screaming innocents until she woke up, covered in sweat.

She remembered the stories about the Age of Laughing Madness, a time of such devastation that those few who survived were driven insane. Now, Jin Li Tam wondered if perhaps this boy had met a similar fate.

But he didn't have the eyes of a madman. Full of sorrow and despair, yes. But not madness. She knew that look all too well these days.

Jin Li Tam looked around the tent to be sure no one listened. "Sethbert wants you to tell him what you saw," she said in a low voice. "He wants to hear how Windwir fell, but not for any noble purpose. Do you understand?"

The boy's face said he didn't, but he nodded.

"Your story is what you are worth to him. As long as he thinks you are willing to tell it, he will keep you alive and well cared for." Jin Li Tam reached a hand across the table to cover the boy's hand. "If he thinks you cannot or will not tell it, he will discard you. Living or dead, I do not know, but he is not a kind man." She squeezed his hand. "He is a dangerous man."

She stood up and whistled for a servant.

A heavyset woman appeared in the doorway of the tent. "Yes, Lady?"

"A guest should not be sat to table in his own filth. Clean this boy up and find him fresh clothing."

"I offered him bathing water, Lady, but he declined."

Jin Li Tam let the anger edge her voice. "Surely you have children?"

"Yes, Lady. Three."

She willed her words to soften. "Then you know how to bathe a child."

"I do, Lady."

Jin Li Tam nodded once, curtly. "This boy has seen more

darkness and despair than any have seen since the Age of Laughing Madness. Be kind to him, and pray that you never see what he has seen."

Then Jin Li Tam left the tent, knowing she could wait no longer. She'd put it off the last two days, uncertain of the best route. But now she knew there was no chance of her staying. There were coops of message birds scattered throughout the camp. She would find a bird that would not be missed for at least another day. She would fling it at the sky with her simple message, tied with the black thread of danger:

Windwir lies in ruin. Sethbert has betrayed us all.

And after, she would sleep with a pouch of magicks beneath her pillow, ready to flee at a word.

Rudolfo

Rudolfo's Gypsy Scouts found the metal man sobbing in an impact crater deep in the roiling smoke and glowing ruins of Windwir. He crouched over a pile of blackened bones, his shoulders chugging and his bellows wheezing, his helmet-like head shaking in his large metal hands. They approached him silently, ghosts in a city of ghosts, but the metal man still heard and looked up.

Gouts of steam shot from his exhaust grate. Boiling water leaked from his glassy jeweled eyes. Nearby lay a mangled metal leg.

"Lla meht dellik ev'I," the metal man said.

The Gypsies dragged him to Rudolfo because he could not stand on his own and refused to be supported. Rudolfo, from his tents outside the ruins, watched them return just like the message bird had promised.

They dragged the metal man into the clearing and released him, dropping the leg as well. Their bright colored tunics, cloaks and breeches were gray with ash and black from charcoal. The metal man gleamed in the afternoon sun.

They bowed and waited for Rudolfo to speak. "So this is all that's left of the Great City of Windwir?"

To a man, they nodded. Slow, deliberate nods.

"And the Androfrancine Library?"

One of the Gypsy Scouts stepped forward. "Ashes, Lord." The scout stepped back quickly, head bowed.

Rudolfo turned to the metal man. "And what do we have here?" He'd seen mechanicals before. Small ones, though, nothing quite so elaborate as a man. "Can you speak?"

"Llew etiuq kaeps nac I," the metal man said.

Rudolfo looked again to his Gypsy Scouts. The same scout who'd spoken earlier looked up. "He's been talking since we found him, Lord. It's no language we've ever heard."

Rudolfo smiled. "Actually, it is." He turned back to the metal man. "Sdrawkcab kaeps," he told him.

A pop, a clunk, a gout of steam. The metal man looked up at Rudolfo, at the smoke-filled sky and the blackened horizon that was once the world's largest city. He shook and shuddered. When he spoke, his voice carried a depth of lament that Rudolfo had only heard twice before. "What have I done?" the metal man asked, his breast ringing as he beat it with his metal fist. "Oh, what have I done?"

᠀

Rudolfo reclined on silk cushions and drank sweet pear wine, watching the sunset wash the metal man red. His own personal armorer bent over the mechanical in the fading light, wiping sweat from his brow while working to reattach the mangled leg.

"It's no use, Lord," the metal man said.

The armorer grunted. "It's nowhere close to good but it will serve." He pushed himself back, glancing up at Rudolfo.

Rudolfo nodded. "Stand on it, metal man."

The metal man used his hands to push himself up. The mangled leg would not bend. It sparked and popped but held as he stood.

Rudolfo waved. "Walk about."

The metal man did, jerking and twitching, using the leg more as a prop.

Rudolfo sipped his wine and waved the armorer away. "I suppose now I should worry about escape?"

The metal man kept walking, each step becoming more steady. "You wish to escape, Lord? You have aided me. Perhaps I may aid you?"

Rudolfo chuckled. "I meant *you*, metal man."

"I will not escape." The metal man hung his head. "I intend to pay fully for my crimes."

Rudolfo raised his eyebrows. "What crimes are those, exactly?" Then, remembering his manners but not sure if they extended to mechanicals, he pointed to a nearby stool. "Sit down. Please."

The metal man sat. "I am responsible for the razing of Windwir and the genocide of the Androfrancines, Lord. I do not expect a trial. I do not expect mercy. I expect justice."

"What is your name?"

The metal man's golden lids flickered over his jeweled eyes in surprise. "Lord?"

"Your name. What is your name?"

"I am Mechoservitor Number Three, catalog and translations section."

"That's no name. I am Rudolfo. Lord Rudolfo of the Ninefold Forest Houses to some. General Rudolfo of the Wandering Army to others. That Damned Rudolfo to those I've bested in battle or in bed."

The metal man stared at him. His mouth-shutters clicked open and closed.

"Very well," Rudolfo finally said. "I will call you Isaak." He thought about it for a moment, nodded, sipped more wine. "Isaak. Tell me how exactly you managed to raze the Knowledgeable City of Windwir and single-handedly wipe out the Androfrancine Order?"

"By careless words, Lord, I committed these crimes."

Rudolfo refilled his glass. "Go on."

"Are you familiar, Lord, with the Wizard Xhum Y'Zir?"

Rudolfo nodded.

"The Androfrancines found a cache of parchments in the

Eastern Rises. They bore a striking resemblance to Y'Zir's later work including his particular blend of Middle Landlish and Upper V'Ral. Even the handwriting matched."

Rudolfo leaned forward, one hand stroking his long mustache. "These weren't copies?"

The metal man shook his head. "Originals, Lord. Naturally, they were brought back to the library. They assigned the translation and cataloging to me."

Rudolfo picked a honeyed date out of a silver bowl and popped it into his mouth. He chewed around the pit, spitting it into a silk napkin. "You worked in the library."

"Yes, Lord."

"Continue."

"One of the parchments contained the missing text for Xhum Y'Zir's Seven Cacophonic Deaths—"

Here Rudolfo's breath rushed out. He felt the blood flee so quickly from his face that he tingled. He raised his hand and fell back into the cushions. "Gods, a moment."

The metal man, Isaak, waited.

Rudolfo sat back up, drained off the last of his wine in one swallow and refilled the glass. "The Seven Cacophonic Deaths? You're sure?"

The metal man shook in one great sob. "I am now, Lord."

A hundred questions flooded Rudolfo. Each shouted to be asked. He opened his mouth to ask the first but closed it when Gregoric, the First Captain of his Gypsy Scouts, slipped into the tent with a worried expression on his face.

"Yes?" he asked.

"General Rudolfo, we've just received word that Overseer Sethbert of the Entrolusian City States approaches."

Rudolfo felt anger rise. *"Just?"*

Gregoric paled. "Their scouts are magicked, Lord."

Rudolfo leaped to his feet, reaching for his thin, long sword. "Bring the camp to Third Alarm," he shouted. He turned on the metal man. "Isaak, you will wait here."

Isaak nodded.

Then General Rudolfo of the Wandering Army, Lord of

the Ninefold Forest Houses, raced from the tent bellowing for his armor and horse.

Petronus

Petronus sat before his small fire and listened to the night around him. He'd ridden the day at a measured pace, not pushing his old horse faster or farther than it needed. He'd finally stopped and made camp when the sky purpled.

Not far off, a coyote bayed and another joined in. Petronus sipped bitterroot tea with a generous pinch of Holga the Bay Woman's herbal bone-ache remedy boiled into it. It washed the old man in warmth deeper than the dancing flames could touch.

He watched the northwest. The smoke had largely dissipated throughout the day. By now, he thought, Rudolfo and Sethbert would both be there with their armies, ready to assist if there was anyone or anything left to help.

Of course, he doubted they would find anything and he suspected he knew why. The longer he thought about it, the more sure the old man became. And each league that carried him closer to Windwir paralleled an inner journey across the landscape of his memory.

~

"We've found another Y'Zir fragment, Father," Arch-Scholar Ryhan had said during the private portion of the Expeditionary Debriefing.

Petronus was forty years younger then, more of an idealist, but even then he'd known the risk. "You're certain?"

The arch-scholar sipped his wine, careful not to spill it on the white carpets of Petronus's office. "Yes. It is a nearly perfect fragment, with overlap between the Straupheim parchment and the Harston letter. It's only a matter of time before we have the entire text."

Petronus felt his jaw clench. "What precautions are you taking?"

"We're keeping all of the parchments separate. Under lock and guard."

Petronus nodded. "Good. They're not safe even for cataloging and translation."

"For now, yes," Ryhan said. "But young Charles, that new Acolyte of Mechanics from the Emerald Coasts, thinks he's found a way to power the mechoservitor he's reconstructed using firestones. He says according to Rufello's Notes and Specifications, these mechanicals can be erased after a day's work, told in advance what to do and what to say, and given even the most complex instructions."

Petronus had seen the demonstration. They'd needed a massive furnace to generate the power, but for three minutes, Charles had asked the blocky, sharp-cornered metal man he'd built to move his hands, to recite scripture and to answer complex mathematical equations for the Pope and his closest advisors. Another secret they had mined from the days before that they would keep close to their hearts, releasing it to the world when they felt it was ready for the knowledge.

"They could read it," the arch-scholar said. "Under careful instruction. If Charles is right, a mechoservitor could even be instructed to summarize the text without reproducing it verbatim."

"If all of the parchments were ever found . . ." Petronus let the words trail off. He shook his head. "We'd do better to just destroy what we've found," Petronus said. "Even a metal puppet dances on a human string."

The look on the arch-scholar's face when he said that was the beginning of Petronus's self-inflicted slide away from Androfrancine grace.

⌒

Coyote song brought Petronus back from the past. The fire was burning down now and he pushed more wood onto it. His fists went white as he clenched them and looked to the northwest again.

They had found the fragments of Xhum Y'Zir's spell.

They had not been careful.

They had unleashed Death upon themselves.

And if Petronus was right about the power of those words, there was nothing left of all their labor. The Androfrancines had spent two thousand years grave-robbing from the Former World and there would be precious little now to show for it.

The rage of P'Andro Whym fell upon him and Petronus bellowed at the sky.

Neb

Your story is what you are worth to him.

The redheaded woman's words stayed with Neb long after she said them.

He'd bathed himself, waiting until the serving woman who brought the water saw him tugging at his filthy robes. The ash and dirt from his body turned the water a deep brown as soon as he settled into it. When he dried himself with the rough army towels, he saw even more ash had turned the white cotton a light gray. Still, he was cleaner than he'd been.

The robes they'd brought him were too large, but he cinched the rope belt tighter and then dumped his own wash water into the patch of ferns behind the tent.

After, he'd tried to nibble at a bit of bread, but his stomach soured after a few bites. Clutching his two books, Neb curled himself onto the cot. He thought about the redheaded woman's words and wondered what made his story so valuable to the Overseer. And why had he seemed so flustered when he learned that Neb couldn't speak? Worse, why had he seemed so excited to hear it in the first place? He knew the lady might tell him if he could ask her, but he also wasn't sure he wanted to know.

Eventually, he rolled over and tried to sleep. But when he closed his eyes, there was no dark, never any dark. It was fire—green fire—falling like a giant fist onto the city of Windwir, and lightning—white and sharp—slicing upward at the sky. Buildings fell. The smell of burning meat—cattle and people alike—filled his nose. And there, in the gate down by the river docks, a lone figure rushing out, ablaze and screaming.

Of course, Neb knew his own mind was drawing that part of the picture in. But in his mind, he could see right to the melting whites of his father's eyes, could see the blame and disappointment there.

Eventually, he gave up on the cot. Instead, he slipped out into the night and went to the cart that, true to their words, the Delta Scouts had brought back. Crawling into the back of it, nestled down among the sacks of mail and books and clothing, Neb fell into sleep.

But his dreams were full of fire.

Chapter

4

Rudolfo

Battlefields, Rudolfo thought, should not require etiquette, nor be considered affairs of state.

He remained mounted at the head of his army while his captains parleyed with the Overseer's captains in a moonlit field between the two camps. On the horizon, Windwir smoldered and stank. At last, they broke from parley and his captains returned.

"Well?" he asked.

"They also received the birds and came to offer assistance."

He sneered. "Came to peck the corpses clean more likely." Rudolfo had no love for the City States, hunkered like obese carrion birds at the delta of the Three Rivers, imposing their tariffs and taxes as if they owned those broad, flat waters and the sea they spilled into. He looked at Gregoric. "And did they share with you why they broke treaty and magicked their scouts at time of peace?"

Gregoric cleared his throat. "They thought that perhaps we had ridden against Windwir and were honoring their kinclave. I took the liberty of reminding them of our own kinclave with the Androfrancines."

Rudolfo nodded. "So when do I meet with the tremendous sack of moist runt droppings?"

His other captains laughed quietly behind their hands. Gregoric scowled at them. "They will send a bird requesting that you dine with the Overseer and his lady."

Rudolfo's eyebrows rose. "His lady?"

Perhaps, he thought, it would not be so ponderous after all.

⌒

He dressed in rainbow colors, each hue declaring one of his houses. He did it himself, waving away assistance but motioning for wine. Isaak sat, unspeaking and unmoving, while Rudolfo wrapped himself in silk robes and scarves and sashes and turban.

"I have a few moments," he told the metal man. "Tell more of your story."

Light deep in those jeweled eyes sparked and caught. "Very well, Lord." A click, a clack, a whir. "The parchment containing the missing text of Xhum Y'Zir's Seven Cacophonic Deaths came to me for cataloging and translation, naturally."

"Naturally," Rudolfo said.

"I worked under the most careful of circumstances, Lord Rudolfo. We kept the new text isolated in a secure location with no danger of the missing words being added to complete the incantation. I was the only mechoservitor to work with the parchment and all knowledge of my previous work with prior fragments was carefully removed."

Rudolfo nodded. "Removed how?"

The metal man tapped his head. "It's . . . complex, Lord. I

do not fully understand it myself. But the Androfrancines write metal scrolls and those metal scrolls determine our capacity, our actions, our inactions, our memories." Isaak shrugged.

Rudolfo studied three different pairs of soft slipper. "Go on."

The metal man sighed. "There is not much more to tell. I cataloged, translated and copied the missing text. I spent three days and three nights with it, calculating and recalculating my work. In the end, I returned to Brother Charles to have the memory of my work expunged."

A sudden thought struck him, and Rudolfo raised a hand, unsure why he was so polite with the mechanical. "Is memory of your work always removed?"

"Seldom, actually. Only when the work is of a sensitive or dangerous nature, Lord."

"Remind me to come back to this question later," Rudolfo said. "Meanwhile, continue. I must leave soon."

"I put the parchment in its safe, left the catalog room and watched the Androfrancine Gray Guard lock it behind me. I returned to Brother Charles, but his study was locked. I waited." The metal man whirred and clicked.

Rudolfo selected a sword in an intricate scabbard, thrusting it through his sash. "And?"

The metal man began to shake. Steam poured out of his exhaust grate. His eyes rolled and a high pitched whine emanated from somewhere deep inside.

"And?" Rudolfo said, sharpness creeping into his voice.

"And all went blank for a moment, Lord. My next memory was standing in the city square, shouting the words of the Seven Cacophonic Deaths—all of the words—into the sky. I tried to stop the utterance." He sobbed again, his metal body shuddering and groaning. "I could not stop. I tried but could not stop."

Rudolfo felt the mechanical's grief, sharp and twisting, in his stomach. He stood at the flap of his tent, needing to leave and not knowing what to say.

The metal man continued. "Finally, I reversed my language

scroll. But it was too late. The Death Golems came. The Plague Spiders scuttled. Fire fell from sulfur clouds. All seven deaths." He sobbed again.

Rudolfo stroked his beard. "And why do you think this happened?"

The metal man looked up, shaking his head. "I don't know, Lord. Malfunction, perhaps."

"Or malfeasance," Rudolfo said. He clapped and Gregoric appeared, slipping out of the night to stand by his side. "I want Isaak here under guard at all times. No one talks to him but me. Do you understand?"

Gregoric nodded. "I understand, General."

Rudolfo turned to the metal man. "Do you understand as well?"

"Yes, Lord."

Rudolfo leaned over the metal man to speak quietly in his ear. "Take courage," he said. "It is possible that you were but the tool of someone else's ill will."

Isaak's words, quoted from the Whymer Bible, surprised him. "Even the plow holds love for splitting the ground; and the sword grief for spilling the blood."

Rudolfo's fingers lightly brushed a polished shoulder. "We'll talk more when I return."

Outside, the sky grayed in readiness for morning. Rudolfo felt weariness creeping behind his eyes and in the tips of his fingers. He had stolen naps here and there, but hadn't slept a full night since the message bird's arrival four days before, calling him and his Wandering Army south and west. After the meal, he told himself. He would sleep then.

His eyes lingered on the ruined city painted purple in the predawn light.

"Gods," he whispered. "What an unexpected weapon."

Jin Li Tam

Jin Li Tam hid the stolen magicks pouch in her tent. As she straightened, she heard a polite cough behind her. She spun.

The young lieutenant—the one that had brought her the horse while they were on the road—stood in the opening.

She pulled herself to full height. "Yes?"

"Lord Sethbert informs you that Rudolfo and his entourage will be arriving within the hour. The Overseer is expecting you at the banquet table."

Jin Li Tam nodded. "Thank you. I will be there."

The lieutenant shuffled uncomfortably, and she could tell that he wanted to say something but was unsure. "Come in from the night, Lieutenant." She studied him. He couldn't have been much past twenty and had the solid look of some minor Delta noble's son, eager to make his mark in the world. She took a step closer to him, but no more because she knew her height might intimidate him, and in this case, for this moment, she wanted his trust. "You wish to say something?"

His eyes moved around the room and he twisted his cap in his hands. "I wish to ask a question." The words came out slowly, then sped up. "But I'm not sure I want to know."

"I may not want to tell you," she said. "But you may ask."

"Some of the men have heard the Overseer talking to his generals over the last two days. Others have overheard the scouts. They say there's nothing left of Windwir but for those metal men and that boy."

"That seems to be true enough," Jin Li Tam said. "Though I hope it will be proven false."

He's not come to it yet, she thought. There's more he wants to ask, but he's not sure he can trust me. She took a risk and used the subverbal finger language of the Delta Houses.

You can trust me, she signed.

He blinked. *You know our signing*?

She nodded. "I do." Even as her mouth formed the words, her hands kept moving. *Ask what you will, Lieutenant.*

His hands fumbled with the hat and he pulled it back onto his head. "It wouldn't be proper for me to question." But his hands now moved too. *They tell us that the Overseer had advance knowledge of Windwir's doom from spies in the city; that we rode out to her aid by way of kin-clave.* His hands went limp and she understood. This young man was on the edge of the blade now.

"You're right," she said. "It would not be proper. He is the Overseer. You are his lieutenant. I am his consort." *The Overseer did have advance knowledge,* she signed back.

"I'm sorry to have bothered you, Lady." And his hands again: *The men have heard him boasting. They say he claims he brought down the Androfrancine city.*

"Please let the Overseer know that I will join him for dinner shortly." Jin Li Tam hesitated. Confirming his fears could lead him down a dangerous path. It was easier to be uncertain than it was to pretend a noble cause or to bury his uniform and flee. *The Overseer's boasting is true,* she finally signed. She watched the color leave his face.

The lieutenant swayed and he dropped his hands. "He must have had good reason," he whispered.

Jin Li Tam stepped closer, now revealing her height as she put her hand on the young man's shoulder. "Once you see the Desolation of Windwir," she said in a low voice, "you'll know there could be no good reason for what the Overseer has done."

The lieutenant swallowed. "Thank you, Lady."

She nodded once, then turned away and waited for him to leave. Once he was gone, she closed the flap to her tent, hid the magick pouch in a different location, and laid out her clothing for the night's event.

As she brushed her hair, she wondered if her father were right about Lord Rudolfo. It was clear now that she must leave sooner rather than later. Sethbert rode a slippery slope on a blind stallion, and no good could come of it. She wondered what her father would say, and she thought perhaps he would tell her to go to Rudolfo. A strategic alliance with the Ninefold Forest Houses—at least until she could return safely to the Emerald Coasts—could keep her about her father's business a while longer.

Sethbert no longer stood when she entered a room. In the early days he had, of course, and certainly during formal occasions he followed the proper courtesies. But he was alone now with his metal man and he was chuckling as it hopped on one foot and juggled plates for him.

"Lord Overseer," she said in the doorway, curtsying.

He looked her over, licking his lips. "Lady Jin Li Tam. You look lovely as always."

As she walked into the room and took her seat, he waved off the metal man. "Wait in the kitchen," he told it.

It nodded and shambled off, clicking and hissing.

"The newer ones are much better," he said. "I think I'll replace him."

Jin smiled and nodded politely.

"And how are you this evening? Have you kept busy?" Sethbert seemed jovial now.

"I have, Lord. I checked on the boy and made sure he was well cared for." When Sethbert frowned, she continued. "I'm sure he'll be talking in no time."

The momentary storm passed from his face. "Good, good. I will want to hear his story."

Jin placed her hands in her lap. "Should I be aware of anything this evening, Lord?"

Sethbert smiled. "You've not met Rudolfo before."

She shook her head. "I've not."

"He's a fop. A dandy of sorts." Sethbert leaned in. "He has no children. He has no wife nor consort. I think he's—" He waved his fingers in a feminine way. "But he's a great pretender. If he asks you to dance—and I suspect he will—dance with him no matter how distasteful it may be."

"If my lord wishes."

"I do wish it." He leaned in. "It goes without saying that the time is not right for him to know of my role in Windwir's fall. He'll know soon enough, but when he does it will be too late for him."

Jin Li Tam nodded. It was sound strategy. The attack on Windwir had knocked a crutch out from under the Entrolusian economy—Sethbert might be mad, but not so mad as to be foolish. For whatever reason he'd destroyed this city, he intended to supplement the Delta's losses by annexation, and the Ninefold Forest Houses were ripe fruit, albeit high on the tree and a bit out of the way. A small kingdom of forest towns surrounded by vast resources. The army, she realized, had never been for Windwir. "I understand."

There was a commotion outside. The tent flaps fluttered and her young lieutenant stood in the doorway. Their eyes met briefly before he looked away.

"Lord Rudolfo rides for the camp. He's bringing his Gypsy Scouts. They are unmagicked."

Sethbert smiled. "Thank you, Lieutenant. Make sure he is announced appropriately."

Jin Li Tam straightened her skirt, pulled at her top and wondered how this last meal as Sethbert's consort would go.

Chapter

5

Rudolfo

Sethbert did not meet him at the edge of his army; instead, Rudolfo rode in escort to the massive round tent. He snapped and waved and flashed hand-signs to his Gypsy Scouts, who slipped off to take up positions around the pavilion.

Sethbert rose when he entered, a tired smile pulling at his long mustache and pockmarked jowls. His lady rose, too, tall and slim, draped in green riding silks. Her red hair shone like the sunrise. Her blue eyes flashed an amused challenge and she smiled.

"Lord Rudolfo of the Ninefold Forest Houses," the aide at the door announced. "General of the Wandering Army."

He entered, handing his long sword to the aide. "I come in peace to break bread," he said.

"We receive you in peace and offer the wine of gladness to be so well met," Sethbert replied.

Rudolfo nodded and approached the table.

Sethbert clapped him on the back. "Rudolfo, it is good to see you. How long has it been?"

Not long enough, he thought. "Too long," he said. "How are the cities?"

Sethbert shrugged. "The same. We've had a bit of trouble with smugglers but it seems to have sorted itself out."

Rudolfo turned to the lady. She stood a few inches taller than him.

"Yes. My consort, the Lady Jin Li Tam of House Li Tam." Sethbert stressed the word "consort" and Rudolfo watched her eyes narrow slightly when he said it.

"Lady Tam," Rudolfo said. He took her offered hand and kissed it, his eyes not leaving hers.

She smiled. "Lord Rudolfo."

They all sat and Sethbert clapped three times. Rudolfo heard a clunk and a whir from behind a hanging tapestry. A metal man walked out, carrying a tray with glasses and a carafe of wine. This one was older than Isaak, his edges more box-like and his coloring more copper.

"Fascinating, isn't he?" Sethbert said while the metal man poured wine. He clapped again. "Servitor, I wish the chilled peach wine tonight."

The machine gave a high-pitched whistle. "Deepest apologies, Lord Sethbert, but we have no chilled peach wine."

Sethbert grinned, then raised his voice in false anger. "What! No peach wine? That is inexcusable, servitor."

More whistling and a series of clicks. A gout of steam shot out of the exhaust grate. "Deepest apologies, Lord Sethbert—"

Sethbert clapped again. "Your answer is unacceptable. You will find me chilled peach wine even if you must walk all the way to Sadryl and back with it. Do you understand?"

Rudolfo watched. The Lady Jin Li Tam did not. She fidgeted and worked hard to hide the embarrassment in the redness of her cheeks, the spark of anger in her eyes.

The servitor set down the tray and carafe. "Yes, Lord Sethbert." It moved toward the tent flap.

Sethbert chuckled and nudged the lady with his elbow. "You could take lessons there," he said. She offered a weak smile as false as his earlier anger.

Then Sethbert clapped and whistled. "Servitor, I've changed my mind. The cherry wine will suffice."

The metal man poured the wine and left for the kitchen tent to check on the first course.

"What a fabulous device," Rudolfo said.

Sethbert beamed. "Splendid, isn't it?"

"However did you come by it?"

"It was . . . a gift," Sethbert said. "From the Androfrancines."

The look on Jin Li Tam's face said otherwise.

"I thought they were highly guarded regarding their magicks and machines." Rudolfo said, raising his glass.

Sethbert raised his own. "Perhaps they are," he said, "with *some*."

Rudolfo ignored the unsubtle insult. The metal man returned with a tray of soup bowls full of steaming crab stew. He positioned the bowls in front of each of them. Rudolfo watched the careful precision. "Truly fabulous," he said.

"And you can get them to do most anything . . . if you know how," Sethbert said.

"Really?"

The Overseer clapped. "Servitor, run scroll seven three five."

Something clicked and clanked. Suddenly, the metal man spread his arms and broke into song, his feet moving lightly in a bawdy dance step while he sang, "My father and my mother were both Androfrancine brothers or so my aunty Abbot likes to say. . . ." The song went from raunchy to worse. When it finished, the metal man bowed deeply.

The Lady Jin Li Tam blushed. "Given the circumstances of our meeting," she said, "I think that was in poor taste."

Sethbert shot her a withering glare, then smiled at Rudolfo. "Forgive my consort. She lacks any appreciation for humor."

Rudolfo watched her hands white-knuckling a napkin, his brain suddenly playing out potentials that were coming together. "It does seem odd that the Androfrancines would teach their servitors a song of such . . . color."

She looked up at him. Her eyes held a plea for rescue. Her mouth drew tight.

"Oh, they didn't teach it that song. I did. Well, my man did."

"Your man can create scripts for this magnificent metal man?"

Sethbert spooned stew into his mouth, spilling it onto his shirt. He spoke with his mouth full. "Certainly. We've torn this toy of mine apart a dozen times over. We know it inside and out."

Rudolfo took a bite of his own stew, nearly gagging on the strong sea flavor that flooded his mouth, and pushed the bowl aside. "Perhaps," he said, "you'll loan your man to me for a bit."

Sethbert's eyes narrowed. "Whatever for, Rudolfo?"

Rudolfo drained his wineglass, trying to rid his mouth of the briny taste. "Well, I seem to have inherited a metal man of my own. I should like to teach him new tricks."

Sethbert's face paled slightly, then went red. "Really? A metal man of your own?"

"Absolutely. The sole survivor of Windwir, I'm told." Rudolfo clapped his hands and leaped to his feet. "But enough talk of toys. There is a beautiful woman here in need of a dance. And Rudolfo shall offer her such if you'll be so kind as to have your metal man sing something more apropos."

She stood despite Sethbert's glare. "In the interest of state relations," she said, "I would be honored."

They swirled and leaped around the tent as the metal man sang an upbeat number, banging on his metal chest like a drum. Rudolfo's eyes carefully traveled his partner, stealing glances where he could. She had a slim neck and slim ankles. Her high breasts pushed against her silk shirt, jiggling just ever so slightly as she moved with practiced grace and utter confidence. She was living art and he knew he must have her.

As the song drew to a close, Rudolfo seized her wrist and tapped a quick message into it. *A sunrise such as you belongs in the East with me; and I would never call you consort.*

She blushed, cast down her eyes, and tapped back a response that did not surprise him at all. *Sethbert destroyed the Androfrancines; he means you harm as well.*

He nodded, smiled a tight smile, and released her. "Thank you, Lady."

Sethbert looked at Rudolfo through narrow eyes, but Rudolfo made a point from that moment forward of looking at the Overseer's Lady rather than his host. Dinner passed with excruciating slowness while banter fell like a city-dweller's footfall on the hunt. Rudolfo noticed that at no point did Sethbert bring up the destruction of Windwir or the metal man his Gypsy Scouts had found.

Sethbert's lack of words spoke loudest of all.

Rudolfo wondered if his own did the same.

Neb

Quiet voices woke Neb from his light sleep. He lay still in the wagon, trying hard not to even breathe. The night air was heavy with the smell of smoke mingled with Evergreen.

"I heard General O'Sirus say the Overseer is mad," one voice said.

A snort. "As if that's anything new."

"Do you think it's true?"

"Do I think *what's* true?"

A pause. "Do you think he destroyed Windwir?"

Neb heard the sound of cloth rustling. "More likely they destroyed themselves. You know what they say about Andro-francine curiosity. Gods only know what they found digging about in the Churning Wastes." Neb heard the soldier draw phlegm down and spit. "Probably Old Magick . . . Blood Magick."

For all their obstinacy toward unsanctified children, the Androfrancines did one thing for them very well. One thing that—apart from the wealthiest of the landed and lords—no one else did for their children: They gave them the best education the world could offer.

For as long as he could remember, Neb had spent most of his days in the Great Library, usually under the care of an acolyte assigned to a group of boys as a part of his own education. The Arch-Scholar Rydlis said it best: The path to learning lies in teaching. And the path to teaching lies in answering the questions of a child.

Neb knew this story very well. The Age of Laughing Madness was brought about by Blood Magick. And part of the charter of P'Andro Whym's followers—codified hundreds of years after their venerated founder had died, nearly five hundred years since the onset of the Laughing Madness—was to keep both magick and science under a watchful eye. The Rites of Kin-Clave had sprung from that same dark time on the edge of histories, forming a labyrinth of ritual and social expectation that twisted and turned back on itself with all the mystery of the greatest Whymer Mazes. Blood Magick was expressly forbidden. Earth Magick was only tolerated during time of war, and never used by nobility. At least not with their own hands.

It made sense. Blood Magick had felled the only home he'd ever had. Such a kind that had not been seen in the Named Lands from the days the Homeseekers had migrated in from the dust storms of the deep south. Such a kind that had not been seen since Xhum Y'Zir, enraged at the murder of his seven sons by P'Andro Whym and his Scientist Scholars, had turned the Old World into the Churning Wastes.

Neb wondered if maybe he couldn't speak now because he'd been driven mad. But then he wondered if the mad could contemplate their possible insanity.

The soldiers moved off and Neb sat up. There'd be no more sleep for him tonight. The stars overhead were swollen, hanging low and heavy in the hazy sky.

Neb slipped from the wagon and returned to his tent. Inside, he went to the table and selected a pear and a piece of bread. While he chewed the pear, tasting its tart sugar on his tongue, he reflected on the soldier's words.

Gods only knew what they found digging about in the Churning Wastes.

He remembered his last visit with his father three or four months ago. He'd just returned from a dig in the Waste and he'd brought Neb a square metal coin that shined brightly despite its age. Brother Hebda was excited.

"We've found a good one this time, Neb. A shrine from the time of the Y'Zirite Resurgence."

Neb remembered this from lessons about the Age of Laughing Madness, the five hundred years after the end of the Old World that were marked by chaos, anarchy and a near eighty-percent insanity rate from the earliest days of the apocalypse to the fourth generation of children. There were some who argued that Xhum Y'Zir had built a hidden eighth Cacophonic Death into his spell after it had been shaped and bargained for in the dark places of the world— a last and final blow for one of his favorite wives who had been captured, raped and beaten to death on his last night in seclusion for his spell-making. But the traditionalists insisted that the exaggeration of ancient magicks was already a large enough problem without adding more to it. But both camps agreed that the insanity was prevalent, and that if it weren't for the Francines—a monastic movement centered around the intricacies of the human psyche, the patterns of human (and primate) behavior—humanity would have murdered itself. The Y'Zirite Resurgence was a small sect of survivors whose particular insanity was the worship of House Y'Zir. They celebrated that fallen Moon Wizard's children for challenging—and later eradicating—the Scientism Movement that had converted P'Andro Whym in his boyhood.

Franci B'yot, the posthumous founder of the Francines, though older than Whym, was influenced by the early days of the same Scientism Movement. Fragments of Whym and B'Yot's correspondence largely led to the sects working together, and eventually becoming the Androfrancines.

So Neb understood why his father had been so excited about the find. A Y'Zirite shrine would have a small library—usually two or three carefully packed jars of parchment. And sometimes mummified martyrs bearing the mark of House Y'Zir burned over their heart.

He turned the coin over in his hand, looking at the image stamped into its surface. "Who is it?" he asked.

"Let me see it." His father took the coin and studied it. "The third son, Vas Y'Zir," he said after a moment. "He was the Wizard King of Aelys." Around them the Orphans' Park was quiet, as the other children were in their classrooms. Brother Hebda always pulled him out of class when he came to visit, and the teachers never minded. He leaned over on the bench, holding the coin in the palm of his hand and pointing to it. "If you look closely, you can see the etching around his left eye—and if you look even closer, you can see that the left eye is actually carved out of nightstone. They said it made him able to see into the Unseen World to make pacts for his Blood Magick." Brother Hebda handed it over.

Neb took it, held it to the light until he could see the dark eye. "Thank you, Brother Hebda."

His father nodded. "You're welcome." His voice lowered and he looked around. "Do you want to know what else we found?"

Neb nodded.

"The arch-scholar didn't let me get too close to it, but buried in the back, behind the shrine figure, they found a Rufello lockbox."

Neb felt his eyes go wide. "Really?"

Brother Hebda nodded. "They did. And it was entirely intact."

Neb had caught glimpses of the mechoservitors Brother Charles, the arch-engineer, had reconstructed from Rufello's Book of Specifications. They were kept in stalls in the lower parts of the library, but once, during a research trip in the care of an acolyte, he'd caught a glimpse of one. It clanked when it walked, steam hissing from its exhaust grate as it moved. It stood about three spans high and it was bulkier than the metal men from the days before P'Andro Whym and Xhum Y'Zir. Still, it was close enough to the drawings that Neb could see the similarities. Neb watched it select a book and slip back into one of the library's many disguised elevators.

"Do you think it may have some of his drawings inside?" Aiedos Rufello was one of Neb's favorite figures from Old World history. His work was old when P'Andro Whym was a boy, and he'd given his life to understanding the scientific mysteries of the First World.

"Unlikely," his father said. "You know why. Show me how well they've trained you in that school of yours."

Neb studied the coin, digging in his memory. He found what he was looking for and looked up with a grin. "Because the Y'Zirites would have no interest in preserving Rufello's science-based work. Xhum Y'Zir saw the Scientism Movement as a threat against his magick, and later, some of its scattered followers murdered his seven sons."

"Exactly," his father said, a proud smile spreading across his face. "But isn't it interesting that all those years later, whoever built the shrine used Rufello's science-based work to protect something they had hidden there."

"Why would they do that?" It had to be important to them, Neb thought.

Brother Hebda shrugged. "It could've been an aberrant Gospel or perhaps part of the Lesser Spell Codex. Regardless, they had me race it back here under a full complement of Gray Guard Elite. We rode day and night; we even magicked our horses for silence. One of the mechoservitors is going to cipher its lock code, but I doubt what's inside will ever be announced."

Neb frowned. "I wish I'd been there." This was one of the digs he'd applied to attend as an intern.

His father nodded. "Someday they'll approve your grant. 'Patience is the heart of art and science alike,'" he said, quoting a passage from the Whymer Bible.

"I hope so."

Brother Hebda slipped his arm around Neb's shoulders. He rarely touched the boy, and Neb thought maybe it was harder to be a parent than an Androfrancine. But now, he pulled Neb close and squeezed his shoulders together with his thick arm. "Give it time, Neb. And if it doesn't happen in the next year or two, it won't matter. I may not have any sway with your headmaster, but I do know a few archeologists that owe me a favor. Once you've reached your majority, we won't need the headmaster's leave. I'll arrange something." He grinned. "It may not be very glamorous, though."

For a moment, Neb felt like his father might actually love him. He smiled. "Thanks, Brother Hebda."

Setting down the pear, Neb felt a stab of loss at the memory. That numb, hollow feeling still licked at the edges of him, but at the core, he felt the twisting of a hot knife.

He would never see Brother Hebda again. There would be no more chats in the park in the shadow of the Orphanage. That first time he'd put his arm around him was the last time. And there would be no assignment with him in the Churning Wastes.

Neb tried to push his grief aside, but it pushed back. And he could not stop the tears when they arrived.

Jín Lí Tam

Jin Li Tam had been sure that of all nights, this would be a night that Sethbert would summon her. She suspected that her father would want her to do what was expected and use the opportunity to learn more about the Overseer's plot. But a part of her wondered if she didn't already know enough, wondered if she shouldn't, instead, slide a knife between his ribs. Of course, at least half the few times—of late—he'd summoned her, he'd had her carefully searched as well.

But Sethbert didn't summon her. Instead, he called a council of his generals and waved Jin Li Tam away in dismissal. She was grateful for it.

She closed the tent flap, tying a set of ankle bells to the silk rope so that the door couldn't move without the subdued tinkling. Jin Li Tam had been trained since girlhood to use all of the accoutrements of her courtesan role to keep herself safe and the information flowing back to House Li Tam.

Slippers and all, she wore her riding silks to bed, her hand wrapped around the handle of her slender, curved knife. Before the banquet, she had hidden a small bundle wrapped in a dark cloak beneath her bed. She could magick herself, slip past Sethbert's patrols, and be to the Wandering Army before morning.

But only if Rudolfo sent a man. And if he did, she would be sure of the hidden message she'd found in his hastily tapped words.

A sunrise such as you belongs in the East with me, Rudolfo had said. But he'd pressed the word "sunrise" harder and he inverted the word "east," and turned his fingers ever so slightly on the word "belongs," giving it a sense of urgency.

The message was that there was compelling need for her to leave the camp and travel west before the sun rose.

But the message behind the message was even more intriguing: Rudolfo somehow knew an ancient form of House Li Tam's nonverbal sublanguage. The "accent"—if you could call it that—was off, giving it an older, more formal tone.

Before the banquet, when she'd made her preparations to leave, she had expected to flee south and west, making her way back to the Emerald Coasts under magicks until she was far enough away to not be recognized.

But now, another offer seemed to be clearly—and cleverly—presented.

This Rudolfo, she thought, may be a bit of a fop. But there was hardness in his eyes and practiced purpose in the way his fingers moved along her wrist.

She willed herself into a light sleep, one ear turned toward the bell on her door.

◦∕

Jin Li Tam awoke to the hand over her mouth. She brought the small knife up and as she stabbed with it, another strong hand snaked in to grip her wrist. She struggled against the intruder. "Easy, Lady Tam," a voice whispered. "I bear a message from General Rudolfo." She stopped struggling. "Would you hear it?"

She nodded and he released her. "I would hear."

The Gypsy Scout cleared his voice, then recited the message. "General Rudolfo bids you good evening and assures you that his proposition is true. He bids you to choose well between he and Sethbert and to consider your father in all of this. It is true that the Wandering Army is small, but as you well know, House Li Tam will launch its Iron Armada to honor its secret kin-clave with Windwir, and when they blockade the Three Rivers and its Delta, it won't matter how small General Rudolfo's army is. Sethbert will be divided, fighting the fight in two theaters."

Jin Li Tam smiled. Her father was right about this Rudolfo. He was a formidable leader.

The Gypsy Scout went on. "Meanwhile, should you choose well, you shall be his guest until this unpleasantness passes and you can be reunited with your father."

She nodded. Of course, her father's secret kin-clave was with the Androfrancines, but Rudolfo's messenger was proof that other alliances were being sought. House Li Tam, a ship-building concern that had established a successful line of banks over five hundred years ago that—known for their political neutrality—even handled the massive Androfrancine accounts. Because House Li Tam had no formal, acknowledged kin-clave with any of the powers, they were free to collect and share information on all of them to the highest bidders.

"What does Rudolfo get out of this for himself?"

She could hear the Scout's smile around his reply. "He said that when you asked that question, I should tell you that one dance with the sunrise will warm him all the days of his life."

She chuckled. "I see. A king who wishes he were a poet."

"We will be waiting to the west for you, should you accept General Rudolfo's offer of aid."

And then she was alone in the dark again. Once more, the bell didn't ring.

Jin Li Tam didn't need any time to make her decision. It had already been made before the scout arrived. But she'd wondered earlier if Rudolfo would make the third gesture, and the scout in her tent was sufficient. Typically, there would be less subterfuge involved, perhaps even a formal gathering. But each of Rudolfo's three gestures bore a subtlety that could be open to interpretation. The first had been the offer to dance in the presence of Sethbert. The second had been another message he had tapped into her wrist, the last words: *And I would never call you consort.*

She had her third gesture. If there had been only one or two gestures within the night, it would have meant nothing. But the third gesture contained yet another hidden message, and she knew for certain now that this Rudolfo was a Whymer Maze of hidden paths behind secret doors. That last hidden message was clearly present, wrapped in the cloak of courtesy to her father. It was the third gesture of a night, a clear point made with subtle grace.

Lord Rudolfo of the Ninefold Forest Houses had announced himself as a potential suitor, following the ancient kin-clave rite prescribed for a Lord seeking alliance between Houses in order to defeat a common foe.

That meant that if she wished to, she could invoke the Providence of Kin-Clave, and by doing so, state without words that she was accepting him as a suitor.

Jin Li Tam wondered how much of this her father already knew, and decided that it had probably been his idea in the first place.

Chapter

6

Rudolfo

Rudolfo slept for two hours in the back of a supply wagon, dreaming of the redheaded Lady, before Third Alarm woke him. He leaped from the pile of empty sacks, drawing his sword and dropping lightly to the ground.

He raced past mustering soldiers and stopped at his own tent. He'd long ago learned the value of not using his own bed or tent in the field. Gregoric stood waiting.

"Well?" Rudolfo asked.

Gregoric grinned. "You were correct, Lord. Entrolusian scouts. Magicked."

"Did they see what they came to see?"

Gregoric nodded. "And left quickly when I called the alarm."

"Very good. That will give them cause to scamper quickly home. And our own scouts?"

"Also magicked and right behind them."

Magicked scouts were nearly impossible to spot when you did not expect them. But Rudolfo *had* expected them. They had come. They had seen Isaak. They had left. And five of his best and bravest Gypsy Scouts had followed after.

"Very well. I will want to hear their report personally."

"Yes, Lord."

Rudolfo turned and entered the tent. The metal man's eyes glowed softly in the dark. "Isaak, are you well?"

The metal man whirred to life. The eyes blinked rapidly. "Yes, Lord."

Rudolfo walked over to him and squatted down. "I do not believe you are responsible for the devastation of Windwir."

"You indicated that may be the case. I only know what I remember."

Rudolfo thought about this for a moment. "What you *don't* remember is possibly more relevant. The missing time between seeking Brother Charles and finding yourself in the streets uttering Xhum Y'Zir's spell." He looked at his sword, watched the light from Isaak's eyes play out on its burnished surface. "I do not think it was a malfunction. Sethbert—the Overseer of the Entrolusian City States—has a man who knows how to write those metal scrolls. He even has a metal man of his own."

"I do not understand. The Androfrancines and their Gray Guard are so careful—"

"Guards can be purchased. Gates can be slipped. Keys can be stolen." Rudolfo patted the metal man's knee. "You are quite a wondrous spectacle, my friend, but I suspect you understand little the capacity we humans have for good or ill."

"I've read about it," the metal man said with a sigh. "But you're right; I do not understand it."

"I hope you never do," Rudolfo said. "But on to other things. I have questions for you."

"I will answer truthfully, Lord."

Rudolfo nodded. "Good. How were you damaged?"

Isaak's metal eyelids flashed surprise. "Why, your men attacked me, Lord. I thought you knew this."

"My men found you in a crater and brought you to me straightaway."

"No, the first ones."

Rudolfo stroked his beard. "Tell me more."

"The fire had fallen, the lightning had blasted, and I returned to the library seeking Brother Charles or someone who could terminate me for my crimes. Nothing remained but ash and charred stone. I began calling for help, and your men came for me with nets and chains. I sought to evade and they attacked me. I fell into the crater. Then the others came and brought me to you."

Rudolfo offered a grim smile. "I wondered. Now I know more. By morning, I will know all."

Isaak looked up. "Lord, you bid me remind you to return to your question about the removal of my work-related memories."

"Ah, that." Rudolfo stood. "Perhaps it will come to nothing. Perhaps tomorrow, we will go down an altogether different path." He extended his hand to the metal man, who took it. The metal fingers were cool to his touch. "But if the winds of fate allow it, I would have work for you in my forest manor, Isaak."

"Work, Lord?"

Rudolfo smiled. "Yes. The greatest treasure in the world lies between your metal ears. I would have you write it all down for me."

Isaak released his hand. His eyes went hot and steam shot out from him. "I will not, Lord. I will not be anyone's weapon again."

For a brief moment, Rudolfo tasted fear in his mouth. A metallic taste. "No, no, no." He reached out, took up the hand again. "Never that, Isaak. But the other bits. The poetry, the plays, the histories, the philosophies, the mythologies, the maps. Everything the Androfrancine library protected and preserved . . . at least what bits you know. I would not have these pass from our world because of a buffoon's ambition."

"That is a monumental task, Lord, for a single servitor."

"I believe," Rudolfo said, "that you may have some help."

Ǝ⁓

The magicked Gypsy Scouts returned from the Entrolusian camp before dawn. They carried a bound, gagged, hooded man between them, deposited him in a chair and removed his hood. Another scout put a large leather pouch on the table.

Servers laid breakfast on the table—oranges, pomegranates, cakes made with nuts and honey, berries with liquored syrup—while Rudolfo studied their guest. He was a smallish man with delicate fingers and a broad face. His eyes bulged and veins stood out on his neck and forehead.

Isaak stared. Rudolfo patted his arm. "He looks familiar to you?"

The metal man clicked. "He does, Lord. He was Brother Charles's apprentice."

Rudolfo nodded. He sat at the head of the table and nibbled at a cake, washing it down with chilled peach wine.

The Gypsy Scouts gave their report; it was brief.

"So how many do they have?"

"Thirteen in total, Lord," the chief scout answered. "They are in a tent near the center of his camp. We found him sleeping among them."

"Thirteen," Rudolfo said, stroking his beard. "How many mechoservitors did the Androfrancines have, Isaak?"

"That is all of them, lord."

He waved to the nearest Scout. "Remove his gag."

The man blustered and flushed, his eyes wild and his mouth working like a landed trout. He started to speak but Rudolfo shushed him.

Rudolfo stabbed a slice of orange with a small silver fork. "I will ask you questions; you will answer them. Otherwise you will not speak."

The man nodded.

Rudolfo pointed at Isaak with his fork. "Do you recognize this metal man?"

The man nodded again, his face now pale.

"Did you change this mechoservitor's script on the orders of Overseer Sethbert of the Entrolusian City States?"

"I . . . I did. Overseer Sethbert—"

Rudolfo snapped his fingers. A scout drew a slim dagger, placing its tip at the man's throat. "Just yes or no for now."

The man swallowed. "Yes."

The knife eased up.

Rudolfo selected another slice of orange and popped it into his mouth. "Did you do this terrible thing for money?"

The man's eyes filled with tears. His jaw tensed. Slowly, he nodded again.

Rudolfo leaned forward. "And do you understand exactly what you did?"

The Androfrancine apprentice sobbed. When he didn't nod right away, the scout refocused him on Rudolfo's question with a point of the blade. "Y-yes, Lord."

Rudolfo chewed a bit of pomegranate. He kept his voice level and low. "Do you wish mercy for this terrible crime?"

The sobbing escalated. A low whine rose to a howl so full of misery, so full of despair that it lay heavy on the air.

"Do you," Rudolfo said again, his voice even quieter, "want mercy for your terrible crime?"

"I didn't know it would work, Lord. I swear to you. And none of us thought that if it *did* work it would be so . . . so utterly, so . . ."

Rudolfo raised his hand and his eyebrows. The man stopped. "How could you know? How could anyone know? Xhum Y'Zir has been dead over two thousand years. And his so-called Age of Laughing Madness has long passed."

Rudolfo carefully selected another honeyed cake, nibbling at its corners. "So my question remains: Do you wish mercy?"

The man nodded.

"Very well. You have one opportunity and only one. I can not say the same for your liege." Rudolfo looked over at the metal man. His eyes flashed and a slight trail of steam leaked from the corners of his mouth. "In a few moments, I am going to leave you here with my best Gypsy Scouts and my metallic friend, Isaak. I want you to very slowly, very clearly and in great detail, explain everything you know about scripting, maintaining and repairing Androfrancine mechoservitors." Rudolfo stood. "You only have one chance and you only have a few hours. If you do not satisfy me, you will spend the rest of your natural days in chains, on Tormentor's Row for all the known world to see, while my Physicians of Penitent Torture peel away your skin with salted knives and wait for it to grow back." He tossed back the rest of his wine. "You will spend the rest of your days in urine and feces and blood, with the screams of young children in your ears and the genocide of a city on your soul."

The man vomited now, choking foul-smelling bile onto his tunic.

Rudolfo smiled. "I'm so glad you understand me." He paused at the tent flap. "Isaak, pay careful attention to the man."

Outside, he waved for Gregoric. "Bring me a bird."

He wrote the message himself. It was a simple, one-word question. After he wrote it, he tied it to the bird's foot with the green thread of peace, but it felt like a lie. He whispered a destination to the bird and pressed his lips briefly to its small, soft head. Then he threw it at the sky and the sky caught it, sent it flapping south to the Entrolusian camp.

He whispered the question he had written. It sounded empty, but he whispered it again. "Why?"

Neb

Neb didn't realize he had fallen asleep until he felt a hand shaking him awake. He opened his eyes, jerking alert. The redheaded woman knelt next to him. She was wearing a dark cloak, but the hood was pushed back and her hair was up.

She placed a finger over her lips. When he nodded, she spoke in a low voice. "War is coming. It's not safe here. Do you understand?"

He nodded.

"Sethbert destroyed Windwir and is giddy with his handiwork. He's keeping you alive so that your story can entertain him. Do you understand?"

Neb swallowed. He'd wondered about that and now he knew. He opened his mouth, thought better before speaking and then closed it. He nodded again.

"I'm leaving now. I want you to come with me."

He nodded, scrambling out of the cot.

"Stay near me," she said, drawing a pouch out from under her shirt where it hung on a cord around her neck. She loosed the drawstrings and poured a handful of powder into her hand. She cast it at her forehead, her shoulders and her feet, then licked the remainder of the powder from the palm of her hand.

Neb watched as her eyes rolled back, then watched as she faded to a shadow in front of his eyes. For a moment, he thought she might magick him as well, and the prospect terrified him. He'd read about scout-magicks and knew how they could affect the untrained and inexperienced. But then she sealed the pouch and dropped it back inside her shirt.

"Follow me," she said. She unraveled a silk string from her wrist and attached it to his wrist as well.

Holding the string, he moved with her as she slipped out of the tent and into the predawn morning. Neb followed her into the darker places of the darkened camp, sliding past tents where soldiers snored and mumbled. He did the best he could to keep track of where they were, but it seemed she changed direction just as he would get oriented.

Finally, they left the camp altogether and moved silently through the forest. As they ran, the redheaded woman's words sank into him.

Sethbert destroyed Windwir. Those words kept at him, pressing him, prodding him, but he did not know why. He'd heard the soldiers earlier, but agreed that Androfrancine curiosity was a more likely culprit than the Overseer, madness or not. But now, this woman not only believed it, but also said war was coming, and she could have just left. But she hadn't—she had come to him first, taking more risk onto herself than she needed.

Neb trusted that.

Sethbert destroyed Windwir. Again, it pressed and prodded. Something behind that wall of words crumbled a bit more, and light peeked through.

Sethbert.

When it hit him, Neb stopped short and the string went taut. The redheaded woman stopped, and in the gray light Neb could see the faintest shimmer of her as she crouched.

"Why have you stopped? We're nearly there."

He wished he could open his mouth and explain to her why he couldn't go with her. He wished he could tell her about the bolt of electricity that passed through him when he realized the truth.

Sethbert destroyed Windwir.

Neb hadn't really killed his father—Sethbert had. And it changed everything.

Because of that, he couldn't leave with her now.

Because of that, he had to go back and kill Sethbert.

Petronus

As the sun rose behind him in a birdless sky, Petronus crested the ridge and looked down on the Desolation of Windwir.

Nothing could have prepared him for it. He'd crested this

ridge hundreds of times, riding out and back on various assignments for the Order. Certainly he'd known this time that he wouldn't see the familiar sights. The large ships at the docks, low in the water with cargo bound for the Entrolusian Delta. The wide, high stone walls that encircled the various quarters that made up the world's greatest city. The spires of the cathedrals and of the Great Library, colors waving in the morning breeze. The houses and shops outside the city gates, nestled up against the walls like calves against their mother.

Petronus slid from the saddle and let his horse tend itself. He stood, shaking, studying the scene that unfolded before him.

He'd known better than to expect any of these things, but he'd thought surely there'd be something familiar to him here.

There was not.

The charred ruins were scattered across the field, and there was no clear delineation where the wreckage of the city stopped and the wreckage of the outlying areas began. Flecked with impact craters and mounds of black rubble, the landscape stretched out and away, ending abruptly at the river's edge. It was bordered by hills to the west and south, and Petronus could see the smoke and flags of the Gypsy camp nestled between foothills.

There was no sign of the Entrolusian camp, but knowing Sethbert, it was hidden away, within reach but not easy reach. A man seldom fell far afield of his father, and from everything he'd heard, Sethbert was every bit as paranoid and problematic as the man who'd raised him and trained him up into his current role. Petronus had once had Aubert removed from the Papal Residence under the watchful eyes of the Gray Guard for threatening the Pope's hospitality staff after accusing them of some kind of treachery or another.

Of course, the same theory would apply to Rudolfo. He'd known the father well enough. Jakob was a fair albeit ruthless man who ruled his Ninefold Forest Houses with a blend of Androfrancine sensibility and uncompromising attention to the Rites of Kin-Clave. He hadn't balked at putting heretics on Tormentor's Row . . . but neither had he been willing to allow the Order access to those prisoners.

Petronus suspected that Rudolfo was made of similar stuff as his father, too. He'd been a boy when Petronus had set into motion his transition out of power. But soon after, Jakob died and that boy was forced to early manhood, taking up the turban of his fallen father. The old man had heard a bit here or there, most notably that he'd stood with the Freehold of the Emerald Coasts in their decision to embargo the City States when they announced their annexation of the Gulf of Shylar and its free cities. Rudolfo had earned a reputation as a brilliant strategist and a competent swordsman during the skirmishes that followed.

He gathered what little he knew about both men and stored it away for future use.

Even now, he told himself, in the face of this devastation, you're scheming and plotting, old man. But why? He'd needed to see for himself that it was gone. He couldn't wait for the birds or the other messengers—no one's description, written or spoken, would've been good enough. He needed to see it himself.

Beyond that, what did it matter? There were two kings on the field, both having kin-clave with the fallen city. And both men were competent—albeit different—leaders.

You've seen what you came to see. Go home now. Return to your boat and your nets and your quiet life.

He turned away from the blasted plain below him, recovered his reins, and then turned back.

"There's nothing here that I can do," Petronus said out loud. "It's not my place."

But in his heart he knew it was a lie.

Jin Li Tam

Jin Li Tam knew they were close when the boy stopped. The magicks had not only enhanced her speed and her strength, but also her sight and her sense of smell. The trade-off was the buzzing in her ears and the shifting headache. Her father had seen to it that she was trained in all manner of subterfuge, including the use of stealth magick even though it was considered unseemly for a noble to use the Elder Ways.

She looked at the boy when he stopped, and what she saw raised the fine hair on her forearms. Alternating waves of anger and relief washed his face, and he kept looking behind them, pulling at the string.

"We're nearly there," she said in a low voice. "Keep moving."

Then he did the unexpected. His hand snaked out, catching the magick pouch that dangled from her neck and tugging it so hard that the cord snapped. With his other hand, he snapped the silk thread that bound him to her. She reached out to grab him, but he was already running back toward the camp.

Cursing beneath her breath, Jin Li Tam followed him. She knew that she could catch him easily, but the sky above proclaimed the cusp of morning and every minute she spent going in the wrong direction was a minute closer to being caught. But she couldn't leave the boy knowing what Sethbert's state of mind was. She moved quickly after him.

She overtook him and caught his shoulder, spinning him around and to the ground. She pounced on him. "I don't know what you're playing at," she whispered, "but nothing good awaits you there."

He struggled against her, his mouth working and his eyes rolling.

I should've drugged him and carried him, she thought. He's less well than I thought.

"I think," a new voice said low in her ear, "that you should release the boy now and stand up slowly." She felt the cold steel tip of a knife pressed in against her ribs, near the back of her heart.

She released the boy and did as she was told. Shadow hands grabbed the boy and pulled him to his feet. More hands gripped her and held her away from him.

A shadow face leaned in to hers. She could make out the

blond stubble on the chin and could smell the roast pork on his breath. A single blue eye took form just inches from her own eye.

Another whisper cut the night, drifting across the forest. "What do you have there, Deryk?"

Jin stayed quiet.

"A woman and a boy." The blue eye blinked. "She's magicked, too."

Another shadow slipped into the clearing. Jin Li Tam carefully looked around. She could see the patches in the soft forest loam where their boots were—or at least had been. She could pick out the faintest breeze as they shifted around her. But the magicks held, and unless they were inches apart, she could not see them. Still, standard Academy tactics suggested a half-squad loosely surrounded her.

She looked at the boy. He seemed unafraid. The pouch he'd taken from her was nowhere to be seen, and she wondered if he'd hidden it in his shirt. If so, they'd find it soon enough.

"The boy looks familiar to me," the voice said again. "Aren't you the lad we brought down from the ridge? The one with the wagon?"

The boy nodded.

The voice moved now across the clearing to Jin's side. Hands fumbled with the hood of her cloak. "And who do we have here?"

Another eye appeared near her face—this one brown and speckled with green. It widened and he gasped. "Well this is a surprise." A smile formed in the shadow.

"You'd do well to release us now and go about your business," Jin Li Tam said, her voice barely above a whisper.

The scout captain laughed. "I don't think you'll convince us of that, Lady Tam . . . no matter how persuasive your courtesan ways may be."

Jin Li Tam relaxed the muscles in her shoulders and in her arms; she willed her legs to unlock. "I can be very persuasive."

The sky was purpling now, and she knew that when the

sun rose, what little of the scout magicks that remained would be half as effective. There was no time for preferred strategies in the face of this present crisis.

"I'm sure you can—"

She dropped before he could finish his sentence, and as she fell to her knees, she flicked her wrist and felt the small knife's handle fall into the palm of her hand. Pitching forward, she ran the knife once around the back of his boot as she rolled toward the boy. As she came up, her hand wove the air, the blade slipping in and out of cloth as she cut where the magicked scouts should be if they were following their own field guides. The howls told her she was not far from the mark.

The one behind her—the one whose knife had pressed into her back—growled and lunged forward, knocking her over. And then she was all knees and elbows, whipping the cloak around his knife hand as she brought her own blade up to the side of his throat.

"Be still," she said. "You don't have to die here today."

But he moved and she didn't give it a second thought. Father trained his daughters very well indeed. Pulling herself into a crouch, she looked around the clearing. She could smell the blood and she could see the wet patches of black on the gray shadows that lay groaning and thrashing on the ground.

The boy was gone now. She could hear him running full on for the Entrolusian camp, and she knew that she could catch him. But what would she do when she did? The look on his face spoke to more than just having left something valuable behind. It spoke of compelling need, of resolution, of a decision being made.

She would let him run. But she would also do what she could to protect him right here, right now. It didn't matter that the injured scouts had recognized her—she would be under Rudolfo's offered protection in a matter of hours. But they had also recognized the boy. And for whatever reason, the boy was returning to Sethbert's care.

One by one, speaking quiet words of reassurance to the

hamstrung scouts, she moved from man to man and cut each throat with careful, practiced precision.

She wiped the blood from her knife onto a twitching, silk-clad corpse and stood, facing west. Then she ran, and the thought came to her again, unbidden but true:

Father trained his daughters very well indeed.

Chapter

7

Rudolfo

It took less than two hours for the apprentice to teach Isaak his trade. When Rudolfo returned to his tent, the metal man sat at the table, sifting through the pouch of tools and scrolls, and the man was gone.

"Do you know enough?" Rudolfo asked.

Isaak looked up. "Yes, Lord."

"Do you want to kill him yourself?"

Isaak's eyelids fluttered, his metal ears tilted and bent. He shook his head. "No, Lord."

Rudolfo nodded and shot Gregoric a look. Gregoric returned the nod grimly and left in silence.

The bird had returned in less than an hour. His question had gone unanswered. Sethbert's reply had been terse: *Return to me the man you took. Surrender the servitor that destroyed Windwir.*

He'd had an hour to ponder the why. Ambition? Greed? Fear? The Androfrancines could have ruled the world with their magicks and mechanicals, yet they hid in their city, sent out their archeologists and scholars to dig and to learn, to understand the present through the past . . . and to protect that past for the future. In the end, he found it didn't matter so much why the City States and their mad Overseer had ended that work. What mattered was that it never happen again.

"Are you okay, Isaak?"

"I grieve, Lord. And I rage."

"Aye. Me, too."

A scout cleared his voice outside. "Lord Rudolfo?"

He looked up. "Yes?"

"A woman met the forward scouts west of Sethbert's camp, Lord. She came magicked and asking for your protection under the Providence of Kin-Clave."

He smiled but there was no satisfaction in it. Maybe later, when all of this unpleasantness had passed. "Very well. Prepare her for travel."

"Lord?"

"She is to be escorted to the seventh manor. You leave within the hour. The metal man goes with her. Select and magick a half-squad to assist you."

"Yes, Lord."

"And fetch me my raven." Rudolfo fell back into the cushions, exhaustion washing over him.

"Lord Rudolfo?" The metal man struggled to his feet, his damaged leg sparking. "Am I leaving you?"

"Yes, Isaak, for a bit." He rubbed his eyes. "I wish for you to start that work we spoke of. When I am finished here, I will bring you help."

"Is there anything I can do here, Lord?"

He doesn't wish to go, Rudolfo realized. But he was too tired to find words of explanation. And the metal man brought something out in him—something like compassion. He couldn't bear to tell him that he was simply too dangerous a weapon to have on the battlefield. Rudolfo rubbed his eyes again and yawned. "Pack your tools, Isaak. You're leaving soon."

The metal man packed, then swung the heavy pouch over his shoulder. Rudolfo climbed to his feet.

"The woman you will be traveling with is Jin Li Tam of House Li Tam. I would have you bear a message to her."

Isaak said nothing, waiting.

"Tell her she chose well and that I will come to her when I am finished here."

"Yes, Lord."

Rudolfo followed Isaak out of the tent. His raven awaited, its feathers glossy and dark as a wooded midnight. He took it from the scout's steady hands.

"When you reach the seventh manor," he told his scout, "tell my steward there that Isaak—the metal man—bears my grace."

The scout nodded once and left. Isaak looked at Rudolfo. His mouth opened and closed; no words came out.

Rudolfo held the raven close, stroking its back with his finger. "I will see you soon, Isaak. Start your work. I'll send the others when I've freed them. You've a library to rebuild."

"Thank you," the metal man finally said.

Rudolfo nodded. The scout and the metal man left. Gregoric returned, wiping the apprentice's blood from his hands.

"Sethbert wants his man back," Rudolfo said.

"I've already seen to it, Lord."

Somewhere on the edge of camp, Rudolfo thought, a stolen pony ambled its way home bearing a cloth-wrapped burden. "Very well. Magick the rest of your Gypsy Scouts."

"I've seen to that as well, Lord."

He looked at Gregoric and felt a pride that burned brighter than his grief or his rage. "You're a good man."

Rudolfo pulled a thread from the sleeve of his rainbow robe. This time, no other message. This time, no question. He tied the scarlet thread of war to the foot of his darkest angel. When he finished, he whispered no words and he did not fling his messenger at the sky. It leaped from his hands on its own and sped away like a black arrow. He watched it fly until he realized Gregoric had spoken.

"Gregoric?" he asked.

"You should rest, Lord," the chief of his Gypsy Scouts said again. "We can handle this first battle without you."

"Yes, I should," Rudolfo said. But he knew there would be time enough for rest—perhaps even a lifetime of rest—after he won the war.

Neb

The Entrolusian camp was at second alarm when Neb slipped back into his tent. He'd run when the woman attacked the scouts, but he'd seen enough to know she was not the typical noble. The magicks had concealed most of her movement, but it was as if a violent wind had rolled across the clearing. Over his shoulder, he heard men shouting and falling, and a part of him wanted to go back and make sure the woman truly was okay. But she seemed the sort to take care of herself and that meant he needed to get as far away from her as he could. Now that he knew what must be done, he couldn't afford to let her take him away from Sethbert, no matter how good her intentions might be.

The genocide of the Androfrancine Order hung upon the Overseer's head and Neb meant to hold him to justice for it. He hid the pouch of stolen magicks. He'd seen the lady use them—the casting seemed easy enough.

He pretended to wake up when the serving woman entered with fresh clothing and a platter of breakfast. She placed the clothing at the foot of his cot and the food on the table, then curtsied at the door. She looked like she wanted to say something, and Neb watched her. Finally, she spoke. "I've just come from the officers' mess. Word is that Rudolfo's war-raven arrived this morning. There was a raid last night. An Androfrancine was taken right from his tent as he slept. The Overseer's Lady, Jin Li Tam, was taken as well. And a half-squad of our scouts were butchered west of camp. These are dangerous days, boy. I'd stay close to the tent if I were you."

He nodded. After she left, he wondered about the Androfrancine. He'd seen glimpses of him—he wore the robes of an apprentice, colored in the drab brown of the Office for Mechanical Study. He wondered if he'd been taken or if he'd left. And the thought of the dead scouts made his stomach sink. At least he was confident she'd gotten away from them. When he'd run, he'd not looked back but he'd also not had any doubt in her ability to protect herself.

Not only was she one of the most beautiful woman he'd ever seen—tall, with copper hair that threw back the sunlight and piercing blue eyes and alabaster skin, lightly freckled in the waning second summer. But now it seemed she was also the most lethal.

Neb moved to the table and ate a breakfast of eggs and rice, chased with a crisp apple cider and a wedge of cheddar cheese. While he ate, he plotted the assassination of the man who killed his father.

He'd never really thought about killing anyone before. Well, that wasn't exactly true. He had thought about it once about two years ago, but it was a brief thought. He'd been thirteen then and the Gray Guard had come to the school to make their annual round for recruits.

He was a big man, a captain named Grymlis, standing tall and broad in his dress gray cap, cloak, trousers and jacket—offset starkly by the black shirt. The blue thread of inquiry woven together with the white thread of kin-clave formed the jacket and trouser piping. The long, slender sword flashed silver as he whipped it in the air.

The orphans fell back, gasping, and the tip of the sword hung in the air, pointed at one of the larger boys. "What about you?"

The boy's mouth opened and closed.

"Could *you* kill a man?"

The boy shot a frightened look to Headmaster Tobel, where he stood near Arch-Scholar Demtras and a few of the teachers. "I'm not . . . I'm—"

But the Gray Guard captain growled and whipped the sword

again. "P'Andro Whym said that one death is a burning library of knowledge and experience," the captain said. "P'Andro Whym said that to take another's life is a graver error than ignorance." He laughed, whipping the sword around, his eyes passing over the assembled boys. "But remember this, boys: He also said that above all things, guard knowledge that it might protect you on the path of change." The sword whipped past Neb close enough that he'd felt the wind from it.

"And in early days of the Laughing Madness," the guard said, quoting the Whymer Bible, "there were soldiers that came to P'Andro Whym in his shattered crystal garden dome and inquired of him—"

—*What must we do? We do not read, nor do we cipher, and yet we are compelled to protect knowledge that light might remain in the minds of men.* The words unrolled in Neb's mind, words from the Eighteenth Gospel. *And P'Andro Whym looked upon them and wept at their devotion to truth and said unto them* —

"—Walk with my seekers, clothed in the ash of yesterday's world, and guard ye what is found. Guard ye the founders. Raise up men who would do the same."

The sword whipped again. This time it pointed to Neb. "What of you, boy? Would you kill for the truth? Would you kill to keep the light alive?"

Neb didn't hesitate. "I'd die for it, sir."

The old captain leaned in, and Neb saw the hardness in his eyes. He leaned in close enough that his bushy white beard brushed Neb's chin. "I've done one but not the other," the old guard said. "But I'd daresay the killing is harder than the dying."

That night, Neb lay awake and thought about the old soldier. He wondered how many men that captain had killed, whether or not Neb could do it if he ever had to. He'd fallen asleep unsure and hadn't thought about it again until now—two years later.

There were practical considerations. So far, he'd only

thought about the magicks. Under the magicks, he could steal a knife or maybe even a sword. Then it was simply a matter of getting past Sethbert's honor guard.

But then there were the deeper considerations. It wasn't hard to figure out that his chances of surviving weren't high. He'd said he was willing to die for the truth, for knowledge. But he'd never really considered that he might die for justice. Until a few days ago, he'd not been able to personally claim any real injustice. Certainly, he'd spent many quieter moments wondering what his life would be like if he'd had a mother and a father—or at least, a father that he didn't address as Brother Hebda. But it was hardly unjust—he was well cared for, educated, clothed and challenged by the best of the Androfrancine Order—a life that was only available to the Orphans of P'Andro Whym. The sons and daughters of nobility attended University in most instances, sometimes even Academy, but they never got past the first corner of the Great Library. Neb and his friends had even walked past the mechoservitor cells, heard them buzzing and clicking in the third basement.

The murder of his father, of Windwir—and, he realized, the murder of the Androfrancine Order—were injustices so massive that his heart could not contain them. It staggered his mind.

Neb didn't know if he would kill to keep the light alive, as the guard had put it. With the city in ruins and the library nothing but charred stone and ash, he doubted if there would be much light to protect.

Neb wondered what that old guard would've said about killing to avenge the light snuffed out.

Petronus

Petronus walked his horse to the edge of the city. He'd told himself that he would turn back, that he just needed a closer look. Something he couldn't name compelled him. Wrath and despair twisted back and forth inside of him, chasing one another around a hollow space at his core.

He walked his horse so that he could feel the crunching of ash and charcoal beneath his feet and know that it was real. He paused every few steps to inhale a lung full of the smell of sulfur, ozone and smoke. And his eyes moved across the blasted landscape, looking for something but he didn't know what.

Petronus certainly knew the Fivefold Path of Grief. He'd started his long road to the Papacy in the Office of Francine Practice, analyzing and manipulating the pathways of thought and behavior. He was moving between the Sword and the Empty Purse for the most part—but found himself back on the Blinded Eye from time to time.

It wasn't that he hadn't seen death and destruction. A few days before he started plotting his own assassination, Petronus had ordered the sacking of a Marsher village in retribution for a raid on one of the free towns upriver. The Marshers had killed half the men and a quarter of the children. They'd also destroyed a small, guarded caravan returning from the Churning Wastes carrying relics and parchment rolls deemed critical for immediate transport for either security or preservation reasons. After burying the dead, the Marshers had returned to their village across the river.

It hadn't been a hard decision, really. Petronus sent in the Gray Guard scouts, magicked and armed with arrows that burned upon impact with a white heat that not even water could put out. Another ancient bit of science kept back from the world so that the Order could keep its edge and limit just how far humanity could go along its headlong path to self destruction.

Petronus sent them in, led by a captain who was already old for the job. Grymlis was the only Gray Guard that Petronus knew could do what needed doing to push the Marsh King back into minding his own and still be able to sleep at night, he thought. So they burned the village on Petronus's orders, killing every man, woman and child.

Afterward, he'd insisted that they ride him out there. It had taken him a day and half. Grymlis had gone with him, though it was obvious that he did not want to, and did not think the Pope should go either.

Petronus had done the same thing then that he did now. It wasn't a large village, but it was larger than he had imagined. And he'd approached it on foot, though an assistant led his horse. Ash crunching beneath his feet, he'd approached the ruined village until he could see it through the haze of smoke that still rose from it. He could make out the charred lumber. The tumbled, steaming stones. The smoldering, black piles that had been . . . what? The larger ones were livestock. The smaller ones children, or maybe dogs. And everything else in between.

Petronus had gasped then, and covered his mouth with his hand, and even though he'd known exactly what he was doing when he gave the order nearly three days earlier, the realization of it shifted like the load of a wagon and it rocked him.

"Gods, what have I done?" he asked no one in particular.

"You did what you must to keep the light alive, Excellency," the captain said. "You've seen it now. You know what it looks like. We need to leave."

He turned around and walked back to his horse. He knew full well that the Marshers would not bury these dead. The Marsher way was simple: You ate or buried what you killed. You did not burn the living or dead—unless it was food.

The Androfrancines had come using fire and they had left those they killed unburied. The message to the Marsh King was clear. And Petronus was smart enough to know that Grymlis had only agreed to escort him back to the village because it added to the message: *Behold, I stand at the edge of your field of dead and turn my back.* The spies they had pointed out to him in the tree line would bear the last of the message back to their Marsh King, and Petronus's neighbors and caravans would be safe for another three or four years.

As he rode back to Windwir from that village so long ago, Petronus had realized suddenly that his life was close to becoming such a lie that he could no longer live it. When he returned, he started plotting against himself with the help of his named successor.

Now it was no longer a village before him. It was the largest, greatest city of the Named Lands. It had been his first lover, this city, and Petronus approached it.

Of course he saw the connection immediately. *I'm identifying with past grief and seeking redemption for perceived wrong.* He'd wondered if the Market Path would eventually show up along the Fivefold way, and here he was, getting ready to bargain.

And certainly that was something he could anchor to within himself—a great sin that he had committed, that he could experience shame over and avoid the larger shame that threatened to swallow him whole.

If I'd been here. If I'd kept the throne and ring, this would have never happened. It would all still be here.

Yet he knew it wasn't true, that evaluating the present based on imagined and different pasts was an unsolvable cipher. Yet he felt it, and it didn't matter that it was a lie. It squeezed his heart and caught in his throat.

If I'd been here.

He ran the Whymer Maze inside himself as he shuffled forward on wooden legs. And then stopped.

He saw it now. What he had been looking for. He'd thought they were sticks, but how could there be so many sticks? And he thought they were stones but they were all nearly the same size, though certainly some where smaller. Bones scattered across the charred and cratered city. Seeing them, Petronus knew what he had to do.

He would bury Windwir's dead.

Jin Li Tam

Jin Li Tam wasn't sure what she expected. The scouts had been waiting for her, and though her own magicks were fading fast, theirs held true. Surrounded by ghosts, she ran with them across the hills beneath a morning sky until they reached the safety of Rudolfo's camp.

The camp of the Wandering Army was ablaze with unbridled color. There was no rhyme or reason to it, no theme that interconnected the rainbow hues of the Ninefold Forest Houses. Unless maybe, she thought, the theme was chaos.

One of Rudolfo's captains had greeted her upon her arrival, explaining that the general himself was busy. They'd even had a bird ready so that she could get word to her father of her recent change of situation. She composed her note over breakfast, using three different codes for the message, and flung the white bird at the sky.

The captain was waiting for her. He was a slight man with the dark green turban and crimson sash of a Gypsy Scout. His beard was oiled and immaculately groomed, dark and short. Two curved long knives rode in buckskin sheaths on each hip, and he carried a narrow longsword by its scabbard.

He appraised her with his dark eyes. "We will be riding to the seventh manor, Lady Tam."

She calculated the leagues. "Four days?"

"Three," he said. "We'll be moving fast."

Jin looked at the hill where the officers sat on their horses and the soldiers gathered. "When do you think the fighting will start?"

He looked at the sky as if the sparse clouds could predict pending violence. "Soon, Lady. And General Rudolfo wants us far away when that happens."

She nodded. "I'm ready to ride."

They brought a roan for her, and she climbed easily into the saddle. A half-squad of scouts pressed in, their stallions magicked to muffle their hooves and increase their stamina and speed. When she looked to the captain, he shifted uncomfortably.

"We have another rider coming."

It was the biggest horse she'd ever seen, its hooves still flecked with the powder that would muffle their sound to a whisper. It was black as midnight, and upon the stallion's back was a robed figure that sat too high in the saddle. The robed figure hissed and clanked as it shifted. A small gout of steam released from high in its back, and Jin realized that the back of the robe had been cut away to expose a small square grate made of metal. From a distance, it would look like an Androfrancine on the ride. But up close, Jin could clearly see the shining hands, the metal feet, the dim specks of golden light from beneath the hood.

"Lady Jin Li Tam," the metal man said, "I bear a message from Lord Rudolfo of the Ninefold Forest Houses, General of the Wandering Army."

As he turned, light fell on his face. This newer mechoservitor was far sleeker, far more refined than Sethbert's older model. She felt her eyes narrow as she examined him.

"I am to tell you," he continued, "that you have chosen well and that Lord Rudolfo will come to you when he can."

"Thank you," she said. Then she paused. "What am I to call you?"

The metal man nodded slightly. "You may refer to me as Mechoservitor Number Three. Lord Rudolfo calls me Isaak."

Jin Li Tam smiled. "I will call you Isaak, too."

The soldiers were double-checking their gear, tightening the straps on their saddlebags and testing their bow-strings.

The captain took the lead. "We leave fast—west, then north, then east—and we don't slow for the first twenty leagues." He pointed to Jin Li Tam and then to Isaak. "I want you two just behind me. The rest will hem us in." He nodded to a young scout with blond hair peeking out beneath his turban. "Daedrek, you'll take first scout. Brown bird for danger, white bird for stop."

Daedrek reached over to take the small partitioned bird basket. He looped it over the pommel of his saddle and laced the pull strings through the fingers of his left hand.

Jin Li Tam watched, fascinated. She'd heard stories about the Gypsy Scouts . . . legends, really, going back to the first Rudolfo, that desert thief who'd led his tribe of Gypsy Bandits into the far off forests of the New World to avoid the desolation of the old one. She'd heard the legends, but she'd never seen them in action.

She hoped they were better fighters than Sethbert's Delta Scouts. From the looks of them, she was pretty sure they were. There were only five plus their captain, but she could see the danger in their narrow eyes, their tight smiles and the way they cocked their heads at the slightest noise.

Daedrek surged forward, and the others waited now until he made the league.

She looked over to the metal man. It explained the larger horse. Obviously the mechanicals weren't nearly as heavy as they looked, but still easily twice that of a large man. Yet he rode well enough. She wondered if he'd ridden before now.

The captain whistled and they took off, riding low and pushing their horses hard. They rode with bows tied to their saddles and swords tucked beneath their arms.

As they moved over the first hill, Jin saw the Desolation of Windwir to her right, an expanse of scorched, pockmarked earth. She thought she saw a horse moving out there along the edge of the wasteland, but she couldn't be sure because the sun came out from behind a cloud and blocked out her view.

They rode for three hours before the white bird flashed back into the captain's short bird net. They stopped then to change out first scouts, then pressed on.

The day flashed by, and when the sun set, they could see the next river's low line of hills in the distance—the beginnings of the prairie ocean that hid Rudolfo's nine forests and their houses. They made a fireless camp, pitching their tents in a ring around the tent she shared with Isaak.

He sat in the corner and she lay in her bedroll. He clicked and clacked faintly, even when he wasn't moving, and she found it both disturbing and comforting.

She tried to sleep, but she couldn't. The events of the past few days would not release her. From the moment she saw the pillar of smoke until now—how much had transpired? How much had the world changed? How much had she changed?

She hadn't killed a man since her first kill when she was still a girl. She'd maimed her share, but at heart she still held on to some of the Whymer beliefs, no matter how impractical they were for her way of life. But today alone, she'd killed five. And she'd sworn off the possibility of children, and saw a magick woman three times a year to keep it that way. And this morning she'd been risking her life to help a boy she did not share blood with.

She'd known Sethbert was slowly going mad. Her father had told her it would be so because every sixth male child in Sethbert's family died in madness, a pattern that generations of kin had still not recognized and rectified. She had expected his gradual deterioration.

But she had never expected that she would be consort to the man who destroyed the Androfrancine Order, or that in the span of a night she would suddenly be kin-clave to the Gypsy King through his announcement as a suitor.

And now she shared a tent with a metal man made from yesterday's magick and science.

She looked over at him. He sat still, his eyes glowing faintly. "Do you sleep?"

A bit of steam escaped his back and he whirred. "I do not sleep, Lady."

"What do you do, then?"

He looked up, and limned in the light of his eyes, she could see the tears. "I grieve, Lady."

She was taken aback. Sethbert's mechoservitor had never shown any sign of emotion. This was new and frightening to her.

"You *grieve*?"

"I do. Surely you know of the Desolation of Windwir?"

She had not expected this. "I do know of it. I grieve it as well."

"It was a terrible thing."

She swallowed. "It was." A thought struck her. "You know," she said, "you're not alone. Sethbert has others—he has all of the others, if I remember right."

Isaak nodded. "He does. Lord Rudolfo assured me of it. He intends for them to help me with the library."

Library? She sat up. "What library?"

Isaak clicked and clacked as he shifted on his stool. "Between us, we contain perhaps a third of the library in our memory scrolls from our work in catalogs and translations. Lord Rudolfo has asked me to oversee the reconstruction of the library and the restoration of what knowledge remains."

She leaned forward. "Rudolfo is going to rebuild the library in the far north?"

"He is."

It was an unpredictable move. She wondered if her father knew of this. It wouldn't surprise her if he did. But the more she learned about this Rudolfo, the more she thought that perhaps this one could even outthink her father, and play the board three moves beyond his five.

That made him a strong suitor.

And his decisiveness. To rebuild the library, three days after the fires of the first had finally died, in the far north, away from the squabbles and politics of the Named Lands. The descendant and namesake of Xhum Y'zir's desert thief, suddenly host and patron to the greatest repository of human knowledge.

A strong suitor indeed, she thought.

"He is a good man," Isaak said, as if he were reading her mind. "He's told me that I'm not responsible for the Desolation of Windwir." He paused. "He tells me Sethbert is."

She nodded. "Rudolfo speaks the truth. I'm not sure how, but Sethbert destroyed Windwir. He was working with an Androfrancine apprentice."

More steam shot from Isaak's exhaust grate. His mouth opened and closed as his eyes shifted. More water leaked out from around the jewels. "I know how Sethbert destroyed Windwir," Isaak said, his voice low.

And in that moment, because of the tone in his voice or perhaps the way his shoulders chugged beneath the tattered

Androfrancine robe, Jin Li Tam realized that she knew, too. Somehow Sethbert had used this mechanical to bring down the city.

She looked for something to say to the metal man, something by way of comfort, but could not find the words.

Instead, she lay awake for a long time after that and wondered at the world they'd made.

Chapter

8

Rudolfo

First battles, Rudolfo thought, set the tone for the entire war.

Rudolfo sat astride his horse and watched the line of forest. Gregoric and his other captains gathered around. "I've had a vision," Rudolfo said to his men in a quiet voice. "The first battle shall be ours." He smiled at them, his hand upon the pommel of his long, narrow sword. "How shall we realize this vision of mine?"

Gregoric nudged his horse closer. "By striking fastest and first, General."

Rudolfo nodded. "I concur."

"We'll send the scouts in first and drive them west like pheasant. Sethbert is no strategist, but his general Lysias is Academy bred—very conservative. He'll see the ploy and try to engage the scouts, judging them to be the inferior force. He'll think to put them between the ruins and the river and call up his contingency to keep the battalion occupied." His voice was low, and Rudolfo watched him make frequent eye contact with the others, measuring them.

One of the other captains smiled. "First battalion will fall back at rapid retreat after a modest effort to hold their ground. If Lysias sees that what he thought was a brigade is only a battalion, he'll most likely pursue."

"Or divide his force when he sees that the scouts are our primary assault," Gregoric said. "Or both perhaps."

Rudolfo smiled, remembering the song very well. "Feint with the cutlass, strike with the knife."

"Then, strike with the cutlass, too," Gregoric said, finishing the lyrics out.

Rudolfo nodded. His father, Jakob, and his First Captain of the Gypsy Scouts had taught them the song to keep time with their blade and footwork. Later, Rudolfo realized, it had really been a strategy lesson, teaching him the Hymnal of the Wandering Army. Three hundred and thirteen songs had never been written down in the two thousand years that Rudolfo's people had occupied the Ninefold Forest. They were written in the hearts of the living, moving fortress that first Rudolfo had built so long ago, the Wandering Army, and sung down to his recruits from the first day of training forward.

"If he pursues the retreating battalion—as I'm sure he will," Gregoric continued, "he'll find three more waiting and we'll net that fish."

"Excellent work, captains," Rudolfo said. "I will ride with the scouts and open this war in a way that is fitting for the general of this Wandering Army."

Gregoric nodded and the others did the same. It pleased Rudolfo that none of them worried about him entering the field. It meant they understood him and respected him as a soldier and a general.

"Very well," Rudolfo said. He turned toward his aide. "And afterward," he said, "I will dine with the men."

Two hours later, Rudolfo hid in the copse of trees surrounded by magicked scouts. He sat on his horse but the scouts around him were on foot. Their magicks would move them at nearly the speed of a horse and hide them from the eye. But at those speeds they would not be quiet. They would sound like wind rushing across the ground.

Gregoric looked at Rudolfo. "General, would you give the whistle?"

Rudolfo smiled and nodded. "For Windwir, my Gypsy Scouts," he said quietly, and then whistled, low and long.

He kicked his horse alive and bolted toward the Entrolusian infantry encamped in the forest across the meadow, smiling at what they would see.

A horse, a single rider galloping forward with a narrow sword lifted high in the air. Around him, a wind low to the ground and roaring towards them.

He lowered himself on the back of his horse, holding his sword low and across the stallion's dark side. He heard his Gypsy Scouts around him, catching slight glimpses of the ones nearest—though very slight.

They raced the meadow, entering the woods at breakneck pace. A few magicked Delta Scouts shouted because there wasn't time to send up birds. Rudolfo assumed one must've decided to brave the rushing, invisible river because he heard the briefest clash of steel and a magick-muffled scream. The first of the Entrolusian soldiers rallied to that shouting, and Rudolfo rode straight into the center of them, Gypsy Scouts mowing over them like a wind of blades. Rudolfo turned then and rode back, laughing and waving his sword. He chose a man and rode him down, then took the ear off his sergeant.

"Where's your captain?" Rudolfo shouted.

The sergeant sneered and lunged forward with his sword, drawing a line of blood along the horse's side. Rudolfo kicked him back and brought the sword down on his neck. The sergeant fell, and Rudolfo whipped the sword over and took the ear off another soldier. "Where's your captain?"

The soldier pointed, and Rudolfo put the sword through his upper arm. He'd not fight in this war again, but he'd have his life for his respect.

Rudolfo spun the horse and rode in the direction the man had pointed.

It did not surprise Rudolfo that Sethbert's worst and weakest were out for this particular battle. It was wired into the Academy to use the worst resources first as a gauge of your opponent. It also told the farmers at home they, too, could die heroic deaths.

He found the captain standing with three soldiers and an aide. The ground moved around him strangely, giving the Delta scouts away, but Rudolfo let his own contingent take care of them.

He slid from the saddle and killed one of the soldiers. One of his scouts—he thought it might be Gregoric—slipped in and killed the other two.

The Entrolusian captain drew his sword and Rudolfo slapped it down and aside. "They send me children," he said, gritting his teeth.

The captain growled and brought the sword up again. Rudolfo parried, then stepped to the side and went in with his knife to slice at the sword hand.

The captain's sword clattered to the ground, and Rudolfo pointed his own sword at the aide. "Ready your general's bird." He nodded to the captain. By now, at least six Gypsy Scout blades pressed in against the shaking captain. "You will write Lysias a message in B'rundic script."

The aide drew a bird and passed a scrap of paper and a small inking needle to the captain. The captain swallowed, his face pale. "What shall I write?"

Rudolfo stroked his beard. "Write this: Rudolfo has slain me." The man looked up, confused. Rudolfo whistled, and a knife tip pricked the young man's neck. "Write it."

He wrote the message and passed it to Rudolfo, who inspected it. He handed it to the aide and watched him tie it to the sea crow's foot. After the bird launched, he pushed his sword into the captain and climbed back into his saddle.

"For Windwir," he said again, and turned back to join his men.

Then, for the next nine hours, Rudolfo helped his Wandering Army send that first message in blood to the man who had snuffed out the light of the world.

Petronus

Petronus skirted the ruined city and followed the river south. Three or four leagues downriver from the shattered and blackened stubs that had once anchored Windwir's piers, Petronus remembered a small town. Once he reached it, he'd recruit what men—or even women—that he could and return to begin his work.

It would be months, he realized, and the rains would be upon them sooner than that. Not far on its heels, the wind and the snow of a northern winter. With the Androfrancines gone, there'd be no one to magick the river. Some years it froze. Some years it didn't. But with the Androfrancines gone, there'd be no need to go upriver with any frequency.

Petronus rode his horse along the bank, careful to keep from the forest. The first battle of the war had gone late into the night—he'd heard bits of it as he'd ridden south—and from time to time, during the day, he saw the birds lifting and speeding off carrying whatever word they carried. He'd also listened to it as he lay in his fireless camp and tried to sleep, before rising early to silence and morning fog.

As he rode in the quiet of the day, Petronus wondered about this new war and what had started it.

The Entrolusians would easily outnumber the Wandering Army, but if Rudolfo was his father's son, he'd be fierce and swift and ruthless.

He was less clear why they were fighting, but wasn't willing to stop and ask, either. It had to do with Windwir, but just what eluded him. Neither of those two armies had anything to do with the city's destruction—that was something the Androfrancines had done to themselves, meddling with what they had no business meddling with.

Still, Rudolfo and Sethbert would have their piss together and see who could go the farthest.

His horse started, jerking its head and frisking. Petronus felt a hand on his thigh, and realized that invisible hands held his horse by the bit. "Where are you going, old man?"

A face stretched up and the light hit it in a way that Petronus could barely see its outline. Magicked scouts. But which?

"South to Kendrick Town," he said, nodding in that direction. "I've business there."

"Where do you come from?"

Petronus wasn't sure how to answer. Caldus Bay was too far for any citizen to have reasonable business so far away. He glanced back over his shoulder, taking in the black expanse of Windwir. "I was bound for Windwir on Androfrancine business," he said. "But when I arrived, there wasn't anything left of it. I just thought any survivors would have headed south."

"We've been instructed to bring any survivors before Lord Sethbert, Overseer of the United City States of the Entrolusian Delta."

Petronus squinted, trying to see the line of the man's face. "So there were survivors?"

"It's not our place to say," the scout said. "We will bring you before Lord Sethbert." Petronus felt his horse being pulled. At first the roan resisted, and Petronus considered doing the same. He'd known Sethbert when the Overseer was a pimple-faced teenager. The young son of Aubert had been in the Academy around the time of Petronus's death by assassin's poison. They certainly hadn't seen much of each other.

But what if he recognizes me? He chuckled. Thirty years had changed him. He was twice the size he'd been and his hair had gone white. He was an old man now, moving a bit slow. Dressed in ratty fisherman's robes. It had been three decades since he'd worn the blue cloak or the white robe. The man that he had been in those days wouldn't even recognize the man he had become.

"Very well," Petronus said with a laugh, "take me to Lord Sethbert."

They moved quickly through the wood. Those places where the sunlight lanced in, Petronus caught shadows of the dark clothing and the drawn battle knives of the Delta scouts. They reminded him of the Gray Guard, and he thought about Grymlis again and the Marsher village.

A black field littered with bones as far as the eye could see.

Petronus shook off the memories. "I heard fighting in the night," he said.

No quick reply and no boasting. These men were defeated, he realized. He'd not press the question to them again.

In silence, they made their way to Sethbert and the Entrolusian camp.

The camp was alive with activity, a small city of tents blended into a forested hillside, invisible until you were within it. He saw servants, war-whores, cooks and medicos all busy about their trade. For the whore, his escort even paused for a moment, laughing and pointing at the young lieutenant she was riding.

Finally, they stopped outside the most lavish array of connected tents Petronus had seen. It even out-glamoured the silk Papal Suites that the Gray Guard accompanied around the Named Lands during the Year of the Falling Moon, that time each century when the Pope wandered the Named Lands to honor the settlers who homesteaded the New World.

They walked Petronus to the side of a large open canopy, and whispered for him to dismount.

"Wait here. When Lord Sethbert is finished, he'll send for you." Then, taking his horse, they left him there. He couldn't help but hear the one-sided conversation.

"I just hope you'll be able to speak soon," the voice said. "I'm running out of patience, boy. You are the only witness and I must hear your story."

Petronus looked for the voice, and saw an obese man sitting upon a folding throne that creaked beneath his weight.

He was chastising a boy in robes not dissimilar to his own. With Sethbert's tone, he would've thought the boy would hang his head, but instead, he was looking all around.

He's counting the guards, Petronus realized, and with no subtlety. But Sethbert wasn't noticing as the boy cased the open air court.

What's he up to? Perhaps a spy from the other camp. But Jakob would've certainly never used a boy in such a hapless way. Surely Rudolfo could not be so very different from his father? Then he saw the line of his face.

He'd had a professor of human studies at the Francine School named Gath. "Show me the line of a man's face," Gath would say to his classroom, spanning the students with his finger, "and I will tell you the intentions of his heart." Petronus stayed late after class three afternoons per week and asked that old professor every question he could think of.

It had never failed him, and he knew exactly what the line of the boy's face meant.

The intention of his heart was to kill Sethbert, and as careless as he was studying Sethbert's circumstances, Petronus was fairly certain that his intentions wouldn't matter once the guards saw what he was doing.

Petronus shouted and raced beneath the canopy.

Jín Lí Tam

Jin Li Tam rode across the prairie ocean and watched the metal man beside her. He'd been silent most of the day, his eyes fluttering as the lids flashed up and down. He was drumming his long, slender metal fingers on the saddle.

Every time she looked at him, she remembered his tone when he'd told her he knew how Sethbert destroyed Windwir. Somehow, Sethbert had used this mechoservitor to bring down a city and end an era where knowledge of the past was carefully preserved . . . and protected.

She shuddered. "What are you doing, Isaak?"

His fingers and eyelids stopped, and he looked over at her. "I am ciphering, Lady. I'm calculating the supplies and surface area necessary to rebuild the Androfrancine Library."

She was impressed. "How can you possibly do that?"

"I've spent a number of years logging expeditionary expense ledgers and cataloging the financial reports of various holdings," he answered. "Once I'm finished, I will modify my numbers based on the economic growth patterns between now and the day the reports were written." A gout of steam from his back. "These will merely be initial inquiries," Isaak said. "I will have to present Lord Rudolfo with something far more accurate."

She smiled at the metal man. "You really mean to do this, don't you?"

He turned to her. "Of course I do. I must."

Jin Li Tam chuckled. "It's a giant task."

"It is," he said, "but a pebble shall fell a giant and a small river make a canyon over time." She recognized the quote from the Whymer Bible. She couldn't pinpoint the exact passage—and she certainly couldn't find it if you pushed that heavy, square book into her hands.

"Hopefully you'll have help."

"I'm sure Lord Rudolfo will free my brothers." He paused and blinked. "But of course, there will be other Androfrancines that were not in Windwir when I—when it fell." He looked away.

Others, she thought. *Others.* The expeditions, the scattered schools, missions and abbeys. They would be out there, and soon—if not already—they would hear about the fall of Windwir.

"What do you calculate the library holdings outside Windwir to be?" she asked.

"Ten percent. The mechoservitors—all of us—account for another thirty between us."

"Gods," she whispered. She thought about all that was lost, but it was quickly burned out with what they could save. Forty percent of that massive library would still be a significant trove of knowledge. This was what Rudolfo had chosen when faced with the end of an age. And he'd made this decision, sending them north to the Ninefold Forest, *before* he made his final decision about going to war.

That was a rare thing. A man who thought of what to guard before he thought of what to kill. She smiled at this. Of course, this Rudolfo seemed to be a man who could do both at the same time.

And she smiled at that, as well.

"I am hoping you will help, as well, Lady Tam."

Now it was her turn to blink. He was clever, this metal man. "I see."

"Your father's bank holds the Androfrancine accounts," Isaak said. "I'm sure that Lord Rudolfo intends to combine some form of Entrolusian reparations supplemented by Androfrancine holdings in order to fund this venture. It far exceeds the Ninefold Forest Houses' economic capacity."

"I'm certain my father will be interested in this endeavor of Rudolfo's."

He certainly would be. She wouldn't be surprised at all if there were a bird waiting for her already, encouraging an alliance with the Gypsy King to keep House Li Tam connected with what little knowledge of the First World remained.

She wasn't sure she minded that at all.

Neb

When the summons arrived, Neb decided to use it as an opportunity to see exactly what he was up against. He listened to the Overseer's chiding, all the while counting the guards, counting the steps he'd need to take and planning his route to and from the Overseer's assassination.

Sethbert was well guarded, especially since yesterday's defeat at the hands of the Wandering Army. They'd at least doubled the contingent of honor guard that took up positions within view of the Overseer and his creaking wooden throne. And there had to be Delta scouts nearby, though Neb couldn't see them.

Magicked or not, he doubted he'd survive the attempt. And he wasn't even sure he'd be successful. The Overseer was easily three times his size, and Neb had nothing but his rage to guide him. Beyond a few fistfights with the other boys, he'd never raised his hands in violence . . . much less raised a knife.

The woman's words came back to him: *Sethbert has destroyed Windwir.* He felt the anger stir inside him, and he summoned a memory of his father, Brother Hebda, with his arm around him sitting in the park. He reminded himself of how that would never happen again because of this man, because of what he'd done.

Even if it cost his own life, Neb had to go through with it. He could think of nothing else to do.

He heard shouting, and looked up.

An old man was running toward him, shouting a name he did not recognize.

"Del," the old man said, "thank the gods I've finally found you." He looked vaguely familiar; Neb couldn't place it.

He was a large man—not nearly the size of Sethbert, but broad shouldered and powerfully built. He had to be approaching seventy, but he moved like he was younger. His white beard stood out from his face, long and unruly, and beneath his straw hat, wisps of white hair poked crazily out. His eyes were set in laugh lines and crow's-feet, and before Neb could react, he'd been swept into the man's embrace, squeezed and lifted by those massive arms. Putting him down, the old man gave him a stern look. "I told you to wait for me."

Neb looked at him, not sure what to do or say.

Sethbert cleared his voice. "You know this boy?"

The old man looked surprised, then turned. "Yes, certainly. Humble apologies for interrupting, Lord—I was overcome with relief."

Sethbert squinted at him, too, and Neb wondered if the old man seemed familiar to him as well. "You're the old man my scouts took by the river."

He nodded. "Yes, Lord. We were returning to Windwir when the city . . ." He let the words trail off. "I'd been looking for survivors when—" he patted the boy's shoulder and Neb felt the strength in the large hand that settled on him "—when Del here must've wandered off."

Neb opened his mouth to say something, but then closed it. What was this crazy old man doing?

Sethbert looked at him then, his eyes cold and calculating, his lips pursed in thought. "I was under the impression that he had seen the city fall. My medicos believe some trauma or another has stolen his voice."

The old man nodded. "Aye," he said. "But we only arrived after." His voice lowered. "His mother passed some days ago; he's not spoken since." Then he leaned in closer and whispered. "He's never been altogether right if you know what I mean, Lord."

Sethbert's eyes narrowed. "What is his relationship to you?"

The old man blinked. "He's my grandson. His father was an Androfrancine. They wanted to put him into their orphans' school but I wouldn't allow it." He met Sethbert's eyes. "I don't hold to their secrets and their smugness. His mother and I raised him."

Neb had never seen anyone lie so quickly, so competently before. He studied the old man's face, looking for some tick that would betray him. Nothing.

He realized Sethbert was speaking to him, and looked up. "Is this man your grandfather?"

Looking at the old man, he realized he'd seen him before. In the Great Library . . . but where? It hadn't been so long ago, either. Or perhaps he looked like someone else—someone well known to him. But why would he lie to Sethbert, creating an elaborate story about a grandson and a dead mother?

Their eyes met and the old man raised his eyebrows. "Well, Del? Are you going to answer the Overseer?"

Slowly, Neb nodded once, then twice.

"And you did not actually see the city of Windwir fall?"

Looking at the old man again, Neb felt a stab of memory. The fire, the lightning, ash falling like snow on the ruined landscape. The screaming, hot wind that blasted out from Windwir, the ships burning and sinking in the river even as they cast off their lines to drift south.

Neb shook his head.

Sethbert scowled. He leaned in to the boy, his voice cold and hollow. "I should teach you to be more truthful."

"I intend to do just that, Lord," the old man said with a firm voice. "Though I'm sure he was just confused. These are dark days for all of us."

Neb wasn't sure what to expect next, but a scout signaled Sethbert, and the Overseer motioned him closer. Sethbert looked once more at Neb and then at the old man.

"You were bound for Kendrick when my men took you?"

The old man nodded. Neb knew Kendrick. It was a small town not too far south of Windwir. He'd been to it a few times on various errands. "I thought there might be survivors there."

Sethbert nodded. "I find it odd that you did not tell my men about your missing lad."

The old man went pale and stammered for a moment. "I beg your forgiveness, Lord. I heard fighting the night before and I was uncertain of how much to say."

The Overseer smiled. "These are, as you say, dark days."

The old man nodded.

"What is your name then?"

"I am called Petros." It was a common name, the name of P'Andro Whym's indentured man, the one who had served the scientist-scholar beyond the terms of his agreement and had been named in one of the gospels as the greatest of the least.

Again, Sethbert squinted. Neb did, too. Even the name seemed familiar.

There was a fluttering, and a gray bird dropped heavily onto the arm of Sethbert's chair.

A winded bird-keeper raced beneath the tent. "Apologies, Lord Sethbert, but this one refused our net."

Neb saw the markings on the bird, but they were unfamiliar. Sethbert waved the bird-keeper off. Instead, the Overseer hefted the bird, pulled its message pouch himself and unrolled the small script. As he read it, his face grew red and his eyes grew narrow.

He looked up at them again. "I'm afraid I've pressing matters to attend to." He paused. "You're free to go . . . but no farther than Kendrick. I may have other questions of you."

But Neb was fairly certain he would not. Sethbert's interest in him had been the story of Windwir's fall. No doubt so that he could bask in his handiwork.

For a moment, he considered opening his mouth, somehow protesting this turn of events. Certainly, this old man Petros had some reason for the lies. Neb might have thought him mad, but he'd seen the hardness in the bright blue eyes and could see that the old man was playing Sethbert like a Marsh whistle. That and the familiar face and the familiar name were enough for Neb to know that he would have to figure out how to kill Sethbert another time.

As they walked out from under the canopy, he felt the pressure on his shoulder shift, and realized the old man had been speaking the entire time. His fingers, moving ever so slightly, had been tapping a message out into his shoulder. Of course, Neb didn't know what it meant. He'd just started nonverbal language training this last year. If the school had not been destroyed, he'd have been at least competent by the end of his last year.

Once they were out of earshot, Petros leaned over. "I've just saved you from a foolish path."

And suddenly Neb knew where he'd seen this man's face

before. Certainly, he was older and larger now . . . and dressed quite differently. But this old man bore a striking resemblance to a portrait Neb had walked under a thousand times in the Hall of the Holy Sees in the Western Wing of the Great Library, where the faces of the Popes gazed down from the walls with sober faces, careworn faces. The second newest painting—hung next to Introspect's—was the only face that smiled, though it was slight.

Petronus.

Of course, it couldn't be. That man had been dead for over thirty years.

Chapter

9

Rudolfo

Rudolfo spent the day with his captains directing intelligence skirmishes on the Entrolusian advance camps. The first battle had cost the Overseer six young officers and one seasoned master sergeant along with a host of infantry. They'd also accounted for a half-squad of Sethbert's elite Delta scouts, though there could've been more. It was hard to tell until the magicks wore down.

A good first battle. And he had a bird this morning from House Li Tam. Vlad Li Tam's iron armada steamed for the Delta now and would blockade the mouths of the Three Rivers. It was a small armada, but even small it could easily handle the City States' navy. The Androfrancines had seen to that, not wanting the bank that stored such a significant percentage of their wealth to be unprotected. And the Li Tam shipbuilders had been the only shipbuilders that could build the iron ships, even with the specifications the Androfrancines had reconstructed from the ruins of the First World.

House Li Tam's engagement was a start, nothing more. Rudolfo knew that the Emerald Coasts had no foot soldiers or cavalry to spare. They would keep what they had near home, knowing that the City States had more to contend with than the three brigades that had ridden north to Windwir.

But the armada would help. And as word spread, others would join. Rudolfo couldn't imagine any of the Named Lands entering the war on the side of the Entrolusians. He'd already sent a dozen birds to a dozen lords, careful to use words like The Desolation of Windwir and This War of Entrolusian Aggression. Even those who hated the Androfrancines—and there were few who did—would not be able to find common ground with someone who had burned away that city's knowledge. Those few who sneered at the ancient Order did so out of jealousy. Rudolfo had no doubt that they'd have killed the Androfrancines, too, without a moment's hesitation. But they would never have touched the library.

For two thousand years, the Androfrancines had built that library, storing knowledge dug from the ashes of the Old World. The wonders they'd dared share with the world—the scraps they'd doled out carefully over time—were amazing to behold. But who knew what wonders they'd kept hidden away, knowing that the world was not yet ready? Who knew what wonders they had yet to sell as humanity grew out of another adolescence, when its adulthood was cut short by the Third Cataclysm known as the Age of Laughing Madness.

For a moment he thought of Isaak, that extraordinary mechanical man, riding north in the robes of an Androfrancine acolyte. He had felt an immediate fondness for him despite the suspicions he held. There was an innocence about him that Rudolfo sometimes wished he could remember having inside of himself. And between what he held in his metal head and what his counterparts held in theirs, Rudolfo hoped to bring back at least something of what had been lost.

It had been an easy decision.

Now Gregoric nudged him. "Here they come, General."

Rudolfo looked, and down the ridge from them he saw the grass bending back as something—or several somethings—came in their direction. A brown bird lifted from their midst, and he smiled. "Excellent," he said. "They've driven back another camp."

"It's a good start," Gregoric said.

Rudolfo looked at him. They'd grown up together, Gregoric just a bit older. He'd been, surprisingly enough, the son of his father's First Captain of the Gypsy Scouts. Later, when Rudolfo's father lay dying and the mantle of the Ninefold Forest Houses was new upon Rudolfo's twelve-year-old shoulders, he'd promoted Gregoric's father to General. It had been his first decision, knowing that despite their seclusion in the northern, prairie-hemmed forests, the world would be watching for signs of strength in the young, new lord.

Gregoric had followed his father into the First Captaincy, and he'd been a flawless leader for the scouts. Even under crisis, it was obvious that he was getting his sleep, unlike Rudolfo. He ran a hand through his short dark hair.

"It's a very good start," Rudolfo agreed. "It will get harder as he applies his better assets. He's ever been the overconfident sort—I expect he's fared worse than he thought he would. I even think," he continued, "that we may have done better than Lysias expected, judging by his response yesterday."

A low whistle cut up the hill and Gregoric returned it. The underbrush rippled as the squad of Gypsy Scouts slipped into the perimeter.

"Captain," said a nearby voice, "and General."

"What have you learned?" Gregoric asked.

"We have another confirmation that they're only three brigades strong. We also learned they had a survivor—a boy. Beyond that, nothing more."

"Excellent work," Gregoric said. "Scrub down, get your men fed and get some sleep."

"Aye," the first scout said. "You heard the captain."

Rudolfo waited until they were out of earshot. "A survivor. That's new."

Gregoric nodded. "He has another seven brigades. That's what concerns me."

"And he's still not brought forth his best effort," Rudolfo said.

"He'll have to pretty soon," Gregoric said, looking down the slope. Rudolfo followed his gaze and saw another wave of movement sweeping in through the high grass.

This time a white bird flew up, and both of them drew their swords. The infantry on the perimeter saw the bird, too, and drew blades as well. Rudolfo shot a glance to the Captain of the Archers nearby, and the captain nodded.

Gregoric started down the hill and Rudolfo followed. At the foot of the hill they waited, and the squad raced past.

"They're just behind us," the lead scout hissed as he slipped past Gregoric.

And they were, only these weren't the magicked scouts they'd so easily mowed through yesterday. This pack was made of harder stuff. Rudolfo felt a searing pain in his side and realized even as he swung his sword down that a knife had slipped in and cut him.

Gregoric went to one knee, his thigh suddenly bleeding.

No one called attention to it. They wouldn't want their opponents to know who'd been injured. But the Gypsy Scouts pressed in, both those who had just returned and the half-squad set aside for these very reasons, and they slowly pushed the Delta Scouts out of the tree line. Rudolfo had managed to wound one of them, but held back once his own scouts were in the fray.

Medicos raced to the front as soon as the fighting had moved back, and they supported Gregoric while running him back up the hill. Rudolfo followed without assistance.

Back in camp, he drank chilled pear wine and ate orange slices and warm sweet bread. Leaning back on his cushions, he reread the note from Vlad Li Tam.

My kin-clave with Windwir is now yours. It was a brief letter, but these closing words grabbed him. He chuckled.

"A formidable woman," he said out loud. She had told her father about his three gestures. In other words, she had publicly acknowledged him before her father. Which meant in a good game of Queen's War, she'd moved on the tower he'd threatened with and in turn now threatened his paladin.

And of course, her father had now responded with subtle grace. The symbol Vlad Li Tam had chosen for kin-clave was an old one that had fallen out of use.

It indicated the unity of houses through strategic marriage.

A formidable woman indeed, Rudolfo thought.

Jin Li Tam

Jin Li Tam's quarters at the seventh forest manor were far simpler than what she'd had at the Overseer's Palace, and the simplicity impressed her. It was a suite of rooms accessed through a wide set of double doors on the third floor. The closets were already stocked with a few items that seemed to be her size. She bathed, dressed in summer gowns and went down to the dining room.

Though he didn't eat, Isaak was waiting there for her. Sitting away from the table, along the wall on a servant's stool.

Jin pointed to an empty chair at the table. "Please, Isaak," she said. "Join me."

"Thank you, Lady." He stood and limped over to the empty chair.

She noticed he was wearing a clean robe and it prompted her to smile. "Why are you still wearing your disguise?"

He looked at her, looked down at the robe, and smoothed it with his metal hands. "I do not know. It seemed appropriate."

He had his hood down, so she knew it wasn't that he

meant to hide himself. Something else then? "Are your quarters satisfactory?"

He nodded. "They are, Lady Tam."

The smell of fresh baked bread and venison stew filled the room as the kitchen door swung open. A servant hastened in, carrying a steaming platter. She placed it in front of Jin Li Tam and then retreated.

Jin paused, trying to decide between the stew or the bread. She broke off a piece of the hot bread. "When will you start your work?"

Isaak buzzed and a bit of steam jetted out. "I'll start tonight by cross-referencing the mechoservitor work logs—I translated them last year—and see exactly what we might still have between us. Scrolls are replaced or cleared from time to time, but it's rare."

She nodded, dipping her spoon into the stew. She held it beneath her nose, smelling the fresh onions, carrots mingled with venison roasted in herbs and spices that made her mouth water. "How long will that take?"

"Two weeks, five days, four hours and eight minutes," he said.

"And after that you'll recalculate your ciphers?" She chased the stew with iced apple cider.

"Yes." A breeze blew in from the forest carrying the faintest scent of evergreen and wood smoke. The light from the candle reflected off his metal face. "After that, I will go to the last of the Androfrancines and appeal for aid."

The door opened and the steward walked in. "Lady Tam," he said, "I've just received a bird from your father. Would you prefer it now or after you've finished?"

She dabbed her mouth with a napkin. "Now, please."

He handed the small scroll to her and she unrolled it, holding it to the light.

The surface message was simple and nondescript. *I'm glad you are well,* it said. But under the surface, triple coded and buried, was the longer message: *I approve of your choice; you will assist in the rebuilding of the library.* And the tense he used and the slightest blurring of the dot of an "i" told her that Vlad Li Tam considered his forty-second daughter betrothed for purposes of kin-clave.

She looked at Isaak and then back at the note in her hands. This was not entirely unexpected, but the timing was at a faster pace than she'd planned for. It confirmed her suspicions, certainly, that her father was involved in Rudolfo's plan to rebuild the library before she'd known of it. She looked again at the metal man, wondering what lay ahead of them in the upcoming months. She thought about the man she was betrothed to, now, and wondered what lay ahead of her, and Rudolfo as well.

When she spoke, it could've meant either or both. "We should discuss the strategy of it," she said.

Neb

Neb couldn't help but stare at the old man as they drove their wagon south to Kendrick. Neb had dragged him to it, pointing, and the old man had made a big show of hitching the horses to it and tying his own to the back.

"I'm glad you didn't let this get away, Del," he said with a wink.

Neb watched him scan the back of it, saw his eyes light up at the tools, and then climbed into the seat beside him.

When the guards had escorted him to the edge of their camp and pointed them southward, he'd thanked them profusely. Once they were out of sight, he leaned in to Neb.

"We're not out of it yet, lad. They'll have scouts shadowing us most of the way."

Neb nodded.

They rode in silence, stopping briefly to eat stale bread and hard cheese from the old man's saddlebags. Neb lay back against the wagon wheel, stretching himself out. In the forests that edged the river road, birds flitted in the shadows and chirped at them. A kingfisher dove the river, coming up from the slow, wide waters with a fish in its bill.

He couldn't speak to ask the old man if he was who he thought he was—but he also wasn't sure that he should ask anything with Entrolusian scouts nearby. After all, if Sethbert had hated the Androfrancines so much that he crushed them like a garden snake beneath his boot, he couldn't possibly love an Androfrancine Pope.

Neb still wasn't sure if leaving the camp was the best of all possible choices, but the old man had made that happen without leaving him much room to protest. Perhaps, he'd seen Neb assessing the Overseer's security. Neb wondered if he'd been that obvious.

And if the old man had seen it, others may have as well. So it was possible that Neb owed him his life. It was also possible that Neb had now missed his first, best chance to bring down the madman who had killed his father and robbed the world of Androfrancine light.

Now they rode for Kendrick with a wagon full of supplies meant for the Gamet Dig, far south and east, in the Churning Wastes. Questions rattled him, poking at him as if he were in a cage.

He glanced at the old man again. He was checking the back of the wagon, rummaging through one of Brother Hebda's pouches as if it were his own. Neb leaped to his feet, feeling a surge of anger that he wasn't sure what to do with.

The old man saw the look on his face. "I'm looking for the Letters of Credit and Introduction."

Hot shame flashed through him, and Neb opened his mouth to speak. A flow of garbled words poured out, sentence fragments from the Nineteen Gospels, the Francine Codex and the other scattered bits that made up the Whymer Bible. He closed his mouth, then tried again with the same results. The old man grabbed up the pouch and pushed it into Neb's hands. He leaned in close, speaking quietly. "There's paper in here. And pencils. This will help our rather one-sided conversation. But do nothing until we know we're clear of Sethbert's men."

Neb nodded. Later, once they were safely shut into a barn

along the way or if they actually pressed through and found an inn in Kendrick, they would have many questions for one another.

The old man climbed into the creaking seat, and Neb climbed into the back this time, holding Brother Hebda's pouch to his chest. There was the snap of a crop and a high, sharp whistle. The wagon lurched forward.

As they rode, Neb's mind wandered. A mad Overseer smothering the world's best light and plunging them all into darkness. A beautiful woman with the sunrise in her hair and secrets on her lips. An old, strong Pope back from the dead to avenge his desolate city.

It belonged in a story—like one of the hundreds he'd read on those quiet days spent in the library. And the memory of it was so strong that Neb could smell the parchment as the rocking of the wagon and the warm afternoon sun gentled him to sleep.

Petronus

Petronus heard the boy's quiet snores from the back and looked over his shoulder. It was good that he slept. He looked like he hadn't slept for days, and Petronus could understand that. He'd not had a full night since the day he saw the cloud. And though he didn't need much these days, he'd take what he could.

While he drove, he wondered about the boy.

It was obvious that he could speak at one time and he was certainly intelligent. Well educated, too. Probably one of the orphans—they received the best education in the world, better than any lord's child. They received the education reserved otherwise for the Androfrancines. Hells, they were Androfrancines as far as Petronus was concerned. And they didn't really get a choice in the matter. By the time they were old enough to have minds of their own, they had already been filled with the backward dream, the constant looking to the past to mitigate the future. Most of the orphans joined the

Order when they reached their majority. Even the girls served in some way, though their prospects were less glamorous within the male-dominated knowledge cult.

Petronus had certainly strayed from the vows from time to time—especially during his early years in the Order. But he'd always taken care, and his dalliances hadn't lasted long enough for him to worry overmuch.

But others weren't as careful, for reasons all their own. It was easy enough—especially for an Androfrancine, with access to the potions and powders for either man or woman who wished to avoid offspring. Maybe, he thought, life longs to recreate itself.

Still, if his assumptions were correct, the boy in the back was one of hundreds that the Androfrancines had brought into the world and then dropped into their orphanage as if the world's best education among the world's brightest scholars could make up for a mother who baked fresh bread and a father whose hands stank of fish.

And he saw Windwir fall. Gods, what a terrible thing to see at any age. This lad couldn't have been more than fifteen. Yet apart from not being able to steer his vocal chords, the boy still had his wits about him.

Enough to plan an assassination, it seemed, though with more bravery than discretion.

And why Sethbert? The line of the boy's face couldn't lie. He'd meant to harm the Overseer either then and there or sometime later. Yet he'd not balked at Petronus's intervention.

Petronus hadn't found the letters he was looking for in the courier pouch. They should've been with the wagon, but then again, the boy wasn't old enough to be an acolyte. Perhaps an internist or an assistant, though even those were usually in their majority. So certainly there were others along at one point in time. The wagon was clearly bound for the Wastes—routine by the looks of it, and not carrying anything of value to merit a Gray Guard escort.

So both the letters and at least one other Androfrancine was missing.

And then there was the war. The two nearest armies had ridden to Windwir's aid and were now fighting each other. Why? One of his favorite Whymer quotes was P'Andro Whym's response to the question put to him about finding truth.

The truth, the Seventeenth Gospel said, *is a seed planted in a field of stones beneath a stone and guarded by snakes. To have at it, be strong enough to move the stone, patient enough to dig the hole and fast enough to dodge the viper's fang.*

He would continue his excavation when the boy woke up, when he could be sure that there were no ears or eyes but their own. And he would not forget that vipers came in many shapes and sizes.

Chapter

10

Jin Li Tam

For Jin Li Tam, the seventh forest manor and the town that surrounded it teemed with rainbow-colored life. The house itself was set upon a slight rise, and the town around it gathered in close—a collection of cobblestone streets and one- or two-story buildings made of finely planed lumber, and glass windows painted in a multitude of colors. The people wore cottons primarily, though she occasionally saw the silks that her own Emerald Coasts were famous for.

She wondered why she'd never visited before, but quickly brushed that thought aside. There'd been no reason to. The

Gypsies kept to themselves, far from the machinations and intrigues of the Named Lands. Once in a while, she'd heard of Rudolfo riding south with his scouts to attend various functions. But they were never the functions she attended, and for the most part the Ninefold Forest Houses kept to their edge of the world.

She walked the streets alone, mindful of the scouts who followed her at an appropriate distance. They meant to give her the illusion of independence, but she suspected that it wouldn't take much to bring them running. Of course, this far from the war, she should be safe enough. The scouts weren't even magicked.

As she walked, Jin listened to the voices around her, picking up fragments of day-to-day life in the forest. A patchwork quilt of hunting stories, rumors about the war and about Windwir, bits of gossip about who was sleeping with whom and what so-and-so's son had seen limping about the seventh forest manor.

Jin paused.

"He was dressed as an Androfrancine, he said. But made entirely of metal."

She had wondered how long before the secret was out. Certainly, most people were familiar with the mechanicals that the Androfrancines had gradually revealed to the world. Small things like the bird her father kept in their indoor gardens, beneath the crystal dome. The little golden bird was unlike any other she had ever seen, and it could sing in sixteen languages. It could also say small phrases—simple things like asking for water it could not drink or food that it could not eat. It had been a gift from one of the Popes, she thought, years ago.

But Isaak was different. Fully the size of man—perhaps even a head taller than average—slender yet solid in build, and perhaps the most amazing spectacle she had ever seen. At one time, according to some of the heresies, there were nearly as many metal men as people. Those were the days long, long before the Age of Laughing Madness. But when P'Andro

Whym walked the ruined basement of the world with his scattered band of diggers and scribes, the metal men were all but extinct.

And now they'd been brought back—at least, a handful had. And if Rudolfo had his way, she realized, those few—built from the parchments and scraps found in the Wastes—would be here, helping Isaak rebuild what Sethbert had destroyed.

"Lady Tam," a voice said beside her. She looked. One of the scouts had slipped to her side.

She looked at him. He was young but not a pup, and unlike Sethbert's Delta Scouts, Rudolfo's men did not swagger. "Yes?"

"The . . ." He paused, looking for the right words. "Isaak would like to see you."

She was surprised. She'd seen him just an hour before and had asked after his planning and his correspondence with the Androfrancines. "Very well."

She walked the half league back to the manor and met Isaak in the courtyard garden. He held a scrap of paper in his hands and he stood there, eye shutters blinking at it.

"What is it, Isaak?" she asked, stepping toward him.

The metal man limped toward her, his dark robe hiding the angles of his lean steel frame. "I've word from the Papal Summer Palace," he said. His eyes flashed open and shut.

"That was very fast," she said.

"It was not in response to the message."

Curious, she thought. "What word does it bring?"

Steam blasted from his exhaust grate. "It is a Papal edict, decreeing that all remaining Order resources and personnel are to be inventoried at the Papal Summer Palace."

She felt her brows furrow. "How can that be? Surely the Pope is dead?"

"I—" He stalled, whirred and clacked. She regretted the words instantly. But he recovered and continued. "Androfrancine Succession is complex—there have been volumes written on it over the last two thousand years.

Though traditionally the Offices are passed on through the laying on of hands, there are contingencies upon contingencies. Pope Introspect could very well have passed the Office on in some manner before his—" Isaak stopped. His eyes blinked back water and he looked away.

Jin put a hand on his shoulder. "Do not forget, Isaak, that Sethbert was the hand that moved you."

Isaak nodded. "Regardless, the edict bears the mark of the ring."

Could it be something that had slipped past her father? She doubted it, but anything was possible given the events of the last week. She knew the answer to the question before she asked it, but she asked anyway. "What does it mean?"

"It means that I cannot stay here," Isaak said, head downcast, his voice sounding weary—something she didn't think possible in a man made of metal. When he looked up at her, she thought perhaps that she'd never seen such a look of conflict on any human's face, and it amazed her that she had already assigned such human features to this metal man based on how his eyes or mouth moved and how he held his head. "I am the property of the Androfrancine Order," he finally said. "Constructed to do their bidding."

And if her suspicions were correct, he was also the greatest weapon the world had seen in over two thousand years.

He stood there, not moving. "Is there more?" she asked.

He nodded slowly. "There is. Pope Resolute's first act as Holy See was to sign a Writ of Shunning."

A Writ of Shunning. Now the Entrolusians would truly stand alone, cut off from the world. A Shunning from the Androfrancine Pope would sever all ties of kin-clave between the scattered governments of the Named Lands and whoever it named—a powerful tool that had only been used (to the best of her recollection) three times in the history of the Named Lands.

"That's good news," she said. "That will only aid Rudolfo's cause."

Isaak shook his head. "No, Lady. You misunderstand."

She looked at him and she felt her mouth drop open. "You mean . . . ?"

"Yes," Isaak said, "the Writ of Shunning named the Nine-fold Forest Houses and Lord Rudolfo, General of the Wandering Army, as culpable for the Desolation of Windwir, and declares his lands and holdings to be held in escrow until a Conference of Findings has convened and made a final determination."

Jin Li Tam felt the air go out of her. Shouting for a bird and paper, she stormed into the manor, her mind already coding the message to her father.

Petronus

Petronus and the boy sat down with the paper as soon as they closed themselves into the barn. They'd hit the outskirts of Kendrick as night fell, and had happened across the farmer.

"I've a coin for the use of your barn," Petronus said.

The farmer approached their wagon, squinting to see them in the fading light. "Are you from Windwir? What news do you bring?"

Petronus climbed down from the seat. The boy watched, rubbing sleep from his eyes. "The city is gone entirely. The Entrolusians are warring with the Gypsies. I'm not sure why."

The farmer nodded. "Androfrancines, then?"

"I've worked for them on occasion. My name is Petros." He turned to the boy and caught a glimpse of a smile when he gave his name. "This is my grandson."

"I'm Varn," the farmer said, extending his hand. Petronus shook it. "You can keep your coin. These are rough times for the Order. Sheltering you is the least I can do."

After they'd settled in, and after they'd torn into a basket of fresh bread, pickled asparagus and roast rabbit that Varn had brought out to them, they filled their metal cups with wine from one the wagon's three barrels and sat down with the paper by lamplight.

Before Petronus could ask, the boy scribbled quickly onto the paper and held it for him to see. *My name is Neb,* it read.

"It's good to finally know your name," Petronus said. "How did you come to be in Sethbert's care?"

For the next two hours, Petronus asked the questions and Neb answered them, his hand working hard to keep up with the old man's tongue. Petronus took it all in—Neb's eyewitness account of the city's fall, his capture by the Delta Scouts, what he'd heard the soldiers talking about, what the redheaded lady had said . . . and how she'd tried to take Neb with her.

Sethbert destroyed Windwir. He had to read those words three times. "Do you have any idea how?"

Neb shook his head.

Petronus pondered this. He'd paid someone, promised something, made some kind of deal to get his hands on the spell. The wasteland where the city once stood had to be the work of Xhum Y'Zir's Seven Cacophonic Deaths. Somehow, the Androfrancines had put the fragments together and Sethbert had used it to his advantage. Somewhere along the way, all of the intricate safeguards, the locked boxes and vaults, the subterfuge of two thousand years of protecting humanity from itself, had failed.

If I'd stayed, this would not have happened.

Petronus felt a hand at his sleeve and looked down at the paper. *Can I ask you some questions?* Neb had written there. He nodded. "Please."

Why did you stop me?

Petronus put his hand on Neb's shoulder and looked him in the eye. "If I could see your scheming, it was only a matter of time before one of Sethbert's scouts or guards picked up on it. How did you imagine you'd be able to assassinate one of the most powerful men in the Named Lands?"

Petronus watched Neb's face. The corner of his mouth twitched and his eyes shifted. It was obvious that he was wrestling with how much truth to give. "You don't have to say, son."

The boy's hand reached into his shirt and came out with the pouch. Petronus recognized it immediately and chuckled. "Clever," he said. "But that alone wouldn't have seen you to safety, even if you'd managed to kill the bastard."

But even as he said the words, Petronus realized that the boy didn't care at all about being seen to safety. That hardness in his eyes, and once more, the line of his face, said without words that Neb would've gladly traded his life for that of the mad Overseer.

"Listen well," Petronus said. "Taking a life—even a life like Sethbert's—robs your own soul in the end. I agree with you that he deserves death for what he's done. A thousand deaths couldn't be enough. But Androfrancines do not kill," he said. *Unless you're the Pope,* he thought. *Unless you merely give the words to the most seasoned captain of your Gray Guard and close your eyes and pretend that there is no connection between your own words and the deeds of others.*

He felt the tug at his sleeve again and looked down. *I am not an Androfrancine.*

"No," Petronus said, "I suppose you are not. But someday you may be. And last year's ghosts haunt next year's forests."

The boy thought about this, then wrote more. Petronus read it. "What now? I don't know. I suppose I'll try to find someplace for you to stay here in Kendrick. I'm only here long enough to rally some men, and then I'm back to Windwir."

When the boy looked at him, eyebrows raised in question, Petronus's felt his own jaw tighten. "I've a city to bury," he said in a quiet voice.

The boy scratched more words onto the tablet, and Petronus was surprised to see it was a statement, not a question.

I know who you are, Father, the crisp handwriting declared, starkly black on the gray paper. Petronus stared at the words and said nothing, knowing his silence said enough.

Neb

Neb watched Petronus work the town all that next day. He stopped at the inn to talk with the lumbermen at their breakfasts. He wandered through Kendrick speaking with women and paused in the crowded village square. The large open space had filled up with the tents and carts of those waylaid en route to Windwir, waiting in shocked silence for some better destination to drop into their minds. And still waiting.

He spoke in hushed tones with the mayor while Neb watched from a distance. At first the mayor was agitated, waving the old man away. Then he was nodding, brows furrowed with anger. In the end he looked intent, and when they shook hands, the mayor left to call an emergency council meeting.

It was easy to see now how this man had become the Order's youngest Pope. Neb had remembered his lessons— Petronus hadn't merited much mention in The Works of the Apostles of P'Andro Whym, but there'd been a bit. He'd been the youngest. He'd been assassinated. He'd been a strong King and Pope. Though the book didn't say so, Neb had heard the old men talking from time to time. "His tongue's as silver as Pope Petronus" had become a common phrase among that generation of Androfrancines. Now Neb saw it firsthand.

The mayor sent riders out into farmlands, sent runners throughout the village, and called in everyone willing to listen within two hours ride. By the time the couriers had gone out, Petronus had sent birds to Caldus Bay and two other villages Neb didn't recognize in care of names that Neb wasn't close enough to read. Last, he wrote a long note in a script Neb recognized as from somewhere on the Emerald Coasts. This he attached to the strongest, fastest looking bird, and he whispered longest into its ears before lifting it to the sky.

When they finished Petronus took Neb to the inn, and they stuffed themselves on catfish stew and fried bread.

As Neb wiped the last of the stew from the bowl with his last crust of bread, he smiled at the old man.

Petronus smiled. "We've done a good day's work."

Neb nodded. They had. And though he really hadn't done much himself, he'd learned in a way that he'd never learned in the Orphan's School. Watching this man work, building trust here and suspicion there—grabbing a grin from this one and a nod from that one. He'd never seen anything like it, and it stirred a part of him. He was suddenly pushed back into his past.

"But I don't know what I want to be," he'd told his father during one visit.

Brother Hebda smiled. "Do not be what you do," he said. He'd been trained in the Francine Disciplines and Neb had always enjoyed seeing them lived out in real life. "Doing and being aren't the same."

"But isn't who I am determined by what I do?"

His father's face broke into an even wider smile. "Sometimes. But what you do can change from situation to situation. Can a good man kill?"

Neb shook his head.

"But the Gray Guard kill . . . are they good?"

Neb thought about this. "I think they are. Because they are doing their job to protect the light."

Brother Hebda nodded. "They are. But say they were ordered to kill a man because he was a heretic, but really he was an enemy of a spiteful cuckold? Are the Gray Guard then defined by what they do?"

Neb laughed. "I only said I don't know what I want to be when I grow up."

Brother Hebda laughed, too. "Oh. That's easy, then."

"Really?"

His father nodded and leaned in. "Watch for the ones who leave your mouth hanging open. Study them, find out what they love and what they fear. Dig the treasure out of their soul and hold it to the light." He leaned in even closer now, so that Neb could smell the wine on his breath. "Then *be* like them."

He remembered thinking in that moment that Brother Hebda was a man he wanted to be like. That very winter, Neb turned in his first grant request to study in the care of an expedition to the Wastes, preferably assigned to Hebda Garl as a student apprentice.

Now, after a day of watching Petronus—or Petros—at work, he'd found someone else he could want to be like.

After dinner, they went out to the gathering crowd. It wasn't a large crowd. Not everyone had come. But enough had. And they stood in the square among the tents and carts, near the open doors of the inn. They stood around an overturned tub that the old man climbed onto, holding a shovel over his shoulders.

Neb watched from the side. The mayor, all agreement earlier, now seemed agitated and anxious to speak. Neb wondered what had changed.

"I'll be brief," Petronus said before the mayor could try to introduce him. He dropped the shovel from his shoulder and pointed north with it. "You all know what happened to Windwir. It's a field of ash and bones for as far as you can see." There were muted gasps in the crowd. "We are all the Children of the New World, and at some place in our lineage, we are each kin-clave unto one another. We know this to be true." He waited for heads to nod, a few voices to speak out. "I'm not a man to leave my kin unburied," Petronus said.

Then the old man went on for another fifteen minutes, laying out a plan of action that astounded Neb with its simplicity.

"Those who can," Petronus said, "will come and help as they can." Shifts of a week on and a week off by thirds—two men at home looking after their neighbor's farm as well as their own while that good citizen was away. Women working in similar shifts. And those who had nowhere else to go—

they would leave with Petronus and Neb in the morning and go set up their camp.

"What about pay?" someone asked.

And Neb's mouth fell open at Petronus's words. "Those who need it will get it. Those who don't will work for love."

Petronus hopped down from the washtub and winked at Neb. "How did I do?"

Neb nodded, wishing he could say something. Then he heard another loud voice and looked. The mayor had climbed onto the washtub now and was holding a scrap of paper up in the air. "I have a word to share as well," he said. "Though I hate to contradict our well-spoken guest."

The mayor waited for the crowd to quiet. "I have word to-day that Bishop Oriv at the Papal Summer Palace has been named the Pope of the Androfrancine Order and King of Windwir. His Excellency has ordered all Androfrancine re-sources and personnel be gathered there to be inventoried in the light of this great tragedy. He also sends along a Writ of Shunning against the Ninefold Forest Houses and an Exer-cise of Holiness."

Neb gasped. A Shunning was an Old World practice that had carried over to the New World through the wisdom of P'Andro Whym. It severed all ties of kin-clave, making its recipient fair game for anyone and an enemy of the light. It had only been used a handful of times, and usually as lever-age to manipulate a Pope's desired outcome. But during the Heresies, it was used as a mask for open war.

And the Exercise had fallen out of fashion for over a thou-sand years. But there was a time when once in seven years, the Pope declared an Exercise of Holiness, calling for Windwir to be closed to the outside world for an entire year. Twice, it had been used to wait out schisms—a year of separation could quell most arguments. Enforced by the Gray Guard, violators early on were killed . . . but later merely punished and evicted.

If Neb had wondered about its meaning, it would've been clear on Petronus's face.

"There will be Gray Guard at the Summer Palace," Petronus said in a quiet voice. "Not many. Not enough to enforce this."

The mayor continued. "And out of kin-clave with Windwir, Lord Sethbert, Overseer of the Entrolusian City States, has agreed to provide guardianship and enforcement of the Exercise. His Excellency, the Pope, compels all townships within the Providence of Windwir to comply and assist as required."

Neb watched the crowd to see how they would respond. And he watched Petronus, too. The old man's face was hard and unreadable. The mayor climbed down and no one moved.

Finally someone spoke up, and Neb was surprised at the voice. It was *his* voice, clear and marching forward with every word.

"I am not a man to leave my kin unburied," Neb said.

And when he said it, he couldn't help but think of Brother Hebda.

Rudolfo

Rudolfo sat in the shade of a fir tree, alone, and thought. There was dried blood on his sleeve and his boot, but it wasn't his. He'd killed a magicked sapper the night before when they breached the perimeter. Rudolfo's men had taken a beating had held their ground. Three of his Gypsy Scouts—*three*—lost in one night.

Gregoric slipped beside him and sat. "General Rudolfo," he said.

Rudolfo nodded. "Gregoric. What do you think?"

Gregoric shook his head. "I don't know."

The bird had arrived two hours earlier bearing news of the new Pope and the Writ of Shunning. Rudolfo had immediately sent word to House Li Tam and the Seventh Forest Manor. Just as he'd finished, his Captain of Intelligence had approached with more bad news. "We've word that two more brigades of Delta infantry are northward bound. And Pylos and Turam are sending contingents."

That's when Rudolfo slipped from the camp into the forest in order to think. Of course he'd known that Gregoric, still magicked from the morning patrol, had followed at a distance. And after sufficient time had past, his first captain had done as he always did and came to sit with his friend.

Rudolfo sighed. "I think we may have to pull back and find new vision. This new Pope has changed the pieces about on the board."

"Aye," Gregoric said. "We still have some time. A few days. We can do what we can and then divide the army."

Rudolfo nodded. "And I will be needed elsewhere."

Tomorrow, with his own half-squad of Scouts, Rudolfo would ride for the Papal Summer Palace to parley with this Pope. Behind him, his Wandering Army would fall back to their forest islands until their general called them back to war.

For the first time in a week, Rudolfo wondered if he truly would prevail.

Chapter

11

Jin Li Tam

The halls of the seventh forest manor were wide and long, with hardwood floors and wood paneling on the walls, dressed up with thick silk carpets and framed portraits. During her brief stay, Jin Li Tam explored what rooms she could, finding few locked doors in the large four-story building. Most of the rooms were spacious, including the servants' quarters, and even boasted running water, heated in a large metal furnace and gravity-fed through copper pipes. Another gift from the Androfrancines.

She'd walked most of the manor on the first day. But now, she sought out the floor she had avoided. She took the wide sweeping staircase that passed the second and third floors, going directly to the fourth.

There, at the end of a short wide hallway, stood the double doors and stained glass windows leading to the Family Quarters.

She looked in on the rooms for children. There were many, all empty now but for one—the room of a small boy, she gathered, complete with scattered toys and a small silver sword hung over the bed. An unwrapped turban lay draped over the back of a chair, and a small boot jutted haphazardly from beneath the bed.

It had been carefully cleaned, but she could tell that the room had been this way for a long while.

A dark, unlocked door marked Rudolfo's quarters—a suite of rooms that included a den and connected to another suite through a large bathing room. The bathing room was impressive. It smelled of fresh lavender, and at its center was a large, round marble tub. An elaborate golden nozzle was set into the ceiling, along with long cords tipped with golden tassels for bathers to pull and bring down the hot rain.

Jin walked through the room, her hand moving over the edge of the tub. The marble was cold to the touch.

Beyond the bathing room a similar suite waited, and the softer colors told her that someday soon, if her father's will held despite the recent Papal Writ, she would be moving from the guest quarters into this space as Rudolfo's bride.

She'd known that someday, when her father willed it, she would either be released to seek a mate for reasons of her own, whether love or convenience, or she would be wed for strategic purposes to advance House Li Tam's interests in the world. Of course, some of her sisters had chosen to stay home instead.

She'd always thought that if she were left to her own heart, she'd neither wed nor stay home. Instead, she'd go to the places she wished to instead of the places her father sent her.

She reached out a hand and touched the thick quilt folded at the foot of the large canopied bed. Certainly, this place would have been one that she would've wanted to see. The ancient forest islands in an ocean of prairie, and their ruthless Gypsy kings—tied by their past to the legacy of Xhum Y'Zir, evidenced by their Physicians of Penitent Torture and their redemptive work. Yet Rudolfo's forebears had blended that dark blood magick rite with the mystic teachings of T'Erys Whym, the younger brother of P'Andro Whym who for a time succeeded his brother and led the leftovers of the world until the Francine Movement, of all things, brought them back to reason as the principal tenet.

Yes, she would've wanted to visit this place. But would she have chosen to stay here?

Probably not, she realized. Instead, if she had her way, she'd spend some time in the Great Library, possibly tour the edges of the Churning Waste, and then move south and sail the channel islands.

Instead, she thought, I am to be here in the shadow of a new library.

Of course, all of that hinged on the Writ of Shunning and its resolution . . . and on her father's wishes. She was certain he'd shift his strategy and she'd been certain that a bird would come. But instead, a note from Rudolfo had arrived that morning.

Pay no mind to this emerging Pope's Writ, it read. *I ride to deal with him. Stay with Isaak.* Only the word "with" had been tilted just ever so slightly to give it the subtext of "near," lending it the weight of great importance.

She'd smiled. Another code was buried in it, too. It was simple and unexpected, woven into the note with the jots and tittles of the Bank Cipher script. *I'll dance with the sunrise yet again,* the equation said.

Jin Li Tam heard limping footfalls in the hall and went to the door.

"Lady Tam?" she heard a metallic voice call.

She poked her head out. "In here, Isaak."

The metal man stopped and turned. He still the wore robes—dark and long. "I've come to wish you well," he said.

The words hit her. "What do you mean?"

He blinked. "I'm leaving for the Papal Summer Palace."

Stay with Isaak. Near him, she thought, because of his great importance. "I don't think Lord Rudolfo would permit this."

Steam left the exhaust grate. "I know. I received his message this morning as well. But regardless of Lord Rudolfo's instructions, I am compelled to obey my Pope. I am the property of the Androfrancines—it is written into my behavior scrolls."

She watched his eyes, looking for an awareness she knew she couldn't see. But she knew from the tears that leaked out from them that he understood at least part of the equation. If this mechanical wonder had indeed brought down the City of Windwir with his very words, what risk could he be to the last of the Androfrancines?

But the other side of the equation would not bother him at all, she knew. He'd welcome it, even ask for it, in the hopes that it would help him shed the weight of guilt she saw him bear with every step. She doubted even the hope of rebuilding the library could be strong enough to lift something so heavy from him.

Stay with Isaak, Rudolfo had written.

But it wasn't Rudolfo's words that moved her. No. It was the other side of that equation that sent Jin Li Tam down the stairs to pack what little she had in preparation for her journey with the metal man who had been Sethbert's sword at the throat of a city.

She didn't worry that Isaak could ever be used in such a way again. She was certain he would not permit it. But then there was the other side.

What risk would the last of the Androfrancines be to him?

Petronus

Petronus led the small group of men over the last rise, and those who hadn't already seen it fell back, gasping, at what they saw there.

They pushed wheelbarrows full of tools, and those with mules or horses pulled small carts along behind them. Petronus looked them over and shook his head.

Damn Pope Resolute and his Exercise of Holiness. It had cost him two thirds of the crowd. No one wanted to tangle on the wrong side of Sethbert's army. They were all smart enough to know that the Exercise was to keep people from digging, and gravediggers were diggers nonetheless.

He looked down at the boy. He hadn't spoken again for two days now, but Petronus was fairly certain that he could if he wanted to. "But you don't have to," he'd told Neb when he realized that he hadn't spoken since, "if you don't want to."

As they crested the rise, Petronus saw birds fly out of the forest, moving north of them, their wings beating furiously. He read their colors and smiled. A horse pulled out from a copse of trees not far from the edge of the blasted area. It rode toward them, and Petronus saw ripples of wind in the grass to the left and right of the rider.

He waited until the young lieutenant pulled up and hailed him. "Windwir is closed," he said.

The wind rippled out as the magicked scouts took up positions around them.

Petronus pointed. "Windwir is a field of bones. We aim to bury them."

The faintest hint of surprise registered on the young man's face. "I'm afraid I can't let you pass."

Petronus stepped closer. "What is your name, Lieutenant?"

"Brint," the young man said. He studied Petronus and the motley band of travelers.

"Have you not faced a loved one's passing?"

Petronus watched the young man's face. He saw the stab of loss rise to the surface and then quickly vanish as the officer forced his emotions aside. It was just slight enough that the untrained eye might miss it, and Petronus suddenly realized he wasn't dealing with the spoiled son of an Entrolusian noble.

Petronus's hands moved close to his body so that others could not see. *Whose are you?* he signed, first in the intelligence subverbal of the Forest Houses and then in the hand dialect of House Li Tam.

The lieutenant blinked but kept his own hands still. "I have seen several loved ones pass," he said in a quiet voice.

Petronus leaned forward, his voice also low. "Did you bury them or let them lie where they fell?"

The first look was anger, but it was followed by a look of deep weariness. The lieutenant said nothing for a full minute, then stared down at Petronus. He whistled, and the wind blew back from around them as the Delta Scouts retreated. When they were out of earshot, he leaned down from his saddle and spoke in a quiet voice.

"Be watchful. I can let you pass but I cannot keep you safe."

"The light will keep us safe," Petronus said, quoting the Whymer Bible's opening admonition.

The young lieutenant shook his head. "There is no light now." He looked around again, scanning for any sign that his men were nearby. "And the one now asked to guard it is the same who snuffed it out. You will not be safe here."

Then, he turned his horse and rode off in the direction of the wind.

By nightfall, Petronus and his ragged band of gravediggers had set up their camp by the river, just outside what had once been the river dock gate and clearly in compliance with the Exercise of Holiness. That area had been granted special Dispensation to keep the supply chain moving through the duration of the Exercise in years past.

The one good thing about having been Pope was understanding the rules one had to play by.

Rudolfo

Rudolfo and his escort rode northwest to the Papal Summer Palace high up and secluded in the Dragon's Spine. Riding high in his saddle, he could see the purple line of those jagged peaks on the horizon. Once they reached the foothills, they'd turn west and follow them until they found the Waybringer's Path and followed it up to the palace and the village that had sprung up around it to care for the Androfrancine foothold when it was not in use.

He'd left two mornings ago, slipping out of the camp before the sun rose, dressed in subdued colors and trading his turban for a black hood. His half-squad of scouts rode, too. He would not have it otherwise, and he would not approach this so-called Pope with magicked scouts regardless of the war.

"What will you do?" Gregoric had asked him as he climbed into the saddle.

Rudolfo had settled himself in, whipping his dark cloak over his shoulder. "I will tell the truth," he said, smiling despite the weariness that pulled at him. "Though I'm not sure they will hear it."

He'd seen the note declaring the Exercise of Holiness and had crumpled it into a ball when he saw that Sethbert had been deputized by the new King of Windwir.

That pompous cesspool carp had sent him a note three days before the Papal decree. Rudolfo should have expected this sudden setback.

You will pay for what you have done, the note read, and Rudolfo knew that though on the surface it could be read in many ways, it was about the Lady Jin Li Tam. It had taken some time for the spies to take word back to the Overseer—largely because the one Physician of Penitent Torture Rudolfo had brought along had not yet finished redeeming them, turning them to Rudolfo's cause. Rudolfo was pleased to send those spies back to Sethbert with news of his betrothal to Jin Li Tam.

Perhaps, he thought, that had been an error in judgment.

The forests and grasslands stretched out before them now and they raced north, stopping only when they had to. The narrow road—more a track really—passed through a few scattered settlements, but the riders stayed low on their horses, their eyes fixed on the line of mountains.

They rounded a corner and a white bird dropped from the sky into Rudolfo's net. He held up his hand and they halted. They waited, and Lieutenant Alyn, the lead scout, made his way back to them ten or fifteen minutes later.

"There's an Androfrancine caravan yonder," he said, pointing to a point where the road disappeared around a slight rise. "Mostly on foot. A few with carts or wagons."

Rudolfo stroked his beard. "Are they armed?"

The scout nodded. "A few guards—none in gray. They look to be up from Pylos or Turam."

Making their way to the Palace, he realized, compelled to obey their Pope. "Very well," Rudolfo said. "I will ride forward. You will accompany me." The others looked uncomfortable but unsurprised. "The rest of you—follow at a distance."

Rudolfo rode ahead and Lieutenant Alyn fell in just behind. He reached beneath his cloak and loosened his sword in its scabbard as he went.

As he cantered around the bend, Rudolfo raised his hand in greeting. He quickly scanned the collection of carts and old men in tattered robes, sized up the handful of guards, and whistled a tune from the Hymnal of the Wandering Army low enough for Alyn to hear it. The lieutenant nodded once, slowly.

"These are dark days for pilgrimage," he said to the guard who approached him. "I've a half-squad of scouts and would offer you escort if you ride to heed the Pope's homecoming call."

The guard, riding a tired old paint, scratched his head, pushing his steel cap back as he did. "You bear the coloring of the Gypsy Scouts," he said.

Rudolfo nodded. "We do."

"You'd do best to ride on then. There is no longer any kin-clave for the Foresters." He waved to the Androfrancines, some of whom were now standing and looking in their direction. "Especially with this lot."

Rudolfo studied them. "Really?"

The guard lowered his voice. "Me, I'm a Turam Bookhouse guard on half-rations and half-pay to see these oldsters back to their new home. I care little for the politics of kin-clave. The rumor birds say Sethbert brought down Windwir with a spell."

"It's true," Rudolfo said. "I've seen it."

"Yet the Writ of Shunning is to the Foresters and their Gypsy King . . . that damned Rudolfo."

Rudolfo shrugged. "Who can know what to believe?" He watched the other guards as they also approached now. "Still," he said, "you are short a few blades for the work ahead."

The look on the guard's face brought a smile to Rudolfo's lips. "What work do you speak of?"

Rudolfo stretched high in the saddle and pointed north and east. "That line of scrub there marks the bank of the First River. You'll pass within two leagues of it, and those are Marsher lands."

The guard nodded. "Aye. We planned to slip past the Marsh King's skirmishers in the night."

Rudolfo sat back down in the saddle. "Perhaps you will succeed," he said. "Perhaps you will not." He shrugged. "I'm offering myself and my half-squad of Gypsy Scouts. If the Writ of Shunning is your concern, we'll ride apart from your charges and watch out from afar."

An old Androfrancine broke from the group and approached. "What is the concern here, Hamik?" he asked. True, he wore a simple, tattered robe, but Rudolfo saw the ring upon his finger.

"You're the arch-scholar of this concern," Rudolfo observed.

The old man nodded. "I'm Cyril. Of the Turam Francine House. You've the look of a Forester about you."

Rudolfo nodded and bowed slightly with a flourish. "I'm sure I must."

"He's offered his blades to ours. He claims a half-squad of Rudolfo's Gypsy Scouts."

He watched at least three emotions wash over the arch-scholar's face. At first, surprise. Then anger. Then weariness. *These are the only currency our hearts can spend now*, Rudolfo thought. He added his own voice to that of the guard's. "I am also bound for the Papal Summer Palace to parley with Pope Resolute regarding the Desolation of Windwir. I am aware of his Writ of Shunning but remain confident that the matter shall be resolved peaceably in its own time and manner." He patted the pommel of his sword. "Meanwhile, my blade and the blade of my men for the true children of P'Andro Whym. We will keep our distance if it pleases you."

A hard look crossed the arch-scholar's face. "And you want nothing for this?"

He smiled. "Only the chance to restore faith in my questionable name."

Both the guard and the arch-scholar's eyes widened a bit, and Rudolfo savored their silence as if it were a fine, chilled wine.

Finally, the arch-scholar nodded and spoke. "Very well, then." He paused and Rudolfo could see the question he wanted to ask next forming on his face before forming on his tongue. "And what is your name?"

Rudolfo threw back his head and laughed. "But of course I am Rudolfo, Lord of the Ninefold Forest Houses, General of the Wandering Army." He inclined his head, doing his best to bow from the saddle. "And I am at your service."

Neb

Neb stood at the river's edge and watched the setting sun. They'd made their camp the day before, setting the tents up carefully outside the place where the city's walls had once stood, near the river. Petronus—Petros, he reminded himself—was a crafty old fox. He'd studied very little Androfrancine Law in the Orphan School but he'd read enough of the codices and Council of Findings volumes to know that it was more complex than a Whymer Maze.

He wasn't sure it would work, but he hoped it would.

They'd spent the day digging trenches in the charred earth, long shallow trenches.

"We start with those who fell outside the city," the old man had told them when they gathered up that morning. "We'll work in the daylight, and should anyone approach, I will deal with them."

They worked all day digging the trenches, but no one approached. At one point, Neb thought he'd seen a rider at a distance, but the rider turned south and vanished.

Now, he stood by the river and stripped out of his clothes. They were black with soot, along with the rest of him.

Neb could've bathed in camp. There were tubs of heated water that a few of the women had put on for the diggers. But the day had worn into him like a wagon wheel on a familiar road and he'd needed to slip away from the others to recollect himself.

He waded into the cold waters, and jumped when his foot moved across something round and slippery. The skull floated to the top, pulled downriver by the slow current. He watched it go and realized suddenly that he felt nothing at all.

"This is my life now," he said to the skull as it bobbed away.

Wind he could not feel caught at the ashy ground and put up a small cloud of gray. "Hail, boy," a voice said from the cloud.

Neb looked, seeing nothing, silently cursing himself for not bringing a knife. He crouched in the water, his hand feeling for a rock. But knife or rock, it wouldn't matter. Even if he could bring himself to wield either, it would do nothing against an enemy he couldn't see.

"You've nothing to fear from me," the voice said.

Neb's eyes moved over the shoreline. But the sun was lower now, and any chance of picking up a glimmer of light, even if it could slide somehow over the magick, was rapidly fading. "I'll not go back to Sethbert," he said in a low voice.

The scout chuckled. "I don't blame you for that. I'm not from Sethbert."

A Gypsy Scout then, he thought. "You're from the Nine-fold Forest Houses, then?"

"Aye," the voice said. "And you're with the gravediggers." It was a statement, not a question.

Neb nodded. "I am. I . . ." He didn't know how to finish his thought. "I used to live here."

Now the voice moved downriver a bit. "I'm sorry for your loss, then. Sethbert has wronged the world with his treachery." A pause. "But don't worry, boy. He'll pay for it."

Neb hoped the Gypsy Scout was right. He hoped it with everything inside of him. "How goes the war?"

Now, the Gypsy Scout sighed. "Not good, I'm afraid. The Pope has issued a Writ of Shunning against us. He's been somewhat *misinformed* about matters."

"He's no Pope," Neb said, and regretted it as soon as he said it.

Fortunately, the scout did nothing with it and continued. "General Rudolfo rides even now to parley with him. We're dividing the Wandering Army, and most are falling back to the Ninefold Forest."

Most. The thought lingered before he asked. "Most?"

The voice was upriver from him now. "Some of us are staying behind. We will be keeping watch over you from the shadows while you do your work. Tell the old man we would speak with him here at the river when the sun rises tomorrow."

Neb nodded. "I will tell him." He paused, thinking about it for a moment. "There was a woman with red hair. From House Li Tam. She fled Sethbert's camp a week past for yours."

"She is safe," the Gypsy Scout said. "Rudolfo spirited her away along with the metal man before the first battle."

A mechoservitor, Neb thought. Another survivor of Windwir. He wondered if there were others. It seemed odd to him that the mechanicals would survive the destruction, but he welcomed what little of the Androfrancines' light remained in the world, though he wondered what a mechoservitor's role in this different world would be.

And the woman—her blazing green eyes and her copper hair filled his memory. She'd towered above him, standing a full head over Sethbert even. "I'm glad she's safe," he said.

A low whistle carried across the charred landscape. "I'm needed elsewhere," the Gypsy Scout said. "Pass word to the old man. Tomorrow at dawn. Tell him it's Gregoric, First Captain of the Gypsy Scouts."

Neb nodded. "I will."

Silence, then the faintest whispering of wind along the ground.

The sky was purple now and the light was leaking out of it quickly, turning the water as dark as the field of ashen bones that stretched west from the river as far as he could see.

With so many of the dead watching, Neb scrubbed himself clean as quickly as he could, then ran back to the camp to find his Pope.

Chapter

12

Resolute

Pope Resolute the First had chosen his name quickly. Until ten days ago he'd simply been Archbishop Oriv, and that really hadn't been much as far as he—or anyone else for that matter—was concerned. He'd climbed the ranks of the Order, starting out as a digging acolyte and working his way into a paralegal role researching and scripting matters of Androfrancine Law for the Office of Land Acquisitions. Somehow, in his later years, he'd earned the favor of Pope Introspect III and had found himself suddenly a bishop. The leap from that role into archbishop—assigned to oversee the Order's vast property holdings throughout the Named Lands—had been a relatively short one.

But this leap, he thought. Gods.

He stood up from his desk and turned his back on the mountain of papers that cascaded there. He walked across the carpet, his slippered feet whispering as he went, and paused at the large open doors that led out to the small balcony attached to the Papal Offices of the Summer Palace. Second Summer had arrived, and the mountain air hung thick with heat. He walked out into it and looked out.

The balcony faced south, giving him an expansive view of the small village with its stone buildings and wood-shingled, high-pitched roofs. Beyond the village, the foothills of the Dragon's Spine rolled down to forest and the forest stretched on for league upon league. The day was clear, and a hundred leagues distant he could see the sunlight thrown back from the surface of the Marsh Sea, spillover from the headwaters of the First of the Three Rivers.

Ten days ago, he'd been downstairs in the quarters reserved for the higher ranking members of the Order. The Summer Palace was first and foremost for the Pope, but it was also for the Pope's friends, and the Archbishop Oriv had certainly been a friend through the years, using his knowledge of Androfrancine Law to bend around the various corners of kin-clave and protect the Order's best interests at home and abroad.

And when the Pope's own nephew had come up implicated in a scandal that involved Order holdings being sold for a pittance, Oriv had done his part to protect the light by keeping that particular corner utterly in the dark.

And now, I am Pope. Of course, he wasn't. He may have

specialized in the laws of property and holding, but you couldn't touch those laws without understanding the other laws that held them up. Especially the Laws of Succession.

He'd been drinking hot brandy in the later part of the day that seemed now so long ago. It was a day, he realized, that people would someday ask about.

"Where were you," they would ask, "when you saw the pyre of Windwir?"

And those who had been close enough to see it—surely most of the Named Lands, if the reports were true—would say where they had been, and the room they were in would grow quiet with loss and grief remembered.

That day, he'd looked up at a word from one of the acolytes who made up the staff of servants in the Summer Palace and he'd seen the pillar of smoke far south and east, rising into the sky. He'd disbelieved it, of course. There were certainly other explanations, other places along that line of sight; but when the birds arrived a day and a half later, he'd finally believed enough to call an Assembly of the Knowledgeable to determine the senior Order member. By the time that handful had gathered, more birds had come in—all with questions rather than answers.

They put forth the questions to identify the ranking brother. He'd known by looking around the room that it would be him.

And after, he'd gone alone into the Papal office and pulled the heavy iron key down from the wall. He'd taken one scholar, one scientist and two members of the Gray Guard contingent with him then, down into the cellars far below, walking the winding stone stairs until he stood before the vault.

He'd opened it, found the Letters of Succession from his friend, Introspect III, and carried them back up to the Assembly.

They named him Steward of the Throne and Ring first. When reports of the devastation arrived, he named himself Pope provisionally. It was understood—but not said—that he would lay down the office should someone from Introspect's named list of successors turn up alive.

When Sethbert's bird arrived, Oriv took his final step, and no one argued though all of them knew it was not the proper form. He burned the Letters of Succession for all of them to see and took his new name.

"I am resolved," he said to the gathered Assembly, "to right this wrong and avenge the light extinguished."

No one argued, even though it went against the teachings of P'Andro Whym. He named himself Pope Resolute the First and immediately issued the Writ of Shunning against the Ninefold Forest Houses and the man who his cousin, Lord Sethbert of the Entrolusian City States, had identified as the Desolator of Windwir.

He used your own light against you, Dear Cousin, the coded note read. *It was a metal man who spoke the words of Xhum Y'zir and finished the Wizard King's work of long ago.*

It didn't surprise him. Most kept clear of the Ninefold Forests because of those ancient ties, though on paper they shared kin-clave with many. But it was a kin-clave in the shadow of a past betrayal. The first Rudolfo had fled the Old World with his wives and his children and his band of desert thieves to hide in the far reaches of the north. But he'd fled before that Wizard King had sent his death choirs out into the land. Some legends even said that he betrayed P'Andro Whym and his tribe of scientist scholars for the murder of Xhum Y'zir's seven sons in the Night of Purging, revealing their location to the old Wizard King. Because of that Y'zir had warned him of the doom to come and had given him ample time to migrate from Old World to New.

Walnuts fall from walnut trees, he thought.

He heard a quiet cough behind him and he turned. "Yes?"

One of the Gray Guard—an old captain who should've been put to field years ago but had been retained to recruit new blood—stood in the center of the room. "We've more news, Father."

It had been a flurry of news. Bird after bird bearing note after note, all flagged by various threads of the rites of kin-clave. Red for war. Green for peace. White for kin-clave. Blue for inquiry. "What now, Grymlis?"

"The Wandering Army has fallen back."

"They've retreated?"

The captain shook his head. "They vanished in the night."

He nodded. "What else does Sethbert say?"

"His consort is in the gypsy's care. Li Tam has approved of the pairing."

Now this was surprising—and disconcerting. With Wind-wir gone, House Li Tam would now hold the bulk of the Or-der's wealth. Perhaps, he thought, Vlad Li Tam had approved of the match before his Writ of Shunning had arrived. "Very well," he said. "Would you ask the birder to see me?" Nor-mally he'd ask his aide, but they were all busily inventorying the holdings of the Summer Palace and working around the clock to lay in the supplies needed for the Androfrancine Remnant to come home.

The captain nodded. "I'll see to it."

Pope Resolute sat back down to his desk, pulled a strip of message paper and dabbed a needle in the ink.

He'd finished the message by the time his birder arrived with the fastest and strongest. Pulling the gray thread of ur-gency from his scarf of mourning, he handed it and the note over. "House Li Tam," was all he said.

After the birder left, Pope Resolute the First walked back onto his balcony and stood waiting. When he saw the hawk lift off, beating its wings against the sky, he felt his jaw tighten.

I am the Pope, he thought.

Shaking his head, he went back inside and closed the doors against the afternoon sun.

Rudolfo

The Marsh skirmishers struck suddenly and swiftly, their sling stones dropping one of the guards and two of the

Androfrancines before Rudolfo's scouts could converge on their position.

A stone bullet whizzed past his head, and he drew his sword with a high whistle. Two of his half-squad slipped from their horses, pulling pouches from beneath their shirts. They hit the ground and rolled, the powder rite only taking a moment. Rudolfo saw them lick their hands and they were gone, fading into evening shadows. He heard the murmur of steel against leather and turned his horse in the direction of the skirmishers. He raised his blade and shook it.

"Mind yourselves," he shouted at the caravan as he galloped past. Already, they were tending to their wounded, though by the looks of it, at least one of the fallen wouldn't make it. Rudolfo took it all in with a blink and followed his men into battle.

Two magicked and three mounted besides Rudolfo . . . against how many skirmishers?

It wasn't quite dark and it surprised him that the Marshers had come out so early. Usually, they preferred the cover of darkness for their work. He heard shouting and the sounds of a struggle ahead and spurred his horse toward it. They were already scattered, a ragged line of ragged men dressed in the stinking rags of the Marsh King's finest. Whistling three bars from the Fortieth Hymn of the Wandering Army, he moved to the right as his other horsemen moved left. In the dark, beneath the powders his River Woman had ground from the roots of the ground and the herbs of the field, his two magicked scouts moved silently behind them, avoiding contact and conflict until Rudolfo whistled the Hymn's sweeping chorus.

Rudolfo had not fought the Marshers in years. From time to time, as kin-clave required, he'd ridden out to exact some price or another upon them. The Marsh King held a violent court, sending his skirmishers out past the edges of his land on a whim. They would bring their war to some small village or some outlying house, bury the dead they made, and then ride back to their swamps at the base of the Dragon's Spine.

Back in his father's day, Lord Jakob had faced down the Marsh King himself when the tattered monarch decided to test the western borders of the Ninefold Forest. He'd taken him prisoner, brought him in chains to Tormentor's Row and shown him the work of his Physicians of Penitent Torture. Rudolfo had been a young boy—younger even than when he'd ridden with his father to Windwir for the poisoned Pope's funeral—but his father had let him walk with them. As they walked, his father had been careful to stay between Rudolfo and the filth-covered king, despite the proximity of the Gypsy Scouts. After an hour on the observation deck, Jakob had ordered his scouts to take the Marsh King back to the edge of the Second River and release him.

Jakob crouched down so that his eyes were level with Rudolfo's. "Never underestimate the power of mercy," he told him. He thought for a moment. "But neither rely upon mercy overmuch."

Now Rudolfo nodded, remembering his father's words so long ago. He held his sword arm down, blade pointed out to the side, as he lined up on a skirmisher.

He whistled the chorus and charged forward. The Marshers rarely used magicks—raised up from the insanity of those first years in the Named Lands, they kept themselves apart from such things. Descendants who had never quite shaken the mantle of madness Xhum Y'Zir had placed upon their forebears. Even as Rudolfo's stallion reared and brought its iron shod hooves down on a Marsher skull, his sword darted out like a serpent's tongue, tearing through cloth and rotting hide to pierce a shoulder.

The magicked scouts launched their own work now, and Rudolfo listened for them as they danced the line with their long curved knives. A blade glanced off Rudolfo's thigh as he twisted in the saddle. His horse bellowed and he spurred him forward, over the top of the Marsher he had wounded.

Then he spun, brought his sword down again and made another pass.

Around him, he saw that the rest of his men fared just as well, coming silent to the task at hand. The Marsh skirmishers howled and growled and spoke in their ecstatic tongues as they rallied. They outnumbered Rudolfo's half-squad three to one but they were on foot and hadn't expected to face the Gypsy Scouts.

It took less than five minutes to bring them down. When it was over, the two magicked scouts held their headman by his arms and let him watch as the rest of the half-squad killed off his wounded men.

When the sounds of the battle faded, the Androfrancine guard approached. Behind him, Arch-Scholar Cyril followed at a distance. Rudolfo broke away from the others and rode to them.

"How are the wounded?" he asked. "We'll need to move quickly when we're finished here."

Cyril spoke up. "We lost Brother Simeon. The bullet took him in the throat. The others will be fine."

Rudolfo nodded. "We need shovels."

The arch-scholar looked puzzled.

"You're Androfrancines," Rudolfo said. "Surely you have shovels?"

Cyril nodded. "I'll send them over. Do you need men, too?"

Rudolfo shook his head. "We'll bury them ourselves."

Even Rudolfo climbed down from the saddle and took up a shovel. They worked quickly, digging out a large square hole in the soft ground. The two magicked scouts held the headman, and he watched them work with narrow eyes.

They pulled the bodies into the open grave, and then as they shoveled earth onto them, Rudolfo approached the sole surviving skirmisher. When he stood before him, he remained quiet for a minute, taking him in.

He was much taller than Rudolfo, his hair and beard the tangled, matted mess befitting his rank in the Marsher tribe. He wore stained and tattered cotton trousers, a hide shirt—

buckskin, though it was caked with mud and cracking—and low boots that seemed newer than the rest of his effects. Probably taken recently, Rudolfo thought.

He stood before the man and nodded to his magicked scouts to release him. "Do you know this tongue?" he asked, and when the man stared blankly at him, he shifted easily into one of the nonverbal languages.

But you know this one, don't you? he signed, in the ancient hand language of Xhum Y'zir's dark house.

The skirmisher's eyes widened. Rudolfo needed no further prompting.

Tell your Marsh King that Jakob's boy has buried his own dead. He waited and the man nodded. *Tell him the Androfrancines are under Rudolfo's protection by Rite of Kin-Clave regardless of what he may hear.* The man nodded again.

Rudolfo looked at the empty patch of twilight and his hands moved again, this time in the language of his Gypsy Scouts. They fell back, and Rudolfo turned his back on the skirmisher, climbing back into the saddle of his horse.

When he looked back the skirmisher was running eastward, and the moon, blue and green and full, was slowly lifting into a charcoal sky.

Jin Li Tam

The half-squad met Jin Li Tam and Isaak at the great arching doorways of the Seventh Manor. Their lead, a slight man with a long mustache and a neatly kept beard, stepped forward.

"Lady Tam," the scout said, "I've been instructed to request that you stay."

One of her eyebrows arched. "And if I do not wish to stay?"

She'd dressed in loose trousers and an equally loose shirt, complete with a set of high, soft riding boots cut from doeskin. Isaak stood beside her, carrying her pack. She had her knife, tucked away beneath her shirt, but was otherwise unarmed. Though she couldn't fathom Rudolfo's men using force to keep her.

"We will not keep you against your will, but we cannot permit the metal man to leave."

Isaak stepped forward. He'd put on clean robes, and because they were outside, his hood was up. His dim eyes lit the dark recesses of it as they flashed and shuttered. "You cannot hold me," he told the scout. "I am the property of the Androfrancine Order and am compelled to obey the instructions of my Pope. It is not a matter of choice for me." He turned to her. "You are under no such compulsion. It would be safer for you to remain here."

She had no doubt of that. *Stay with Isaak,* Rudolfo had said.

He pulled himself up to his full height, towering above the scouts—taller even than Jin Li Tam. He limped forward.

The scouts moved to block his way and he kept walking. When they put their hands on him, he pushed through and pulled them off their balance. "Please desist," he said. "I do not wish you to be harmed."

And he kept walking, his damaged leg catching as he went. Jin Li Tam watched as he moved down the cobblestones toward the manor gates. He was not moving fast, but she hadn't thought he would. Obedience might be written into him, but at least he could control the pace at which he moved. She had no doubt that he could walk without effort, day and night, following the most likely bird-path to his destination far to the northwest. She looked at the scouts, who stood by watching their lead expectantly.

"Whatever else he is," Jin Li Tam said, "he is a machine made for service to the Androfrancines. You'll not stop him. His script requires obedience to them."

The lead nodded. "We've been told to expect as much. But we had to try." He sighed and looked to his men. "And we've readied a horse for you as well, Lady Tam."

She smiled at him. "I see that Rudolfo's Gypsy Scouts are formidable as well as intelligent."

He bowed slightly. "We emulate our leader."

She returned his bow, careful to bend slightly less as fitting for her station. "Shall we ride then?"

Ten minutes later, they overtook the metal man easily at the edge of town. He moved slowly, limping down the road, as if every step took him where he did not wish to go. He paused as they approached and looked from Jin to the lead scout.

"If you don't mind," the lead scout said, "we'll be joining you."

The scouts rode out ahead and Jin Li Tam hung back, matching her speed to Isaak's. The air hung heavy with the smell of evergreen and baking bread. Tonight, she thought, would be the full moon.

"What do you think awaits you?" she asked Isaak quietly.

But when he looked at up at her, saying nothing, she knew it couldn't possibly be good.

Petronus

Petronus waited by the river in the last dark gray before night became morning. He was glad the boy had spoken again and he was intrigued by the message. He'd urged Neb to say nothing to the others and then, when his bladder woke him and told him the night was nearly past, he rolled from his blankets and shambled quietly down to the river.

The moon hung low in the sky, and as he urinated into the river, he watched that blue green globe and wondered at the power of the Younger Gods. Once, in the oldest, oldest times, it had been gray and barren. But according to the legends, the Younger Gods had brought it water and soil and air, turning it to a paradise. He'd even read one surviving fragment from the Hundred Tales of Felip Carnelyin, who claimed to have traveled there to see many wonders, including the Moon Wizard's tower—a structure that could be seen with the naked eye on some nights. Of course, the fragmented parchment of Carnelyin's exploits was now gone forever, reduced to ash in the ruins of the Great Library. He sighed and dropped his robes, turning away from the moon and the river to look back on the field of ash and bone. The moonlight painted it in deep, shadowed tones.

"Are you here yet?" Petronus asked in a low voice.

He heard a chuckle. "I've been here. I just didn't want to interrupt your business with nature."

Petronus snorted. "I didn't splash you, did I?"

He felt the faintest breeze. "No."

And in the light of the setting moon, he saw the shimmer of a man so close he could reach out and touch him if he wished to. "So you're Rudolfo's First Captain?"

"Aye. I am Gregoric." Petronus watched the ghost move, pacing like a cat. "And who might you be?"

Petronus found a large stone by the water's edge and sat on it. "I am Petros." He thought for a moment. "Of Caldus Bay."

"You had the look of a fisherman," Gregoric said.

Petronus nodded. "All my life."

The Gypsy Scout chuckled again. "For some reason I doubt that. You've been somewhat more than a fisherman, I'll wager, though just what I'm not sure."

Now Petronus chuckled. "I think you just expect too little of fishermen."

The shadow crouched, leaning forward. "I have a man in Kendrick. He heard you work the crowd over. He watched you win them to this work. And I've watched you build your camp and dig your graves. I've seen how well you skirt the spirit of the law by following its letter. You've worked in statecraft *and* warcraft, I suspect."

Petronus inclined his head. "I think fishing is a bit of both, actually. Regardless."

"Regardless," Gregoric said. "You don't need me to tell you that Sethbert will not tolerate your toying with the law."

Petronus smiled. "They've stayed away so far." But he knew the scout was right. So far, they'd been fortunate. Riders in the distance, coming close enough to see them with their shovels, then racing south. But any day, he expected them to close the gap and approach, to challenge them and perhaps even drive them off. Or try to.

"I have it on good authority," Gregoric said, "that you've had some help."

The lieutenant, Petronus thought. "We're doing the right thing here. I think there are many who would agree."

Petronus could hear the exhaustion in Gregoric's voice. "Aye. It would be unseemly to leave the bones of Windwir to bleach in the sun."

Petronus rubbed his temples. He still wasn't sleeping well. His dreams were full of fire and screams, but he couldn't tell if it was Windwir that he imagined burning or if it was that Marsher village so long ago. Either way, he slept less and less each night.

"Did you call me out to tell me what I already know? That the mad Overseer will come for us soon enough?"

The shadow rose and stepped back. "No," Gregoric said. "I came to tell you more than that. I think you are more than you are telling me. I think you are a man who needs to know what has transpired." He paused and changed position again. "Sethbert used a metal man to bring down Windwir. He bought a man inside the walls of Windwir who wrote the scrolls for these mechanicals and scripted one of the mechanicals to recite the Seven Cacophonic Deaths of Xhum Y'zir in the central square of the city."

Petronus shuddered. He felt his heart stop a moment, felt his skin go cold. "I wondered how it went." He paused, wondering how much he should trust this Gypsy Scout. But then he continued. "I thought at first that the damned fools brought it upon themselves—that somehow they called down the city upon their heads." He picked up a rock, weighed it in his hand and then tossed it out into the river. "I guess I wasn't too far from wrong."

"No," Gregoric said. "I guess you weren't."

Petronus stood. "So why have you told me this?"

"I thought you should know what kind of man you're

up against," Gregoric said. "You've heard the new Pope's decree—otherwise, you'd not be so careful to remain outside the city's gates." He waited a moment. "His accusations against Lord Rudolfo are untrue. Sethbert killed the Order with its own sword."

Petronus's eyebrows went up, but he said nothing.

The silence grew uncomfortable, then Gregoric spoke. "We found the metal man that Sethbert used. Lord Rudolfo sent him back to the Ninefold Forest with Sethbert's former consort, Jin Li Tam of House Li Tam."

Petronus felt the ice again moving over him. He remembered the mechoservitor that the young acolyte had demonstrated for them. They'd kept at it, after all. They'd built their metal servants and they'd continued their study of the spell.

And in the end, they'd brought doom upon themselves.

"I told them they should burn it," he said to himself quietly.

"Burn what?" Gregoric asked.

Petronus didn't answer. Instead, he turned toward camp. The sky was graying now and he could see their tents huddled together between what had once been the docks and what had once been the wall of the best and brightest city in the Named Lands.

"If Sethbert could do this to an entire city, I can't imagine dealing with a bunch of interlopers would give him much pause," Gregoric said. "We'll watch out for you, but you should know that there are not many of us. Lord Rudolfo has sent the Wandering Army back to the east and has ridden for the Papal Summer Palace to parley with Resolute the First."

Petronus nodded. "Any help you can give us would be appreciated. We've much work to do here." He started walking toward the camp, suddenly aware of how utterly tired he was, feeling the exhaustion soak through him, dragging at his feet and pulling at his head.

Gregoric whistled low, then called out to him once more. "Why are you doing this, old man?"

Petronus stopped and turned. "We all have debts to pay at one time or another," he said.

He glanced at the moon again, that blue green sphere that was now merely a sliver on the horizon. He wondered what the Younger Gods would think of what their wayward sons had done.

Chapter

13

Rudolfo

The gates of the Summer Papal Palace were closed and under heavy guard when Rudolfo and the caravan approached. They'd seen the piled-up stack of old stone buildings shoved in against the high peaks of the Dragon's Spine from a long way off, but it was midday before they were near enough to see the somber men in gray positioned at its entrance.

The remainder of their journey had passed without incident, and along the way they'd picked up a few more stray Androfrancines making their pilgrimage at the new Pope's request. The first small group was a document-retrieval expedition that had been waiting at Fargoer Station near the edge of the Churning Waste for the Gray Guard to escort them home to Windwir. Watching from his place on the far fringes of the caravan, Rudolfo studied them. They were quiet and kept to themselves, a small locked box between them. Their robes were deep blue, marking them clearly as set apart from the others.

The second group they added to their number was a handful of Whymers—including a medico and a mechanical engineer—accompanying a cartload of books to the Papal Summer Palace.

Rudolfo shook his head. Ordering the return of all Androfrancines and Androfrancine property seemed an error in judgment on the part of the new Pope, though others might see it as sound strategy. And he understood the motivation beneath it. The Order had been dealt a mortal blow by the Desolation of Windwir, and when light fades, huddling in the dark with what and who were left seemed the right course of action.

Better to scatter, to disappear, to wait until morning, the Gypsy King thought. As his Wandering Army had done.

By now, they would be home and quietly preparing to defend Rudolfo's prairies from the armies that even now were marching on Windwir to support Sethbert.

Twice along the way, birds had found their way to him. The first, from Vlad Li Tam, had encouraged him. The shipbuilding banker stood behind him, his iron armada in place around the massive whitestone port cities of Entrolusia. But Rudolfo knew that despite the best intentions and despite the new arrangement between them, House Li Tam was one house against many. And with a new Pope wearing the ring and crown, even *that* ally could waver.

Still, it had been welcome news to hear the Ninefold Forest Houses had a friend.

The second note had disturbed him. Certainly, he couldn't expect his words to weigh more than a Pope's, but he'd hoped that Isaak and Jin Li Tam would stay put in the relative safety of the Ninefold Forest. Learning that even now they journeyed toward him blackened his already dark mood.

When they were close enough to see the gates and the guards, he called his scouts to a halt and rode in when Cyril beckoned him closer.

The arch-scholar extended a hand up to Rudolfo and he took it, gripping it firmly. "You've seen us through," Cyril said. "You've earned my gratitude for that."

Rudolfo forced a smile to his lips. "I am happy to help."

"If I can return the favor," the arch-scholar said, "I surely will."

Rudolfo nodded. "Do you know this Pope Resolute the First?"

Cyril glanced from left to right to make sure he was out of earshot. "A newer archbishop—one of Introspect's back-scrubbers. He worked in acquisitions and land law. I believe he's kin to the Overseer of the Entrolusian City States."

A key turned in a lock somewhere buried in Rudolfo's brain. Interesting, he thought, that this archbishop was away from Windwir and now suddenly the Pope after Sethbert's move against the Androfrancines. His hand moved up to his beard and he nodded slowly. "I see."

"I'm sure he'll treat fairly with you," Cyril said.

Rudolfo studied the old scholar's face. Dark circles hid his eyes and a week's stubble grayed his face. "Let us hope so," he said.

He looked up to the gates beyond the cluster of stone out-buildings that made up the surrounding village. The guards there were watching them but not moving to investigate.

Cyril shifted uncomfortably on his feet. "I'm not sure what happened to Windwir. I'm not sure anyone *can* know it with any certainty. But I *do* think it had less to do with the Houses of the Named Lands and more to do with the children of P'Andro Whym. We've long played with ancient fire; it would not surprise me if we did this to ourselves."

Rudolfo nodded but said nothing. Sometimes telling an entire truth could put one at a disadvantage.

We will all know the truth soon enough, he thought.

He rode back to his men, signing his instructions to them from the saddle. He saw their downcast, angry eyes but knew his orders would hold. Had Gregoric been here, perhaps it would've been different. Perhaps his old friend would've read Rudolfo's intentions underneath the hand signs and nonverbal cues and refused to obey.

But Gregoric was four hundred leagues distant, watching that curious old man and his entourage of diggers.

As his Gypsy Scouts vanished back down the road, away from the Papal Summer Palace, Rudolfo brushed the dust from his cloak, straightened his turban and rode to the gate.

"I am Lord Rudolfo of the Ninefold Forest Houses," he said to an Old Gray Guard captain waiting there. "I am General Rudolfo of the Wandering Army. I would parley with your Pope Resolute the First, Displaced King of Windwir and Holy See of the Androfrancine Order."

When they brought forth irons for his wrists and feet, Rudolfo smiled and offered himself up to them.

Sethbert

Lord Sethbert, Overseer of the Entrolusian City States, took his breakfast in the late morning sun. He speared the pickled asparagus with a small golden fork and lifted it to his mouth.

General Lysias stood before him, and Sethbert made a point of not inviting him to sit. "Well, Lysias," he said, talking with his mouth full. "What word today?"

Sethbert swallowed the asparagus and washed it with chilled coffee, cooled in the river three leagues west and brought in to him by runner on demand.

The old general looked well rested finally. But there hadn't been much for the old bugger to do of late. The Wandering Army had vanished four days ago. Their tents had come down in the dark, and by sunrise the field they'd occupied was barren. Of course Lysias had sent in the scouts, but none had returned. They found their bodies hidden in the wood the following morning.

"A patrol found scout-sign last night," Lysias said. "They're good—but not so good to have covered their tracks entirely. Regardless, there aren't many of them."

Sethbert smiled, selecting a slightly larger fork to stab a large slab of beef and raise it to his mouth. He tore a bit off with his teeth and chewed it down to meat pulp before speaking. "Rudolfo's a clever fox," he said. "He means to keep an eye on me."

"I suspect so, though they're staying near the city. Which brings me to another matter."

Sethbert felt his eyebrows arch. "Yes?"

"We still have the matter of the trespassers to resolve."

Sethbert laughed, bits of meat spraying the table. "Still digging their graves?"

Lysias nodded. "They've not violated the Exercise of Holiness . . . yet."

Sethbert nodded. "Another clever fox. What do you know of this Petros?"

Lysias shrugged. "Not much. After he left with the boy, he went to Kendrick and held some kind of council there with the townsfolk. Most that came back with him were refugees and traders with no real destination beyond Windwir."

Sethbert shook his head. "And he means to bury them all?"

"All that he can, Lord," Lysias said. "Scouts to the west and south say word is spreading and more are on their way."

The sun had moved in a way to obscure the general's face, but for a moment Sethbert thought he saw admiration painted upon it. "I should speak to him," Sethbert said.

"I'm not sure that would be prudent, Lord."

"Perhaps not prudent," Sethbert said, "but at least proper. I do have guardianship of Windwir for the time." He loved the irony of those words. He wondered what his cousin, Oriv, would think if he knew the entire truth? Or if he realized the intricate puppetry that had spared this new Pope the fate of Windwir? Sethbert had paid a small fortune to ensure his mother's sister's firstborn son was safely away before he shook the cage of Heaven and taunted down the anger of the Gods.

"If my Lord wishes," Lysias said, "we could ride out this afternoon."

Sethbert nodded. "That would be fine, General." He sipped from the chilled coffee. "Is there more?"

Lysias looked uncomfortable. "Word of your—" he

struggled to find the right word to say "—*involvement* in the fall of Windwir is spreading through the camp." He paused. "At the moment, it is mere rumor. Overheard bits between officers. You've not been careful in your boasting."

Sethbert laughed. "Why should I be? Call the camp together and I'll tell them all gladly. *You* were the one who felt it should be kept quiet. I've indulged you, General, as much as I am wont to."

Lysias was a conservative, Sethbert knew, relying on the control of information as a part of his wartime strategy. Academy trained, this old veteran was brilliant at his work but shackled to a way of doing things that no longer mattered.

Because of me, Sethbert thought, smiling. *I've changed the world.*

The general gritted his teeth. "I thought you understood, Lord Sethbert, the importance of discretion in this matter."

Sethbert waved his words away. "The rumors are inconsequential. Let me show you." He clapped and a servant entered. "Which one are you?" Sethbert asked.

The servant bowed. "I am Geryt, Lord."

"Geryt, do you believe I destroyed the city of Windwir with one of the Androfrancines's metal playthings?"

The servant looked from Sethbert to Lysias, obviously unsure of how to answer.

"Well?" Sethbert said.

Pale-faced, the servant finally spoke. "I've heard such, Lord Sethbert, even from your own lips."

"Yes," Sethbert said slowly, leaning forward, "but do you believe it?"

The eyes came up and locked with Sethbert's. "I do not know what to believe, Lord Sethbert."

Sethbert smiled and sat back, waving the servant away. "My point exactly, General Lysias. No one knows what to believe. One will believe Sethbert speaks the truth, another will say that it is madness to believe one man could bring down a city." His smile widened. "And some will even believe it was that damnable Gypsy King."

Lysias nodded, but the dark look in his eyes told Sethbert that the general didn't agree. It didn't matter. The old general certainly was right, but Sethbert couldn't tell him so. Sethbert had been a bit too vocal when he'd first seen the fruit of his labor. The pillar of smoke, the blasted city, even the look of utter desolation on that Androfrancine boy's face had been the most potent of liquors, driving him giddy with accomplishment.

After all, he thought, who wouldn't feel a bit drunk after saving the world?

Jin Li Tam

Jin Li Tam sat outside her small tent with Isaak, picking at the bowl of steamed rice and dried vegetables while she listened to the scouts talk in low voices.

So far, they'd encountered nothing but scattered groups of Androfrancines making their way north. They'd moved off the roads to avoid them, and she was grateful that Isaak had permitted this. A part of her had feared he'd wish to join them.

But he hadn't.

And part of her had thought perhaps he'd not tolerate their need to make camp, to take food, to take sleep along the way.

But he'd quietly acquiesced.

"You don't want to go back," she told him between bites.

He looked over to her. He'd pulled back his hood, and the last of the sunlight glinted off his round head. "I am a danger to them," he said in a matter-of-fact voice. "I am a danger to the entire world."

She'd put as many of the pieces together as she could, and out of respect—if a machine could be shown respect—she'd not pressed for more. But now, just two days away from the Papal Summer Palace and Gods knew what awaited them there, it was time to check her assumptions.

"Sethbert used you," she said. "This much is obvious. The

Androfrancines unearthed some ancient weapon and Seth-bert somehow bent your script to his own dark purposes."

Isaak said nothing for a moment, his eye shutters flutter-ing like steel moths. When he spoke, his voice was low. "I understand that the sons and daughters of House Li Tam are among the best educated in the world," he said. "You are fa-miliar with the history of the Old World?"

She nodded. "What of it we know. Most of it is lost."

"When P'Andro Whym led the extermination of the Young Wizard Kings—the Seven Sons of Xhum Y'Zir—their father shut himself away for seven years, and at the end of that time, brought forth a spell—"

Her breath went out from her. "The Seven Cacophonic Deaths," she said.

Isaak nodded. "He sent his Death Choirs into all the lands, singing their blood magick and calling down the wrath of that grieving archmage."

Jin Li Tam knew the story well. After that Third Cata-clysm, the Age of Laughing Madness settled upon what gen-erations to come would call the Churning Wastes. A few had survived, but they were driven mad by what they'd seen. A few—a very few—had hidden themselves beneath the ground or in the mountain caves of the Dragon's Spine that cut across the far north. These had come forth later, digging the ruins and gathering up what little remained for what was left of the world. Of course, by then that first Rudolfo had al-ready disappeared north and west, beyond the Keeper's Wall, to hide himself away in that ocean of prairie at the far end of the New World.

Jin's voice lowered. "You have the spell?"

Isaak nodded. "I sang it in the central courts of Windwir and watched the city reel from it."

Jin shuddered. "How could such a thing happen?"

Isaak turned away. "My script was modified. They were al-ways so careful with us. Brother Charles expunged my mem-ory each night, careful that I should not keep such knowledge.

But his apprentice—under Lord Sethbert's instruction—altered my activity script."

Jin shook her head. "Not that. I can piece that together myself. Sethbert has fingers on many strings. What I don't understand is why they would even undertake such dangerous work in the first place?"

Isaak looked at her, and steam trickled from his exhaust grate. "The preservation of all knowledge is at the heart of the Androfrancine vision."

Jin knew this was true. Along with an abiding curiosity about how and why things work. She'd heard stories of fabulous machines and intricate mechanicals kept locked away in the hidden vaults of the now dead city. Her father, along with others close to the Order, had benefited from this. There was the mechanical bird in his garden—a trinket really. But more practical than that, there were the iron ships at his docks, powered by engines that the Androfrancines had built from ancient specifications and housed in high, broad iron-shod cruisers. It made House Li Tam the most formidable naval power in the Named Lands.

Perhaps, she thought now, the root of Windwir's fall lay exposed in that.

They hid in their city, guarded by Gods knew what in addition to their Gray Guard. And they doled out scraps of knowledge and innovation to those they favored, withholding it from those they did not. They held on to what they learned until they felt the world was ready for it.

They'd been so cautious about those outside of their city but had somehow not brought the same level of care within their own Order. Somehow, Sethbert had learned of the spell and had then learned how to use it to bring down the Androfrancines.

She looked at the metal man across from her. She wondered if he wasn't another example of their failure to watch themselves as well as they watched the world. "I'm curious about you, Isaak," she said.

He blinked at her. "Why would you be curious about me?"

She shrugged, smiling. "I've never met a metal man before. You are somewhat of a rarity."

He nodded. "There was a time when there were thousands of us. When Rufello drew up his Specifications and Observations of the Mechanical Age, he was working with the broken and discarded remains of mechoservitors found in the ruins of the Eldest Days, broken artifacts from the Age of the Younger Gods."

Jin finished chewing her rice before speaking. "When were you built?"

He hesitated, and Jin noted that hesitation. *He's not used to speaking about himself.*

But then he continued. "My memory scrolls have been replaced at least twice since my first awareness. I have no record of those times. My first memory is Brother Charles asking me if I were awake and could I recite the Fourteenth Precept of the Francine Accord." He paused, and she watched his eyes alternate between dim and bright as the gears in his head whirred. "My last awakening was twenty-two years, three months, four weeks, six hours and thirty-one minutes ago. I'm not sure when I was built, though I suspect that knowledge is stamped somewhere onto me. Brother Charles was a meticulous craftsman."

She studied him. His chest bellows moved in and out to keep whatever strange fire burning in him hot enough to boil the water and keep him moving, to keep air moving through him to power his voice. His eyes were jewels of some kind— dull yellow and glowing with varying degrees of brightness. His mouth was more of a flap that opened and closed— probably to humanize him more than for anything else. A wonder of the ancient world, brought back carefully by adapting old knowledge to present-day capability.

"He was indeed a meticulous craftsman," she said.

Isaak looked at her and the eyes dimmed. "He was . . . my father."

The bellows began to pump faster and harder. Water

leaked from around the eyes—another humanizing characteristic: A machine that could cry. A high pitched squeal leaked from his mouth.

She put down her bowl and reached across, placing her hand on his shoulder. It was hard beneath the coarse wool robe. "I don't know what to say, Isaak," she told him.

In the end she said nothing, and simply sat with him while he cried.

Neb

Neb looked up from the wheelbarrow and saw the riders from the south, a large group of them. He started counting horses but gave up—there was no way he could count them. There were too many.

Dropping the load of bones, he turned and ran for Petronus, shouting at the top of his lungs. The old man looked up from across the blackened field, but he was too far away for Neb to see the expression on his face. Other nearby workers stopped what they were doing until Petronus waved and shouted at them to get back to the task at hand.

Neb ran as fast as he could, but the riders still overtook him and he fought his way through the storm of ash they kicked up. As it cleared he saw they had surrounded Petronus, and a large man on an enormous stallion—Sethbert, he realized—leaned down to speak with the old man.

Neb approached but stayed off to the side, listening.

"I thought," Sethbert said, "you were in Kendrick."

Petronus bowed. "I went, Lord. I've come back."

Sethbert snorted. "I see that. And what exactly are you doing?"

Neb watched as the cavalry around Sethbert surveyed the group, quickly counting heads. An unfelt breeze lifted ash from the ground and he heard a low whistle. "We're here," a voice said in the faintest whisper. Neb nodded and his stomach went to water.

"We are burying our dead," Petronus said.

"Surely," Sethbert said, "you are aware that an Exercise in Holiness has been decreed?"

Petronus nodded. "We've been very careful not to enter the city itself. We were going to wait until we had your permission to suspend the Exercise for humanitarian reasons. It is my understanding that precedence was set for this by—"

Sethbert raised his hand. "I know, I know. I'm not a fool, old man. I know a bit about Androfrancine Law. But we can move past that. I will do far more than grant you permission."

Neb saw a pained look cross Petronus's face, as if he knew what Sethbert was going to say next and dreaded its outcome.

Sethbert straightened himself up as high as he could in the saddle, his jowls shaking as he jiggled around. "Bring them in," he shouted to his men. "Bring them all in." The soldiers started herding the workers.

He smiled down at them, and his horse danced a bit while they waited. When everyone was gathered, he addressed them.

"I commend you all," Sethbert said, "for the work you have undertaken. It is a noble thing that you do." His eyes scanned the crowd, making contact with theirs if he could. "Petros here has said there is a loophole in Androfrancine Law that would allow me to grant you permission to enter Windwir for humanitarian reasons. I will go further than that," he said, his voice raising as he said it. "I will underwrite this venture on behalf of the Androfrancine Order and as Windwir's appointed Guardian, I will protect you as you work. Every one of you will get a fair day's wage for a hard day's work and I'll send a contingent of cooks and supplies."

Perhaps he expected a cheer to go up. It did not. Petronus looked at him, his eyes hard. "We don't do this work for money, Sethbert. We do it because it needs to be done."

Sethbert snorted. "Exactly." He leaned down. "Look, old man, whether you want it or not, you'll have my help or you'll not be permitted to enter the city."

Petronus gritted his teeth. "It won't change how the world sees you when it knows what you have done," he said quietly. Then he spit at Sethbert.

Neb watched the look on Sethbert's face shift from shock to fury. He wiped the spittle away, and when his foot shot out it was fast and hard. The boot hit Petronus's jaw, and the old man was spun around as he fell. Neb raced in but wasn't able to hold him up. They fell together into the ash. Sethbert glowered down at them. "One last condition," he said. "Anything you find here belongs to the Androfrancine Order. I will send men daily to collect whatever you may happen to find. I already have at least one spy in your camp and I will know if you try to cheat me." Sethbert smiled. "Do you understand me?"

Petronus rubbed his jaw, his eyes bright and dangerous. "I understand you."

Then Sethbert noticed Neb. "Did you find your voice, boy? Are you ready to tell me the story of the Desolation of Windwir?"

Their eyes locked and Neb felt himself shiver. He couldn't move.

Sethbert laughed. "I didn't think so."

As he turned and rode away, Neb watched him go. Suddenly, he wished he'd never met Pope Petronus. If he hadn't, perhaps he would've found a way to kill Sethbert.

But the look on Petronus's face, the fire in his eye, the ice in his voice—they resonated deep inside Neb. *It won't change how the world sees you when it knows what you have done.*

Perhaps, Neb thought, someone else would make Sethbert pay for his sin.

Chapter

14

Rudolfo

Rudolfo prowled the high-windowed prisoner's quarters in the western tower of the Summer Palace. They'd removed his shackles at the door, marching him through the compound in chains for show more than anything else. They locked the door behind him, and he noticed immediately that there was no way to open it from inside. The windows were set high enough and deep enough into the stone that there was no way a man could squeeze through. And the colored glass blocks looked too thick to break.

The suite of rooms was more than adequate. The living area contained a full bookcase—a treasure of books, Rudolfo saw from a glance, ranging from the tragic dramas of the Pho Tam Period to the mystic poetry of T'Erys Whym—along with an ornate desk and a sitting area near a golden furnace.

His boots were hushed by thick carpets as he strode across the room and opened the door to the bedchamber. The bed was large, with heavy timber posts and heavy wool blankets and quilts. Once he'd seen the entire suite, he returned to the desk and sat at it. He found paper and started crafting messages that he doubted he'd be allowed to send. Still, it kept him focused to write them.

He was finishing his fifth message when he heard a key at the lock. He looked up and watched as an older man in white robes trimmed with blue stepped in, accompanied by two taciturn guards.

"Lord Rudolfo," the man said with the slightest nod.

Rudolfo stood and then bowed. "Pope . . . *Resolute*, is it? I wish we met under more favorable circumstances."

The Pope nodded, then gestured to the sitting area. "Let's sit and talk for a while." He walked to a large, plush chair near the furnace and waited until Rudolfo joined him.

Rudolfo walked to the chairs and then sat. He adjusted himself until he was comfortable. "You've issued a Writ of Shunning against me, and your guards arrested me on sight," Rudolfo said. "I would know why."

The Pope's eyes narrowed. "You know why. You know damned well why."

Rudolfo kept his voice low, his tone calm. "I did not destroy Windwir."

Resolute's next question was edged with urgency and anger. "Where is the metal man?"

Rudolfo hoped his next words were truthful. "Somewhere safe."

"I've issued orders for all Androfrancine resources to be gathered for inventory here at the Summer Palace. All resources, including the mechoservitor."

"I understand this."

"Yet you ride to me alone and empty-handed?" The Pope leaned forward. "You are harboring a fugitive."

Rudolfo matched his posture, leaning forward himself. "I'm safeguarding the Named Lands—and *you*, I might add, the Last of the Androfrancines—from the most dangerous weapon conceived in recent history."

The Pope smiled. "So you admit it?"

"To holding him? Yes." Rudolfo's eyes narrowed. "But I did not destroy Windwir. Your cousin did that."

Resolute sat back, his mouth open and his eyes wide.

"Certainly I know Sethbert's your kin," Rudolfo snapped. "I make a point of knowing." But the disdain—much like the cockiness—was a sham intended to provoke.

Inwardly, he felt grateful for the look of surprise on the Pope's face. It meant he did not know what Rudolfo knew. Of course, the Androfrancines no longer had the intelligence resources available that they had once had. To be sure, the Order maintained a vast network of operatives, but it would take months to pull it back together under the vastly different circumstances.

If it *could* be pulled back together. Rudolfo suspected that it would be an impossible task.

Do I press or hold? He pressed his hands together, forming a tent beneath his chin. Hold, he thought. Wait.

Resolute's face flushed. "And you say my cousin Sethbert destroyed Windwir? Those are lofty charges."

"And yet I imagine he made the same allegations to you regarding me," Rudolfo said.

"He did."

"With what evidence?"

The Pope didn't even think. "You *do* happen to have only one of the fourteen mechoservitors. And the one you happen to have is the one that supposedly brought down the city. We also have the body of Arch-Mechanic Charles's apprentice, allegedly killed by your men."

"All of these are true enough," Rudolfo said. "I do not hide it. And tomorrow, I will tell you my tale and you may judge for yourself." Rudolfo offered an apologetic smile. "I am tired and would present my best case to you, not the mumblings of an exhausted general." He stood. "I will also have messages to send," Rudolfo said, "in accordance with the Rights of Monarchy spelled out in the Rites of Kin-Clave."

More surprise. Whatever kind of archbishop he'd been, this Oriv hadn't learned the subtle dance of kin-clave politics.

Finally, the Pope stood and smoothed his robes. "Tomorrow, then," he said. "And I will consider your *request*."

Rights are not requests, Rudolfo wanted to say, but didn't. Instead, he waited, counting the steps, until Pope Resolute the First reached the doorway and raised his hand to knock.

"Excellency?" he said, stepping forward and raising his hand.

The Pope turned. "Yes?"

"I would just have you ask yourself one thing on my behalf."

The Pope's jaw clenched but he forced the words out. "What is that?"

"I do have the metal man. And I did kill the apprentice—or rather, I had him killed. But how would I have known anything about the discovery of the Seven Cacophonic Deaths?"

Pope Resolute frowned. "Spies. Someone in the upper echelons. Anyone can be bought at the right price."

Rudolfo smiled. "Even a cousin?"

Resolute's face went white. He turned back to the door and knocked on it three times. When it opened to him, he left without saying a word and his guards followed after.

Rudolfo watched them go, and inventoried everything he had just learned.

Vlad Li Tam

Vlad Li Tam's summer office was on the eighth patio of his seaside estate. The building was layered like a pyramid, each level smaller than the one before it until the eighth and last—the highest point in a hundred leagues or more. There, reclined on cushions and smoking his pipe, he asked questions and gave answers as he saw fit each day, every day.

"What news have we of my forty-second daughter?" he asked, drawing in a lungful of the kallaberry smoke.

The aide found a string on his stack of pages and followed it to the appropriate message. "She comes under the color of knotted blue."

Ah, he thought. An admonition couched in inquiry. She was a clever one. He'd named her for the water ghosts that once raced the oceans—the Jin of Elder Times. Quick and unseen and too deep to be caught.

She'd lived up to her name.

"What is her admonition?"

The aide shuffled papers about. "Her admonition is that the metal man is returning to Pope Resolute."

Of course, Vlad Li Tam thought. He is dangerous and in danger all at once. He didn't need for her to say that she would accompany the metal man. He knew that she would. "And what is her inquiry?"

"Do you still mean for her to wed Rudolfo?"

He knew his daughters well, and now he smiled. Once the new Pope issued his decree, Vlad Li Tam had known she'd write and ask. Not because she thought his strategy might've changed—though she'd tell herself that. She would ask because there was a part of her, deep down, that saw marriage as the hunter's snare—something to poach but not be caught in.

He laughed. "Of course I do. Resolute the First will come to nothing."

"Lord?"

He inhaled from his pipe and watched the green waters of the Inner Emerald Coast. "What else do you have?"

The aide pulled the dark purple thread—a color not on any message scarf but known to be that of silent kin-clave. "I've word from Resolute," said the aide, "ordering significant credit transfers of guardianship custom to Sethbert."

"How significant?"

"Certainly enough to offset part of the impact from destroying the major pillar in the Delta's economy. For a short while, anyway."

Vlad Li Tam smiled. "He only needs it for a short while. The Writ of Shunning coincides nicely with Sethbert's guardianship of Windwir. It's not a stretch to assume he intends to take the Ninefold Forest under his care as well."

But why? Vlad Li Tam did not ask this question out loud, though. He did not want his aide to know that he did not know—it was better for them to believe he knew everything.

Most days, he *did* know everything. But today, he did not know why Sethbert had turned on Windwir, why he'd brought her down so utterly without any warning or posturing.

The plan was well conceived. The cousin conveniently away at the Papal Summer Palace. The apprentice paid for. The metal man's script rewritten. Sethbert had managed to bring down the city, prop up his economy and position himself to annex the Ninefold Forest and provide the muscle for an Androfrancine Remnant.

But why?

"Rudolfo also rides for the Dragon's Spine," the aide said, pulling another string. "His Wandering Army's vanished."

Vlad Li Tam sighed. He'd known the army would vanish. He'd wondered whether or not Rudolfo would go to face the Pope. Now he knew something more about Rudolfo.

The aide shuffled paper. "That is all of the *unquiet* business of the day."

"And the quiet business?" Vlad Li Tam said.

"Pope Petronus has voided our letters of credit in the Windwir Effort, with apologies."

Vlad Li Tam leaned forward. "Because Sethbert is tending to it?"

The aide nodded. "Yes, Lord."

"Good. Tell Pope Petronus that I will keep his secret. For now."

"I will send the message immediately." The aide stood, bowed and left.

Three days, he thought. *In three days I will tell everyone that I am going to the Dragon's Spine as well.*

Vlad Li Tam inhaled the deep salt air. It was nearly as soothing as the kallaberry smoke.

"I wonder what we are making, daughter," he said to the sea below.

Jin Li Tam

Jin Li Tam approached the Gray Guard at the gates of the Summer Papal Palace before any of the Gypsy Scouts could.

"Hail, keepers of the light," she said. "I would speak with Pope Resolute." She cantered her mount closer. "Tell him it is Jin Li Tam, former consort of his cousin Sethbert, forty-second daughter of Vlad Li Tam, and most immediately, betrothed of Lord Rudolfo of the Ninefold Forest Houses and

General of the Wandering Army." She inclined her head to them. "Tell the Pope I have personally escorted his metal man home."

Getting in, she realized as the gates creaked open, is never the problem.

The Pope insisted on seeing her immediately, personally escorting her to the guest quarters. He did not understand the taking and giving of kin-clave, she realized. And he did not understand that because of this, she knew everything there was to know about him in less than seven minutes.

"My father was very specific," she told him, smiling through the lie, "that I was to personally escort and supervise the mechoservitor until this matter of Windwir is resolved. He said that you of all men would understand why this was so important in light of recent events." Her tone was dark and she lowered her voice. "House Li Tam has acted as a neutral party in many negotiations of kin-clave."

The Pope nodded. "We will accommodate his request."

She nodded. She knew full well it had nothing to do with anything other than money. This new archbishop's only bridge to what remained of the Order's treasury was her father, and doing what her father wanted was prudent for him. "Also, there is the matter of consummating my betrothal to Rudolfo."

The Pope stammered. "Yes. I did not know until today."

"My father only recently announced it. I'm assuming that the Order does not forbid conjugal visits of their prisoners?"

"It can be arranged, certainly."

"My father would appreciate that," she said. Already, the betrothal was working in her favor. It had to be her father.

After the Pope left her, she bathed and perfumed herself and oiled her hair. She unrolled the one gown she'd found among the clothes laid out for her at the seventh manor and she hung it near the hot water so that the steam could lift the wrinkles.

She moved easily and naked around Isaak as she prepared.

"We will see Lord Rudolfo tonight then?" Isaak asked.

"We will," she said. "We have much to discuss."

She arranged to have her dinner served in Rudolfo's chambers, and ten minutes before, she and Isaak went to the staircase that led to the tower where the Gray Guard waited. They did not bother to search her, though they looked Isaak over thoroughly, exchanging furtive glances of trepidation between themselves. Still, her father's wishes—even those she manufactured—would be followed. Of this, she had no doubt.

Finally, they worked a large key in the door and opened it for her. She walked in, Isaak close behind, the thick carpets shushing his metal feet.

The Prisoner's Quarters were nearly indistinguishable from her own. Wall hangings of hunting scenes woven in tapestry took the place of a wide glass window—this room's windows were set high and narrow in the ceiling. She saw a desk with scattered sheets of paper filled with cramped script in at least three languages, and behind it, a bookcase. A door led off the main room into what she supposed was the bedroom and bathing room. Across from it, a small dining table was set for three, and in the center of the room stood a golden furnace surrounded by a low couch and three armchairs.

Rudolfo stood from the couch and bowed. She watched his eyes move over her quickly, pausing in the right places. "Lady Tam," he said, "you are a vision in my desert."

She curtsied. "Lord Rudolfo, it is agreeable to see you again." And it was. It surprised her just how agreeable. He was dressed in a pair of dark green trousers and a loose-fitting silk shirt the color of lightly cooked cream, tied together by a crimson sash. A matching turban accentuated the midnight of his eyes. He looked at the metal man, and his smile widened.

"Isaak," he said. "Are you well?"

"I am not, Lord," the metal man said. "I fear—"

Rudolfo raised a hand. "After dinner, my metal friend."

He walked to Jin's side and offered her an arm. She let him take it. He seemed taller than she remembered, but certainly shorter than she was. She felt his fingers moving along her arm, pressing and releasing.

I hoped to spare you this, he tapped. "Let me seat you," he said aloud.

She nodded and smiled as he moved her toward the table, placing her hand on his wrist. *My father had other plans it seems,* she replied.

He pulled out her chair and pushed it in as she sat. Then she watched as he circled the table to stand behind his own chair. "Come and sit with us, Isaak," he said, pointing to a third place at the table.

"I do not eat, Lord Rudolfo," Isaak began, but Rudolfo waved his words away.

"Join us anyway."

Isaak limped to the table and sat, staring down at the place settings arranged before him. He looked up at the dome-covered dishes and the bottles of chilled wine. "May I at least serve, Lord?" the metal man asked.

Rudolfo shook his head. "Certainly not." He winked at Jin. "Tonight is our betrothal dinner, and I intend to do all of the serving."

Jin watched him as he moved from one side of the table to the other, now by her side again and holding a dripping bottle of wine wrapped in a white cotton towel. He raised his eyebrows and she nodded. He filled her glass, then filled his own and sat.

He raised the glass and leaned in. "I would have cooked," he said, "if Resolute had given me free run of the kitchen."

Jin smiled, shifting easily into another nonverbal language. She sipped her wine, moving her fingers and shrugging. *Resolute knows little of statecraft,* she signed to him. She licked her lips, wishing the wine were tart and a bit drier. "This is an excellent choice," she said.

I concur; we can use that to our advantage, he signed back. He returned her smile. "I'm glad you approve."

He turned to Isaak. *How has he been?* Rudolfo signed to her, moving his fingers along the stem of his glass while touching the table cloth with his right forefinger. "How have you been, Isaak?"

Remorseful, she answered.

"I am functioning properly, Lord Rudolfo."

He nodded and turned back to Jin Li Tam. "It's a tradition in my house that the groom-to-be prepare a feast for his betrothed. When my father took my mother into his house, he spent a week in the kitchens and three weeks before that in the Great Library poring over recipes to make the perfect selections for her." Rudolfo chuckled. "He spoke of it often as his greatest test of strategy. He sent runners across the Named Lands gathering the ingredients. A bottle of apple brandy from the cave-castles of Grun El. Peaches from Glimmerglam, of course. Rice and kallaberries from the Emerald Coasts."

Her father had spoken of Lord Jakob. He'd not spoken of the lady, though. Under better circumstances, her father would have fully briefed her on the history of Rudolfo's house. When she'd accepted the role of consort to Lord Sethbert, she'd spent nearly a month locked away with everything her father had gathered on that man and his family.

Now, the stakes were higher—a full betrothal—but she knew far less about this man she was to marry.

She shifted in her seat, suddenly feeling the weight of those stakes. Perhaps her father had changed his strategy.

She doubted it. If he'd intended to do such a thing, word would've waited for her here and she'd not have been allowed to see Rudolfo.

Your father must protect Isaak, he signed to her as he stood again. "Alas," he said, "we'll celebrate our occasion with less glamour."

Rounding the table, he took her plate and served her. He watched the look on her face as he lifted each lid, and she noticed how well he read her expressions, leaving off those dishes that elicited a less than favorable response from her.

He reads people well, she thought, as he speared asparagus onto her plate. He left off the drizzle of butter and roasted garlic and continued.

She smiled at him as he put the plate in front of her. "You are quite good at that."

He nodded. "I am a student of the masses."

He served himself quickly, and filled fresh wineglasses with something red and unchilled. She lifted it to her nose and knew already it would be tart and dry on her tongue.

Rudolfo raised his glass. "To formidable partnerships," he said. His other hand moved slightly, but she followed with her eye. *May we find happiness in one another despite the circumstances that bring us together.*

She raised her glass as well and repeated the words that he had spoken aloud. She was too surprised to reply to the words he had not spoken, the words he'd signed in the non-verbal language of House Li Tam.

She'd not considered happiness as something important to this Gypsy King. She wondered what else would surprise her about him.

Petronus

Two days after Sethbert's visit the first supply wagons pushed their way along the ash-strewn road, delivering tools, food and clothing to the workers.

Petronus tasked Neb with inventorying and assigning them. The boy was quick with a pencil and ciphers. Over the days, as word spread to the outlying villages, more workers drifted in. A few refugees—tradesfolk who'd relied on Windwir for their livelihood—showed up. And at least two Androfrancine caravans had stopped, en route to the Summer Palace to heed Pope Resolute's call. When those wagons—and their Gray Guard contingents—stopped, Petronus marked his face with soot and talked to the ground, though he knew it was unlikely that anyone would recognize him.

But the boy recognized you, some part of him chided. Of course, the amazing thing about boys was that they actually paid attention to busts and portraits even when it seemed like they didn't. But someday, he thought, someone who really knew you will recognize you. *You were lucky with Sethbert,* the same voice said.

Now that Introspect was dead, there were no other Androfrancines who knew about Petronus. And back at home, in Caldus Bay, the few still living who knew his secret were too grateful to have their limerick master back to ever break it. And of course, Vlad Li Tam had known. He'd helped locate the roots and flowers that Petronus's particular poison had required, and had arranged for and financed the runaway Pope's escort home after an appropriate period of time in hiding at House Li Tam on the Inner Emerald Coast.

The past hounds us all.

After leaving Neb, Petronus walked north, away from camp. When he'd first seen the wagon, he'd felt a surge of anger far more powerful than he expected. As if all his rage towards Sethbert for this senseless act of genocide was focused into one white-hot flame that could only see a wagon of tools and supplies. The anger was so powerful that it shook him, and now, at least thirty minutes later, he still felt the tension of it. As he walked, he found himself suddenly moving into a Francine meditation he used frequently when he'd been in Windwir.

He stopped and chuckled.

"Why are you so angry, old man?" he asked himself aloud.

Petronus felt the stirring of wind and heard the voice nearby. "Do you often talk to yourself?"

Petronus squinted but saw nothing. "I see you're still around, Gregoric."

"I am," he said. "We ran in with the wagon. We've been gathering what information we can on Sethbert's strength here."

Petronus thought for a moment he saw the faintest ghost of a dark silk sleeve. "Do you think the Wandering Army will return?"

"Unlikely."

Of course, Petronus thought. If Rudolfo wars alone against the Named Lands, he'll not make a stand here in the open.

He'll force a fight where he is most likely to win it—at the end of his opponent's long march into the Prairie Sea, with winter fast approaching and Rudolfo's Wandering Army defending their home from a backyard they no doubt knew how to use as a weapon.

"But it is good to know what you are up against," Petronus said.

"And I fear we're up against quite a lot," Gregoric said. "I've had birds that say there are two armies on the move in addition to Sethbert's."

"They're marching here?" Petronus asked, a bit surprised.

"They'll stop here," Gregoric said. "A good leader shows his men what they fight for, gives them a night to get drunk and rage over it, then points his army like a burning arrow straight at the heart of his enemy."

"They're riding east, then?"

"Aye," Gregoric said. "They are."

Petronus chuckled, but it was a grim sound. "Then they're fools."

"Aye," he said again. "They are. But they'll come angry to our back door. We'll still have all of the advantage . . . but also all of the risk."

"Any word from Rudolfo?"

Gregoric didn't say anything. After a moment, he changed the subject. "What were you so angry about?"

Petronus nodded slowly. "I was angry about Sethbert's wagon of supplies. The hypocrisy of it enraged me."

He saw the faintest glimmer of a dark eye. "Perhaps it isn't hypocrisy at all," Gregoric said. "He's burying his own dead—Marshers would hold him in high regard for such a thing."

He felt another stab of anger that twisted into remorse. "Marshers are—" He stopped himself.

"In the end," Gregoric said, "it doesn't really matter as long as your men are fed and clothed. The rains are not so far away, afterwards the winds and snows. It's already miserable work without the cold and wet. The outlying villages might be able to help some but that would be impossible to manage once the weather goes."

Petronus wanted to tell him that he'd already solved that one. The arrangements he'd initiated with Vlad Li Tam before he learned that this clerk turned archbishop had gone and declared himself Pope would have ensured supplies and eventually guards and skilled laborers for as long as the work required.

"As long as the work gets done," Petronus finally said.

"Be well, old man," the Gypsy Scout said.

"Be safe, Gregoric," Petronus answered.

Once he was alone, he turned back and looked across the expanse of black, studying the forest of bones. He could see now those places that were clear, and he could see the trenches where they dumped the wheelbarrowed dead.

He's burying his own dead, Petronus thought. That's what Gregoric said.

Petronus looked out at that field again.

And I am burying mine, he realized.

Chapter

15

Rudolfo

When they finished dinner, Rudolfo led Jin Li Tam to the sitting room and brought a bottle of cinnamon scented liquor and two metal glasses with him.

Before sitting, he looked back at Isaak. "And you're certain that you can do this?"

Isaak's eyes shuttered. "My limited understanding is that in matters of Shunning, communication privileges are not withheld. Your request does not interfere with my adherence to Androfrancine protocol."

Rudolfo nodded. "Very well."

He'd spent days in this room, hating the cage, and writing out carefully coded instructions to his scouts, to the stewards of his Ninefold Forest Houses and to the pontiffs. Of course, he'd assumed the messages would never be seen; it was more for *his* benefit that he wrote them. He would have burned them eventually . . . until the old Gray Guard captain had poked his head in to say he would be dining with his betrothed and the mechoservitor that was not to leave her side.

Now, Isaak sat slowly reading each document. Then later, in the same way Rudolfo hoped to rebuild the library, Isaak would conjure back each page exactly as Rudolfo had written it. Truly a miracle of mechanics.

After Isaak reproduced them, Jin Li Tam could pass them to the Gypsy Scouts that arrived with her. They in turn would run them to the half-squad that Rudolfo had left outside.

Rudolfo sat and poured liquor into the glasses. He held one out to her.

She took it and he found himself admiring her long slender fingers. He followed them, then caught the line of her wrist and lower arm. The gown she wore accentuated the line and grace of her and he'd found it hard to take his eyes off her.

Her father's acceptance of him as suitor and declaration of their betrothal had surprised him a bit, but more surprising was that he'd not reversed it when Resolute took power. Of course, it also said something about the man. He was a Whymer Maze, to be sure, and he knew something or he would not gamble with his forty-second daughter.

But even more surprising than all of that was the sheer fairness of her. And the fierceness, too, Rudolfo saw. It was not unheard of for a woman to be taller than him, but she towered—and she held that poise as power in her fists. Her red hair, now pulled back and pinned to reveal her long neck and the curve of her jaw, threw back the lamplight. She was not overly slim, she had muscle to her. But she also had curves and the gown played to all of them.

Beyond the beauty, intelligence shone in her eyes and wit played on her tongue and Rudolfo felt utterly charmed.

He studied her face, sipping the warm liquor. "How do you feel about this . . . *arrangement*?"

She shrugged. "I am a daughter of House Li Tam. I am about my father's business."

Rudolfo smiled. "A proper response." He leaned forward. "Are you always so careful, Lady?"

She took a drink from the metal cup, then put it down on the small pine table nearby. "Are you always so direct?"

"I am known for it when it suits me."

He watched her face, finding her harder to read in this instance, now that the reading went deeper than food and drink. "I am intrigued by my father's choice of strategy," she finally said.

Rudolfo stroked his beard. "Your father studied with the Francines as a boy, yes?"

She nodded. "He did."

"His move to humiliate Sethbert by so quickly aligning with his enemy—and so quickly endorsing our betrothal— shows that he learned well from them." One of probably hundreds of actions Vlad Li Tam spun into his web in order to influence outcomes to his advantage. "I have always admired his strength."

Jin inclined her head slightly. "My father has spoken highly of you and your house, as well."

"Then you are not displeased with his decision?"

Her words were careful again. "My father is a brilliant man. I trust his judgment implicitly."

Rudolfo refilled their cups. Back in the Ninefold Forest, they called this liquor Firespice. It was a blended spirit his people had brought across the Keeper's Wall when the first Rudolfo settled the Prairie Sea. It was strong, and if the night went where it could, he thought it might help prepare them.

He sipped it and put down the cup. He looked over to Isaak, who sat at the table, humming quietly as he read Rudolfo's stack of notes. The mechoservitor looked up and their eyes met for a moment.

Jin Li Tam followed his eye. "He is a wonder to behold," she said.

Rudolfo leaned forward. "He is amazing, to be sure. But truthfully, Lady Tam, you are the only wonder in this room."

She blushed, then went redder when she realized it. She shifted uncomfortably in the seat, her poise lost for just a moment. But she recaptured it, and her blue eyes narrowed. "You flatter me, Lord Rudolfo. And yet you do not need to. I can assure you that I will—"

He raised his hand and she went quiet. "It is not required," he said in a quiet voice. Her eyes narrowed even further. "I recognize," he said, "that you are well versed in the rites of kin-clave and the highest machinations of statecraft. But these are dark days upon us, and your father's strategy is sound. We do not need to invoke our flesh in these matters."

Her mouth opened but he continued. "I am fully aware of the expectations upon you as a daughter of House Li Tam. I am fully aware of the Articles of Consummation in the Fourteenth Overture of Kin-Clave by Betrothal. You do not need to bring those to bear in this conversation. It is the two of us," he gestured to Isaak, "and a metal man. If you wish it, we can go into the bedchambers, close the door to Isaak and let the world believe what it will. We need do nothing but sleep, yet we can both claim it to be the most rewarding and exhausting night of passion either of us have ever known."

He did not think it was admiration on her face. It might have been surprise or perhaps even uncertainty. But for the slightest moment, he thought he saw relief there. Then it became amusement, and she smiled. "You are a kind man to ask after my feelings on the matter."

He inclined his head. "I believe some journeys are best taken slow. The Desolation of Windwir has changed us all. It has changed the world and we do not know what will come of it. It is enough; I would not add more change to it, strategy or no." He paused. "Though, I must tell you that I am pleased with your father's work so far."

Jin Li Tam stood and walked to him. "Change," she said, quoting the Whymer Bible, "is the path life takes."

Rudolfo stood, and when he did, she bent down and kissed him softly by the side of his mouth. He placed his hands on her hips, feeling the solid warmth of her, and stretched up on his tiptoes to return her kiss. "A fortuitous undertaking," he said quietly. Pressing his fingers into her hip, he sent her another message, and she blushed again.

You will ever be my sunrise, he told her.

Then, because he knew that it was important to her that it be her own idea and that she lead in this particular dance, he let her take him by the hand and guide him into the waiting bedchamber.

Closing the door, they left Isaak to his work and he left them to theirs.

Neb

Brother Hebda haunted Neb's dreams that night.

They were in the Androfrancine Cemetery, near the high, ornate gates that led to the Papal Tombs. His father met him there and they walked. Overhead, the sky looked like a bruise—green, purple, blue, shifting and sliding like oil on water.

"It's going to get worse, son," Brother Hebda said, putting his arm around him.

"What do you mean, Father?" Neb asked. Somehow, in his dreams he was able to take that leap, to give that title to this once large, once jovial man who visited him occasionally.

Death was unkind to Brother Hebda. He'd lost weight and his features had sagged with the weight of despair. He pointed to the south and then the west. "A Lamentation for Windwir has been heard across the Named Lands . . . and beyond, even. Armies converge here to grieve and rage with their eyes upon our bones. They ride east from here to avenge us upon the wrong house."

Neb scanned that direction, but in his dream, the Great Library and the Office of Expeditionary Unction blocked his view. Of course, this part of his dream made sense—just before bed, Petronus had told them all the Gypsy Scout's news. He felt a bony hand on his shoulder, felt the steel in Hebda's arm as he steered Neb and pointed to the north.

"Curiosity is stirred in the north; the Marsh King brings his army into play, honoring a kin-clave older than our sojourn in this land."

This piqued Neb's curiosity. Petronus had not mentioned this. He realized suddenly that they had stopped walking, and he looked around. Now they stood at the foot of Petronus's tomb. His name stood out from the rest, being the only Pope in the last millennium or better to take his given name as his holy name.

Hebda ran his hand beneath the name. "He will bring justice to this Desolator of Windwir and will kill the light that it might be reborn."

Neb felt his stomach lurch. "Father, I don't understand."

Brother Hebda leaned down. "You do not have to. But you will play a part in this. When the time is right, you will stand and proclaim him Pope and King in the Gardens of Coronation and Consecration, and he will break your heart."

Those gardens were a memory now. Of course he'd never seen them. They were opened only during the Succession. But he'd walked by them and he'd seen their design drawings in the library. They were smaller than he thought they should be.

He didn't know what else to say. Something grabbed his heart and squeezed it. He felt his throat closing. He was afraid. He stammered but could not find his words.

"Nebios," his father said, invoking his full name, "you came into this world a child of sorrow, destined to be a man of sorrow." His father had tears in his eyes. "I am sorry, my son, that I have no hopeful word for you."

Neb wanted to say that he'd gladly accept sorrow just for the hope of seeing his father again, but before he could open his mouth, he fell awake and realized he was shouting.

Petronus was by his side in an instant. "Dreaming again?"

Neb nodded. Not just shouting, but also sobbing. His hands went to his face and came away wet. His shoulders were still shaking. He caught his breath. There was something he needed to tell Petronus, something that seemed more important and more urgent than anything else from his dream.

Curiosity. Stirred. He remembered.

Looking up at Petronus, he said the words slowly and carefully. "The Marsh King brings his army into play."

And Petronus winced when Neb said it.

Petronus

Petronus cursed all the way back to the northern edge of camp.

He had no idea why the boy's words had resonated so true with him, but they had. And Petronus may have been the Pope of the Androfrancine Order, but he was a fisherman at heart, and despite decades of Francine training still gave credence to the dead who spoke in dreams.

He went to the sentry. This one was an Entrolusian infantryman. Sethbert had been sending them down so that the gravediggers weren't pulling double shifts between digging and guarding. "How goes the watch?"

"Fine enough," the soldier said, leaning on his spear. "Nothing stirring but the coyotes."

Petronus looked north. If they were coming, they'd come from the north. But how? If they were skirmishers, they'd come in, kill, bury and then pull back. And if the boy were correct—if it was the Marsh King himself, bringing an army—then it would be something else altogether.

The Marsh King had not left his exile in five hundred years. And that time, he'd left to lay siege to Windwir for half of a year until the Gypsy Scouts and the Gray Guard had pried them off the city and sent them back to their marshes and swamps.

Petronus looked at the guard. He was young—maybe twenty—and wide-faced.

"Any news?" Petronus asked.

The soldier studied him, sizing him up. "You're the old Androfrancine that runs this camp."

He nodded. "I am he. Though I'm not much of an Androfrancine anymore."

"There are armies riding in from the west. They will be here tomorrow . . . maybe the next day. Most of us will ride on for the Ninefold Forests. Some of us will stay here and aid you in your work."

Petronus nodded. "I've heard as much. Which do you hope for?"

The soldier frowned. "The first battles were over before I saw action," he said. "But after seeing this—" he turned and tipped his spear toward the ruined landscape "—I don't know."

Petronus thought about this for a moment. "Why?"

"Part of me wants justice for this. Part of me wants to never cause harm to another."

Petronus chuckled. "You'd have been a good Androfrancine, lad."

The soldier laughed. "I suppose," he said. "When the other boys played at war, I dug in the woods for artifacts beyond my family's farm."

"I was like that as a boy, too," Petronus said. "Now I dig graves."

The soldier pushed back his leather cap and scratched his short blond hair, returning to the question. "I'll follow my orders when the time comes," he said. "Want doesn't come into it."

Petronus felt a sudden kinship with the young man and reached out to squeeze his shoulder. "Want rarely does," he told him.

Petronus turned back to the north. The moon was still visible though no longer full. It cast eerie light onto the fields and hills east across the river and on the line of forest to the north.

Of course it had just been a dream, he thought. And his Francine sensibilities told him, regardless of his upbringing, that dreams were the working of the deeper places inside. Bits of truth and lies we told ourselves, all fruit to be sorted as our bodies slept.

But why would Neb dream of the Marsh King?

He stood with the sentry until he was relieved and a new guard—this time one of his own men—took over. He chatted with the sleep-muddled trader for a few minutes, then turned back to try and get an hour of sleep before the sun rose and they went back to their work.

When Second Summer passed, the rain would be on its heels. And after the rain, snow. They didn't need any further complications than what the changing seasons could provide.

He was halfway back to the camp when he heard the shout behind him. Petronus stopped and turned. He moved quickly across the shattered ground, feet crunching in the ash.

By the time he reached the line again word had been passed, and the camp moved into Third Alarm. The lieutenant that Sethbert had attached to the camp—the same one that had let them pass what seemed forever ago—met them at the line.

The three men stood, facing north, staring.

At first, Petronus thought, it seemed the forest moved in on them. The moving branches rippled in the dim light of the blue-green moon as it set over the hills.

An island broke away from the larger body and moved closer to them. A cluster of horses, Petronus realized, in formation around a larger horse at the center. A voice, amplified by magicks to carry across the river valley, bellowed out from it.

"I am the Marsh King," the voice said in an archaic

Whymer Tongue that few would recognize in this present age. But Petronus recognized it immediately. "Those who war against the Gypsy King war also against me."

The guard and the lieutenant both looked to Petronus, their eyes wide with either fear or surprise. Petronus glanced at them, then stared back at the small island of mounted men and the contingent of foot soldiers behind them.

Petronus wondered what else Neb had dreamed. And he wondered, at the same time, if he really wanted to know.

Jin Li Tam

Jin Li Tam crept out of the darkened room holding her clothing against her naked skin. Rudolfo had pretended to sleep, she knew, sparing her the awkwardness of the morning after.

She pulled the bedroom door closed behind her and glanced around the room. Isaak now sat near the furnace, burning page after page of Rudolfo's notes, just as the Gypsy King had instructed him over dinner. "You've finished then?" she asked.

He nodded, looking up at her. "And your betrothal is consummated?"

She chuckled at his directness. "It is indeed."

"May your firstborn be strong and wily and inhabit the New Land with grace and awareness," Isaak said, quoting one of P'Andro Whym's lesser admonitions.

His words surprised her. Of course, she took powders for that. Betrothal was one thing; motherhood was another. Still, she imagined at some point, if her father's designs held true through present events, she would walk that road.

"Thank you, Isaak," she said.

She dressed quickly, putting herself back together but not nearly as well as she could have. It was important that they see they had indeed cemented the new arrangement. She was certain that the Pope would have the captain of his Gray Guard watching.

Rudolfo had surprised her yet again. Initially, she wondered if Sethbert's assessment of him were true, but midway through dinner she'd known of a certainty that Sethbert was quite wrong. And in that time between the table and the bed, she'd even reached the conclusion that the Gypsy King was probably quite skillful in many matters, both private and public.

He'd confirmed this when they moved into the bedchambers. He'd confirmed it three times that night.

She'd approached the work with the same resolve and aloofness she had with the others before, giving only the parts of herself to him that her father—and custom—required. But he had worn her down with passion and gentleness, his hands moving over her body, pressing messages into her skin that disarmed her at the time and alarmed her now.

No, she corrected herself, the messages weren't alarming. How she rose to them was.

And that final time, just an hour earlier, all of those words, spoken with his tongue and his hands across the landscape of her body, reached an unexpected and powerful crescendo.

Jin Li Tam prided herself on control in all things. And in the bedroom, she came (and went) as she pleased, keeping vigilant guard over her body's responses to those who visited it. Of course, the visitors knew what she wished them to know. In some instances, they needed to know they had failed and that she had fabricated her end result. In others, she did not even bother to fabricate. And with a few, she had relieved the guards and given herself to the pleasure.

But Rudolfo had laid his siege, bribed her sentries and, eventually, taken the city. Some part of her could not—or would not—stop him, and that alarmed her.

A fortuitous undertaking, he had said again after she had cried out that final time. Then they had fallen asleep for another hour, tangled in silk sheets and one another.

She pulled on her shoes and checked herself in the small wall mirror.

"Are you ready, Isaak?" she asked.

The metal man stood. "I am ready, Lady."

They walked to the door and she knocked on it. When it opened, the Gray Guard's face was unreadable. "Thank you," she told him, inclining her head toward him.

Returning to her chambers with Isaak in tow, she selected a few pieces of fruit from the bowl in her sitting room. She drew a stack of parchment from the desk and placed it near a pen and a small bottle of ink.

While Isaak went to work, she took the fruit into the bathing room. She drew a bath and climbed into the large granite tub of steaming water.

Biting into a pear, she found her mind wandering back to the night before, then leaping into an imagined future.

There was a strength beneath Rudolfo's foppish exterior, a steel that reminded her very much of her father. And considering that Vlad Li Tam was the greatest—and most formidable—man alive, this could not be a bad thing. But she wondered at the same time how the Gypsy King would deal with his changing world.

She knew enough of him. A life spent on the move between nine manors and a hundred small forest towns. A deep passion for good food, chilled wine and . . . She found herself blushing and settled deeper into the tub.

But if—or perhaps now it was simply *when* —they solved the present dilemma of the Papal Writ, and if Rudolfo did somehow manage to rebuild some portion of the Great Library far away in his northern woods, how well would the General of the Wandering Army take to being rooted in one place?

And how well would she?

But moving the center of the world came with consequences and sacrifice. So did shifting history, that wide and strong river, in a new and unexpected direction.

Chapter

16

Rudolfo

Pope Resolute spent most of a week interrogating Rudolfo at his leisure. Most of those meetings occurred in the sitting area of Rudolfo's quarters, but at least twice the Gray Guard had escorted him—shackled, of course—to the Pope's office on the top floor. Apart from that first night, Rudolfo had not seen Jin Li Tam.

Resolute, he thought, was learning his job.

But this time, when the Gray Guard came for him, they did not shackle him. And he was surprised to find Isaak and Jin Li Tam both sitting in the office with Resolute.

"Lord Rudolfo," the Pope said, looking up from his desk. "Please sit."

Rudolfo nodded to Jin Li Tam and she returned the nod.

"It is good to see you, Lady Tam," Rudolfo said.

"And you, Lord Rudolfo."

Rudolfo sat. "And, Isaak, what of you? Are you well?"

The metal man opened his mouth to speak, but Pope Resolute spoke for him. "The mechoservitor is in working order. I am grateful to your betrothed for its safe escort."

Rudolfo's eyes quickly searched the room. There was more paper on the desk than there had been two days ago. The Pope himself looked less well rested, and the door behind his desk was closed against an overcast sky. The weather was cooling—he'd felt it in the last several days. Soon, rain would drum his thin, high windows. And this far north, the snow was just behind it. It was a conservative and predictable strategy. Something right out of an Academy textbook. They'll hide here, Rudolfo thought, and assess what they have. In the spring they'll know what to do, what to become. He suspected it wasn't this Pope's doing. Someone had to be advising him. Someone from the military.

Rudolfo couldn't be here that long. He couldn't be here even close to that long.

Pope Resolute leaned forward on his desk. "I've brought you here, Lord Rudolfo, to outline the next steps of this investigation."

"You do not intend to recall the Writ of Shunning?" Rudolfo asked.

"I have no evidence indicating I should do so," Pope Resolute said, moving papers across his desk.

Jin Li Tam spoke, her voice sharp. "And you have no evidence that you should *not*. The mechoservitor corroborated—"

"The mechoservitor corroborated only what Rudolfo had told him. I do not doubt at all that Brother Charles's apprentice changed the mechanical's script. I do not doubt at all that this mechoservitor spoke the spell and destroyed Windwir. Beyond that, I know nothing."

Jin Li Tam's fingers moved along the arm of her chair. *He stalls.*

Yes, Rudolfo signed. "I can appreciate your position, Excellency," he said. "Please continue."

"In light of this, you will continue to be my guest. We continue to gather our people and our resources—every day, a few more respond. Soon enough, I'll be able to convene a Council of Investigation."

Rudolfo nodded. "A fair solution, I'm certain."

There was a knock at the door. Resolute looked up. "Yes?"

An aide materialized, moving quickly to the Pope's side and leaning down to whisper in his ear.

I cannot stay, Rudolfo signed.

I concur, Jin Li Tam signed back.

When the Pope looked up, his face betrayed surprise. The aide left quickly, and Resolute released his held breath. Rudolfo thought he might even look more pale than usual. He glanced at Rudolfo, then stared at Jin Li Tam.

"I have surprising news," he told her.

But before he could continue, the doors opened. Pope Resolute stood, and Rudolfo took it as a cue to do the same. Jin also rose, and out of the corner of his eye Rudolfo saw surprise now color her face as well. A slight man in saffron robes and short red hair shot through with gray entered the room. Two young men dressed in black silk accented with saffron colored sashes accompanied him, and Rudolfo immediately saw the resemblance in the faces and the posture. Brothers with their father, he noted.

But he saw more than that. He glanced at Jin Li Tam again to be sure, and there was no doubt. They had the same eyes.

"Lord Tam," Resolute said. "It is an unexpected honor to meet you."

"Some messages should be delivered personally," the slight man said, his eyes sharp and hard. "I will be brief, Archbishop Oriv."

Curious, Rudolfo thought, that he does not address him as Pope.

Resolute noticed it, too, he realized. The man's eyes narrowed. "When I've concluded my business with—"

Vlad Li Tam waved aside the words like so many gnats. "I believe you will find that my business takes precedence." He looked at Rudolfo and offered a tight smile, then he looked to his daughter and the smile widened. "It is good to see you, daughter."

She bowed. "You also, Father."

"I promised to be brief," Vlad Li Tam said, turning to Pope Resolute.

"I will have my guests escorted—"

Again, Lord Tam waved the words away, interrupting. "That will not be necessary, Archbishop. What I have to say is for their ears as well."

Resolute sat heavily, a dark look crossing his face. "Very well."

"The matter of your succession to the throne of Windwir and the Holy See of the Androfrancine Order appears to be in dispute," Vlad Li Tam said in a matter-of-fact tone. "There is another Pope—one with a more direct line of succession. I can personally verify this."

Rudolfo watched Resolute's eyes widen. "Another Pope? How is that possible?"

Vlad Li Tam shrugged. "Those questions are for another to answer. But as a steward of the Androfrancine treasury, I am required to inform you of this officially before suspending your access to the Order's holdings. I could have sent a courier but I felt such news should come directly from me."

"Where is this Pope then? Why has he not announced himself?"

Vlad Li Tam smiled. "I cannot say. He remains . . . *discreetly* anonymous. In light of recent events, I'm certain you can appreciate that discretion."

Resolute sat back in his chair. For a moment, he looked deflated. Beyond him, framed in the glass door, dark clouds broke open and rain fell. "This is highly irregular," he said. "And you claim he has clear rights of succession?"

"It is not for me to make that claim. I simply say it is a more *direct* line of succession. It will be a matter for the Order to investigate. It would be improper for me to speculate further on the intricacies of Androfrancine law."

Resolute's face went red. The surprise is wearing off, Rudolfo thought. Anger touched the edges of his voice. "Certainly, there will need to be further investigation," the Pope said. "Meanwhile, I have an Order to rebuild and that requires access to funds. How do you propose I handle that?"

"I would not presume to tell you," Vlad Li Tam said. "I am merely fulfilling my obligation to convey this information to you."

Resolute glared. "This is entirely unacceptable. You can't—"

For a third time, Lord Tam dismissed him with a gesture of his hand. "It is," Vlad Li Tam said slowly, "what it is." He paused and Rudolfo knew that it was not to choose the right words but to set the stage for them. Vlad Li Tam's words were chosen before he'd left his office on the eighth patio of his seaside manor. "You of all people should appreciate the importance of taking great care with what little remains of P'Andro Whym's Order."

The Pope looked from Vlad Li Tam to Rudolfo. Then he looked at Jin Li Tam. Rudolfo watched him calculating, saw the hardness growing in his eyes. "I understand entirely," he said, his jaw tight.

Vlad Li Tam inclined his head. "Excellent. I have urgent matters to attend to. I'm afraid I must return to the Emerald Coast immediately."

Without a word to his daughter, Vlad Li Tam spun and strode out of the room. Rudolfo caught Jin's bemused look out of the corner of his eye.

Resolute looked again at Rudolfo and Jin Li Tam. "I will have you escorted to your quarters, Lord Rudolfo. I'd speak with Lady Tam about this unexpected turn of events."

Rudolfo stood and smiled. "If Lord Tam speaks true, your Writ of Shunning has no teeth."

But the two Gray Guards that stepped quickly to either side of Rudolfo, hands on the pommels of their short swords, were all the teeth this pretender required.

Jin Li Tam

Jin Li Tam waited for the archbishop to speak. Her father's sudden arrival had surprised her. His sudden departure had not. He was a man given to a strange blend of effectiveness and attentiveness. He would ride the length and breadth of the Named Lands, deliver his message and then ride back.

And the news of another Pope also surprised her, though it was no shock at all that her father knew of it. He was ever at the center of the web—and often, the web was of his own design.

"This is most unexpected and unacceptable," the archbishop said. "How are we to resolve it?"

Jin Li Tam pushed a strand of hair back from her face. "I am my father's daughter, always about his business. But the matter of succession is not my matter to resolve. My interest lies with Lord Rudolfo and the Ninefold Forest Houses. I want him released immediately."

Resolute chuckled. "When I needed your father's good favor that might have had clout with me."

The insolence stunned her momentarily. When she spoke, her voice was low, even menacing. "You will *always* need my father's good favor," she said. "And you will never have his without mine."

"Regardless," Resolute said, "Rudolfo remains with me. As does the mechoservitor." When she opened her mouth, he continued, not giving her a chance to interject. "Do you dispute that this mechanical belongs to the Androfrancine Order? Matters of succession aside, I am at the very least an archbishop of the Order and the ranking member accounted for thus far."

She looked at Isaak, then back to Resolute. *Oriv* is his name, she reminded herself. She would not allow herself to think of him as Resolute any longer. "I cannot dispute that."

"Very well. I think given the strained relationship that presently exists between House Li Tam and the Androfrancine Order, it would be best for you to leave the Papal Summer Palace. The Gray Guard will escort you and your Gypsy Scouts to the gates tomorrow morning. Until the matter is resolved, you will not be permitted to return. Do you understand?"

She nodded and stood. "I do. Thank you, Archbishop."

He flinched when she said it and she was glad for it. The more she dealt with him, the more she thought he must be Sethbert's puppet. He probably was not in on the plan to destroy Windwir, but he was certainly a part of it. Sethbert had ensured his cousin's survival somehow, and now pulled the strings that made him dance.

Once more it brought her back to the question that had plagued her since she'd first learned of Sethbert's act of genocide. Why? Madness, she thought, and yet the plan was better conceived than she had initially thought.

Jin Li Tam left the room, her eyes darting left and right at the Gray Guard who stood in the shadows just outside the open office door. But they did not move as she walked quickly past.

The Gypsy Scouts were waiting for her in the guest barracks on the back of the palace. She slipped out the servant door and into the cold rain, knocking lightly on the door. The lead scout opened it. "What news, Lady Tam?"

She pushed past him and into a spacious room lined with bunks and chests. "House Li Tam has suspended all fiscal transactions with this so-called Pope," she said. "My father claims there is a more direct successor. The pretender intends to hold Rudolfo and to enforce his Writ of Shunning. Sethbert intends to ride on the Ninefold Forest."

The scout nodded, his face hard and unreadable. "What about the mechoservitor?"

"He is Androfrancine property. And Isaak will not dispute that, Pope or not." Unless, she thought, someone with more authority than the archbishop directed otherwise.

"Very well," the lead scout said. "I will send word to the others."

He whistled and a scout stepped forward, pulling parchment and ink-needle from his kit. Another drew a small brown bird from a belt cage.

Jin Li Tam smiled. She had read Rudolfo's instructions before passing them on to the scouts. Having nothing but time on his hands, he'd written up instructions for every possible circumstance he could imagine. She'd spent most of a day reading them, her respect for the man growing with each page. He was perhaps the most strategic thinker she'd ever known. He wasn't quite as meticulous and careful as her father, but he was very close.

"So tonight, then?" she asked the Gypsy Scout.

"Tonight," he answered.

Leaving them to their work, she returned to her quarters. She locked the door first, then went to her bed. Reaching below the pillow, she drew out the note she expected to find there.

It was a simple letter—the kind one would expect a father to write a daughter. It even included congratulations for her betrothal, and she smiled at this. It had been her father's work and will—yet he congratulated her for it. But buried within the banality of the letter was another message. She read it twice to be sure. Then she read it again before crumpling it and pushing it into the furnace.

War is coming. Bear Rudolfo an heir.

Neb

It took three days for violence to erupt on the plains of Windwir. Neb watched the tension grow for those days, working quickly as the first of the rains fell. The ruins became a treacherous soup of wet ash and Neb slipped and slid behind the wheelbarrow as he jogged it to the nearest open grave.

When the snows came, he wondered what they would do. Surely Petronus didn't intend for them to work when the bones were frozen to the ground and buried beneath a foot or two of snow.

"Riders," someone shouted.

Neb looked up in time to see a line of horses, the soldiers they carried riding low in the saddles. He drew a line out from the horse's noses and saw that they were riding for the Entrolusian line. They were Marshers by the looks of them, but it was hard to tell from so far away—harder still with four armies encamped about the ruins.

He dumped his load into the trench and moved back out to

the line of shovelers. He saw Petronus approaching through a haze of rain.

"Whose were they?" he called out when he was close enough for Neb to hear him.

"I'm not sure," Neb shouted back. "Marshers, I think."

Petronus looked worried. He'd not been the same since the night the Marsh King arrived. For the rest of that night and all of the next day, the Marsh King had preached from the northern edge of camp, his magicked voice blasting out across the ruined city. He railed against the injustices the Androfrancines had delivered upon his people, he quoted long passages from obscure, apocryphal gospels that Neb had never heard of, and at some points over the course of his oratory, he even babbled in ecstatic utterances.

It was unsettling. Several of the diggers dropped their shovels and left. Even the Entrolusian sentries seemed shaken in the end. But when the other two armies arrived the long oration wound down, and the Marsh King's voice no longer boomed across the blasted lands.

From there, the tension had built until now. Petronus stood by Neb, and together they watched the riders gallop south. They watched a group of riders break from the forests to the south, riding north.

Neb couldn't look away. The horses met and passed each other amid the distant sound of shouting. Some of the horses rode on without riders as spears and swords found their marks, bringing men from both sides out of the saddle and into the black soup. He felt Petronus's hand on his shoulder and he looked up. The old man was pointing to the northeast where more riders, these followed by a scattered cloud of foot soldiers, advanced south as well.

"The Marsh King is to war now," Petronus said.

Neb watched as the two cavalries made another pass before breaking off. Then he watched as a group of soldiers and horsemen moved north to meet the next wave of Marshers. But these weren't Entrolusians—more likely the Honor Guard of the Queen of Pylos. At least that's where Neb thought their camp was. "He's outnumbered—three armies to one." He looked at Petronus. "Why would the Marsh King enter into this war? And why on the side of the Gypsy King?"

"I'm not sure, but he does. He has a long hatred of Windwir. Perhaps he thinks Rudolfo brought down the city as the so-called Pope has said."

Neb had studied the Marshers a great deal in school. They had a history of skirmishing with Windwir and the outlying villages under Androfrancine protection. The Marshers had come to the Named Lands early as well, a ragged tribe made up of those the Madness had particularly tainted. They'd arrived not long after the first Rudolfo and they'd settled into the valleys along the banks of the Three Rivers. But after a generation or two proved that the Madness had not purged itself, they were gradually pushed back—under the auspices of the early Androfrancines—into the swamplands and marshes near the headwaters of the Central River.

Neb turned back to his wheelbarrow. "I should get back to work," he said.

Petronus squeezed his shoulder. "I should, too."

Neb finished out his shift and cleaned up in the bathing tent. The temperature had dropped considerably in the last few days. He scrubbed his robes while he danced around the lukewarm shower, rubbing the same rough bar of strong soap over them as he did himself. After drying and slipping into clean clothing, he went back out into the mud long enough to hang his wet clothes in the tent he shared with Petronus, then went to find dinner in the galley.

He sat alone, holding a metal cup of venison stew close to himself, eating it slowly and savoring the wild taste of the young deer cooked with turnips and potatoes, carrots and onions.

That voice had stayed with him. The scriptures and the ecstatic utterances raised the hairs on his arms even now.

I sounded like that. Not as loud, certainly. Yet the Marsh King's words had marched out strong and clear, not jumbled and squeezed together like sausage into skin.

And when he said them, he said them as if those words were the most important words ever spoken.

Neb finished his dinner and crawled back into his tent. Yesterday, Sethbert's wagons had arrived with long wooden pallets and they'd laid them in the mud within their tents and along the causeways where they walked the most. There weren't nearly enough of them, but it was a start.

Neb wrapped himself in his blankets and listened to the water running beneath his pallet.

In the distance, he heard the Marsh King's voice start up again, too far away to hear clearly despite the magicks that enhanced it.

But Neb heard the laughter at the end of this night's brief sermon clearly enough.

It haunted his dreams.

Petronus

"You must pull your people back," Gregoric said, his voice sounding both weary and angry at the same time.

Petronus shook his head. "I'll not. Not until this work is done."

One of the other Gypsy Scouts had found him in the galley, pressing a scrap of paper into his hands—a call to the river. He'd dumped his stew back into the communal pot, grabbed a chunk of dark, sweet bread that was only partly stale, and made his way to the place where he'd first encountered the Captain of the Gypsy Scouts.

"Sooner or later, you'll start losing men," Gregoric said.

Petronus's laugh was more of a bark. "It's already happening. And with the rains coming on, there are fewer showing up to help."

"I don't mean just attrition," the scout said. "You're caught between four armies, old man. One of them is bound to fall on you."

Petronus knew this was true. Today's battle had been within sight and sound and he'd watched it drift closer and closer to where his men worked with their shovels and wheelbarrows. Talking to the Entrolusian lieutenant, he'd learned that the Marsh King had surprised them all. No one had expected him to ride down from the north and declare some strange kin-clave with Rudolfo. They'd waited and watched, but when he sent horse-bound skirmishers across the fallen city to attack Sethbert's forward cavalry, the waiting and watching evaporated into warfare.

"Let them fall," Petronus said. "We will do this work and trust the Gods to watch out for us."

In the rain, Gregoric was easier to make out. A sheen of water along a shoulder, drops of rain rolling off him to splash lightly into the mud. "We've work of our own to do, by the bird."

Petronus felt his eyebrows raise. "You have news?"

"Aye. A message from General Rudolfo at the Summer Papal Palace. We were to follow the armies on their way east and slow them as best we can. Every day is one closer to winter and we have the advantage in our home-woods. But the Marsh King's arrival may be all the delay we need."

Petronus nodded. "What else?"

Gregoric chuckled. "Sethbert went into a rage this morning. There are rumors that his Androfrancine funding ran out. More rumors that there is a second Androfrancine Pope with a more direct line of succession than Resolute the First."

Petronus hoped he was able to mask the surprise he felt. "Where is this second Pope?"

"We do not know for certain," Gregoric said, "but if he's making life hard for Sethbert, then he's fine by me."

Petronus nodded. "A second Pope would complicate matters."

Gregoric's voice took on a thoughtful quality that alarmed him. "Particularly if he announced himself. It could break the alliance against General Rudolfo and even up the odds."

But at what cost? Petronus looked to the river. "It would bring a war like nothing we've had in the Named Lands."

"We will get there with or without this second Pope," Gregoric said. "It's only a matter of who fights for whom. Word of the Desolation has spread across the Named Lands. Rumors continue to fly—some claim Rudolfo brought down the city, honoring some ancient kin-clave with Xhum Y'Zir. Others say Sethbert, though they offer no compelling reason why. A handful believe it is the beginning of some darker shadow that falls across us all. Fewer and fewer believe the Androfrancines brought this doom upon themselves." Gregoric paused.

And how long has it been now? Just a month, slightly more or less? Barely enough time to see beyond the fog of shock that hemmed them all in. "The rumors will settle down," Petronus said.

"Aye," Gregoric said. "But unless something changes, the truth may be buried before they do."

Yes. Petronus saw that clearly enough. Rudolfo was incapacitated, his Wandering Army fallen back into a defensive posture. Sethbert and Resolute controlled the flow of communication to the rest of the world by simply being the only authorities speaking to the crisis. But Vlad Li Tam controlled what remained of the Androfrancine accounts, and that old fox had no doubt used his knowledge of Petronus to slow down their rapid evaporation and complicate matters for Sethbert's cause.

Shine the light of knowledge upon the sins of the past, the Twelfth Gospel of P'Andro Whym said, that you may be watchful for the morrow. The scrutinized truth is the safest path to follow.

But how much light and how much truth?

What would Whym do with this? Of course, that ancient founder of the Order knew nothing of Popes and crowns and rings. He was a scientist-scholar who raised his fist against the Wizard Kings and, when that brought down the world around him, helped to dig what he could out of the ashes.

"What of the Marsh King?" Petronus asked, but his heart wasn't in the question. It was sinking fast, like skulls in the river, and he wondered how deep it would sink before it dragged the bottom.

Gregoric stood from where he crouched. Petronus felt his movement more than he could see it. "I've attempted parley with him. He will only speak to Rudolfo."

"He realizes that Rudolfo is Resolute's guest for the time being?"

"He does. One of his captains told my scout that the Marsh King dreamed Rudolfo will return to us shortly."

Marsher mysticism. As if somehow that ragamuffin king had heard his name, his voice boomed out again in the Whymer tongue. Time again for the nightly sermon, the admonitions and warnings, threats and promises.

"It's time for me to make the rest of my rounds," Gregoric said. "We expect Marsher raids on the Queen of Pylos sometime before dawn. We'll keep the Entrolusians distracted if they attempt to come to their aid." He was quiet for a moment, and Petronus felt his eyes upon him. "You're looking tired, old man. You're not resting enough. If you fall, this work of yours will end."

Petronus forced himself to his feet, his legs numb from the rock he'd sat on. "I thought you wanted me to pull my workers back?"

"I do." Gregoric laughed, but it sounded hollow and devoid of any real humor. "Forget I said anything."

Petronus heard the slightest of splashes, barely discernable from the sound of the rain. Once he knew he was alone, he cursed Vlad Li Tam loudly.

Then he returned to his tent. He'd hoped to sleep, but now, while the stub of a candle guttered at the small crate he used as a table, he carefully crafted a proclamation he had hoped he wouldn't have to write.

Chapter

17

Rudolfo

Rudolfo picked at his dinner, thinking of the night to come. He'd dressed in his darkest clothing. He'd stretched, listening to his joints pop and his muscles crack as he loosened himself up.

He saved the game hen for last, then ripped into it with his hands. He found the small pouch hidden in the carcass and put it beneath his red cloth napkin on the off chance that his dinner was interrupted.

I did not want this, he told himself. He hated that violence was now necessary, but Oriv brought it on himself. Rudolfo preferred stealth—particularly in a sensitive matter of state. Tonight's antics would not look good for him nor his Ninefold Forest Houses.

Still, he hoped Vlad Li Tam's revelation of another successor to the Windwir throne would work to his advantage. Perhaps it meant that the world would not stand against him after all.

Rudolfo took the pouch into his bedchambers and finished packing what few belongings he'd brought. Then, he took the pouch and dumped its contents into his hand. He stared at the mixture of powders with open distaste.

It was unseemly for a lord to magick himself, even under the most dire of circumstances. His father had insisted that he learn the way of the scouts—including the proper application of the magicks—but had also insisted that if he did his work well, he would never need to use them. Rudolfo counted it as a personal failing that now, in this moment of need, he had come to this place.

He flung the powder at the five points—forehead, shoulders, feet. Then, bracing himself, he licked the bitter powder from the palm of his left hand, and felt the world shift and bend around him.

The colors around him leapt out in dazzling force, an explosion of light that narrowed until he could pick out a crumb on the carpet in the dining area beyond his open bedroom door. Sound exploded too, as his own heartbeat filled the room. He felt the first wave of nausea and swayed slightly on his feet. His Gypsy Scouts practiced with the magicks, forcing their bodies to adjust to them. They could wear them for months on end with only the slightest discomfort. But he'd been closer to ten the last time he'd used the River Woman's powders.

He remembered throwing up on his father's boots that cold morning so far back in his memory.

He steadied his breathing, waiting for the room's movements to stop. When it did, he moved through the room, dimming the light as best he could.

When he heard the commotion in the hall, he went to the door.

It opened, and a breeze that smelled of lilacs moved over his face. "Are you ready?" Jin Li Tam asked.

He moved in the direction of her voice, leaning in to see the faintest outline of her against the dim light. "I am. Where are my Gypsy Scouts?"

The slightest of stirrings. "We are here, General," a voice said.

Rudolfo looked into the hallway at the body of the Gray Guard, stretched out on the floor. Already, one of the scouts pulled at it. Under any other circumstances it would be comical, watching the corpse slide—seemingly of its own volition—across the threshold and into the Prisoner's Quarters. Once it was in the room, he stepped over the body and into the hall.

Invisible hands closed the door and locked it.

A belt was pushed into his hands, and he felt the sheathed scout knives, magicked with the oils that kept them as silent and invisible as the scouts that danced with them. He pulled the belt around his narrow waist and buckled it.

"What of Isaak?"

Jin Li Tam's voice was near his ear now, her breath warm on the side of his face and smelling like apples. "He is with the archbishop."

"Excellent."

Rudolfo let the Gypsy Scouts lead the way, staying to the sides of the long, wide halls, finding the shadows where they could, and quickly dowsing lamps where the light was most likely to betray them.

They slipped past acolytes and scholars, guards and servants. Once, he and Jin Li Tam waited in an alcove while the two scouts found a better route. Once more, when no better route could be found, they waited while another Gray Guard was killed.

The Palace went to Third Alarm just as they reached the middle point of the stairs that swept up to the Papal Offices. Below them, the main doors burst open and a squad of Gray Guard, led by that ancient captain, poured in. They locked the door behind them, posted sentries, and scattered.

Rudolfo grinned at the danger of it. When two guards pounded up the stairs, he crouched and pressed himself against the hand carved railing. Once they passed, he continued up, feeling Jin Li Tam's hand on the back of his knife belt.

The four Gray Guard at Oriv's door did not have time to shout. Blades whispered and two of them fell, their shouts muffled by the scarves shoved quickly into their mouths. Rudolfo felt Jin Li Tam move past him quickly, and watched as the third guard's throat opened to her knife in a red line that moved with a quick, careful stroke. Blood spilled onto his gray uniform.

When the fourth guard hesitated, his mouth opening, Rudolfo danced forward with his own blades, pushing one into the soft tissue beneath his chin and the other through the left side, into the heart.

He heard scrambling behind the door, and pushed it open quickly. Oriv was on his feet behind the wide desk, fumbling with a drawer, his eyes wide with terror. The archbishop raised a strange cylindrical device—a metal tube bound to an ornately carved pearl handle—and worked a small lever on it with his free hand.

Rudolfo saw the spark and ducked, feeling the heat from it as it singed the left side of his head. Behind him a heavy form fell, and he heard the sound of bubbling blood and the drumming of soft boot heels on the floor.

Roaring, Rudolfo pounced across the desk, pulling the archbishop to the floor. The weapon fell to the carpet, and the archbishop resorted to his feet, his nails and his teeth. Rudolfo fought back, keeping his grip on the archbishop as well as his knife. Finally, he worked the tip of the knife into the would-be Pope's ear. He shifted so that his mouth was close to the other ear. "We've done this your way," Rudolfo whispered. "Now we do it mine."

The others moved into the room, leaving the bodies where they fell and quickly working the locks of the door. "We've lost Rylk," the remaining scout said. "Whatever it was, it put a hole through his torso the size of a child's head."

Rudolfo resisted the urge to push his knife farther into Oriv's ear. "Is anyone else hurt? Lady Tam?"

"Singed but otherwise fine," she said.

Rudolfo looked around the room. He saw Isaak in the corner. "Isaak, are you well?"

"I am functional, Lord Rudolfo."

"Good. Ready yourself for travel. We're leaving."

"But Lord Rudolfo, I am the property of—"

Rudolfo ignored him. He twisted the knife just a bit. "Release the mechoservitor into my care until this unpleasantness is past." He felt Oriv's muscles tense, and he pushed the knife. "You'll realize soon enough," Rudolfo said, "that my restraint has limits."

"Killing me only reinforces your own guilt." Panic laced the archbishop's voice, and it pleased Rudolfo greatly.

"And yet," he said through his smile, "you'd still be dead. Now do as you're told."

They stayed long enough to scoop the papers from the cluttered desk into a carrying pouch along with the strange weapon. Two minutes later, with Isaak bringing up the rear and Oriv under knifepoint at the front, they made their way down the stairs.

Soldiers waited at the bottom, swords drawn.

Rudolfo smiled and twisted the blade again, savoring the melody it made. Sweeter than any choir, the archbishop screamed for the Gray Guard to stand down, and they obeyed their so-called Pope.

Neb

It was Neb's turn to inventory the artifact wagon. Petronus did it himself most of the time, but over the past several days, the old man had become further withdrawn. He'd started trusting Neb with more of his responsibilities, and Neb didn't mind that at all.

He approached the wagon now, keeping the rolled parchment and pen hidden beneath his robe and out of the rain. They'd rigged a canvas covering with a system of ropes and poles. The wagon waited beneath it, guarded by an uninterested merchant who muttered and moved about to avoid the water that flowed in channels off the makeshift roof.

The merchant looked up as he approached. "How long?"

Neb looked over the side of the wagon at the muddy items stacked inside. He poked at it with his walking stick. "Two hours, I'd say."

He nodded. "I'll be back then," he said, and shambled off to find some hot soup.

Neb pulled himself up into the back of the wagon and picked his way to the front. He spread the parchment out on a dry patch on the seat. Then, sitting amid the day's collection, he started inventorying each item.

The workers gave a cursory look at anything they found. Initially Sethbert's man had insisted they bring everything, but they quickly saw that the sheer volume exceeded the capacity of several wagons. Now they left the more mundane scraps they found, and saved only the most important pieces for the daily wagon.

Neb—or Petronus on the days when he did it—was the second pass through the items, giving them one more opportunity to pull out a cup or a blade or some other implement that had found its way in amid the mechanical birds or the copper globes.

The first hour always went fast and the last hour always went the slowest. Some days merited a third or fourth hour, but today the wagon was only a third of the way full. Neb typically went through everything all at once, tossing the unwanted items over the side and into the mud. After that initial pass, he then inventoried what was left.

But then, an hour into his inventory, he saw it in the corner of the wagon.

He was not surprised that he missed this particular artifact on the first pass; it wasn't very large at all. The fact that anyone had found it was probably a small miracle. Perhaps the light had caught it just right there on the skeletal finger of the man who had worn it.

It was a simple affair—a plain ring made of a strange metal, dark as iron but light as steel. The signet itself was clogged with ash and mud, but Neb knew it before he spit on the corner of his robe and used it to clean the dirt out of it.

He'd seen pictures of this ring all of his life. And he'd seen the stamp of its signet on thousands of documents throughout the Great Library. He'd seen it on the finger of every man whose portrait hung in the Hall of Kings.

It was the signet ring of the Androfrancine Pope.

He looked around, unsure what to do. He knew Petronus wouldn't want the ring to fall into Sethbert's hands. It was just a ring, certainly. It had no magicks about it. But it was one of the oldest symbols of the office, something that could not be reproduced. And news was all over the camp that some other Androfrancine—someone keeping quiet but at least known to a few—had a more direct line of succession to the Windwir throne. Of course, Neb was the only one around who knew the truth about Petronus. He certainly hadn't shared that information, which meant someone else knew. Or perhaps, he thought, it wasn't Petronus at all that they were referring to. Perhaps it was another archbishop vying for the crippled Order's highest office.

Still, during the time they'd worked together, Neb had quickly come to think of the kind, strong old man as the true Pope. Though it wasn't anything he could conceive of proclaiming—regardless of what Brother Hebda told him in his dreams.

In the end, he slipped the ring in his pocket. At the very least, he could keep it from some pretender's finger. At the very best, if Petronus took back his rightful place the ring would be nearby.

Neb resumed his inventory, feeling the weight of millennia in his pocket and not knowing quite what to do with it.

Jin Li Tam

They rode for a night and a day, only stopping for minutes at a time. Jin Li Tam and Rudolfo galloped their stallions side by side, riding without words.

By morning, she'd felt her senses falling back into their normal place. By early afternoon the last of the magicks had burned out, and she felt the weariness of withdrawal aching in her limbs. Scouts spent years practicing the magicks, learning the rhythms of their bodies and picking up the tricks of the trade that made withdrawal less of an issue. The fact that magicks were only used during time of war—and by only the most elite of soldiers—also made a difference.

Though not officially a scout, she'd spent enough time

with the scouts. Still, these she rode with now could stay mag-icked for days at a time—even weeks—without undue effect. She could barely handle a day of it.

They were a full squad now, between Rudolfo's escort and her own, less the man who'd been killed by the archbishop. They kept her and Rudolfo in the middle with Isaak as they rode, and they kept their blades tucked back beneath their arms, ready to bring them forward with a moment's notice.

When it was well past dark, they stopped to make camp. They rode their horses into a forest of old growth pine a league or better from the muddy track that served as the soli-tary road this far north.

Rudolfo pulled away with his lead scout while the others set up camp. Jin Li Tam tried to make herself useful, but in the end she was only in the way. The Gypsy Scouts moved with precision, quickly putting up tents and laying in a small fire.

Of course, Oriv would be a fool to have them followed. His already limited Gray Guard had been thinned by a handful of men. He'd not risk losing more or leaving his Palace un-guarded. If he went looking for vengeance—and Jin was not sure he was the sort to do so—he would hire it out. Or turn to his cousin. She had no doubt that birds were already winging their way rapidly south and east, carrying news of Rudolfo's escape.

Isaak had not spoken since leaving Oriv's office, and for the first time since they'd left she realized he no longer wore his Androfrancine robe. How had she missed that? He sat against a tree, staring out through the woods at nothing. His bellows shook from time to time, as if he heaved sighs that his chassis was not designed for. She could see the intricacies now of his metal frame and musculature. His long, slender arms and legs and his helmetlike head with his jeweled eyes all glistened dully as the Gypsy Scout struck the sparks for their fire. His mouth opened and closed periodically.

Jin Li Tam walked to him and crouched. "Isaak?"

He did not respond. She reached out a hand, hesitated, and

then lowered it onto his cold, metal shoulder. He spun, eye-lids flashing to life as his hand came up. He paused. "Apologies, Lady Tam."

"Where are your robes?"

His eye-shutters flitted and steam released from his back. "Pope Resolute ordered me to remove them. He said it was unseemly for a mechanical to wear the habit of P'Andro Whym."

"I suspect," Jin Li Tam said, "that P'Andro Whym would have been glad for you to wear it." She waited, wondering if she should continue. "Is that what troubles you?"

Isaak looked up, his eyes full of a sorrow of such magnitude that she had only seen once before. "No, Lady Tam. I am troubled by another matter."

She felt her eyebrows knit together. "What other matter?"

"I fear," Isaak said, "that I am malfunctioning. I do not believe I will serve well to assist with restoration of the library." He paused, and his mouth clacked open and closed in a metallic stammer. "I am no longer . . . reliable."

"In what way?" Around them, the scouts put the last finishing touches on the camp. She could smell the onions that the cook sliced as he prepared dinner.

Isaak looked back out at the forest. "Pope Resolute asked me many questions. Difficult questions. About my role in the Desolation of Windwir." He paused. "Then he asked me if I could reproduce the spell from recall, in writing."

Jin Li Tam felt her stomach clench. But she couldn't bring herself to ask it.

Isaak continued, still staring off into the forest. "When he asked me to, I told him I could not. I told him that part of my memory scroll had been damaged in the execution of the spell."

Jin Li Tam sighed. "And he believed you?"

"Of course he believed me. Mechanicals cannot lie."

She nodded. "You are worried that you are malfunctioning because you lied to the archbishop?"

"Yes," Isaak said, turning back to look at her. "How can a

mechanical lie? I think—" He sobbed, and the violence of it cause Jin Li Tam to jump back. "I think perhaps the spell altered me."

It changed all of us, she thought. "If it did, Isaak, then it was for good. You are carrying the most dangerous weapon the world has ever known. A spell that killed a world to satisfy a father's wrath. A death for each of the seven sons P'Andro Whym executed in his Restoration Scientifika pogrom. Those Deaths must be kept hidden in you, Isaak. The Androfrancines were the best and noblest of us—with infinite patience, studying their matrices and working their ciphers, only releasing to the world what secrets and wonders it was ready for. If *they* couldn't safeguard this secret, no others of us could. You are the safest tomb for it until it can be removed and destroyed." She paused, charting her course of words carefully. "If you must lie to keep this secret, then lie." Her eyes narrowed. "There is no price too high, Isaak."

She waited to see if he would respond. When he didn't, she put her hand on his chest, her fingers splayed out. Where his shoulder had been cool, his chest was warm. "Change is the path life takes," she told him. "Maybe the death you have seen has brought you life."

"It is an odd sensation," he said in agreement.

She opened her mouth to speak again but Rudolfo interrupted her as he swaggered in from the forest. "Hail, Isaak," he shouted, and tossed a bundle toward the metal man.

Isaak caught it and stared down at it.

"I thought perhaps you could use it. I picked it up on our way out."

Jin Li Tam looked at the bundle now too, and felt the smile pulling at her mouth.

In that moment, she suddenly knew that love was planted in her heart toward the laughing Gypsy King, Rudolfo.

She smiled at Rudolfo while Isaak stood and dressed himself in Androfrancine robes.

Vlad Li Tam

Vlad Li Tam was not even halfway to the Emerald Coasts when the bird found him. This bird always found him. He was riding when it settled upon his shoulder and nibbled playfully at his beard. He'd petted it and raised his fist to signify a halt. They helped him down from the saddle, and he pulled the message.

While he read it, his servants hastily erected a tent and chair for him to sit in. He summoned his master sergeant and his aide. "There has been a significant change in the course of events," he finally said after leaving them in silence for a time. "I have in my hands a decree from our invisible Pope. Of course, he doesn't name himself. But he has the tone of authority, the confident positioning of his words."

Vlad Li Tam stopped, took the message and passed it to his aide, who sat quickly and began to study it, making ciphers in the margins. "He's moved faster than we thought he would," the aide said.

"But without his name," Vlad Li Tam, "we have nothing but words."

The aide went back to reading. "He encourages the continued gathering of resources at the Papal Summer Palace and commends Archbishop Oriv for his strategic effort on behalf of the Order." Then he shook his head, amazed. "And then exercises his Right of King by way of kin-clave to declare war on Lord Sethbert, Overseer of the Entrolusian City States."

"Note that," Vlad Li Tam said, accepting his kallaberry pipe from the servant who was setting luncheon. "He does not declare war on the City States themselves."

The aide chuckled. "He is allowing them a way out. They can deliver Sethbert or they can support him."

Vlad Li Tam nodded. "Mark him, Arys. Petronus is the wiliest of men."

But, he thought, for all of his wiliness, he still hid himself from the world. Vlad Li Tam had spent a year fishing with Petronus when they were both young. Vlad's father, Tal Li

Tam, had insisted that his first son spend a year without privilege. Of course, every Tam father realized that a true first son would think beyond the edges of the light. So they offered the families that took them in a stupendous amount of currency to ensure that the experience truly was without privilege. Because these boys—the first sons—would someday inherit the lucrative and invisible network that the Li Tam shipbuilders had created when they turned to banking both currency and information. And that inheritance demanded a broad range of experience to give a broad range of knowledge.

He'd lived with Petronus and his family, had eaten at the table with him, taken his share of beatings with him, fishing daily the wide waters of Caldus Bay.

Even then, he remembered Petronus's love affair with the Androfrancines. He showed him the excavations he'd led to his own backyard forest, pointing out the holes he'd dug in search of artifacts that did not exist in the New World.

"Maybe someday," Vlad Li Tam had said to Petronus as they mended their nets at the end of a day, "you'll be Pope."

Petronus had laughed and he had joined in. But he wasn't surprised at all to read about a young Archbishop Petronus in his intelligence training with Father. By the time Petronus was made Pope, Vlad Li Tam had already seen his twenty-third daughter into the world, fully managing House Li Tam. They rekindled their friendship as if twenty years hadn't passed.

Though they didn't see each other often, they met occasionally at affairs of state. Three times, they met in conference at the Summer Papal Palace over Androfrancine accounts. Vlad's most vivid memory was the summer before Petronus's so-called assassination. They were sitting in the office on the upper floor, the afternoon sun spilling into the room through glass doors wide open. They'd pored over the papers from morning until night and only had the afternoon left because of Li Tam obligations that called him elsewhere.

After a particularly challenging conversation on asset liquidation, Petronus paused, and a pained look crossed his face. "Do you ever wonder what your life would be if you weren't Lord Tam of House Li Tam?"

"I can't," Vlad remembered saying. "I was made for this. I can't imagine being anyone other than who I am."

Petronus had thought about this and nodded. "But do you ever miss fishing?"

Vlad Li Tam laughed. "Every day."

Five minutes later, the staff and servants at the Papal Summer Palace did not know what to do when their Pope came bellowing down the hall for bait and tackle and wine.

Now all these years later, Vlad Li Tam still believed the answer he'd given his boyhood friend. He had thirty-seven sons and fifty-three daughters, all honoring him in some fashion. At no time had he wondered what it might have been like otherwise.

I do not believe in otherwise.

It's what he was made for. Somehow, he had to make his friend see the same thing for himself.

Vlad Li Tam turned to the Master Sergeant. "We will need the birder to order a flock. You'll have a day to set up the bird-tents." He looked over his aide. "You'll have the same day to rescript the proclamation." He drew in on the pipe as his servant held a long stick match to it. "The next day, we ride for Windwir."

He dismissed them with a nod, and they stood to leave.

I'm coming, Petronus, he thought.

I'm coming to remind you what you're made for.

After they left him, not even the kallaberry smoke could lift his spirits.

Chapter

18

Rudolfo

Rudolfo arose early, as was his custom, and walked alone through the forest. He whistled, long and low, to warn his sentries that he approached. They whistled back to acknowledge him, but after years of riding with their general, they did not approach or interrupt.

He loved the mornings most of all. It was a time when the world still slept and he could be in solitude, apart from everything. It was a time for processing strategy and plotting the day's schemes.

The rain let up sometime in the night, but the ground and foliage were still wet. The air hung heavy with moisture—ribbons of mist moving low across the ground in the deep gray of predawn.

They would ride hard today and put yet more distance between themselves and the last of the Androfrancines. But soon enough, that small remnant would be the last of Rudolfo's concerns.

War was coming. A bigger war than he'd imagined when he launched that dark raven with its scarlet thread what seemed so long ago. Then, he'd thought it would his Wandering Army against Sethbert. But much had happened in the weeks that followed.

Vlad Li Tam's message intrigued him and he wondered how this new development would play out. A second Pope, one with a more direct line of succession, could mean divided loyalties. At the very least the Writ of Shunning would not stand, though he was certain Sethbert and his cousin would force the issue for as long as they could. The Androfrancines' leadership crisis would reproduce itself around the world as the houses of the Named Lands were forced to pick a side.

You get ahead of yourself. Rudolfo chuckled.

For all he knew, this Pope was also in Sethbert's pocket. Though he doubted it very much. Li Tam's involvement would have been different if that were the case.

Of course, the papal succession aside, there were other developments that also intrigued him. He'd seen the messages and knew now about the Marsh King's sudden declaration of kin-clave with him. A strange and unexpected alliance that prompted him to send birds to the Forest Manors, sending his stewards into the records archives to search for some shred of information about kin-clave between the Gypsies and the Marshers. The only connection Rudolfo could make was the Marsh King's capture when he was a boy.

Still, the Marsher Army was a formidable force when pulled together. Less predictable even than the Wandering Army, they relied on chaos—even madness—to prevail. Known mainly for their skirmishing raids, those few times the Marsh King's army had been called together over the last thousand years were formidable for those they faced. They rarely won when strategic minds came into play against them, but they never really lost, either. They slunk back north to their swamps and marsh grass, daring generals and kings alike to enter their demesnes and fight on Marsher land.

Few did, though the Androfrancine Gray Guard had forced the issue with them a time or two, exacting a price on skirmishers who raided the villages and towns that Windwir protected.

Why would the Marsh King side with the Ninefold Forest Houses?

And alongside that strange and unexpected alliance, there was another. His sudden kin-clave with House Li Tam through betrothal to Vlad Li Tam's forty-second daughter. It was a surprise that Rudolfo still did not know quite how to measure.

The consummation had been effective and even pleasurable. Though it wasn't the physical act that defined the pleasure of that night for him. Certainly, she was skilled enough. And judging by her response to him, their skills were well matched for the deed. But his pleasure had been deeper than their bodies pressed together or his hands tangled in her long, honey-scented hair or their mouths moving along one another's bodies. There was something deeper. Something sparked by their mutual conquest of one another. For though he took great pride in wearing her down and at long last commanding her body to pleasure, the truth of it was that she had done the same thing for his heart, and he was compelled now to think of her, to wonder about her, to wish to see her.

He'd considered going to her that night. Their eyes had caught across the fire and they'd traded brief smiles. But in the end, they'd slept side by side but in their separate tents.

Gods, what a woman.

And her father had not changed his strategy to the best of his knowledge. Nor would Rudolfo change his. He would align himself with this new Pope—if he were a man of reason and moderate strength—and he would win that new Pope to his way of seeing. When the war was finished, he would rebuild the library in a place where he could watch over it, a place far from the meddling of men like Sethbert.

Rudolfo heard a whistle behind him. It was too high and it did not warble at the end.

Setting his jaw, he crouched near a thick evergreen and drew his long, curved knife. He did not return the whistle, and after a moment he heard soft footfalls.

"Lord Rudolfo?" It was Jin Li Tam's voice.

He stood, putting his knife away. "I'm here, Lady Tam."

She slipped through the foliage with the ease of a Gypsy Scout. "I don't quite have the whistle down," she said.

Rudolfo smiled. "It's nearly there. You learn quickly."

She curtsied. "Thank you, Lord. May I join you for your walk?"

He'd just started to think it was time to turn back, time to rouse the last watch from their few precious hours of sleep and strike camp for the long day's ride ahead. "Please," he said.

She came alongside him, and they were both careful not to touch. "You are well?"

"I am. And you?"

"Yes," she said. "Better now that we're on our way."

They walked together, side by side, and her measured footsteps impressed him. She moved like a scout, confident and light with her step. The ferns and branches around her only trembled lightly as she went past; they did not leak the water that had collected there.

The sky lightened above them, patches of it showing through the canopy of forest.

Rudolfo enjoyed the silence as they continued together. Eventually, they reached the edge of the wood and looked southeast and downslope to see the edge of the wide, wide river—this was the Third River, the largest of the Three but also the most desolate. They stood and watched the sunrise.

After it climbed onto the horizon, they turned back and walked slowly toward camp.

"What will you do now?" Jin Li Tam asked.

"I ride for Windwir," he said. "I still have men there."

"What of Isaak?"

Rudolfo stopped. The way she said it—the tone of concern and the expectation of a favorable response from him—suddenly reminded him of the way his mother had spoken to his father about him when he was a child. Of course, she didn't know Rudolfo listened. When his father showed the five-year-old heir a myriad of passages and tunnels built into and beneath the Forest Manors, Rudolfo spent his free time learning the arts of espionage and found his parents were easy marks.

By six, he'd abandoned it. Wise to his ears, they'd begun fabricating tales of buried artifacts and ancient parchments in the gardens and forests surrounding the manor. Of course, he came back empty-handed at least a half dozen times before he realized their strategy. Disappointed with espionage, he'd moved into pickpocket training.

He blinked the memory away. *She cared for him like a child.*

"I was hoping for your assistance," Rudolfo said, walking again.

She glanced at him. Ahead of them, a rabbit bolted. "How may I help?"

"Stay near him. Use the pretense of helping him with the library." Rudolfo reached out, gently pulling a branch aside for her as they walked. "Your father knows who this second Pope is. Perhaps he would speak to him on your behalf, asking that this invisible Pope authorize Isaak under your care to gather the necessary data to rebuild and restore what can be found."

Jin Li Tam nodded. "With all plans and specifications subject to his Excellency's approval? And generous terms through House Li Tam?"

He smiled. "Exactly."

Her brows pulled together. "I've been meaning to ask you about the library," she said.

Rudolfo paused midstep, looking at her, then resumed walking. "Yes?"

"Why do you wish to do this? You intended to do this before the archbishop declared, even before I proposed you as a suitor to my father. You meant to do this and finance it yourself."

He chuckled. "Sethbert would have paid for it. He still will if I have my way."

"But why would you do this? You do not seem to be the sort who would keep what light remains to yourself. The strategy beneath it suggests that you mean to keep the library in a place where it can be protected."

Like she protects Isaak, he thought. *That* was the quality of parenthood he heard in her voice.

He shrugged. "I am not a young man. I stand just past the middle of my road. I am only now taking a wife. If I cannot give my Ninefold Forest Houses an heir, then at least I can give them knowledge. Something to love and defend fiercely in this world."

Her next words surprised him. "Doesn't it also atone for the first Rudolfo's betrayal?"

He laughed. "I suppose perhaps it does."

"Regardless," she said, "I think it is a wise and wonderful thing that you do." They settled back into silence before she surprised him again. "Do you want an heir, Rudolfo?"

Now he stopped entirely, a smile widening on his mouth. "You mean now? Here?"

"You know what I mean."

He shrugged. He'd been with many women. For a time, he'd used the powders to dull his soldiers' swords. And he'd certainly taken them through enough gates. But when he had finally tried to make a child with a consort sent from the Queen of Pylos as a matter of kin-clave courtesy, he'd been unable. And they'd tried for nine pleasurable months. After that, fearing that he couldn't sire, he left off with the potions and redoubled his efforts with the women on his rotation. No discreet notes arrived by bird from his stewards, no reports of a girl (or three) heavy with child and claiming his patrimony.

He'd heard that the Androfrancines also had magicks for this. But even if it were true, it felt contrary to him for no reason he could discern.

He looked at Jin. "I've certainly considered it at length," he said. "Alas, I'm afraid my soldiers have no swords."

When he said it, he was certain that she would look relieved. Though she was quite demonstrative and capable in the midst of their consummation, Rudolfo did not believe for a moment that this formidable woman had any interest in children.

She surprised him for a third time. Instead of relief washing her face, she took on a thoughtful aspect. And she didn't speak.

As they continued walking slowly back to camp, they slipped into an agreeable silence and Jin Li Tam's hand slipped into his.

Petronus

Petronus stood at the center of Windwir, in the square where he had once addressed his people from the high balcony of the Office of the Holy See. All that remained of that massive structure was a mound of stones. He turned slowly from that point, taking in the view around him. Here and there, he saw scattered patches of workers as they pushed their loads or shoveled their trenches. As the rains increased, his help decreased. A few more left each day, promising to return with the spring. Sometimes it was a wash as newcomers joined up, but at the end of any given week, there were still less than they had started with at the beginning.

He'd had Neb rework his numbers, and it looked as if they could be finished before spring if the winter followed the cycle of the last few years and stayed more mild than fierce. And if he didn't go below thirty men. And if the war didn't swallow them all. Regardless, he wasn't willing to stop the operation. Those who could stay would stay. He would be one of them, and they would work at the pace they could. If there was still more to be done beyond spring, so be it.

Of course, there would always be more work. He'd seen to that with his proclamation.

You're a fool, old man.

He just couldn't leave well enough alone. He'd written the proclamation, forcing himself into the middle of something that every part of his soul screamed for him to flee. So many complained of not having the power to do right, making great boasts of what they would do if only they had this or that. He had that power, but it felt hollow from where he stood. Still, he'd put the light back onto Sethbert where it belonged. And by not acknowledging the Writ of Shunning, he'd made it nonexistent. Taking the time to reverse it meant acknowledging it in the first place and he could not afford to let the Named Lands see Oriv as any more than a subordinate archbishop doing the best he could in light of dark times.

He would wait now and see what Oriv did next. If Sethbert truly pulled the strings, he would bluster and cry foul and try to press on, even without the support of House Li Tam and without access to the Androfrancine fortunes they held in trust.

Vlad surprised him. He'd lost sleep wondering what that old crow played at. He'd heard nothing further about the iron armada or the blockade against the delta cities, dispatched early on, then pulled back to patrol the waters and wait. Then, using his knowledge of Petronus as a reason to sever Oriv and Sethbert's access to funding complicated matters further.

He's forcing something and I am a part of it, he thought. It was a game of queen's war they played, each moving based on the other's previous movement. Petronus did not doubt at all that Vlad had hoped for a full declaration followed by a quick succession. He'd given him something less—a guarded proclamation issued under the Fourth Article of Preservation, citing the safety of King and Pope as critical for the well-being of the Order, and allowing for a measure of secrecy.

But what Pope had ever used that secrecy to hide himself entirely? To remain hidden from view? This game of queen's war was not a game Petronus could win. He could only hope to move fast enough to stay ahead of his opponent—and the world that watched them play. And move well enough to stay in the game until the stone rolled down the hill so fast that he could slip out the back and find someplace to wait out the rest of the storm.

Unless.

Petronus looked around again. Overhead the sky was charcoal on steel, but it hadn't rained all day. It was quiet. The occasional skirmishes between the Marshers and the other armies had toned down considerably after the first few days.

So far they'd avoided any kind of pitched battle, and Petronus suspected that the generals were all trying to decide what to do about this new arrival. Uniting their forces against the Marsh King would certainly be sufficient to drive him back, but it would leave them weakened for the long march east.

Time that allowed the Wandering Army to strengthen its position, though how effective they'd be without their leader remained to be seen.

It was as if the Named Lands themselves were the board upon which they played.

Unless. The thought nibbled at him and his eyes widened at the strategy unfolding in his mind.

He wondered how much of this Vlad Li Tam had planned from the start, and he wondered how much Rudolfo knew of it.

Most of all, he wondered if Sethbert realized that he'd been used.

Sethbert

Sethbert's hands shook with rage as he fought to suppress the violence inside of him that demanded release. He forced his eyes back to the report.

"This," he said slowly, "is entirely unacceptable." He looked up to lock eyes with Lysias. "How many?"

"Forty-seven, Sethbert."

Sethbert noted that the general failed to use his title. "Forty-seven deserters in two weeks? We're not even fully engaged."

Sethbert watched a look of disgust march across the general's face. "It has nothing to do with cowardice. It has *everything* to do with your indiscretions. Men will not willingly follow a monster."

"Surely you can break their will?"

Lysias shook his head. "You don't have enough loyal officers to do that. You will leak resources slowly. It is time to relieve these and bring forward fresh faces. You do not want to mix the bad in with the good. The spoiled pear always takes the barrel."

"Fine," Sethbert said. "Make it so." He looked to his aide. "And you have a message for me?"

The young man stepped forward and passed the unrolled paper to Sethbert. "It isn't good news, Lord."

Of course it wasn't. The day had brought no good news. There'd really been no good news since the day the Marsh King showed up across the valley, blasting his nonsensical ramblings across the night, every night, for how long now?

Shortly after that mud-bugger showed up, he'd received word from Oriv—Pope Resolute, he reminded himself—that their funds had been frozen by House Li Tam. He'd flown into a rage to hear it. He'd known it was a risk—that there might be someone higher placed than his cousin out there somewhere. And after the first week, because no one had come forward disputing Resolute's succession, he'd assumed no one would.

Of course, there had also been mixed news. As angered as he was about Rudolfo's escape, he was pleased to learn that they had resorted to violence. It meant they no longer needed to keep up the pretense of civility in their dealings with him.

"How did it arrive? And from whom?" he asked, squinting at the message.

"It came under Androfrancine thread from House Li Tam, Lord."

He read the note, feeling his anger rebuilding. He saw everything right in front of him. House Li Tam again. His consort now Rudolfo's betrothed—an alliance formed. Perhaps, he thought, Rudolfo was involved from the start. In bed with the Androfrancines along with Vlad Li Tam and, though he did not know how, the Marsh King as well.

What would they gain by the Desolation of the Named Lands at the hands of those robed tyrants? That question bothered him, but not overly so.

What bothered him more was that now they played a Pope of their own onto the board. Convenient that he was in hiding, invoking some obscure Androfrancine codex. And even Sethbert knew enough of their law to realize it was a stretch of that rule's intent.

He read the proclamation, his lips moving as he followed the words. When he finished, he crumpled the note and cast it aside. While the aide scrambled for it, Sethbert kicked over a chair.

"There is another Pope," the Overseer finally said.

"What does he say?" Lysias asked.

At Sethbert's wave, the aide passed the note to Lysias. He scanned it quickly. "This changes the war," Lysias finally said. "It is now a contest of words *and* swords. It will shift loyalties but it is impossible to say which. Or how we'll stand in the end."

"We need to fix the problem within our ranks. We will punish the men who fled."

"We don't have the resources to track them down," Lysias said.

"I have a better idea," Sethbert said. "I will address it personally."

Lysias nodded. "And what about the gravediggers?"

Sethbert thought. "We'll continue to subsidize their work in the name of the true Pope, Resolute the First."

"Very good, Lord."

He smiled at the respect he had purchased at some small price. Or at least the form of respect. He doubted Lysias had ever truly respected him. A man like that wouldn't appreciate Sethbert's strength of character.

After the general left, he turned to his aide. "Cross-reference the deserters with their homes of record. Send a bird to the Overseer's Watchmen. I want a wife, a child, a mother, a sister. But don't kill them. Blind them. Mute them. Tell them why."

The aide paled. "Lord?"

Sethbert smiled, thinking about lunch and hoping it was pheasant or pork. "And when it's done, have word leak to the men of it."

"Yes, Lord."

"Now, fetch me a mechoservitor and tell the chef I'll take my lunch outside today."

The aide bowed and walked quickly away.

Alone, Sethbert righted the chair he had kicked over in his rage. Then he sat on it, and wondered what Rudolfo would do now that he was free. He'd been delighted to hear that the Gypsy King had delivered himself over to Resolute in the first place, and he'd known that he would not stay away from his Wandering Army and his Ninefold Forest for too long. His cousin was barely competent and no match for the wily fop.

But now, with Rudolfo's alliance with House Li Tam through strategic marriage, his role in this deepened considerably more than just a Gypsy King enraged at the death of a city.

Sethbert took no pleasure in his lunch that day.

Neb

Neb read the proclamation again, his fingers moving over the ring buried in his pocket. He looked at the haphazard sketch of the Androfrancine Papal seal, a great finishing touch on the message, then returned to the beginning of the proclamation.

Oh My People it began, and it continued in perhaps one of the most moving documents he had ever read. It read with the resonance of ancient greatness, something that one could study but never emulate. Within it he felt the death of something beautiful, and the solemn, humble work of saving what could be saved knowing full well that nothing would ever be as good as it had been.

This truly was a man he could want to be like.

Of course, Neb saw Petronus's mastery even in the way he led the gravediggers. At some point, Brother Hebda said he would proclaim him Pope. Maybe it was figurative, he thought. Maybe he was supposed to give him the ring.

He'd thought about it a dozen times since he'd found the damned thing. And each time, he pushed it back out of his mind for reasons he could not fully conceive.

He looked up again, and realized in his headlong walk out of camp he'd wandered pretty far into the ruins of the city. He looked around, trying to use the hills and the river to determine where he stood within the city. He was close to where the Garden had once been, or at least he thought he was. Not having walls and buildings to navigate by made it a difficult chore. But he picked his way north the equivalent of half a block, then west, then north again.

When he was reasonably sure he'd found it, he sat down in the ash and pulled his knees to himself. They'd already been through this part of the city, raking the ash for bones and artifacts.

Neb pulled the ring from his pocket and studied it for the hundredth time. It was simple and rare—the way that life should be. He'd cleaned it carefully by the light of a guttering candle when Petronus made his rounds around the camp at night. Now, it shone dully in his hand. He looked at it, turning it in the gray daylight of emerging winter.

"My king would speak with you," a heavy, guttural voice whispered to his left.

Neb jumped, looking around but seeing nothing. Still, this darker light was perfect for scouts. "Who is your king?"

The voice moved now. "My king is the Reluctant Prophet of Xhum Y'Zir, the Unloved Son of P'Andro Whym, Most Beautiful of the Northern Marshes."

Neb hesitated as the voice continued away. He looked back toward camp, so distant now that he could barely make out the figures that moved along its edges. He looked north, in the direction that the voice went, and saw the line of dark trees. Behind the trees, smoke drifted into the sky from the Marsh King's camp fires.

The voice returned. "My king would speak with you," it said again. "You will not be harmed. You will return bearing his grace to your people."

"I think you're mistaken," Neb said. "I think perhaps he wants to parley with Petron—Petros, our leader."

"No," the scout said, moving away again. "No mistake. You are Nebios, son of Hebda, who watched the Great Extinguishment of Light, the Desolation of Windwir?"

Neb swallowed the sudden fear in this throat and nodded.

"My king would speak with you." Now the voice grew more distant, and Neb looked back to camp once again.

Then, turning north, he ran after the Marsh King's ghostly messenger.

Chapter

19

Rudolfo

Rudolfo and his party made their last camp together twenty leagues northwest of Windwir. In the morning, they would split up. He would ride with his escort to meet Gregoric and his company of Gypsy Scouts well beyond sight of the armies encamped around Windwir. While he turned southeast, Jin Li Tam and Isaak would ride northeast with their escort and make for the Prairie Sea with all haste.

A cold rain fell as the sky shifted to twilight, and the sun slipped behind them to vanish colorlessly. Tonight they would forgo a fire, never certain how far afield the various scouts and patrols might go. Between Sethbert's forces and those of the neighboring nations Pylos and Turam, the southern and western hills would be well covered. And now the Marsh King dominated the north.

They huddled beneath canvas tarps hung low, using the pine trees as natural cover as much as possible. Rudolfo looked at Isaak, the rain beading and rolling off his metal surface.

"You'll not rust, will you?"

"The alloy composite of my chassis is resistant to rust and other forms of erosion, Lord Rudolfo," the metal man said.

Rudolfo nodded. "Well enough." He leaned against the tree. A few paces away, he watched Jin Li Tam lay out a tent and pull it together and up with the practiced skill of a soldier. He watched her as she worked, enjoying the places where the water clung to her clothing, accentuating her curves. "I want to speak with you about the work ahead," he told Isaak, his voice dropping.

"Yes, Lord Rudolfo?"

"I've asked Lady Tam to assist you. She will speak to her father on behalf of the library and try to get sanction from this new Pope he spoke of." Rudolfo turned from watching her and studied Isaak. "I will get you more help as soon as I possibly can. Meanwhile, start planning."

The metal man's head swiveled around to face him. "Have you given any thought to the location of the new library?"

Rudolfo thought about this. "There is a hill near the seventh forest manor—on the outskirts of town. I had intended it to be a Whymer Maze. Is it of sufficient size?"

Isaak's eyes flashed bright and then dim, the shutters working quickly as he calculated. "If we build into the hill and above it."

Rudolfo nodded. "Once we have secured the patriarchal blessing, I will hire the best architects, engineers and builders in the Named Lands to realize this vision. I will hire the carpenters of Paramo to design and build the furnishings required. Your role will be to tell us what we need to properly house the holdings you think can be restored."

Steam chugged out of his exhaust grate. "Your faith in me continues to astound, Lord Rudolfo."

"You are a marvelous wonder, Isaak. You may even be the very best of the Androfrancines' work among us."

Certainly the most dangerous and the most innocent at the same time, he thought.

"I will strive to exceed your expectations."

Rudolfo smiled. "I have no doubt that you will."

"I had started my preliminary research before the summons arrived. I will resume that work now, by your leave."

Rudolfo nodded. "To your work, my metal friend."

Isaak limped off and Rudolfo watched him as he went. His armorer had done the best he could, certainly, never having worked on a mechanical before. Perhaps he could do better for the metal man with enough time to properly study his musculature and metallic skeleton. Maybe as they cataloged what was left in the memory scrolls of the mechoservitor corps, they would even find the ancient drawings from Rufello and have done with that limp.

Part of him wondered, though, if Isaak would permit that or if he would bear the limp along with his great remorse, a constant reminder of a pain that defined him.

Rudolfo had talked with Jin Li Tam about the metal man's lie. It was an interesting development in the mechoservitor's character.

Change is the path life takes. Perhaps that meant Isaak was truly alive. He wondered at the implications of such a thing. A man made by a man.

That night, as the coyotes howled beyond their camp, they ate cold rations and washed them down with colder wine. They talked briefly, voices low, about the next day and the work ahead.

"I'll see to the Marsh King and plumb this sudden kinclave he's declared towards me," Rudolfo said. "I'll send word when I know. Until then, the Wandering Army stays at home. We need to see what this new Pope will mean for present loyalties."

Jin nodded. "I think Queen Meirov is tenuous at best in her alliance with Sethbert. He's not been a good neighbor to her people."

Rudolfo stroked his mustache. "She is a strong queen with a weak army." Pylos, the smallest of the Named Lands, used their army primarily to police the border they shared with the Entrolusian City States. He'd had kin-clave with her in the past. "Perhaps I will call upon her after I've parleyed with the Marsh King."

"My father will also send word to her," Jin said. "She relies on House Li Tam for her small fleet of river ships, and no small amount of her treasury is held with him as well."

Rudolfo smiled. "What do you think your father will do about the City States?"

She shrugged. "It's hard to say. I'm sure he'll follow this new Pope's lead. He can put the blockade back in place in a matter of days."

And in two weeks, Rudolfo knew, those iron ships—powered in some similar way to the Androfrancines' metal men but on a much larger scale—could cripple the supplies and replacements that Sethbert relied on his wooden riverboats to deliver.

Gradually, as the clouds broke overhead and the stars shined out, swollen with wet light, they fell into silence. The scouts moved about the camp, some restringing bows and preparing to go on watch, others crawling into tents for a few hours of sleep. Beneath his own tarp across from them, Isaak sat with his eyes flashing and his bellows wheezing slightly as he ciphered.

They sat in silence for an hour, listening to the forest as it moved about them. A wind carried the faintest sound—a bellowing voice carried across long distances—and it stirred the fine hairs on Rudolfo's neck and arms. Everyone knew of the War Sermons of the Marsh King—they sprung from the pages of that people's violent history in the Named Lands, though they'd not been heard for more than five hundred years.

Rudolfo turned and tried to pick out the words, but it was in the ancient Whymer tongue—a language he was largely unfamiliar with.

Jin leaned closer to him. "He's prophesying now. It's fascinating."

Rudolfo's eyebrows shot up. "You understand him?"

"I do," she said. "It's faint. Something about the dreaming boy and a Last Testament of P'Andro Whym. A coming judgment on the Named Lands for the Androfrancine Sin." She paused, and Rudolfo admired the line of her neck and the strength of her jaw as she cocked her head and listened. "The Gypsy King will . . ." She shook her head. "No, it's gone. The wind carried it off."

They fell back into silence again and another hour passed. Finally, Rudolfo stood, bid his company good night and crawled into the low battle tent they had set up for him.

He lay still, listening to the low voices outside and to the sounds of the wind as it played the evergreen ceiling. Was it so long ago that he dreaded the idea of staying still? When one bed or one house was not enough for him? He'd spent his life moving between nine manors. From the age of twelve, when he stepped into his father's turban, he'd spent more of his life in the saddle and tent than he had manor or bed. And he'd loved that life. But that pillar in the sky created a longing for something else within him. Perhaps it was a temporary fixation. The Francines would say to follow the thread of his feelings backward. It was grief connecting to grief— today's sadness reaching back into yesterday's and gathering strength.

You've lost your light young, he remembered his father telling him when he lay dying in the amber field. First his brother at five, then his father and mother at twelve. Windwir's destruction found that grief and worried it, creating inside of him a longing for home and rest that he could not remember ever knowing before.

He jumped when she slid alongside of him into the narrow bedrolls. She moved as silently as a Gypsy Scout, perhaps more so. And when she had entwined her arms and legs with his, she pinned him down and kissed him on the mouth.

"For a great and mighty general," she whispered, "you are not so very bold."

Rudolfo returned her kiss, amazed at how in the moment he finally longed for home, home appeared and welcomed him.

Petronus

Petronus was rounding the corner, approaching the galley tent, when the muddy bird flapped into camp. It squawked and hopped about until he scooped it up and slipped the unthreaded message from its foot. He opened it and saw Whymer runes.

Your grandson is our honored guest, it read.

Petronus checked the tent first. Then the wagon and the galley and the bathing tent. When Neb didn't turn up at any of those places, he went next to the sentries. But the sentries were pulled in closer now that defense was warranted, and at sundown, the guard had changed.

After he'd done that much, Petronus returned to the camp and organized a search party. The War Sermon started up as they moved into the city.

But midway through the search, Petronus called them together and sent them back to the camp. The Marsh King's note was specific enough that he knew they wouldn't find the boy. While the others drifted back, Petronus stayed on the northern edge of the city and watched the line of forests. Tonight, the War Sermon was particularly cryptic—a string of prophetic utterances about a boy, obscure references to texts Petronus had heard of but never seen. Texts that not even the Androfrancines had seen these two thousand years. Only the memory of these texts survived as references in newer works.

He understood the words but did not understand their meaning.

"He's in the Marsh King's camp," Gregoric said.

Petronus turned in the direction of the voice. "You've seen him then?"

"Aye," the scout said. "We saw him running with one of their scouts."

Petronus felt anger, sharp and focused. "And yet you did not stop him?"

"No. For many reasons I'm sure you can cipher out."

Yes. It would have meant giving away the Ninefold Forest House's continued presence at Windwir. Petronus did not like the mathematics of it, but it was what it was. He would hope he'd choose differently, but knew that he had been in that position before. Sacrifices for the greater good. Memories of that burning village chewed at him. "Have you seen their camp?"

Gregoric's voice moved again. "I have not. They're better woodsmen than Sethbert's men. And they seem to have kin-clave with us."

"I found that surprising," Petronus said.

"We did as well. But we'll have some better idea of it in the next few days."

Petronus raised his eyebrows, waiting for Gregoric to finish, but he didn't speak right away. When he did, his voice was far away and he was running fast. "We will also inquire about your boy."

Those words settled him somewhat. He still felt the strain pulling at his neck and back, and he swung his arms as he turned back toward camp.

There's nothing more that you can do here, old man.

As he walked, he thought about the Gypsy Scout's words. Most likely, it meant that Rudolfo was near and intending to parley with the Marsh King. It would be a first, and to Petronus's recollection, there had been a rather brief and nasty war between the Ninefold Forest and the Marshers. Four, maybe five years before his assassination. Jakob had captured the Marsh King and showed him his Physicians of Penitent Torture. Then he released him, and the Marshers never bothered the Forest Houses again.

Now they were Rudolfo's only kin-clave remaining in the world apart from his alliance with Vlad Li Tam.

And they had Neb.

Petronus stopped and looked behind him at the dark line of trees against the sky. Remnants of his upbringing as a Gods-fearing boy momentarily usurped his Androfrancine sensibilities. It happened infrequently, but when it did it reminded Petronus of how fragile the human heart and mind can be when faced with potential loss.

All the way back to camp, Petronus prayed.

Neb

The Marshers defied Neb's imagination.

He'd run as fast as he could to keep up with the scout, tearing through the underbrush, ducking and weaving to avoid the branches that slapped him. The scout was fast and big, making no attempt now for stealth.

Neb ran for what felt like leagues before he realized the forest had changed. Fishing nets interwoven with branches concealed mud-smeared, tattered tents. Unkempt men and women, many slack-jawed and empty-eyed, wandered the camp. They wore unmatched bits of weaponry and armor scavenged from two thousand years of skirmishing, and they moved to and fro in silence.

Neb's guide vanished, leaving him at the edge of camp. A young girl approached him. She was covered in filth, just like the others, her hair shot through with mud and ash, and Neb suddenly realized that it wasn't simply different values around hygiene. They did this to themselves, painting themselves with earth and ash, for reasons that were sacred to them.

The girl smiled at him, and beneath the caked dirt, he could see that she possessed a coltish kind of prettiness. She was nearly as tall as he was, and he thought perhaps her hair was a mouse brown beneath the mud. Despite the dirt, she had it pulled back from her face and wrapped with a bit of red ribbon.

"The Marsh King summoned you," she said. It wasn't a question.

"Y-yes," he said.

She took a step closer to him and he smelled her. It was a distinct scent—the musk of sweat, the smoky smell of the ash, the traces of sulfur and clay in the mud. And apples, he realized. She extended her hand to him. "I will take you."

He took her hand and felt her gently tugging him along, walking at a quick gait. He studied her as they went. She wore mismatched boots and a long man's tunic cut down to fit her. Beneath it, a long-sleeved shirt that had once been white. Her calves were bare and gray with dirt. She wore no weapons that he could see.

The Marsh girl led him through a maze of trees and tents, dodging in and out of the Marsh King's silent soldiers. "Why are they so quiet?" he asked, his curiosity finally getting the better of him.

"It is our faith. We have one voice in war—the voice of our king. So we only speak when necessary."

Neb took her hint and remained quiet until they approached a tent slightly larger than the other, snug against the side of a low hill. "The Marsh King awaits you in there," the girl said pointing.

Before Neb could thank her, she vanished, running quickly and vanishing around the side of the hill without looking back.

He swallowed and approached the unguarded tent. Dim light danced inside the filthy canvas structure, and as he pushed aside the free-hanging flap, he realized that the tent was just a foyer. A tunnel had been dug into the side of the hill, widening into a cave with tangled roots for its ceiling and mud for its floor. Sitting in the center of that cave at the foot of a large triangular idol was the largest man Neb had ever seen. Bits of twigs and food hung in his large black beard, and on his lap he held a massive axe, the head of which glistened in the lamplight like a mirror, throwing back the light and intensifying it. He wore armor of a similar sort—silver and mirrored like nothing Neb had ever seen before. The giant fixed his dark eyes on Neb, then looked quickly to the left to the idol. It was a meditation bust of P'Andro Whym, from one of the earlier heresies.

"Come forward," the Marsh King bellowed in the Whymer tongue.

Even without the magicks, the voice was compelling. Neb shuffled forward. He looked around the room as he went. It looked like there was a back entrance—much smaller, certainly too small for the Marsh King, and shrouded with a heavy curtain hastily staked into the ceiling. There were scattered reed mats and piles of ratty blankets.

Neb wasn't sure what to do next, so he erred on the side of caution and lowered himself to his knees. "I am here, Lord."

Again, the Marsh King stared down at him and then looked away to the idol. "I will preach about you tonight," the Marsh King said. "I will call you the dreaming boy because I have seen you in my dreams." He looked to the idol, nodding slowly. "Now is set into motion the time of judgment, and the unloved children of P'Andro Whym will be the firstborn of the new gods." Neb looked at the idol himself but saw nothing there but an old metal god. The Marsh King leaned down. "Do you understand any of this?"

Neb shook his head. "I do not."

Another glance to the idol, head cocked to hear, then the deep voice continued slowly. "Do you understand what it means to be the reluctant prophet of Xhum Y'Zir? Because someday, you will be."

"I do not understand, Lord," Neb said. But the words, when they washed through him, left him shaken. He'd studied the fundamentals of the mystic heresies and he understood the straying from Androfrancine truth. His own dream of Hebda, dead and speaking with him as if he weren't, was powerful regardless of whether or not it was real. Who wouldn't listen to the ghost of their dead father?

But the Francines were clear: The ghost was just an aspect of himself, working out problems in his sleep.

Except for the part where those dreams came true, the Marsh King and his army had perfect proof of that.

"How is it that you invade my sleep, Dreaming Boy? What are the things that you show me?" The Marsh King waited, glancing quickly to the idol. "Who is this resurrected Pope that will avenge the light by killing it?"

The fear worked its way into his stomach and it lurched. He knew about Petronus somehow. His hand wanted to go to the pocket now and check it again, make sure it was still there. But he didn't. "I do not know, Lord," he said again.

The Marsh King roared and leaped to his feet, moving past Neb quickly and moving to the tent flaps. "I will speak with you in the morning." Neb watched him draw a large silver drinking horn and hold it to his lips. When he brought it down his face was covered in what looked like blood, and his satisfied sigh shook the walls of the tent.

The Marsh King strode into the night, his War Sermon booming out, a storm of words that could be heard as far as twenty leagues away.

Neb was still watching him when the girl approached. He jumped when she touched his shoulder and he turned. The curtain still swayed where she came from. "He will be all night," the Marsh girl said.

"He's preaching about me," Neb said.

She nodded. "He is. The dreams were very powerful."

"What do they mean?"

She laughed. "If I knew what they meant, why would the Marsh King summon *you*?"

Neb looked at her. She didn't look as dirty as he'd thought she did. Or maybe it was the light. Her large brown eyes crinkled at the edges, as if she laughed a lot. But there were deep places there that suggested she cried a lot, too. When she smiled, her teeth were straight and white.

"Maybe they don't mean anything," Neb said.

She shook her head. "It is unlikely. Most dreams mean something." She sighed. "But I hope you're right."

Neb saw that the thought of it relieved her. "Why do you hope I'm right?" he asked.

She looked to the idol herself for a moment, then back to Neb. "Because the dreams said that many would go to their second death in the fire for the Androfrancine sin." She shuddered as she said the words.

"And I had something to do with it?" Neb asked, his voice suddenly small.

"You were in the dreams. If the Marsh King knew why, you would not be here." She extended her hand to him, and for the second time he took it.

He'd actually never held a girl's hand before. He'd never really thought much about it. The orphans were discouraged from the opposite sex in the male-dominated Order. Certainly there were some provisions for Androfrancines to marry—but not many, not even when unexpected children were involved. Her hand was gritty and dry and firm—not ever what he would have expected for this first. He let her lead him up through the back door of the cave.

Neb wondered about the girl. She must be the Marsh King's servant. Perhaps even a daughter, which seemed odd to his sense of the world since the other armies would never think to bring children into the battlefield.

But she wasn't quite a child. Probably within a year of him. Perhaps even a bit older.

Of course, these were Marshers. Perhaps she was here for darker reasons than he wished to imagine.

Neb followed her as she led him to a lean-to that sheltered a fire and a large steaming kettle of thick stew. She found broken bits of pottery to use as spoons and scooped two wooden bowlfuls out of the sticky mess. It smelled sweetly pungent beneath his nose.

Sitting in the mud beside the Marsh girl, Neb ate his stew and listened to the War Sermon as it bellowed out into the night.

Vlad Li Tam

Vlad Li Tam listened to the voice on the wind and nodded slowly. "He preaches again," he said. His aide brought a long match to the bowl of the ornate pipe, and Vlad Li Tam inhaled a lungful of the kallaberry smoke.

It cleared his head by slowing down his mind. It bolstered him in a warm sea of euphoria that kept him alive and gave him the edge he needed to do what must be done.

They camped in the open with nothing to hide—a small caravan of wagons ringed around their tents. He fully expected to parley with all parties involved excepting perhaps the Marsh King. House Li Tam had given up that part of the world long before Vlad's time. He wasn't sure how many sons or daughters of Tam had been sent north to buy their father's way into that stunted place. None had been accepted. Some had been killed. At least three hundred years ago, they'd stopped trying. He'd read about it in the archives.

He expelled the purple smoke, watching it disperse into the night air.

"I will wear armor tomorrow," Vlad Li Tam told his aide and his master sergeant. "And a sword."

They both nodded.

"I suspect Petronus will require his hand forced," he said, looking at them both, his eyes narrow. "I suspect that I will betray my friend."

"Hail the camp," a distant voice called out. Vlad Li Tam looked up and nodded as his guards scattered to reinforce their positions.

"Hail, Gypsy Scout. What news do you bring?"

"Lord Rudolfo sends regards and will join your parley on the morrow."

Vlad Li Tam nodded. "Excellent. Is my daughter with him?"

"She has returned to the Ninefold Forest with the metal man. Your presence here was unexpected. Otherwise, I'm certain she would have delayed her travel."

Far better for her to stay near the mechoservitor. She could be trusted to watch out for it, to keep it from the wrong hands. It reminded him of another matter. "Tell your general that after the parley we will move quickly against the City States if they do not lay down arms. Our Pope will want the mechoservitors that Sethbert is holding. They are critical for the reestablishment of the library."

"I will tell him," the scout said, never staying still yet never entering the camp's ring of light.

After the scout left, Vlad Li Tam called for a bird and laid his pipe aside to compose a message, coding it in double and triple Whymer loops that only an Androfrancine Pope could read. After he'd finished writing it, he went back over it, layering in yet more code in the slightest brush strokes of his pen, the seemingly hapless smearing of a letter here or there.

He tied it to his strongest, smallest bird and whispered the direction to its tiny head as it fluttered against his hands.

Vlad Li Tam tossed the bird into the sky, watched its wings unfurl as it caught the light breeze and shot east, flying low to the ground.

Chapter

20

Jin Li Tam

Jin Li Tam rose early on her first morning back in the seventh forest manor. She slipped into plain cotton trousers and a loose-fitting shirt, pulling a light cloak over both to keep her dry in the cold autumn drizzle. In her absence, they had moved her into the room adjoining Rudolfo's, outfitting it with everything she could possibly need. She left her hair down and shoved her foot into the low doeskin boots the steward had provided.

In the hall, she paused at the door. Once more her eyes went to the children's quarters, and she thought again about the one furnished room. Despite the early hour a servant passed, and Jin Li Tam reached out to touch the girl's arm.

"What is that room?" she asked, pointing.

The servant shifted uncomfortably. "It's Lord Isaak's room, Lady Tam."

She felt herself frown. "I don't understand. Why would Isaak need a child's room?"

The girl blushed and stammered. "Not for the—" She struggled, looking for the right word. "Not for the mechanical," she finally said. Her eyes wandered the hall, only pausing to meet Jin Li Tam's eyes for the briefest of moments. "I'm not sure it is proper for me to speak of it. You should ask Steward Kember or perhaps Mistress Ilyna."

Jin Li Tam nodded. "Very well."

Looking to that closed door one more time, she turned and moved down the hall, her soft boots whispering across the carpet. She took the stairs two at a time, springing lightly, and nodded to the Gypsy Scouts that waited for her at the main doors. They fell in behind her, and she smiled beneath her hood. She'd grown familiar with the half-squad Rudolfo had assigned to her, and most of her life she'd had guards of one kind or another. Sethbert was the first to not assign an escort to her, and she knew it had more to do with the message he sent to her father—like his insistence that she be considered a consort and nothing more.

They were very different men, Sethbert and Rudolfo. Rudolfo carried a certain ruthlessness about him, but it was the carefully chosen path that blended menace with charm in order to achieve a goal. Sethbert's had been more the meanness of a large bully accustomed to imposing his will for the pleasure it brought him more than to any purpose.

Rudolfo, as she had observed before, was more like her father. Prepared and cautious, but with an aloof and light touch.

Even the men he'd chosen for her escort showcased this. They followed, often just one or two, but they stayed far enough back to not invade her privacy.

As she passed through the gate, a movement on the hill outside of town caught her eye. A lone figure moved along the top of that cleared surface and she knew it was Isaak, pacing out the space there. The structure would be massive and for a moment, she stood still and took it in. How would this sleeping town respond in the shadow of this undertaking? Certainly, Rudolfo had considered this. She was too new to the Ninefold Forest to know what it would mean when the library opened its doors and became the centerpoint of the Named Lands, so far from the centers of commerce and statecraft.

Of course, that was the first vision of the Androfrancines. And though Windwir was easily the most powerful city in the world, it had never been the largest. The children of P'Andro Whym, with help from their Gray Guard, had kept it to a size that they could manage, turning away the universities that sought to locate near that vast receptacle of knowledge. Instead, they'd allowed small groups of students to visit in shifts throughout the year, mostly the children of nobles. And Androfrancine scholars traveled out to the schools, carrying what knowledge the Order deemed appropriate.

She found herself wondering how this new library would work. The Order's back had been broken and it would not soon come back. Two thousand years of careful growth had made them insular as it was. But now, with possibly only a thousand Androfrancines left in the world—one percent or less of their former numbers—she did not see the Order coming back into its strength any time soon.

She resumed her walk, glancing over her shoulder to be sure the scouts were following.

The town stirred to life, a few women out to the bakery and a few hunters gathering outside the locked tavern, waiting for the owner to throw open the doors and feed them before they went after their game.

A carpenter worked beneath a canvas canopy, planing a length of wood in long, slow strokes.

Jin Li Tam moved through the streets until she reached the narrow river that ran through the center of town. She followed the river north until the rest of the town fell away to a scattering of houses and huts. The steward's wife, Ilyna, had told her where to go. There were never any signs but most towns had at least one apothecary.

She'd sent a bird to her oldest sister on the outer shores of the Emerald Coasts, now the wife of a Free City Warpriest, and the finest apothecary House Li Tam had ever produced. She'd studied at the Francine School disguised as a young man and fooled those old monks for three years. Much older than Jin Li Tam, Rae Li Tam had lived a lifetime making potions and powders for their father's work, and her medicines, magicks and poisons were legendary.

She had replied to Jin's note immediately, and the coded recipe waited for her when she and Isaak and their half-squad arrived at the seventh manor the night before. Jin had translated the recipe into a common script late that night, working by candlelight and feeling the knots in her stomach as she did so.

Smoke trickled from the small ramshackle hut, and an older, plump woman squatted at the river, her head inclined toward the water. "Aye," she said without looking up. "Dark times indeed." Then, as if finishing her conversation, her head rose and her eyes met with Jin Li Tam's. She blushed. "Lady Tam, an unexpected grace." She bowed.

Jin returned the bow, inclining her head and offering a smile. "I have need of your services, River Woman."

The River Woman smiled. "Magicks for the Lord's new Lady? Or will it be powders of another sort? Whatever my Lady needs, I'm sure we can find it in the elements given."

The Gypsy Scouts lingered at the edge of the clearing, waiting. Jin Li Tam bit her lip. There was still time, even after this, for minds to change. But her father's strategy seemed clear to her. "I doubt you'll have seen this particular powder," she said quietly.

"That will be quite unlikely," the River Woman said. "But let's discuss it over tea."

She led Jin into the small hut and put water onto the stove. The River Woman's home was crowded with cats and books and jar upon jar of herbs and powders, dried mushrooms and berries, crushed leaves and lengths of root. The house smelled sweet and bitter at the same time.

Once the tea was poured, Jin Li Tam slipped the recipe from her belt purse and palmed three square House Li Tam coins. She passed the recipe across the table, and the River Woman studied it, her eyes narrowing and widening intermittently. When she finished, she pushed it back to the center of the table. "You are correct. I've never seen such a thing. How did you come by it?"

Jin Li Tam shrugged. "The Androfrancines guard their light." She waited, willing herself to ask the question. "Do you have the ingredients to make it?"

The River Woman nodded. "Aye. Or at least, I can. I may need to send away for some. Caldus Bay may have what I lack."

Jin Li Tam brought the three coins out and placed them on the recipe. "I will require your utmost discretion in this matter."

"You shall have it. A woman's body is a temple of life, and she must open or close that gate as she pleases." The River Woman glanced at the recipe again, clucking at it. "And you think this will work?"

She smiled. "We will see for ourselves soon enough."

"Finally, an heir," she said. The old woman chuckled. "You know," she said, "I delivered both of Lord Jakob's boys to him."

Jin Li Tam leaned in. "Both?" The room, again, with its small boots and its small sword hanging on its wall.

"Lord Isaak and Lord Rudolfo," the River Woman said.

"Both strong, beautiful boys." She must have seen the realization dawning on Jin Li Tam's face. She blushed. "No one's mentioned Lord Isaak to you?"

Jin Li Tam shook her head. "I did not know Rudolfo had a brother."

"A twin brother," she said. "Just two hours older. He died rather . . . unexpectedly . . . in his fifth year."

Jin Li Tam felt something she could not name. It pulled at her, and she felt the knots in her stomach tighten. "How?"

The River Woman looked around as if there might be other ears within hearing. Her voice lowered to nearly a whisper. "They said it was the red pox that took him. They cremated him immediately."

It wasn't uncommon, though it was unnecessary. They'd had the red pox powders for over a thousand years now. Still, some children did not respond to the powders and, of course, they weren't available to all children. Just to children of privilege. But the River Woman's tone suggested doubt. "You do not believe it was the red pox?"

"I do not. I gave him and Rudolfo both the powders. I do not think it likely that it would work on one but not the other." She paused, looking around again. "I think he was poisoned. Though I know of no poisons that hide behind a mask of the pox."

Her stomach clenched again, and she wrestled to keep her composure. She looked at the recipe again and thought of her elder sister.

She felt a shadow stirring in her heart, and wondered how deep the layers of her father's strategy might go.

Petronus

Petronus's bellowing nearly drowned out that of the Marsh King and his War Sermon. "I will not," he roared, shaking his fists at the west.

He could tell by the bird's markings that it was a Tam

courier. And by the fact that it came straight at him to drop lightly onto his shoulder with a chirrup, in the dark of night, as he patrolled the outskirts of the city for the boy.

If you do not declare publicly, I will declare you myself in three days' time.

It was code within code buried in the text of a message regarding a House Li Tam donation of foodstuffs for the gravedigging effort.

Buried alongside the coded threat, there was another message. A generous petition from Lord Rudolfo to assist in the establishment of a new library using the memory scripts of the mechoservitors in Sethbert's camp to rescribe as much of it as was stored within their scrolls.

But not even that was enough to hold his anger at bay.

If you do not declare publicly, I will declare you myself.

He bellowed again, his fists clenched, kicking at the ground. "Damn you, Tam," he shouted.

Of course, he'd known he would have to. There would be no getting around it. Nothing would be left if he stood back. And if his suspicions about Vlad Li Tam's strategy were true—and he did not doubt them—he did not know if he could be a part of that game of queen's war. But he had no choice now, and he'd known that it would come to it when he'd written the proclamation.

You've done this to yourself, old man.

Yes, he thought. Yes, I have. And he would pay the price for that and come back from the dead because it was the only honest thing he could do. But he would name the time and place.

He drew his needle and ink and wrote his reply on the back. *I will do it myself in my own time and if you do not honor this, you do not honor me or my house.*

He tied the message to the bird and threw it at the sky.

As he walked back to the city, he heard the War Sermon and listened to the Marsh King prophesy about the dreaming boy. He finally calmed enough to think about the other aspects of the message. Rudolfo's petition intrigued him. The idea of the Great Library—or what could be saved from it—sparked a hope within him that he had not expected. He'd remembered that first mechoservitor, and wondered if it was possible that they had come so far as to remember an entire library? It *might* be possible. But it didn't seem likely. There would be the vaulted knowledge—everything that had already been cataloged, translated and cross-referenced against other fragments.

But how much of the library could they bring back?

Anything that they could build would be a miracle more than he had expected. And positioning it in the far north put it out of reach of the masses, kept it safe. Its only nearby threat would be the Marshers, and recent events suggested an unexpected alliance there. And it was not too far from the upper gates of the Keeper's Wall, beyond which lay the Churning Wastes. It made far more sense than the Papal Summer Palace, where the first Popes had thought to build their library, huddling against the Dragon's Spine as far from the Named Lands as possible. It had not worked then and it would be the same now. The bitterly cold winters precluded any commerce whatsoever for a large portion of the year, and they were quickly realizing that a waterway would be necessary if they were to truly shepherd the Named Lands through its sojourn in the New World.

He had no difficulty agreeing to the petition and issuing an order for Sethbert to surrender the mechoservitors in his care. But he could not do this without proclaiming himself, and he was not ready to go back to honoring that lie on behalf of a backward dream.

Ready or not, Petronus knew he did not have much time.

Neb

After they ate their stew, the Marsh girl led Neb back to the Marsh King's cave. She passed him a pile of tattered blankets and pointed to a corner in the damp, earthen room. He rolled himself up into the corner and watched her do the same thing across from him. The idol glowed dully in the dark, offering light and heat. From where he lay, he saw that the idol clutched at a mirror, the face of P'Andro Whym contemplative as he modeled self-examination.

Once she was beneath her blankets, she propped her head up on one hand and looked across to him. "I can't imagine what it was like," she said in a quiet voice.

He wasn't sure what she meant, but he had an idea, and he swallowed back the sudden terror that gripped him. He felt a lurch in his groin, a squeezing ache that made him want to throw up.

Her eyebrows furrowed. "I'm sorry, Nebios ben Hebda. I shouldn't have said anything."

Nebios ben Hebda. A Marsher name. "It's fine. I just can't talk about it yet." His stomach lurched again. "You don't think the Marsh King will make me talk about it, do you?" Suddenly, he wanted to run as far from this camp as he could.

She shook her head slowly. "The Marsh King would not force such a thing. There is grace in the Marshlands."

So far, the Marshers had been nothing like he had expected. Very little was shared about them in the parts of the Great Library that he was permitted to study from. They weren't the half-crazed savages that legend painted them. Oddly customed, to be sure, but not—to his eye, anyway—the lunatic children left over from the Age of Laughing Madness. Children who perpetuated their violent insanity from generation to generation according to the lecturers and texts of the Orphan School. And whose king heard the future from a bust of P'Andro Whym and roared out that word beneath the Moon Wizard's tower.

They were a complex and spiritual people.

He studied the girl for a moment longer, then realized he had no idea what her name was. He asked and she laughed at him.

"I do not have a name like yours," she said. "You would laugh to hear it."

He smiled at her and shook his head. "I would not laugh."

She lay on her side, facing him, her hair spilling around her gray-streaked face. "My name is Winters."

"Winters?"

She nodded. "Winteria, actually. I did not name myself."

Neb changed the subject, his mind wandering quickly back to the morning. "What do you think he will want to talk to me about?" he asked.

She frowned and thought about this. "I suspect he will ask what you know of the gravediggers' camp, of Sethbert's camp, whether or not you've seen Lord Rudolfo yet or caught sign of his scouts." She shifted in her blankets, and Neb was surprised to see a bare shoulder peeking out from beneath them. He felt the heat rise to his cheeks. "He'll also want to know what you know of the metal man and the Lady Jin Li Tam." She paused and her voice softened. "But I'm sure he will not ask you about the other," she said.

He sighed. "And afterwards, he'll let me go?"

She laughed again and rolled over, her back to him now. "You can go now if you want to, Nebios." She looked back over her shoulder at him and smiled. "Or did you think perhaps I was assigned to you as your jailer?"

He laughed, too. "I didn't know what to think."

She shrugged. "It's hard to know what to think when your dreams become entangled with another's."

Neb lay still and watched her back. Her shoulders slowly started rising and falling, and when he was certain she was asleep, he drew the ring from his pocket and held it up to the idol's light. They were cast of the same metal, he realized.

Slipping the ring back into his pocket, he pulled the blankets over his head and ciphered himself to sleep.

When his dreams swallowed him into that hopeless burning vision of Windwir's fall, he looked around to see who might be watching, but saw no one whatsoever.

Rudolfo

Rudolfo kept the others waiting for a fashionably appropriate time, taking longer than needed to prepare himself. For the parley, he selected his best turban and matching sash in the brightest green he had, trimmed with the purple. He wore these along with a shirt the color of burnt cream, all over the top of the mesh armor he had received from Pope Introspect for a small heresy he helped suppress.

He selected his best sword—a long slender affair with a hard steel basket and a light blade that could shave a man. He strapped it on, climbed into the saddle and rode with his Gypsy Scouts for the appointed place.

A cluster of scouts from all sides gathered at the bottom of the hill. The only one who came alone was the one Rudolfo assumed to be the Marsh King. He was a giant of a man, maybe the biggest man he had ever seen. Beneath his stinking, filth-matted furs he wore silver armor, and in his hands he held a massive silver axe. He rode a giant stallion that danced beneath him as he listened to the people around him.

Nearby, Rudolfo saw a petite woman sitting sidesaddle on a roan, her golden hair piled high upon her head and tucked beneath her shining crown. She wore a gold breastplate and greaves, but her arms were draped in red silk that matched her battle-skirt. She was still beautiful, though the years were catching up to her. He'd bedded her a handful of times, both for business and for pleasure. She was adequate but took few risks.

It explained the Queen of Pylos in many regards besides just the bedroom.

Rudolfo nodded to her and smiled. She did not return the gesture, but instead stared at him with open contempt.

He looked further but saw nothing of Sethbert. The fat goat had sent his General Lysias on his behalf, making his feelings clear on this matter without speaking or even appearing. Rudolfo was not surprised.

He was also not surprised to see Ansylus—the Crown Prince of Turam—next to Lysias. His family had married into Sethbert's to the point that the resemblance between them all was uncanny. It was obvious that he viewed those gathered here with disdain, and Rudolfo doubted he'd even speak.

Vlad Li Tam looked up as Rudolfo sidled in closer. "Lord Rudolfo," he said. "It is agreeable to see you again."

He tipped his head. "Likewise, Lord Tam."

Then Vlad Li Tam looked to the Entrolusian general. "It is best that your master did not attend. I would be frank with you."

General Lysias glared. "I'll not ask you to be."

Vlad Li Tam smiled. "Regardless, I shall be. But in just a moment." He turned to the Queen of Pylos. "Queen Meirov, you are radiant as summer." She took her eyes off Rudolfo long enough to smile demurely at Lord Tam. Vlad then looked to the Marsh King. "You grace us, Lord."

The Marsh King grunted but did not speak.

"Now, to business," Vlad Li Tam said. "The Pope is calling for the cessation of hostilities and the immediate arrest of Sethbert." He looked at the General. "Here is my frankness, Lysias. Your Overseer brought down Windwir and broke the back of the Androfrancine Order."

"That is absolutely false," Lysias said, but Rudolfo saw the lie on his face before he told it. Lysias pointed to Rudolfo. "There is a Writ of Shunning against this man."

"A worthless writ," Vlad Li Tam said. "For the man who issued it is, as you no doubt have heard, not the true Pope."

Lysias spit. "That will be known when he declares himself and the Order has opportunity to investigate his claims." He looked around at the others. "Until then, Pope Resolute the First is the heir of P'Andro Whym."

Vlad Li Tam sighed and shook his head. "Even now, word of the new Pope spreads across the Named Lands. Some claim they have seen him, traveling under heavy guard, dressed in the rags of an Androfrancine abbot, never staying in one town for very long. In only a few months' time loyalties will begin to shift, and you will see the Named Lands descend into war like they have never known. In the end Windwir will lie desolate, and yonder gravediggers will have more unfinished work ahead because of Sethbert's folly."

He pointed in the direction of the city, and Rudolfo followed his finger. He could just make out a line of men working with shovels in the rain while others pushed wheelbarrows through the mud.

"I plead with you," Vlad Li Tam said, "leave men behind to help the gravediggers with their work, but let these be the last graves we dig for a season. War will not mitigate our loss."

General Lysias spun his stallion. "We'll not stand down. Resolute is our Pope."

The Crown Prince looked around at them. Finally, he spoke. "I've heard nothing to convince me otherwise." He turned his horse as well.

They rode off and the Queen of Pylos watched them. When they were out of earshot, she spoke. "I have no love of Sethbert, it is true. But I must concur. I do not need proof as he does of your invisible Pope, but I do need to know that he indeed *is* Pope, and for that to happen he must declare himself."

Vlad Li Tam nodded. "And you, Lord Rudolfo?"

Rudolfo nudged his horse forward, giving the queen a hard look. "I had no argument with the Androfrancines. I rode here to honor my kin-clave when I saw the pillar of smoke. I found a metal man in the ruins who spoke backward, and I learned over time that Sethbert had paid a mechanical apprentice to rescript the metal man to bring down Windwir." His eyes narrowed, never leaving hers. "On my honor, I did not do this terrible crime, Meirov." He turned to Vlad Li Tam. "I am pledged to the light, Lord Tam. I will follow your Pope and will extend my Gypsy Scouts to him should he require their services."

Vlad Li Tam nodded. "Very well." He looked to the Marsh King, who said nothing. "I am certain that the Pope will reveal himself soon."

Queen Meirov turned her horse and moved down the hill toward her waiting men. "I should hope so, Vlad Li Tam. If

Sethbert indeed brought down Windwir and your Pope proves true, I will serve the light as well."

Vlad Li Tam smiled. "Excellent. We will discuss remuneration for your assistance and arrange the appropriate letters of credit when the time comes."

She gave Lord Tam one final, brusque nod and rode back in the direction of her camp.

Lord Rudolfo watched her go. He quickly signed a message to Vlad Li Tam. *Tonight then?*

Vlad Li Tam nodded. *Run them north to the other.*

When darkness settled on the city and when the Marsh King's next War Sermon bellowed out into the night, Rudolfo and his Gypsy Scouts would liberate the mechoservitors that Sethbert kept hidden in his camp.

He turned his horse and started down the hill. He was surprised when the Marsh King fell in beside him. The large man looked at Rudolfo, sadness etching his face. "I care nothing for Popes or metal men," he said. "But your success is mine and my people's. Come to my camp and parley with me as you will."

The Marsh King spurred his stallion to a gallop, and Rudolfo watched him ride until he was nothing but a speck on the horizon, moving north.

As he watched, he decided that he would indeed go to the Marsh King's camp and parley, perhaps even bring a bottle of chilled peach wine, made in the orchards of Glimmerglam and shipped by barrel downriver to stock each of his nine manors.

Rudolfo wondered what he would wear for such an occasion.

Chapter

21

Neb

Neb woke up to a hand on his shoulder and sat up quickly. Winters crouched near him, dressed in a burlap dress that clung to her emerging curves. This close, she smelled of earth and smoke and sweat.

"I brought you breakfast," she said, pointing to a chipped bowl set at a small table.

Neb rubbed the sleep from his eyes. "You're not eating?"

She shook her head. "I fast today. The world is changing."

He kicked himself out of the blankets and stood. She stood, too. "Is the Marsh King back?"

"Soon," she said. "Eat first."

He went to the table and sat on the rickety wooden stool that waited for him there. The bowl was filled with boiled oats that still steamed, and the smell of buttermilk, honey and dried apples made his stomach growl. Near the bowl was a plate holding an assortment of roasted chestnuts, a chunk of bread and a bit of white, strong-smelling cheese.

Winters sat across from him, watching as he ate the food and washed it down with cold water from a metal cup.

"There was a parley this morning," she said. "All of the lords attended, including Lord Tam of House Li Tam."

"Did the Marsh King go?"

She nodded. "Our people were represented."

He tried the cheese. Its sharpness saturated his mouth, driving out the sweet and sour flavor of the boiled oats. "What do you think will come of it?"

"Nothing but war," she said. "Though when this hidden Pope declares, I think alliances will shift." She looked at him. Her large brown eyes hardened. "Of course, the Marshfolk care nothing for Named Land statecraft and even less for Androfrancine politics."

"Then why has the Marsh King brought his army south?"

Winters scowled. "Curiosity and kin-clave," she said. "The Marsh King's dreams have long foretold an end of the Androfrancine light. As have the kings that went before. For many years we even warred with the Androfrancines, thinking perhaps we could bring about that end."

Neb looked up from his breakfast, surprised. He'd known all his life about the skirmishers, but had never heard a sufficient justification beyond ancient grudges and the residue of madness in the Marsher line. "But why?"

She smiled, and in the soft light of the cave it carried a sweetness that he felt tugging at his heart. "Because when the light goes out," she said, "the dreams of the Marsh Kings will be realized and we will be guided to our new home."

She reached across the table now and laid her hand on Neb's cheek. "Dear, dreaming boy," she said. "If you could see the Marsh King's dreams, you would weep with joy from the beauty of it. Your father has seen them, and the power of them brought him back from death to parley with you in your sleeping hours."

Neb wasn't sure which made him more uncomfortable, the Marsher mysticism or Winters's hand cupping his cheek. He felt warmth moving through him, and something fluttered in his chest and stomach.

Winters dropped her hand, and he realized from the look on her face that she'd felt the discomfort, too. She looked away and blushed.

"I don't understand," Neb finally said. And he meant both the strange feelings this ragamuffin girl stirred up inside of him as well as the Marsh King prophecies.

"We are at the end of our sojourn, Nebios ben Hebda," she said. "When all that was left of our peoples came to this New

World from the lands beyond the Churning Wastes, the first Marsh King wore sackcloth and ashes, bathing himself in the dust of the earth that he came from and calling upon his children to do the same. Strangers in this land, we eschewed the Androfrancines and their light, loving shadow more because we knew the knowledge of the past could not create a safer future—it would merely remake the past. Even P'Andro Whym knew that a day was coming when his sins would be visited upon his children." Her words tumbled out fast, her eyes alive as she spoke and her sentences rushing together. "A home-seeking is upon us and by the waking and the sleeping dreams, you are the one who leads our pilgrimage homeward."

Suddenly she was speaking in tongues like the Marsh King, her eyes wide with wonder and fear. Neb saw the muscles tighten in her jaw and neck as she tried to fight the ecstatic utterance, but she couldn't.

Neb opened his mouth to ask her if she was okay, if there was anything he could do, but his mind wasn't able to pull the words together into a question. He felt something like panic growing in him, starting in his stomach and spreading throughout his body. He felt arousal and fear and rapture as his body tingled head to toe.

He opened his mouth to ask what was happening to him, and when he did he found himself suddenly speaking in tongues with the Marsh girl, their voices weaving in and out of one another as they finished one another's sentences in a language that was no language but longing and terror and terrible sadness.

Her eyes had rolled back into her head now, and she fell away from the table to twitch on the floor. Neb felt his own muscles pulling him down as well, but he forced himself to his feet and went to Winters before falling to his knees before her.

Her arms snaked out around him, her strong fingers digging into his skin and pulling him down to the dirt. Holding her close to himself, Neb let his words wash through him and out of him, dancing with her own words as they held one another on the floor. Finally, the fit of language ceased and they lay still, eyes closed, their ragged breath the only sound in the room.

When he opened his eyes, she was staring at him. He felt the ache in his jaw and the rawness in his throat, ragged from words he was unaccustomed to speaking. "I don't understand what happened," he said, his voice rough and quiet. "I don't understand how I could have any part in this."

She stretched her neck toward him and kissed him on the cheek. "Dear, sweet, Dreaming Boy," she said with a voice that seemed far away. "Understanding is not always necessary."

Neb's muscles were sore now, and he realized suddenly that he was still entwined with the girl. The tingling had become something different. The warmth of her body and the firmness of her hands as she held him were building toward something in him that was frightening and exhilarating all at once.

He disentangled himself quickly, scrambling to his feet. She did the same, and he realized that her face was as red as his. "I'm sorry," he said.

She laughed. "There is nothing to be sorry for. The spirit moves as it will, so also the body."

He looked at his half-eaten breakfast at the table, but knew already he wouldn't be able to finish it. "I think I should go back to Windwir soon. They will be worried for me."

A sad looked passed over her face. "I understand. I will see if the Marsh King has returned from the parley."

She walked close to him, near enough for him to feel her warmth. Then the Marsh girl Winters quickly touched his cheek once more, and left through the back entrance of the cave.

After she'd gone, he sat and thought about her and her people.

A home-seeking is upon us.

Neb hid all of her words in his heart and wondered about the world that had changed.

Pecronus

Vlad Li Tam's wagons of donated supplies arrived in the late morning, and Petronus met them at the edge of camp, glaring at Tam as he smiled down from his horse.

"I would talk with the captain of this company," Vlad Li Tam said to the sentries who stopped him.

"That would be Petros," one of the guards said, turning to look for him.

Petronus stepped forward. "I'm here."

"I come bearing the grace of House Li Tam and the Pope of the Androfrancine Order," Vlad Li Tam said. "I would speak with you about your work here."

Petronus gritted his teeth. "I'd gladly speak with you about our work, Lord Tam."

The slight, older man dropped from his saddle, heavy in the armor he wore beneath his canary colored robes. "Let us walk together."

They moved away from the camp and toward yesterday's work. Petronus guided them toward a recently filled trench, feeling the anger build in him with every step. When they were out of earshot, he rounded on Tam.

"What game do you play at?" he asked, not even trying to mask the rage.

Vlad Li Tam smiled. "I play at the game of survival, Petronus. I play at the game of keeping the light alive." He paused, his eyes narrowing as his smile faded. "I should ask what game *you* play at, Petronus. You could have stayed dead. You could have stayed in Caldus Bay. But here you are."

Petronus knew Tam was right, and he knew that at least part of his anger was directed inward, toward himself. "I had to see it," he said, his voice thick with loss. "I had to see what they'd done to themselves."

"And then you had to bury them?" Vlad Li Tam's voice wasn't chiding, it was matter-of-fact, as if he were stating some obvious truth about Petronus's soul.

He nodded. "I did." He waved his arms around, taking in the four points of the compass. "These others weren't prepared to do it. They're too busy posturing and pointing fingers." He stared at Vlad Li Tam. "We both know who really brought down Windwir."

Vlad Li Tam's eyes flashed. "They've done this to themselves. We both knew they would when they started playing with words that should not be played with. It was only a matter of time."

Petronus felt his fists clenching and unclenching. "You claim House Li Tam had no part in this?"

Vlad Li Tam shrugged. "We monitored increased intelligence gathering in the City States coinciding with the discovery of the final fragment. My forty-second daughter, Jin Li Tam, was Sethbert's consort until recently. She'd known something was under way but not exactly what. I knew an event of some kind was likely." He stepped closer to Petronus and put a hand on his shoulder. "When or who—these facts eluded the best work of my sons and daughters." He leaned forward. "But I do know this much—word of the final fragment was not initially leaked by the Androfrancines. They were most cautious."

"And you did not leak it yourself?"

Vlad Li Tam shook his head. "I did not."

"But you knew of it?"

He nodded. "I did. I had been approached years ago about storing something of great value and great danger in the Li Tam vaults. There was talk of scattering the fragments under Pope Introspect, but it was quickly abandoned."

Petronus studied the man, then studied the line of his face, and tried to gauge the truth of his words. But Vlad Li Tam was a master of queen's war and a master of himself. There were no telling movements, no revealing posture, no hints whatsoever to catch him in a lie. And not even the best Francine training could see through that perfect mask. "Then we need to know how Sethbert discovered the spell and what compelled him to take action."

Vlad Li Tam shook his head and chuckled. "An Androfrancine to the end."

Petronus felt his blood rise. He pointed to the filled-in trench, then pointed to a line of diggers closer to the center of the city. "A city lies dead, Vlad. A way of life is ended. What little remains of the light is guttering. If it weren't for the mechoservitors, it would be all but extinguished now. I want to know why."

"We all do, Petronus. But strategy would dictate that first, we shore up what remains." Vlad Li Tam sighed, looking away for a moment before meeting Petronus's eyes. "I'm afraid I have not been completely truthful with you."

Petronus felt his eyebrows furrow. "What do you mean?"

Vlad reached into his belt pouch and drew out a yellowed scroll, rolled carefully and tied with Androfrancine purple. He passed it to Petronus.

Petronus read the note and paled. He read it again, this time more slowly, and the words finally came together. He looked up. "These are plans for the relocation of the Order, away from Windwir."

He nodded. "Under Introspect's seal."

Petronus's mind spun. "Why would they do this?"

"Defensive posturing," Vlad Li Tam said. "It seems they had a sense of what was coming, too."

Petronus racked his brain, trying to find some scrap of memory that might make sense of this. For two thousand years, the Great Library and the Order had occupied Windwir. They were the backbone of the Entrolusian economy, centrally located yet distant enough for a modicum of safety and privacy.

Suddenly, he saw Vlad Li Tam's strategy more clearly and understood it. "The Ninefold Forests," he said quietly.

Vlad Li Tam nodded. "I have been under Holy Unction by

the Order for nearly thirty years—really, since just after you left—to groom Rudolfo for this." Petronus studied him, surprised when the line of Vlad Li Tam's face betrayed him in such a small lie.

Longer than that, he realized, but he didn't say anything. The one person other than Vlad Li Tam that could truly say when this started had died in the Desolation of Windwir. But Petronus suspected that the work—both the study of the spell and the plans to relocate Windwir—had started well before he'd stepped down from the Papacy and returned to fishing.

Another reason you should have stayed, old man.

Petronus forced his mind back to the matter. "You mean to continue Introspect's plan, then?"

Vlad Li Tam's eyes were hard, blue glass. "That depends on the word of my Pope."

Petronus nodded. "Does Rudolfo understand exactly what this means?"

Vlad Li Tam shrugged. "He may or he may not. I'll not tell him—I'm bound by Holy Unction. And there have been certain—" he paused to find the right word "—*complexities* in implementing the Androfrancine strategy. You studied the Francine way. Men can be shaped for a role, but it often involves sacrifice."

Petronus's eyes narrowed. "What have you done?"

Vlad Li Tam climbed into his saddle. "These are matters best left in the past." He settled himself and looked down.

"I am your Pope, Lord Tam," he said, his voice taking on a tone that he'd not used in decades. "I would know of these matters."

Vlad Li Tam laughed and turned his horse. "You are a fisherman, Petros, digging graves in the rain. When you openly declare yourself to be more than that, ask me again. Demand it of me, even, and under Holy Unction I will tell you everything." He walked the horse in a wide circle around Petronus. "Rudolfo is taking back the mechoservitors tonight. The spell-caster is already in the Ninefold Forest, planning the library in the care of my forty-second daughter. They will want your input soon so that work can begin with the spring."

Petronus nodded but said nothing.

"Declare soon, Petronus," Vlad Li Tam said. "We've light to guard."

As he rode away, Petronus realized two things. First, that once he declared he probably would not want to know exactly what Vlad Li Tam had done to prepare the Ninefold Forest for this time. Not just for the sake of being able to face Rudolfo, but also because of what it meant for the boy who had once been his friend, who had once shared his home and hearth and boat.

The second thing he realized was the more surprising of the two. The thought stayed with him long after Vlad Li Tam's horse crossed the blackened landscape and galloped up the western hills to be swallowed by the forest.

As he played it out in his mind, following that river of reason with its many branching streams, Petronus realized that he would do whatever he had to do to protect the light.

Even if it meant letting the Androfrancine Order die where it lay, ending its backward-watching dream of two thousand years.

Resolute

Pope Resolute the First looked out at the blanket of white that covered the rooftops and courtyards of the Summer Papal Palace. The first snows of winter had fallen, and judging by the looks of it more would come soon. In the courtyards, staging areas had been hastily erected during second summer to catalog and inventory Androfrancine property returning by his order. From there, the goods were stored in barns, papers and books hauled into the Papal Palace itself. The migration north had grown to a trickle despite the invisible pretender's support of the notion.

Now, another bird from the pretender called for the cessation of the migration as winter set in, deeming the northern routes too treacherous to risk what little remained of Androfrancine resources—human and otherwise. This new word called for Androfrancines to wait out the winter wherever they were, bidding them to remain patient and assuring them that new instructions would follow soon.

The order made sense. He'd sat down to write a similar proclamation, but Sethbert's last message was insistent that he wait as long as possible to make sure the Order's holdings were safe in his keeping, far north and out of the way of the brewing war.

But now, the pretender had given instruction of his own—countermanding Oriv's—in this second proclamation from his so-called exile. Initially, Oriv felt confident of his cousin's sense of statecraft and strategy, but keeping silent no longer felt appropriate.

He heard a quiet cough, and turned away from the wide window in his office. Grymlis, the newly promoted General of the Gray Guard, stood waiting.

Resolute studied the man. Grymlis was short and broad and powerful, especially for his seventy or more years. His short gray hair and beard bristled, and he wore his dress grays creased, the various bits of silver that decorated him shining brightly in the lamplight. He'd been in the service of the light probably longer than Oriv had been alive, retiring into recruitment activities and escorting high-ranking officials. He'd actually led Oriv's caravan to the Palace, seemingly so long ago.

"We've another bird from Sethbert," Grymlis said, extending the small rolled message.

Oriv took it, unrolled it and read it quickly. "Rudolfo is at Windwir without his Wandering Army." He smiled. "Perhaps that bodes well for us."

Grymlis said nothing, and Oriv could feel the hardness of his eyes as the general stared. "What?" the Pope finally demanded.

"I would worry less about where Rudolfo is and more about where the weapon is," Grymlis said.

"It's a mechanical," Resolute said. "I've told you—the mechoservitor is harmless now. They can't lie, you know. They're machines. What they do, what they know, even what they can and cannot say is written onto tiny metal scrolls that they play out in their metal heads."

Grymlis snorted. "Forgive me, Excellency, if I don't share your trust of its word. It brought down a city. Genocide on a massive scale; over two hundred thousand souls lost along with the greatest repository of knowledge and artifacts this New World has ever known. I somehow doubt that lying poses any kind of obstacle in the course of its work." The general's tone softened. "If its script could be modified to recite the spell, then it certainly could be modified to lie."

Oriv sighed. He knew the general was right. But the notion that things could go so very wrong in so many ways disturbed him.

Why? It was the question of the year and it applied to nearly everything these days. Why had Windwir fallen? Why had Oriv been spared? Why had this hidden pretender issued proclamations without having been pronounced and without having even submitted himself for investigation by what remained of the Order? Why had the Gypsy King come all this way under his own free will to turn himself in, only to escape as soon as the pretender emerged?

Questions. Nothing but questions. "I am the Pope of questions," he said quietly. At Grymlis's raised eyebrows he waved the old general off. "It's nothing."

"There may not be answers, Excellency," Grymlis said. "If I may be so bold?"

Pope Resolute nodded. "Yes. Go on."

"Your silence will be your undoing. People crave answers, but in the absence of answers, they will follow the loudest, clearest voice."

"You believe I should answer the pretender's challenge?"

Grymlis nodded. "More than that. If you are the Pope, *be*

the Pope. If you are the King of Windwir in exile, then for light's sake, *be* the King of Windwir." His voice rose, taking on a sharpness that stirred Oriv.

"I am these things," Oriv said. "I am."

Grymlis's next words marched out clear and slow. "You are a clerk hiding in the mountains, tallying up your leftovers while beggars and refugees bury your dead." His voice became a growl. "While your cousin and his alliance play at army and tell you what they wish for you to know. While your banker diverts your Order's funds into the pocket of a pretender you know nothing about. While the greatest weapon this world has ever seen walks and talks and serves Lord Rudolfo his chilled peach wine."

The words stung him, and his first thought was to slap the general. His second thought was to demand his arrest. In the end, he did neither. He felt his shoulders slump. "What would you do?"

"Nothing . . . from *here*." Grymlis strode forward, throwing open the doors to the balcony, letting the cold wind blow snow onto the thick Emerald Coast carpets that lined the office floor. "If you stay a week longer, you'll have stayed too late. Leave the steward in charge. Leave a company of the Guard if you must. Set those who've come home to whatever work you will." His eyes were sharper and harder now than a thousand angry dreams. "But for light's sake, man, go out and be King and Pope. You'll not sway the tide of loyalty up here in hiding."

The words resonated. It was completely contrary to his cousin's direction. But after the week with Rudolfo and the mechoservitor, he'd started doubting how truthful his cousin had been. And he still could not move past the fact that his cousin had known somehow that he was away from Windwir on the day it fell. He suspected strongly that Sethbert might even have had some hand in arranging that. Coupled with that, Oriv knew that his mother's sister's son had no love toward him and no loyalty to blood.

He'd even found himself wondering from time to time if

Sethbert *had* somehow arranged the Desolation of Windwir as Rudolfo had maintained. Some of the refugees spoke of rumors, words passed from soldier to merchant to farmer and so on.

He looked outside again, then looked back to Grymlis. The old guard waited patiently.

"We have a reserve treasury here?"

Grymlis nodded. "Certainly."

Be your name, something deep inside of Oriv whispered. Resolute.

"Very well, General. Ready half of the contingent. They ride with me under your command in three days' time. Am I clear?"

"Perfectly, Excellency," Grymlis said with a smile.

Now, thought Resolute, to be the clearest and loudest voice.

Calling for his birder, he crafted his reply to the pretender's proclamations in as loud and clear a tone he could muster. Next, he wrote to Sethbert in the same tone, instructing his cousin that he would meet him on the plains of Windwir in one week's time.

When he finished, he turned his chair so that he could look out of his window and watch the falling snow.

Jin Li Tam

Jin Li Tam sat at the desk in the makeshift office the steward and house staff had created for her and Isaak, but she couldn't keep her mind on the work.

Tomorrow, she'd return to the River Woman and pick up her powders. There was no guarantee that they would work. These measures were only taken on rare occasions, when other strategies failed. And regardless of the efficacy of the powders, there was still the matter of Rudolfo ingesting them and rising to the challenge of copulation. The former concerned her, but not overmuch—she'd been trained by the best of poisoners, though she smiled at the irony of this particular situation—lacing his food or drink with a substance that would bring life rather than death. As to the latter—she had no worries. The Gypsy King's soldiers might be swordless, but they needed no marching instructions.

She stood and stretched, looking across the room to Isaak. He sat at his own desk, his robes neatly pressed and cleaned, both of his hands blurring as they simultaneously filled two sheets of parchment. The pen-tips scratched lightly at the papers in a kind of harmony with one another, and his eyes flashed as he wrote. It took less than a minute for him to fill both pages and move them aside with practiced efficiency, letting them dry on the stack as he started new pages.

She walked toward him, glancing down. Lists of books and authors and shelf locations from a library that was now a crater of ash and bones. "I'm going to walk," she said.

He looked up, nodded slightly to acknowledge her, then continued.

She let herself out of the manor, and her Gypsy Scouts fell in behind her. She recognized Edrys, a young sergeant that had been with them at the Summer Papal Palace, and she smiled at him.

She turned to them as they left the manor gates. "Today, I wish for you to walk with me . . . not behind. I would know more of my new home."

The two scouts exchanged apprehensive glances. "Lady Tam," Edrys started, "I'm not sure—"

She raised an eyebrow. "Sergeant Edrys, have you been forbidden to have discourse with me?"

"No, Lady Tam. I just—"

She interrupted again. "Am I in some way odious to you and not worthy of your company or your conversation?"

He turned red. "No, Lady Tam. I—"

"Good," she said. "Walk with me."

They both hurried to either side of her, and together they went out into the streets.

A light, cold rain fell, and the air was heavy with the

promise of snow. She'd climbed what they were calling Library Hill the day before and had seen that the Dragon's Spine was wrapped in white like a Marsh bride on her nuptial day. Within days, the snow would reach them here, whiting the forest and turning the Prairie Sea that surrounded the Ninefold Forest into a vast desert of snow dunes. The intense cold would even freeze the rivers in some places farther north.

It was a vast difference from the sunny climate of the City States on the Entrolusian Delta or the tropics of the Emerald Coasts farther south and west.

And this will be my new home.

They walked together at an easy pace, and Jin savored the cold air even as she shivered against it. The furrier was busily crafting her winter wear—boots, hats, heavy coats and pants—but they wouldn't be ready for another week. Until then, she wore a parka she found in the back of her closet. The Gypsy Scouts had gone from silk to wool with the changing of the seasons, dyed bright as the rainbow houses they served.

"I would know more of my husband-to-be," she said to Edrys as they walked.

He paled at her statement. "Lady Tam, I—"

She laughed. "Edrys, you worry too much. I'll not ask anything unseemly. I believe you can know much of a man by the men he keeps near him. Or would you prefer that I know my husband through the prostitutes he keeps on rotation or through the house staff that serves him?"

His face went red when she mentioned the prostitutes, and she smiled inwardly. Those surface details were simple matters to discuss, really. As were at least seven of the hidden passageways within the seventh forest manor. She suspected that each of the nine manors was a world of secrets in itself.

She suspected the same of Rudolfo.

"What would you know, Lady?"

"How long have you served him?"

Edrys did not miss a step. "I've served Lord Rudolfo all my life." She knew this. Many of the Gypsy Scouts were the sons of Gypsy Scouts, raised on the magicks and the blades along with their mothers' milk.

"And what is the single most true thing about him?"

Edrys thought about this for just a moment. "He always knows the path to take." He paused. "And he always takes it, no matter what the cost."

She nodded. This certainly seemed true of him. She'd been trained first and foremost to watch and to listen. She heard the things that were said and unsaid. She made a point of seeing the overlooked and underestimated. "Was Lord Jakob that way as well?"

Edrys chuckled. "I'm far too young to have known Lord Jakob. I was born the year he and Lady Marielle were killed."

Jin Li Tam had certainly heard bits of the story whispered in her father's house. An unexpected and violent coup in the Ninefold Forest led by a charismatic mystic named Fontayne. Fontayne's cousin had been the steward at Glimmerglam, the first forest manor. First, they poisoned the Gypsy Scouts assigned to guard the manor and its family. Then, they butchered Lady Marielle in her sleep. They had not realized Lord Jakob and his heir had slipped out through a hidden passage in order to do some night hunting. Lord Jakob had returned at the sound of the alarm bells and was beaten to death in front of his son by Fontayne and his mob of insurgents.

Jin Li Tam had spent much more time watching and listening after her first visit with the River Woman. For the first time in her life she found herself doubting her father's business, but she could not for the life of her understand why. Whatever must be done to move the world—that's what her father stood by. And she did, too. Or at least she thought she did. It's how she pleasured and occasionally took her pleasure from the men her father sent her to. She did her watching and her listening for him, first and foremost, and passed what she saw or heard along to her father for his work.

But now, she found that she questioned it. But why? It was perfect strategy at a level that not even the Francines could fully appreciate. For the price of a poisoned brother then, a formidable leader now walked the Named Lands. One who, according to the youngest of his Gypsy Scouts, always knew the right path to take and always took that path no matter what the cost.

And a part of that strategy, she realized, had always been that this leader be paired with a daughter of House Li Tam so that her father's good work could be realized.

But *why* did he need this leader? What does he intend for Rudolfo?

And what did he intend for *her*? She thought about the powders that the River Woman made for her. She thought about the work ahead of her, quietly going about the business of giving him an heir. More than an heir, she realized. A child who would grow up to protect the light that grew where it had been transplanted.

Her head ached for a split moment as she thought of the very different life he would inherit. Rudolfo had ridden the plains, laughing and racing his Gypsy Scouts, living from manor to manor. That would change with the library. The seventh manor would become the new center of the world.

She shook her head, realizing she'd stopped walking, and she looked at Edrys, who had lapsed into silence. "I'm sorry, Edrys. My mind wandered."

He nodded. "You were asking about Lord Jakob. My father served with him as well as Rudolfo. He said they were very much alike. According to him, Lord Jakob took the turban early as well, and it made him strong. He raised a strong boy and happenstance brought the same fate to Lord Rudolfo. My father thought he was much like Lord Jakob, only more ruthless because of the circumstances under which he came into his own."

She stopped, and the words settled in. More ruthless because of the circumstances that brought him into his own. *Lord Jakob took the turban early and it made him strong.*

Unexpected tears leapt to her eyes and she blinked into the cold, her mouth falling open with surprise, not from the realization but from her reaction to it.

She saw her father's strategy now, and saw that he had skillfully intersected Rudolfo's life at key points to move the river into the path he deemed best, a path toward a Gypsy King guarding the light of the world instead of a Gray Guarded Pope.

She also understood that she too was a part of his plan for Rudolfo, and she felt both gratitude and despair, a sadness for the price Rudolfo had paid in order to follow a path he had not chosen.

She looked away, wiping her eyes quickly. If Edrys saw, he'd say nothing. She knew this.

"Thank you for the walk, Sergeant," she said, turning away.

He cleared his voice. "By your leave, Lady Tam?"

She looked up. "Yes?"

"You could not want a better man. There isn't a member of the Wandering Army that wouldn't lay his life down for Lord Rudolfo."

"Thank you, Sergeant Edrys," she said.

As Jin Li Tam walked back to the manor, she wondered how it was that her mind could see so clearly the brilliance of this strategy and yet her heart could only grieve it.

Then she wondered: How could her father have known so long ago they would need a strong, non-Androfrancine guardian for the remnants of Windwir?

The first snowflakes of winter drifted down, and Jin Li Tam felt a deeper coldness washing through her heart.

Chapter

22

Neb

Winters avoided Neb's eyes until the Marsh King returned, then she disappeared entirely. They hadn't spoken, they hadn't known what to say, and all of it was just too new and strange for him. Cryptic prophecies, strange dreams, unexplainable fits of glossolalia were not what he'd expected when he'd run after the magicked Marsher scout.

Now, the Marsh King stood before him and held court, asking Neb about the gravedigging operation, about the armies and even a bit about Petronus. Neb answered carefully about the old man—describing him merely as a wandering Androfrancine—and spoke honestly about the Entrolusians and what little he knew of Rudolfo and the Queen of Pylos, the few scraps he'd picked up listening to the soldiers speak.

The giant fur-clad man paused between questions, glancing to the idol of P'Andro Whym and occasionally asking follow up questions. Finally they fell into silence, and after a few minutes of this, the Marsh King spoke.

"You are on the edge of becoming, Nebios ben Hebda," the Marsh King said. "A man is shaped not only by his choices but by the choices of those around him. You are being shaped by the Desolation of Windwir, and where some have taken up the sword you have taken up the shovel. I have seen in my dreams that your shovel will be the salvation of my people." Here the Marsh King leaned forward, lowering his deep voice. "And I have seen in *your* dreams, too, the great sorrow that you will bear because of your great love." The Marsh King paused. "I will summon you again in due time, Nebios ben Hebda. For now, I will leave you to your work and return to mine."

With that, the Marsh King stood and departed. Eventually, Neb left the cave and went to the foyer that the tent created. A few minutes later, Winters appeared.

"I will escort you to the edge of the plain," she said.

They walked slowly through the camp, and once again Neb wasn't exactly sure where the camp gave way to the forest. It was getting colder, and the pools of rainwater were now staying frozen longer into the day.

As they walked, Neb looked at her out of the corner of his eye. How was it that she seemed prettier each time he looked at her? How was it that the dirt and grime seemed less and less prevalent and her eyes and mouth seemed more? And how was it that it felt so good to be near her, to have the musky smell of her in his nose? It perplexed him.

Certainly, he understood human sexuality at least in theory. They'd covered it in school, and he'd seen a bit of it as it played out around him during his life in the city. And he knew that a lot of people followed those promptings of their nature, but everything he knew said that as an Androfrancine, he lived above such things. It never occurred to him to ask his father about his mother or to ask how it was that Brother Hebda had not kept his vows to the Order. It was simple: His father had made a mistake. And the grace of P'Andro Whym covered that mistake, even providing a home and food and education for the product of that mistake.

Perhaps these were the types of feelings that took men down the path of error. Or perhaps the fit of glossolalia they had experienced together somehow bonded them in a deeper way.

Neb wasn't sure, but he did know that the awkwardness grew and that she must feel it, too.

As if reading his mind, she stopped walking and turned on him. "I sense discomfort between us."

Neb stopped. He wrestled to find the words. "I'm not sure what it is." He thought about it some more.

"Is it unpleasant?"

He shook his head. "No. Just uncomfortable. I don't know what it means or what to do or how to act or what to say."

She laughed. "I feel that, too."

Now that he'd started, the words just kept coming. "And then there's your king and his dreams. It's a way of knowing that cuts across the grain of everything I've been taught." He felt a lump growing in the back of his throat, felt water building in his eyes. "And I really just want to go home, to talk with Brother Hebda about his latest dig, to finish my schooling and join the Order as an acolyte. But I can't. Because my home is a field of blackened bones, my father's among them. And there is no school, there is no library and soon enough, there may be no Order. Everything I have ever known and loved is gone from the world."

She nodded, her brown eyes soft with something that might've been concern. "Then you will come to know and love differently," she said, "and learn to live around the chasms. These are hard days, Nebios ben Hebda, but they are the travail of a woman with child. Through this pain, you will lead your people into their new home and it will be a home to you as well. I've seen it in the dreams."

"I don't want to lead anyone anywhere," he said, and he heard the voice of an angry child in his words.

Winters sighed. "I understand that feeling all too well. But we do what we are made for."

Suddenly, her hands were sliding up and around his neck as she pressed herself closer to him. Stretching up on tiptoes, she kissed him lightly on his mouth. Then she stepped back quickly, her cheeks turning red despite the layer of mud and ash. Neb felt his own heat rising along with stirrings elsewhere. "Why did you do that?"

She smiled. "I already told you. We do what we are made for." Then she dug into her pocket and pulled out a small silver vial. "The Marsh King wants you to have this."

Neb took it, and looked at it. "What is it for?"

"It's voice magicks," she said. "You'll need them."

He slipped it into his own pocket, and was going to ask her what he would need the voice magicks for, but he swallowed the question when his fingers felt the ring there nestled beside the Marsh King's gift. One more thing that Brother Hebda had told him in the dream, one more thing that the Marsh King knew without Neb saying.

Winters must have seen the look on his face. "Do not be troubled," she said. She brought her hand up and touched his shoulder.

Then the sound of horses reached their ears and they turned. Moving through the forest, Neb saw a handful of horses—one large and white at the head of them. A slight, bearded man in a green turban and a long golden robe rode high in the saddle with an aloof confidence, surrounded by men dressed in multicolored wool uniforms.

"Is that—?"

Winters interrupted. "It's Lord Rudolfo of the Ninefold Forest Houses. I'm afraid I will have to leave you here." She took both his hands in her own. "Be well, Nebios ben Hebda." She smiled at him, and for a moment Neb thought that maybe—just maybe—there could be some kind of peace or home at the end of this for him. "We will see each other again."

Neb wasn't sure how to respond, so he said nothing. He felt her squeeze his hands and he tried to squeeze back but it felt awkward.

Releasing his hands, she turned and ran back toward the camp.

Neb watched her go, still trying to capture and label the strange feelings she evoked. Then he continued south, breaking from the forest and making his way through the bones and ashes of Windwir.

He was halfway back to camp when something she said struck him as odd.

I've seen it in the dreams.

Shrugging it off, Neb moved south at a quickening pace, anxious to see Petronus and tell him what he could about everything that had happened to him.

Rudolfo

Rudolfo studied the Marsher camp as he rode into it. He had not been sure what to expect and he openly admired their skill at camouflaging themselves and their tents. He and his Gypsy Scouts stayed near one another. They were unmagicked to honor the kin-clave the Marsh King had proclaimed between them, and they were careful to keep their hands in plain view as well as their sheathed weapons and unstrung bows.

He'd never crossed into their lands and his only encounters with them had been with the king his father had captured and the occasional skirmishers he'd faced over the course of his life. He knew what most of the Named Lands knew about their history, and in many ways, he realized there was more kinship between the Marshers and the Ninefold Forest because of the ties to Xhum Y'Zir. Some scholars traced the original Marshers to the house slaves freed by Xhum Y'Zir after his sons were killed by P'Andro Whym. They came to the New World close on the heels of the first Rudolfo so long ago, before the others came led by the Whymers to establish the Named Lands.

He knew little of their culture. They were given to bouts of mysticism, following a system of beliefs unknown to most. Apart from skirmishing and scavenging they kept to themselves, though at one time their skirmishing and scavenging had been on a much grander scale. They used to bring down whole cities. Now they occasionally took farms or caravans but even most of that slowed down ten years ago or more.

Rudolfo brought his horse to a stop in the center of the camp and raised his voice. "I've come to parley with the Marsh King."

The people moved around him, silent, though they watched the mounted riders carefully.

Gregoric leaned over. "They say nothing."

"Marshers vow silence that their king be their only voice in time of war," a girl said, stepping from the crowd.

"And yet," Rudolfo said, inclining his head to her, "you are speaking to us."

"I am." She curtsied. "I will bring you to the Marsh King."

Rudolfo dismounted, leading his horse behind him as he picked his way through the muddy camp. He'd chosen a golden rain robe, wool trousers and a silk shirt over the top of his armor. He'd thought about leaving the light breastplate off, but he'd decided it would be best to humor his Gypsy Scouts.

He followed the girl and his men did the same. They walked to a tent against the side of a hill, and the girl gestured inside. "The Marsh King will join you soon. I will have refreshments brought to you."

Rudolfo nodded. "That would be most pleasant," he lied.

The girl curtsied again and ran off. She was a waif if he'd ever seen one. Long brown hair, tangled and filthy. Dried mud and ash smeared into her face and her plain burlap dress. There wasn't a clean patch on her. And even from the distance they'd kept, Rudolfo had worked hard not to wrinkle his nose at the smell.

He looked over his shoulder at his men, flashing hand signals to them. One of them stayed with the horses. The others took up their positions near the tent. Gregoric slipped into the tent, then slipped back out a minute later.

"It's fine, General," he said. "Filthy but fine. There's a back entrance."

Rudolfo nodded. "Very well. Wait with the men, Gregoric." He brushed past his first captain and into the tent. At the end of the short passageway, he saw that a small table had been set, along with a stool. Nearby stood a massive chair, and near it a meditation statue of P'Andro Whym—the one with the mirrors of self-awareness. It was dented and dirty, but it spoke of centuries past and of the same mysticism that had paved the way for Whymer Mazes and the Physicians of Penitent Torture—dark sides of T'Erys Whym's adoration of his brother.

Rudolfo went to the small table and sat, drumming his fingers lightly on the wood.

A most unusual kin-clave, he thought.

"Lord Rudolfo," a voice bellowed behind him.

He looked over his shoulder, and stood as the massive man pushed his way into the cave. Behind him, two Marsh women followed with trays of food and drink. Rudolfo extended his right hand to the Marsh King. "I do not know what to call you," he said.

The giant looked at Rudolfo's hand, then locked eyes with him. "I am the Marsh King." He continued past him to sit heavily in the chair. He glanced to the idol, then back to Rudolfo. "What is your strategy to win this war?"

Rudolfo chuckled. "You do not waste time with pleasantries, do you?"

The two women unloaded the trays onto the small table. One poured a thick, amber-colored syrup into a glass and set it by Rudolfo's right hand as the other placed bowls of poached salmon mixed with walnuts, apples and onions, loaves of black bread and wheels of strong-smelling cheese. Rudolfo picked up a bit of cheese and nibbled it.

"Pleasantries do not interest me," the Marsh King said, again glancing to the idol. "Have you listened to my War Sermon?"

Rudolfo shrugged. "You speak the Whymer tongue most nights. It is not a language I've kept up on." *But I've kept up on this language,* he signed, using the house language of Xhum Y'Zir.

The Marsh King's eyes widened, but he did not sign back. "The world is changing, Lord Rudolfo. I have dreamed it. On the night before the pillar of smoke, I dreamed of fire consuming the Named Lands for the sins of a father that is worshiped yet forgotten." The Marsh King looked to the idol. "Windwir is just the start of this. But in the end, it will close the Marshfolk's sojourn in the land of sorrows." He leaned forward. "And in my dreams, your blade guards the path to our new home."

Rudolfo picked at the salmon mixture with a small tarnished fork. It had been poached in lemon juice, and tasted surprisingly sweet and sour. He washed it down with a cold brown liquor that turned out to be a thick whiskey. He felt the warmth move through him and he savored it. He looked at the Marsh King. "And because of this you have announced our unexpected kin-clave?"

Rudolfo watched this time, carefully. The eyes always went to the idol before speaking. And after a glance, the words followed. "Your resurrected Pope will save the light by killing it. After, a Gypsy blade will guard that light, and by guarding it, guard our way."

He felt his eyes narrow. "Tell me about this resurrected Pope."

Another glance. "You will know of this soon enough."

"Regardless," Rudolfo said, watching the idol out of the corner of his eye, "you can imagine how odd it is that after two thousand years of scorning the Named Lands and its obeisance to the Rites of Kin-Clave, suddenly when Windwir falls you are quick to ride south and take a side."

Then, before the eyes could shift to the idol, Rudolfo signed: *You are not the Marsh King.*

The man looked to the idol, concern washing his face. He continued the stare at the idol and Rudolfo smiled. Finally, the giant spoke. "Dreams come when they come. I do not bid them."

Rudolfo nodded. "I understand." Then his hands moved. *You are the Marsh King's puppet,* he signed. *You read his hand signs in the mirror.*

Now he looked something like a wash between anger, puzzlement and fear. His mouth opened and closed, his heavy breath rustling his beard and mustache.

Rudolfo sipped the whiskey, then put it down. "I know what you're about," he said, raising his voice. *Tell your puppeteer that Lord Rudolfo has sniffed him out.*

But before he could speak, the girl appeared from her place behind the curtain. She smiled at him, and Rudolfo saw it was the girl who had led him here. "Lord Rudolfo, my apologies for this subterfuge," she said, striding forward and extending her right hand. "You can imagine why it is prudent for the Named Lands to see the Marsh King as something other than what she truly is."

Rudolfo accepted her hand and forced himself to raise it to his mouth, despite the grime and mud. "I understand completely. As long as kin-clave exists between us, I will honor your trust."

She nodded. "Thank you. I know you understand what it means to come into power young and alone."

Rudolfo felt the sting of memory, remembering that first lonely day as the new Lord of the Ninefold Forest Houses. Gregoric's father had been his strength, and not long after brought Gregoric into the position of First Captain so that he could become Rudolfo's general by proxy. "Yes," he said. "It is challenging to earn and keep respect."

She looked at the large man who played her proxy. "My father chose Hanric to play the part of my shadow until I found my own strength. Of course, my people know."

This surprised Rudolfo. "Really?"

She smiled. "Marshfolk are very different from Named Landers."

"Aye," Rudolfo said, chuckling. "As are the Forest Gypsies."

"My role is more spiritual than directive," she continued. "Most of my life is spent writing my dreams, both the waking and the dreaming. I also write out my glossolalia."

Rudolfo pondered this. "These are the War Sermons we hear."

She nodded. "They are. I've written these down for as long as I can remember. My Whymer Seers catalog them and assign them numbers, weaving my dreams into the matrix of dreams from the Marsh Kings that have gone before. My father chose Hanric as my shadow partly for his strength as a warrior, but also because, like me, he remembers everything he reads. He has spent his life preparing for the War of Androfrancine Sin, reading the dreams." She looked to Hanric now. "I will draw numbers tonight and determine their sequence at random. And the Marsh King's War Sermon will continue."

Rudolfo laughed now. "I think we lead our houses very differently."

The corners of her eyes crinkled as she smiled. "We do."

Rudolfo's hand crept up to stroke his beard. "I must admit that this is not what I expected for my parley with you."

"But you saw through my subterfuge soon enough."

The Gypsy King shrugged. "I've had a life of statecraft and intrigue. Until now, I would imagine you spent your life away from that."

"I have," she said. "Though I had an Androfrancine tutor."

Rudolfo raised his eyebrows. "That is quite curious given the history."

"Yes." She looked at Hanric. "I will come for you soon, Hanric."

He bowed and quickly left the cave.

When he left she looked at Rudolfo, and for just a moment her hard eyes became soft. There was a certain prettiness beneath the dirt, and a coltish, awkward strength in her bearing. As young as she was, Rudolfo sensed that she already exhibited the trappings of formidability. "Now," she said, "let's talk strategy for this war of ours."

Rudolfo smiled and reached for the bottle of whiskey.

Petronus

Petronus sat amid the rubble and ash and thought about the past.

He'd waited for Neb to return or for Gregoric to bring

some word, but neither had happened, and eventually he'd wandered into the city. In addition to the boy's disappearance, the work worried him. By his estimates they'd buried nearly a third of the dead, but it was obvious now that the winter was upon them, and their workforce dwindled with each day that the armies waited.

He'd often found that walking helped. One of the things he'd hated about being Pope was that he could no longer simply go for a walk. Gray Guard or archbishops or aides surrounded him everywhere he went, though from time to time he'd managed to slip past them. On those days or nights, he wandered a circuit of streets, always the same streets, head low and hands clasped behind his back, dressed in the simplest robes he could borrow.

Now he had done the same thing, his feet picking out a path that carried him along the backside of the crater where the great library had stood. Before he knew it, he was where the Garden of Coronation and Consecration had once been, where as a younger man he'd taken the scepter and the ring offered to him and had been proclaimed Pope Petronus.

He sat down, thinking about what it meant then to be Pope, contrasting it to what it meant now.

Tonight, Rudolfo would raid the Entrolusian camp. Petronus had his doubts about the success of the operation, but rebuilding the library would be a popular cause in light of the Desolation of Windwir. And it was sound strategy to move the library north. The only unsound part of the strategy was the Androfrancines' continued care of the light. Given their weakness now—from over a hundred thousand souls to maybe a thousand—there was no way they could keep the secrets of the Old World and even the First World safe from men like Sethbert.

You know what you need to do, old man, he told himself. You've known since you learned it was Sethbert. You've known since that clerk proclaimed himself Pope.

Petronus sighed. It was easier then, with the trumpets and the shouting and the crowds. Because on the surface of it, there was nothing to be done. Nothing to be responsible for, not really. Archbishops and Gray Guard and scholars and lawyers shielded him from any silent moment of accountability. The closest he'd come to it was the Marsher village, and only that because he'd commanded that captain to take him.

He heard movement behind him and turned. Neb made his way towards him, walking slowly. Petronus climbed to his feet and went to the boy. "You're back," he said, opening his arms.

Neb walked cautiously into the embrace, and pulled away quickly. Petronus saw that he had his hand in his pocket, fumbling with something.

"We've worried about you," Petronus said. "Our Gypsy friends said they would inquire—I've been waiting for word." He smiled, patting the boy's back. "I'm glad you're back."

Neb nodded. "Lord Rudolfo approached to parley as I left."

Petronus sat and pointed to the blackened piece of masonry nearby. As Neb sat, Petronus said, "The kings all met for parley this morning."

Neb looked at him, and Petronus saw concern on his face. "What will you do?"

Petronus blinked, surprised at the boy's sudden directness. He wondered what had happened to him in the Marsher camp, and would have asked, but Neb's tone commanded honesty and attention. "I do not know what I will do," he said.

Neb nodded. "The Marsh King talked about a resurrected Pope. He said that the end of the light is the end of their time in this land—that there is a new home for them."

Petronus cocked his head. "Marsher mysticism and nothing more."

Neb shrugged but didn't speak.

"Something else happened," Petronus said. It wasn't a question.

Neb looked up, then looked away, his face awash with conflicting emotion. He doesn't want to tell me, Petronus thought. "There was a girl," he finally said.

Petronus chuckled. "This is the age it starts," he said.

Neb looked away, and Petronus noticed that his hand was still buried in the pocket of his robes. "Do you believe that dreams are true?"

"Of course," Petronus said. "The Francines teach us that the dreams are how parts of our mind work out the stimuli of our waking experience."

Neb shook his head. "I mean—can they tell the future?"

Petronus sat back. "It must be possible sometimes. You dreamed that the Marsh King and his army rode south to Windwir, and he did."

Neb's eyes met Petronus's. "That's not all I dreamed that night."

Petronus waited.

Finally, Neb continued. "In my dream, Brother Hebda told me I would proclaim you Pope in the Garden of Coronation and Consecration."

Petronus felt the color drain from his face. Now the boy reached into his pocket, withdrawing something small that glistened dully in the gray winter sunlight. Petronus squinted at it and gasped.

The Papal signet lay in the palm of Neb's hand.

The boy stretched his hand out to Petronus, and it shook slightly.

At first, he did not take the ring. He just stared at it, feeling the fear of it course through him. After what seemed hours, he picked it up and weighed it in his hands.

"You are Petronus," Neb said, "the Missing King of Windwir and the Lost Pope of the Holy See of the Androfrancine Order." Petronus saw the line of tears cutting tracks of white down Neb's cheeks. He felt tears building in his own eyes.

"I am Petronus," he said slowly. Holding his breath, he slipped the ring onto the second finger of his right hand.

Neb stood and drew a vial from his pocket, unstopping the lid. He raised it to his lips, and Petronus shook his head, standing.

"No," he said, taking the vial away. "You've done enough, Nebios. Let me proclaim myself."

Neb let out his held breath, and Petronus took the vial from his shaking hand.

Raising it to his lips, he felt the power of it course through him. Blood magick from its taste, spiced with powders from things grown in dark places. He drank it down and cleared his voice, feeling the wave of sound rumble out from him like thunder.

Then Petronus drew himself up to his full height and shouted at the sky. "I am Petronus," he said. "I am the coronate King of Windwir and consecrated Pope of the Holy See of the Androfrancine Order."

The words blasted out from him, marching for league upon league. Petronus intended to stop with that, but as his eyes took in the blasted city around him, he felt all of the anger he'd kept buried these last few months, and it demanded release.

Pacing the holy ground of his consecration and coronation, Petronus spent the rest of that afternoon delivering a War Sermon of his very own.

Sethberz

Sethbert heard the voice outside and stood from his luncheon table. Over the weeks he'd grown accustomed to the Marsh King's midnight ranting, but they'd been easy to ignore, being in what was for all practical purposes a dead language. He'd had the first few nights translated by an old man he'd kept on for just that sort of thing, but once he'd seen that at least a third of it was unintelligible, another third was disjointed bits of scripture, and the rest a smattering of references from something called the Book of the Dreaming Kings, Sethbert had put the old man onto other work and put the Marsh King's War Sermons out of his mind.

But this afternoon's voice was clear, speaking in the formal language reserved for matters of high ceremony. Sethbert exited the tent and saw he wasn't alone. Soldiers, servants, war-whores, aides and cooks had all stopped, looked up, and went outside to listen.

Sethbert waved over a young lieutenant. "I missed the first part. What did he say?"

"He said he was the King of Windwir and the Pope of the Androfrancine Order," the young lieutenant answered.

Sethbert snorted. "The King of Windwir and the Pope of the Androfrancine Order is at the Summer Papal Palace." He opened his mouth to say more, but swallowed his words when he heard his own name mentioned in the angry outpouring. He felt eyes on him, and at the same time he felt his anger rise. The voice was making charges—true charges, Sethbert realized—and spelling out the consequences for Sethbert's transgressions.

He kept listening, hearing much of the same language he'd read in the written proclamation. Of course, the written proclamation had been kept away from his military at General Lysias's insistence.

He looked now at the listening faces around him, his eyes measuring them. Lysias had protested his handling of the desertions, but they'd dropped off substantially when word spread through the camp of how Sethbert dealt with those who spurned their oath to the Delta City States. He wondered now what this news would mean for his army.

I could tell them the truth. They would hail me as a hero. But Sethbert would not tell them the truth simply because he knew that he shouldn't have to. "Some are kings and some are not and there's a reason for that," his father had told him. Sethbert believed it.

And the longer he kept knowledge to himself, the better control he had over what that knowledge could do. Something he'd actually learned from the Androfrancines.

Sethbert listened to the War Sermon, listened to the rallying call of this Pope, and for a moment he thought the voice and words seemed familiar. It sounded like someone he'd known.

He saw Lysias walking quickly toward him, a perplexed look on his face. Like an Androfrancine clock, Sethbert thought, perfectly on time.

"This does not bode well," Lysias said. "I've a bird back from the front lines. It's coming from the center of the city. Scouts have been dispatched."

Sethbert nodded. "Do we know who it is?"

Lysias shrugged. "Not with any certainty. But . . ." He started the sentence, then paused.

Sethbert sighed. "But what, General? Who is it?"

Lysias set his jaw. "He claims to be Petronus," he said.

Sethbert dropped the wineglass he'd forgotten he still carried. It shattered on the ground. He felt his stomach lurch, and he closed his eyes against it.

The wily old gravedigger and his Androfrancine laws, he thought.

I should have recognized him.

Then Sethbert screamed for his horse and sword.

Chapter

23

Rudolfo

Rudolfo reached the old man first, racing low in the saddle across the wasted land. Behind him, his scouts magicked themselves and ran, sending their horses back to camp with a whistle.

The old man looked at Rudolfo, and their eyes met.

Rudolfo saw anger and despair in those blue eyes, cold as winter stars and sharp as moonshine blades. The force of the stare was enough that he grunted and pulled up his horse. He whistled, and his men, already fading as the magicks took hold and bent light around them, scattered to take up positions around the old man.

Rudolfo saw a boy standing next to the old man. The grandson, he realized. Gregoric had told him about the boy and even pointed him out when they'd seen him leaving the Marsher camp with the girl he later learned was the true Marsh King.

He slipped from the saddle, landing on his feet with ease. He approached, one hand brushing the hilt of his narrow sword. The old man stopped speaking as Rudolfo slowly knelt before him. "You claim to be Petronus," Rudolfo said in a whisper. "What proof do you bear?"

When Petronus replied, it was the voice of many waters. "I watched you with your father at my funeral, Rudolfo. You wore a red turban and you did not cry."

Rudolfo nodded. "It is as you say."

Petronus inclined his head.

Rudolfo drew his sword and laid it at the old man's feet. Then, he kissed the old man's ring.

Petronus nodded, grimly. He looked out across the city, and Rudolfo's eyes followed. A line of horses approached from the north, the south and the west. Rudolfo picked up his sword and stood, holding it outward and down.

Petronus cleared his voice. "Lord Rudolfo of the Ninefold Forest Houses has pledged his Wandering Army to my cause and pledged his fealty to me as the Holy See of the Androfrancine Order. In the absence of the Gray Guard, he holds the Guardianship of the Light." He paused. "You who war on Rudolfo, war on the light."

Rudolfo nodded, whistling to his men. They pulled in closer, forming a shield around the Pope after checking the perimeter. Behind him, Rudolfo knew the Marsh King's army would not be far behind. When they'd heard the proclamation he and the king, Winters, had run out of the tent shouting orders. Her shadow, Hanric, raised the third alarm, and their soldiers—men *and* women—rallied. Rudolfo rode out first with his Gypsy Scouts, but they'd agreed that the Marsh King's army would follow after.

Rudolfo watched the rising cloud of ash on his north, west and south. The Marsh King's shadow arrived next, followed closely by the Queen of Pylos.

She slowed her pale horse to a trot and slipped from the saddle. The silver bow upon her back glistened in the watery afternoon light. "I am for the light," she said. She glared at Rudolfo.

She'd hoped to be first, he knew. To offer her fealty and seek the Pope's favor and currency. Pylos was a small nation with a challenged economy.

Rudolfo smiled. "Queen Meirov," he said. "You are radiant."

She inclined her head, but her face remained a cold mask. She opened her mouth to speak, but closed it as the sounds of shouting approached.

Rudolfo had no difficulty picking out Sethbert's raised voice, and he turned south to watch the fat Overseer's approach. Sethbert had ridden north without his armor, bundled in a fur coat against the cold and brandishing a sword. He pulled up his horse but did not dismount.

"I dispute your claim," he said in a loud, icy voice.

Petronus fixed his eyes upon him. When he spoke his words rumbled out, but already Rudolfo could hear the magicks fading.

"Lord Sethbert," Petronus said, "Overseer of the Entrolusian City States. You are the Desolator of Windwir and enemy of the light. Surrender yourself. We've lost enough because of your senseless act of genocide. We do not need more bodies in this field of ash."

Sethbert sneered. "Senseless act of genocide?" He laughed. "I am a patriot of the light." He leaned in, studying the old man, and Rudolfo gathered his strength, ready to defend his

Pope. "By the Gods," the Overseer said as he looked Petronus over more closely. "It *is* you."

"Then you acknowledge me as your Pope?"

Sethbert's eyes narrowed. "I do not. I simply acknowledge you as Petronus."

Petronus nodded. "That is enough then." He looked around the gathering crowd. Rudolfo looked, too. Now the workers were drifting in too, wide-eyed and slack-jawed at the sight of their leader holding court with nobility. "You all have heard him acknowledge that I am Petronus."

"It does not make you Pope and King," Sethbert said. "The Order has a Pope, Resolute the First, proclaimed in accordance with the Lines of Succession."

One of the Gypsy Scouts whistled, and Rudolfo looked up to see Vlad Li Tam approach, his horse sweaty from the hard gallop. Rudolfo watched knowing glances exchanged between Lord Tam and Pope Petronus. "Pope Petronus," Lord Tam said, inclining his head.

Petronus nodded his acknowledgement. "Lord Tam. We have much to discuss."

Rudolfo watched Sethbert's face turn purple with rage. "You should have stayed on your Emerald Coasts, Tam," Sethbert said. He turned to Petronus. "And you should have stayed dead." He raised his voice then, as loud as he could. "I dispute the Papacy of Petronus."

With that, he spun his horse and rode south to his camps. His men fell in behind him.

Rudolfo looked at the faces of those gathered close to the newly proclaimed Pope. The Queen of Pylos looked uncomfortable but resolved. The Marsh King's shadow stood near her, his face blank. The boy stood near the Pope, his face a wash of emotion that moved freely between sadness and wonder. The only person in the crowd who looked pleased was Vlad Li Tam.

Rudolfo scowled, puzzling out the expression on the face of the man who would soon be his father by marriage.

It was a look of relief, but Rudolfo did not understand how anyone could feel relief knowing what was to come.

As the first snowflakes of winter fell on the Desolation of Windwir, mingling its cold white with the gray ash of the fallen city, Rudolfo's mind spun strategies and intrigue.

The War of the Androfrancine Popes, born in a field of bones, was upon them.

Jin Li Tam

Jin Li Tam raced down the hallways of the manor with her pack slung over one shoulder. She paused long enough to knock at Isaak's door, then opened it. "Are you ready?" she asked.

Isaak looked up from his desk of papers. "I am, Lady."

"And you have your tools?"

He held up the leather satchel containing the mechoservitor tools. "I do."

The bird had arrived the day before, and those members of the Wandering Army from the Seventh Forest Manor and the town that surrounded it gathered in the meadow south of town and prepared to ride west. Over the protests of the steward and the captain of the contingent, Jin Li Tam insisted on accompanying them. And because she was going, Isaak went too. She would use the pretense, if Rudolfo challenged her, that the mechoservitors might require repairs after so long in Sethbert's care.

In two days' time, she would meet Rudolfo at the western steppes of the Prairie Sea. There, she would slip the first of the powders into his evening brandy and give herself to the task of bearing him an heir. Apprehension fluttered in her stomach.

I should stop this, she thought.

And do what? Dishonor her father and the work of House Li Tam by questioning a will and a strategy that stretched far beyond her understanding? Because of a poisoned boy?

Because of an orphaned Gypsy King? It was this strategy and will, both from her father, that shaped a leader for the Named Lands' first catastrophe. If bearing an heir and settling into the life of a Gypsy King's wife was her part to play in this, to create a wily and educated child who would one day take the turban—this was not a chore. This was honor.

Isaak fell in behind her, carrying the large leather satchel of mechoservitor tools. Despite his limp he kept up with her, his feet thudding heavily on the thick carpeted floor. She glanced at him over her shoulder. His eyes were bright. "When will we hear if he was successful?"

"Tomorrow night at the soonest," she said. Coded deeply into the message she'd snatched from the steward's hands was a note that Rudolfo intended to liberate the metal men from Sethbert's camp whether or not the invisible Pope gave him leave. His plan was to pass the metal men over to a small contingent that would run them east and north to Isaak's aid, then return to the front with his Wandering Army.

War is coming, her father's note had read. She could smell it in the air now, and she sensed the tightening of a hunter's snare but she could not quite see it.

There were birds from her brothers and sisters, passed along with her father's approval. The scattered nations of the Emerald Coasts and the pioneer counties of the Divided Isle were teetering on fences. The Androfrancines were woven into the Named Lands—a thread that, when ripped out, unraveled the entire robe. She could read the critical mass as it built throughout, armies being recruited and supplies being stockpiled. They waited simply to be compelled one way or another, and she saw her father's strategy with this invisible Pope now as well. She would expect some grand event soon in that regard, though she was not certain what. Perhaps a public proclamation.

Her Gypsy Scouts waited for her at the door. She stopped, and Edrys stepped forward. "You're certain I cannot dissuade you of this notion, Lady Tam?"

She smiled at him. "I assure you that you cannot."

He nodded. "Very well. We shall accompany you."

She inclined her head, ever so slightly. "Thank you, Sergeant."

As they exited the manor into the snow-blanketed courtyard, she felt for the satchel of powders in the pocket of her coat. She took no pleasure in the deception she must play, but neither did she lament it overmuch. For all she knew, Rudolfo pined for an heir. But her father's work must be done with discretion. Whatever his strategy ultimately was, it required secrecy and care.

So I will deceive the man I marry.

Of course, she'd always known that if she married, deception would be required of her.

She was her father's daughter.

Neb

Neb waited near Petronus's tent. In the last few weeks, the old man had used the tent more and more for work. Eventually, it made more sense for Neb to stay with some of the other young men.

Neb hadn't expected the response to the proclamation. He wasn't sure what to expect, but the sudden convergence of three armies upon the new Pope was an alarming outcome. When the crowd broke and all that remained were the Marsh King, Rudolfo and Queen Meirov, Petronus walked away with them while they talked in low voices. Neb returned to the camp, and after a dinner that he'd barely touched, he waited there in the snow.

Finally, the old man arrived. He saw the boy and offered a grim smile. "It had to be done, Neb," he said.

Neb nodded. "I am sorry for it."

Petronus pulled open the flap to his tent. "You may be. But it's unnecessary." He paused, half in and half out of his tent. "But I do wonder what else you've seen in your dreams."

He couldn't bring himself to tell him. "Nothing that makes any sense," he finally said. "You should rest, Excellency."

Petronus nodded. "Good night, then."

After the old man slipped into the tent, Neb wandered through the camp.

The workers were snoring in their tents, the small Androfrancine heaters venting steam into the cold air through long brass chimneys. Otherwise, the camp was quiet. With the snow falling now, Neb wasn't sure how long they could hold out. With Petronus firmly rooted in Windwir, there would be no more supply wagons from Sethbert. But with Petronus proclaimed, they would have access to the funds in House Li Tam's Androfrancine accounts. The Entrolusian sentries were now simply replaced with Marshfolk or Gypsy Scouts. And he suspected Rudolfo's Wandering Army was on the march.

Thinking of the Marshfolk brought memories of the girl back to him. He couldn't push her far from his mind—she invaded regularly.

He'd already felt drawn to her, but the kiss sealed it. He wondered what she was doing now and if he would see her again. She said he would, but Neb took little at face value these days. For instance, this Rudolfo. On the surface he seemed a fop, but up close, Neb saw steel in that man's eyes. It made him grateful that Petronus had given him the guardianship, and even more grateful that Petronus had put the metal man in the Gypsy King's care.

Neb wandered past the edges of the camp. The moon was up again, high above now, blue flecked with green. Some days the Moon Wizard's tower was barely visible, but only when the moon was low and nearby.

Of course the Moon Wizard was a distant memory from the First World. And all of the books containing the legends of his exploits were ash now. Brother Hebda had once shown him a parchment of an early text about the Czarist Lunar Expedition from the world before the time of P'Andro Whym. They had been talking and walking during one of his father's visits.

"I want to do what you do," Neb said. He'd not been allowed to touch the parchment, but he'd leaned in close to study it well. "I want to find the lost parchments of the Old World."

A shadow formed on Brother Hebda's face. "Not all of them *should* be found," he mumbled in a low voice.

"Brother Hebda?"

He looked up. "I'm sorry, Neb. I'm a bit distracted tonight. I think we found something that would be better off unfound."

Neb looked up at him. "What is it?"

Brother Hebda shook his head. "I don't know. And if I did, I couldn't tell you. But I have a bad feeling."

His father had been right.

Neb heard a low, familiar voice.

"Nebios ben Hebda." He could smell the musky earth smell of her, and without warning he felt warm lips brushing across his cheek. "The Marsh King is very pleased with you," she said.

He jumped at the kiss. At night, the magicks were virtually impenetrable. "Winters?"

But she was already off and running back into the night.

Vlad Li Tam

Vlad Li Tam smiled and sipped at the kallaberry smoke through the long stem of his pipe. He'd replayed the day's events again and again and could not be more pleased. When he'd finally left, Rudolfo, Meirov and the Marsh King had been discussing strategy for the night's work.

Now all he needed to do was wait.

"Obviously my fiftieth son did very well with the ring."

The aide nodded. "He did, Lord."

"I have fine, strong children." He closed his eyes, feeling the smoke lift him. But he wondered if the smoke would lift him past what was coming tonight.

"Your children are legendary, Lord," the aide said. "There is also word from your thirty-seventh son. He rides with Resolute the First."

Vlad Li exhaled the smoke. "He'll arrive to a surprise tomorrow."

"He has a good source on the Guard," the aide said. "He will feed us what he can on their movement and strategy."

Vlad Li Tam pondered this. "Oriv's contingent of Gray Guard is too small to do much beyond protect him. Still, knowing their location will be useful. And perhaps we'll glean something from his parley with Sethbert."

But he wondered how long Oriv would hang on to what small foothold he had now that Petronus had proclaimed himself. Certainly there would be some of the Androfrancine Remnant that remembered Petronus, but the fact that he'd faked his own death thirty years ago would turn some away. It was certainly a challenge to Androfrancine Law. No Pope had ever quit before, let alone gone to such lengths to do so.

But bringing one back from the dead had proven to require equal lengths. Petronus had resisted at every turn. Vlad Li Tam's betrayal had been quietly arranged. A new ring forged with a bit of the Fargoer's steel he'd kept for such an occasion along with specifications for the ring that he had found in the Androfrancines' very own library nearly thirty years ago.

He wasn't sure how the Marshfolk and Sethbert played into it, but Vlad Li Tam sensed a strategy alongside his own—something that even overlapped his own schemes. Scraps of it drifted to the surface from time to time.

His own part was complex. But this other strategy was as elaborate as a Whymer Maze, he knew that much. And he knew that the Androfrancines had been afraid of something. Their quiet, somber tones as they discussed the need for a strong leader, for a new guardian of the light, set apart from the rest of the world.

He took another pull from his pipe, listening to the crackle of the dried berries as they burned beneath the match his servant held. "We will return to the Emerald Coast tomorrow," Vlad said.

Already, he knew his iron armada had redeployed, blockading the river and seaports throughout the Entrolusian Delta. Sethbert's reinforcements would come by foot, and his supply chain would come by land now rather than by water. The lines of war had not been clearly drawn, but at the very least he could see the shape and size of what loomed ahead.

If Rudolfo was as strong as Vlad had made him to be, the war would soon be behind him. The library would be underway. The Order would limp to the shadows and simply die of its wound. His daughter would raise a child that mixed the Gypsy King's strength with the cunning of the Tam. The light would flicker but would not go out.

But at what cost?

Vlad Li Tam sighed and sipped his pipe again.

Chapter

24

Rudolfo

Rudolfo crouched at the forest line and felt the magicks take him. Twice now the unseemly task fell to him, and as much as he disliked it, it was necessary and practical if he were to accompany his men on the raid.

As if reading his mind, Gregoric shifted uncomfortably beside him, and Rudolfo heard the muffled crunch of pine needles. "I wish you'd reconsider, Rudolfo," the first captain said, voice muffled with the magicks. He'd dropped the title . . . something he only did when he was speaking more as friend than soldier.

Rudolfo looked at the patch of night where Gregoric crouched. "You've known me for how long, Gregoric?"

"All of my life."

He nodded. "Then you've known what I would do since we crafted the strategy for tonight's work."

Rudolfo felt a hand on his shoulder. "Aye," Gregoric said, "I've known it. But the world has changed, and so has your role in it."

Change is the path life takes, Rudolfo thought, remembering the words of P'Andro Whym. "You suggest that for the benefit of the library, I take less risk?"

"Not just the library," Gregoric said. "All that's left of the Androfrancines is in your care and in the care of your Nine-fold Forest Houses. You've also a wife and a people to think of now." Gregoric paused, and Rudolfo could read the hesitation in his voice. "If you fall," the first captain said, "this war will be over for us. If you fall, what's left of the light may go out."

Rudolfo loosened the twin scout blades in their sheaths at his belt. He preferred his long, narrow sword, but the magicks were better suited for knife-fighting, especially in the close quarters they allowed. "I will not fall, Gregoric," he said in a low voice.

Rudolfo heard the thunder now, building in the north, and waited. When the Marsh King's army appeared, moving fast and low across the plains and bathed in the blue green light of the moon, it looked like a black ocean rolling across the land. They rode silently, even Hanric, bearing down on the Entrolusian advance camps. Rudolfo stood and stretched. He could feel the magicks in his blood now, itching beneath his skin. He could smell the sweat of the horses behind him, mingled with the scent of ash and snow.

The Entrolusians had expected the attack. They'd leaked word to one of the spies they'd turned and had given him time to get that word to Lysias.

The first Entrolusian advance camp moved to third alarm

and launched their birds long before the Marsh King's army poured over them.

Farther west, another camp went into alarm, and Rudolfo smiled. That would be Meirov's rangers.

"It's time," Rudolfo said, drawing his knives and tucking them underneath his arms, blades pointing behind him.

Gregoric whistled, and the squad moved out.

They ran south and east, the magicks muffling their boots as they whispered across the snow. Rudolfo felt his heart pumping, and the darkness melted back to a gray light as his eyes adjusted to the powders. He could hear the fighting now in the front lines and he picked up his pace, watching the open ground vanish between him and the far side of the meadow.

They hit the forest and spread out, adjusting their course to avoid the pockets of infantry racing toward the front lines.

As they ran, they clicked their tongues lightly against the roofs of their mouths from time to time—the slightest of sound, but with the amplification of their hearing, it was enough to get a sense of their loose formation. Rudolfo stayed in the center and made no sound at all.

Two leagues slipped past in the span of minutes, and they widened their circle in order to flank Sethbert's camp. If Vlad Li Tam's source in that camp spoke true, the mechanicals were stored in the center, near the tents of the Delta Scouts and not far from Sethbert's massive canvas palace.

Behind them, the sounds of fighting grew. It was a simple bit of misdirection, Rudolfo realized, that he hoped Lysias would fall for. They had counted on the mechanicals being guarded, but expected the Entrolusian general to shift resources to Sethbert when the bird arrived.

They rallied at the pile of moss-covered boulders Gregoric had picked for them during his reconnaissance. Rudolfo watched the small bird materialize seemingly out of air. It fluttered in invisible hands before Gregoric released it.

They'd captured one of Lysias's small messengers earlier in the week, and Vlad Li Tam had helped forge the coded message. The urgency of the message, delivered in the midst of an attack on the Entrolusian front lines, should be enough to give them the opening they needed.

Unless, Rudolfo thought, Sethbert had so eroded Lysias's loyalty that the general refused to intervene. But he counted on Lysias's academy training for this. No general from that austere school needed loyalty to do his job, and Rudolfo's strategy relied upon that.

They waited while the bird shot up, then found its mark. The camp was already at third alarm, bustling with activity as fresh squads of magicked scouts raced north to the fighting and took up positions to reinforce the camp's perimeter. But Rudolfo's squad was already inside that perimeter, slipping in through the temporary hole Lord Tam's man had arranged.

Huddled near the boulders, they waited.

Finally, Gregoric's hand pressed the small of Rudolfo's back. *He's taken the bait,* his fingers tapped.

Rudolfo twisted and touched Gregoric's shoulder. *Excellent,* he answered. *Give the whistle when you will.*

He could hear Lysias shouting now, and knew that the Overseer's tent would now be their defensive center. More reinforcements rushed past them into the night, some plain and some with the acrid odor of fresh magicks upon them.

Rudolfo held his breath until they passed.

After they'd gone, Gregoric whistled the first three bars of the First Hymn of the Wandering Army. He whistled it at a pitch Rudolfo's heightened senses could barely perceive. Then, they were off and running again for the center of camp. Spread out, they rushed in, dodging and weaving in and out of people.

"Scouts in the camp," a voice cried out. Other voices joined in and Rudolfo heard the snicker of steel through cloth and skin, the rasp of metal on metal as blades slid past blades and into flesh.

They did not stop, they did not even slow. They pressed, and when an obstacle presented itself they cut through it or went over it. As they ran, Gregoric's sappers spread out into the camp to light their fires.

Gregoric and Rudolfo cut through the back of the mechoservitor tent while the others moved around it and dispatched the distracted guards. Already the shouts spread, and it would only be moments before they realized that the threat against Sethbert had been a Gypsy ruse.

"Mechoservitors arise," Rudolfo said in a low voice. Scattered throughout the tent, amber eyes fluttered open and gears purred as the room rustled.

"We are the property of the Androfrancine Order," one of the mechoservitors said, steam hissing from its exhaust grate.

"I am Lord Rudolfo of the Ninefold Forest Houses, General of the Wandering Army. I am the duly appointed guardian of Windwir, established in accordance with Article Fifteen of the Precepts of Order," Rudolfo said slowly, reciting the words Petronus had given him. By all the Gods, he hoped they worked. "Section three, item six grants me the authority to redirect Androfrancine personnel and property as needed for the protection of the light." Outside the tent, the sounds of fighting erupted. It lent urgency to his voice. "You are ordered to return to what remains of the Great Library at top running speed. You are not to stop. You are to disregard further orders until these orders are carried out completely. Do you understand?"

Thirteen voices echoed in the tent, thirteen forms clicked and clacked to life as they sped into that chaotic night.

In that moment, Rudolfo heard Gregoric cry out.

Vlad Li Tam

Vlad Li Tam did not sleep that night. He rarely did during key moments of strategy. He sat in his tent without the kallaberry pipe and huddled in his blanket, waiting for his aide to bring word.

He'd given his fiftieth son the work he'd trained him for. Of course, when he'd first adopted this particular strategy, his fiftieth son had not been born yet. He'd had no idea which arrow he would fire at this particular target. Ordinarily, a Tam would use others as his arrows, manipulating their environment until they became the right weapon at the right time. But in this regard, he could not afford to let an unknown quantity in the vicinity of Rudolfo after so much work over so many years. So it fell to the only resource a Tam could trust: Family.

He'd sent his son away to earn the knotted cord of a lieutenant in Sethbert's army, setting him apart for the task. And in the fullness of time, Vlad Li Tam raised that hammer in his fist.

So it was that he drove one more nail into Rudolfo's soul—the last one that he would drive, he thought. The rest of it would ripple out now as repercussions, and what he built into his forty-second daughter would be enough to carry things forward.

Their unborn child would inherit the center of the world, and would protect it better than the Androfrancines could.

The tent flap rustled and his aide spoke, thrusting his head into its warm confines. "Your fiftieth son's last words have arrived, Lord Tam."

Last words. Vlad Li Tam reached out and took the rolled parchment. He unrolled it, read it slowly, and then tucked it into his shirt, nestled against his hairless chest. "It is a poem," he said, his voice heavy, "about a son's great love for his father."

The aide bowed his head. "I am sorry for your loss, Lord Tam."

Lord Tam nodded. "Thank you, Aetris."

The tent flap rustled closed and he stretched himself out on his back, staring at the ceiling of his tent as it shifted beneath the snow. It would be at least another hour before he received any confirmation from another source. But his fiftieth son would not have released the bird bearing his last words unless he was certain of the implementation of his own strategy.

He reached up and pressed the note to his chest. His son

was certainly dead by now, and he felt the grief licking at him. When others could see, Vlad Li Tam wore a face of stone, unreadable and unyielding. But here, alone in his tent and without the kallaberry smoke to cut the edge of his pain, Vlad Li Tam wept silently for the son he had killed.

He knew the outcome was worthy of the sacrifice, and he knew his son would have agreed as well, if he'd known what he died to save. But still, Vlad Li Tam felt the ache of that loss, and he hated the powerlessness it visited upon him. It reminded him of another loss that still lay ahead of him on this road.

When the next bird arrived, it bore the news that Vlad Li Tam had expected. He'd gone outside for that one, his breath steaming out into the cold night air as he stamped in the snow. He pressed that message into his aide's hands. "Reply to Petronus with condolences for Rudolfo's loss," he said. "And send the bird to my forty-second daughter."

His aide nodded. "Yes, Lord Tam."

"And spread the word. We strike camp at first light and ride for home."

Vlad Li Tam turned south and east, staring out in the night. The War Sermon had started up at long last, and far away he could see the fires in the Entrolusian camp.

"It is finished," Vlad Li Tam said to the night.

Petronus

Petronus stood with Meirov's rangers and the half-squad of Gypsy Scouts near the crater where the Great Library once stood. They heard them before they saw them, like a wave of sound across the night, a sound like nothing Petronus had heard before. Bellows chugged, gears hummed and oiled legs pumped. It was as if a room of farmers all worked their shears in perfect time together, low and steady amid the chaotic sounds of combat.

He squinted in the direction of the sound, and saw what could have been the dancing of ghost-lights or fireflies if he hadn't known better of this part of the world and time of the year. And if they hadn't flown in thirteen perfect pairs, moving in formation at the same speed.

Petronus watched as they drew near, moving twice the speed of a horse . . . possibly faster. The moonlight washed them in tones of blue and green, casting an eerie light around them as they moved sure-footed across the snow.

They spilled into the crater before halting, and Petronus raised his hands as the rangers counted them. "Behold," he said, "I am called Petronus, King of Windwir and Holy See of the Androfrancine Order."

"Petronus," one of the mechoservitors started, "sixty-third in succession, was the eighth Pope to be assassinated in the Enlightened History of the Androfrancine Order."

"A deception," he said. He held up the ring. "I bear the ring of P'Andro Whym."

The mechoservitors bowed their heads. Petronus had never seen anything like them. Tall and slender, they stood just half a head higher than a man. Their long arms ended in equally long fingers, and the metal plating that lay over the top of their metallic skeleton shifted and moved with the working bellows underneath. A small grate in the center of their backs emitted gouts of steam.

Back when young Charles had worked on them, Petronus remembered that the power was the biggest challenge. How long had that enormous fire gotten them? Three minutes? Five? He couldn't remember now, but it was a massive amount of energy just to power the head and torso.

Somehow, they'd solved it. Something inside of these mechoservitors burned hot enough to boil the steam and power them.

Petronus looked out on the crowd of metal faces. "I am commending you to the care of General Rudolfo of the Wandering Army. All that remains of Windwir's Great Library is housed in your memory scrolls. Rudolfo will take you to Isaak—Mechoservitor Number Three—and you will work with him for the restoration of the library. Do you understand your instructions?" He held up the ring, and their amber eyes followed it.

"Yes," they said in a single voice.

"Which of you is familiar with the cartography of the Named Lands? Step forward."

Four of the mechoservitors stepped forward.

"Should trouble arise along the way, you are to rally at the seventh forest manor of the Ninefold Forest Houses. Do you understand?"

They nodded.

"Very well. Until Lord Rudolfo returns, be seated and close your eyes."

They sat, and the dim light of their eyes went out as they simultaneously brought down their metal shutters.

Petronus turned back to the south, waiting.

Thirty minutes later, the first of the Gypsy Scouts returned. They breathed heavily, coughing into the cold air. Surgeons from the Queen of Pylos did the best they could to wash and wrap wounds they could not see, their hands slick with invisible blood.

Five minutes after, another wave arrived, followed closely by the rear guard.

"We lost three for certain," one of the lieutenants said after quickly taking inventory with his men. "Five are unaccounted for, including Gregoric and Rudolfo."

Petronus cursed under his breath and looked toward the south.

Resolute

Pope Resolute the First had entered the Entrolusian camp just hours before the hostilities broke out. Sethbert had received him coldly, making his displeasure of his cousin's decision obvious with every word. "You've left your people without a leader," the Overseer said, his jowls shaking with rage.

"I am the Pope," Resolute said, his own anger flaring. "I will decide what's best for my people."

Four days on the road and his nerves had frayed. And the first news he'd heard upon arriving was that someone claiming to be Petronus was this hidden Pope Vlad Li Tam had spoken of.

Initially, he'd laughed it off. He'd attended Petronus's funeral when he was a younger man. He'd even had a bit of a roll-about with one of the women who had served at the state banquet afterward. Coming back from the dead was not a hallmark of the Androfrancine Papacy.

But when Sethbert assured him that it was true, it had added to his foul mood.

"You may be the Pope," Sethbert had said, his voice low, "but you have *me* to thank for that."

At that point, the alarms had sounded. Not long after, squads of scouts and infantry flooded the Overseer's tent, and Oriv found himself crowded into the corner with his Gray Guard escort.

"We've word from the spies," Lysias said, out of breath as he ducked into the tent. "Rudolfo's Gypsy Scouts are on the hunt."

"On the hunt for what?" Sethbert asked.

Lysias's reply was nearly a sneer. "You," he said, through clenched teeth.

Resolute watched the exchange. Sethbert's command of this man was tenuous at best. It took no expert in statecraft to see that, just as it took no military training to see that the Entrolusian army was divided and growing more so as the winter came on and the pressure increased.

Sethbert bellowed for his sword, and an aide belted it onto him. They heard the sound of fighting grow outside, and Lysias kept himself between Sethbert and the door. A wall of Delta Scouts, magicks shimmering in the lamplight, crouched with ready blades, and Grymlis and the two Gray Guard drew their swords as well. Then, near the back of the tent Resolute heard another sound, and it caught his attention. He'd heard it before, wandering the library, but that seemed impossible to him. Nonetheless, he heard the gears, heard the pumping bellows and the solid sound of metal feet upon the ground.

"Mechoservitors?" He didn't realize he'd said it aloud until he saw Sethbert staring at him.

"What did you say?" Sethbert's face went pale, then a deep rose color replaced it.

"It sounds like mechoservitors, but . . ." Resolute felt the realization of it grip him. Sethbert had told him all had been lost but for the spell-caster.

"They've freed the metal men," a scout said at the door. "They are running north to Windwir."

"It was never about me," Sethbert said in a low voice.

Lysias cursed and stormed from the tent, barking orders. Sethbert followed.

As the tent cleared, Resolute looked to Grymlis. The old Gray Guard captain studied him, and still feeling short-tempered, Oriv snapped at him. "If you've something to say, Captain, say it."

Grymlis pulled himself up. "I *will* say it," he said. "I know Petronus. If he is truly alive, you will be no match for him." The captain's voice dropped. "And I question the viability of a war of succession."

"I concur," he said. But Resolute's doubts went even further than whether or not this war would be viable.

Deeper than that, he questioned whether or not he should fight at all.

Ride to Petronus now, some part of himself said. Do not let this tragedy become worse than it already is.

But even as the thought crossed his mind, he shoved it aside. It couldn't be Petronus. Petronus was dead. And if, somehow, it truly was that long-dead Pope miraculously back from the dead, then it would be a matter for the committee to investigate.

Meanwhile, until such time as a committee could be convened to their work, Resolute would perform his duty for the light.

Chapter

25

Rudolfo

Rudolfo heard Gregoric's cry and leaped toward him, his blades ready. His enhanced vision picked up the outline of a man, crouching and facing him. Rudolfo slowed and stepped to the right and the crouching figure turned with him. As he drew near, he made out the Entrolusian lieutenant's ripped uniform and saw that the officer now held Gypsy blades. The blades turned as if following Rudolfo's movement.

He sees me, Rudolfo thought. Certainly there were sight magicks, but none so powerful as to see a magicked scout. Though there were rumors that the Androfrancines had a magick to undo all magicks. But how would this lieutenant get access to something like that? Those sorts of secrets were gone now with the Great Library, unless Rudolfo managed to bring some of it back. And to do that, he needed Gregoric. And to get Gregoric, he had to kill this man.

Rudolfo charged with his knives out and ready.

The man did not fight like an Entrolusian. He moved too fast, with confidence and skill. Rudolfo heard Gregoric gasping near his feet and pressed the lieutenant back, sparks striking from the knives as they met.

They spun and thrust and slashed at each other, their knives moving in time with one another.

Rudolfo heard commotion outside, and heard the whistle that meant the mechanicals had cleared the edge of camp. It was time to go.

He heard Gregoric sputtering on the tent floor, and realized in an instant that his first captain was trying to give the whistle to pull back. He feinted with one knife, thrust with the other, and gave the whistle for his men to fall back.

The shouting grew nearer and Rudolfo pressed his opponent, bringing his dominant, left-handed knife to bear after setting him up to follow the right. The Entrolusian lieutenant adjusted fast, and Rudolfo felt the skill and strength in his opponent's two hands.

He is better than me, Rudolfo thought, the realization hitting him as solidly as any fist. And he's trying hard not to show me that.

The tent flaps rustled, and two soldiers entered. They were down before Rudolfo could blink, their throats cut with expert precision. He smiled at the work of his Gypsy Scouts even as he cursed their disobedience.

We must flee.

And as if the Entrolusian heard him, he suddenly opened himself. It was not much of an opening—and one that someone less skilled than Rudolfo or his Gypsy Scouts might not have noticed. But it was an opening, and Rudolfo took it even as he wondered why it was offered.

He put the first knife in through the man's kidney, and because it was Gregoric at his feet, he twisted it until the man cried out and dropped his blades. Then he put his other knife into the man's heart, and as he fell, brought the first up and swept it quickly across his throat.

Before the man fell, Rudolfo clicked his tongue and heard three tongues click in reply. He followed the sounds of Gregoric's labored breathing, and sheathed his knives. "Guard me," he hissed to his men.

More soldiers entered the tent, and his Gypsy Scouts dispatched them with quick brutality.

His hands scrambled for Gregoric, found him and lifted him. He couldn't tell if his first captain was conscious, but he found his arm, wet and slippery with blood, and pressed words into it.

Hang on, friend. I'll see you safely home.

Slinging him over his shoulder, bent beneath the weight of him, Rudolfo left through the back of the tent.

He ran as fast as he could, his tongue clacking lightly against the roof of his mouth. The three scouts who'd stayed behind with him spread out so that two were ahead to clear their path and one was behind to guard their flank. They weaved a shifting line, moving to the left, circling back, then moving to the right. It was a chaotic pattern of movement following a path that few could predict.

When they left the camp and slipped into the forest, they were on the southern side of the camp. When they breached the perimeter, outward bound, they were on the western side. Along the way, the forward scouts had killed six and the rear guard just two.

They stopped at the edge of the forest to bandage Gregoric's wounds as best they could.

When they laid him out on the pine-needled floor, the First Captain of the Gypsy Scouts stirred, clutched the front of Rudolfo's scout tunic, and pressed a message into the Gypsy King's neck.

Leave me. I'm finished.

Rudolfo found his shoulder. *Nonsense. You've a war to win for me.*

Gregoric lapsed back into unconsciousness. When the other scouts tried to lift him, Rudolfo's voice was harsher than he intended. "I have him," he said.

His legs and back ached from the run. Even with the magicks, his strength was not sufficiently enhanced to compensate for this. Still, he crouched, rolled Gregoric up and over his shoulder, and lurched to his feet. They ran west along the edge of the forest, cut north and ran along the base of the foothills, then broke cover and ran the open, snow-crusted plain.

They did not stop running again until they reached what had once been the center of Windwir. The Rangers of Pylos stood watching the south, bows drawn, not expecting them from the west. Rudolfo whistled, high and shrill, and other whistles greeted him.

"I've a wounded man," he said as he crested the edge of crater. He shrugged off the rangers when they tried to lift Gregoric from his back, laying him down himself. "Do we have a medico?"

But Rudolfo didn't need a medico to tell him that somewhere along the way another part of the light had been lost from his world.

Jin Li Tam

Jin Li Tam read the note a dozen times before she finally burned it. And even after she burned it, it stayed before her eyes.

It had arrived early that morning on the bird her father knew could always find her, and she was not certain what it meant until she saw the long faces of her escort.

He will need you now, the coded note read. *Comfort him and you will be his right hand.* Then, buried in a deeper code: *Grieve your brother's sacrifice for the light.*

When she asked the Gypsy Scouts about their downcast countenance, they told her of Gregoric's death, and suddenly the meaning of her father's note struck home. She'd gone to her tent then, and for the first time she could remember, she cried silently in the manner becoming of a daughter of Vlad Li Tam.

She had no grief for her brother. Instead, she felt a rage that spilled over to flood her entire family, her father most of all. The strategy was clear to her, certainly. A man is shaped by the events of his life. The Francines taught this and it made sense, just as they also taught that a man or a group or even a nation could be moved by stimulating their lives in the moments that they needed it. A bit of grief to build their compassion, a bit of loss to instill a value of gratitude, an opportunity for vengeance to temper wrath.

And yet, despite the clarity of strategic intent, she found herself suddenly full of doubt. Her father's work consisted of dozens of living, breathing games of queen's war, the move in this game connected in some way to the move in another. And she had believed—had been taught to believe—that his work was in service to the light, darker in many ways than the work of the Androfrancine Order, but critical for the Named Lands to never go the way of the Old World.

But now, for some reason, his work enraged her. And at the heart of it, it was the perception of Rudolfo's mistreatment at her father's hands.

Is this what love is? If so, she struggled to find anything useful in it. Love, she thought, should be whatever strategy best protected the greatest good. And who was she to question her father's will? For all she knew, he merely added to a work his own father had carried forward. Who was she to question the work of House Li Tam?

This work will keep light in the world. And before she'd seen that pillar of smoke what seemed so long ago, she would've said without hesitation that the nobility of that end justified any and all means. Now, though, she hesitated.

When she knew Rudolfo was a few hours away, she cleaned herself and washed the red from her eyes and dressed in simple woolens and boots. Tonight, she would do her work—her part in her father's work—but she would not dress it up.

Jin Li Tam went to the edge of camp with the others, including Isaak, and watched the line of metal men running in perfect synchronicity across the white ground. Alongside and behind them, as if riding herd, the Gypsy Scouts rode their horses hard. For the first time since meeting him, she could not pick her betrothed out of the group of riders.

Even when they pulled up, she did not recognize him at first. When he slid from the saddle and handed his reins to a waiting aide, she finally spotted him. But she stayed at the edge and watched him, gathering what she could.

He was not himself. He walked more slowly, his shoulders

slouched, and his face was hard and tired and unspeakably sad. His eyes were rimmed red with exhaustion, and the line of his jaw was tense. He wore the winter woolens of a Gypsy Scout, and the dark clothes were stained with darker patches that she knew must be blood. She wondered if that blood was Gregoric's.

She watched him pass instructions to another captain, and finally she could wait no longer. She walked out to him, and when he looked up at her, his expression stopped her in her tracks.

In that moment, something broke inside of her and a realization dawned within her—a certainty took shape—but she pushed it aside. After, she told herself, I will reflect upon this.

He did not express any surprise at seeing her so far afield from the seventh forest manor, and he only nodded and grunted when she told him she'd brought Isaak to look after the other mechoservitors.

She repeated this to the captain who waved Isaak over, but before the metal man reached his kind, Jin Li Tam had grabbed Rudolfo's hand and pulled him after her. He did not resist.

She called for a tub and hot water, for food and drink, and while the servants laid these things out, she sat Rudolfo on the wide cot and pulled at his boots.

The loss was hard upon him, she saw, and soon he'd move along that Fivefold Path of Grief the Francines spoke of. Now, he shook his head and mumbled and kept his eyes cast down and away from her.

Still, he stayed pliant, even lowering himself into the hot bath and suffering her to wash his friend's blood from him. After, as if he were a child, she dried him with thick, heated towels and wrapped him into a heavy cotton robe.

While he sat at the cot and nibbled halfheartedly at a piece of cheese she'd sliced for him, she turned her back to him and poured his brandy.

Swallowing against the lump in her throat, she stirred in the first of the powders. Then she sat with him, forcing him to eat more and to drink down the warm spiced liquor.

After, she lay him back in the bed, blew out the lamps and crawled in beside him. Holding him close, she stroked his curly hair and ran her hands around the back of his neck until he fell asleep.

She lay awake a long time after, thinking of what was to come. She waited the full three hours, then stripped and pressed herself close to him, stroking him and kissing his neck.

When he responded, she pushed open his robe and crawled onto him, taking him into her and finding a rhythm that could sustain them both.

He clung to her but did not make a sound, even at the end. After, he fell into a deep sleep clutching tightly to her.

But Jin Li Tam did not sleep. Instead, she thought about the new certainty she had found when she first saw Rudolfo in his grief, and she knew that she had transcended her father's will.

This child is not for you, she told her father deep in the places of her heart where she was afraid to go. This child is *never* for you.

She rolled over and faced Rudolfo, feeling the heat of his breath against her neck as he moved in his sleep to embrace her.

"For you," she said. "Only you."

As if answering, Rudolfo mumbled.

Jin Li Tam pulled him close and kissed his cheek.

And finally, sleep chased her down into her restless dreams.

Petronus

The men gathered around Petronus in the galley tent, and he looked up with raised eyebrows. Everywhere he went now, magicked scouts moved around him. Meirov's personal Border Rangers formed his private escort. Someone had even dug up a fancy white and blue and purple robe—from the smell of it, a relic from an attic. Petronus had accepted the gift, but knew he'd not wear it. All he'd brought himself to wear so far was the ring.

"Excellency," the group's leader said with a brisk bow. "We beg audience with you."

Petronus chuckled. "You need not start begging now, Garver. Regardless of recent events, I am still myself."

Garver looked around at his companions, twisting his knit cap in his hands. "Yes, Excellency."

Petronus sighed. Everything had changed, and part of him resented the boy, Neb, for his place in that, though he knew it was a road he would've walked with or without the boy. And the Marsh King's role in this was also something he couldn't afford to forget. Why were the Marshers suddenly supporting the Order? Or were they simply supportive of Rudolfo?

He looked up at the men, and lowered his spoon back into the bowl of cooked oats. They'd tried to give him a bigger tent and better meals to go with his fancy robe, but he'd refused those, insisting that he be treated as every other worker. He'd continued to make his rounds, though now under escort, and even stopped to help dig the bones from the frozen ground.

"What can I do for you, Garver?" he finally asked.

The man was clearly uncomfortable now. Before the proclamation he'd had no difficulty speaking his mind to Petronus, and the sudden shift reminded Petronus that this role he now played honored a lie he did not believe in. That somehow his station in the Order set him apart in some way.

Petronus looked across to Neb. The boy sat quietly, looking from Petronus to the group.

Petronus sighed again. "You had no trouble speaking plainly when the latrines needed redigging or when the supply wagon came up short on flour and salt." He offered the best smile he could. "Nothing has changed."

Everything has changed.

Finally, Garver spoke up. "Excellency, we know how important this work is to you, and we've come up with a plan to finish by early spring if the winter is as mild as the past three. We can rotate men and women into the camp just as we've been doing. The new supplies are coming in well, and the workers are overwhelmed by the Order's generous wage."

Petronus nodded. "Excellent." But the look on Garver's face told him that he'd not gotten to a point he was afraid of raising. "And the problem is . . . ?" He let the words trail off.

"I don't know how to say this, Excellency," Garver said, looking around to his companions for moral support. Petronus followed his gaze. He'd brought the best of the lot with him, the smartest and most able.

"Say it plainly, Garver, like you did four nights past in the council tents when we talked about curtailing the hunting because of the armies."

Garver nodded. "Very well, Excellency. We don't need you here anymore." He flushed. "Not to say we don't want you. You've done right by us and by your kin. But we don't think it proper for our Pope and King to dig graves in the snow."

"And I think it's quite proper," Petronus said, feeling the anger rise quickly in him.

Garver swallowed, eyes shifting to the left and right again. "You mistake my meaning, Lord, but it's from my poor choice of words. Any of us here can work a shovel or wheelbarrow. But only one of us can be the Pope." He took a deep breath before continuing. "The world just lost a Pope and does not need to lose another. The fighting has stepped up. You will be safer elsewhere and able to focus on your work."

Petronus studied the faces of each man around him, including the rangers. None of them looked surprised or uncertain. None of them looked as if they were ready to disagree. And if he were honest with himself, he wasn't sure he could disagree with that wisdom either.

"What would you propose?"

Garver released his held breath. "Appoint someone to lead

this effort in your stead. Work with them by the bird if you must, but don't overlook your other responsibilities. The Named Lands need their Pope."

Petronus sighed. "Very well. I'll think on it and we'll discuss it at council tomorrow. Is that reasonable?"

Garver nodded. "Thank you, Excellency."

"Thank you."

After they left, he looked across to Neb. "What do you think?"

Neb chewed a piece of bread, a thoughtful look on his face. "I think they're right, Excellency."

Petronus rolled his eyes. "Not you, too."

Neb grinned but the grin faded quickly. "I think Sethbert's men will come for you here at some point. Or try to. There is no dispute for the ring and the scepter if you are not alive. But more than that, I'm certain you're going to need to convene a Council of Bishops under Holy Unction. There is much work to do beyond digging these graves."

Petronus leaned back, realizing for the first time how much the boy had grown these past few months. Well-spoken and wise, firmly rooted in a classical Androfrancine education and yet so young. "And who do you think I should put in charge of this operation?"

He shrugged. "Rudolfo is in charge, by proxy, as the Guardian. He or one his officers can provide the military support and council we need. You could appoint Garver or one of the others to oversee the gravedigging and the day-to-day logistics of running the camp."

Petronus shook his head. "I'd want someone from the Order for that."

Neb shrugged. "I don't know then. Most of the Androfrancines went to the Summer Papal Palace. There are a few left, but I don't know them."

Petronus smiled. "How strongly do you concur with Garver's recommendation?"

Neb scowled, his brow creasing. "I think you can do more away from here, in a safer place. Regardless of what we believe, there is another Pope competing for authority and attention, and the only way to prevail is to be a better, stronger Pope than he." He paused, and his face softened as he shrugged again. "I concur strongly, I guess."

Petronus stood. "Then you'd best find new robes, Neb."

Neb looked at him, confusion clouding his face.

"I've just made you my aide. Your first assignment is the completion of the work here. Afterwards, you will join me in the Ninefold Forest to assist with the restoration of the Great Library."

The boy was still sputtering and red-faced when Petronus left the galley, chuckling. He hoped he was making a good decision. He'd always been impeccably good at picking out the shepherds from the sheep, but this shepherd was terribly young and these sheep were a motley herd.

Still, the boy had seen the work of Xhum Y'Zir and lived to tell it. He'd been the guest of the Marsh King and the subject of his War Sermons. He'd proclaimed a Pope and buried his own dead.

But more than that, he'd known when to keep Petronus's secret, and had known even better than Petronus when it was time to break that secret onto the world.

That alone was enough for Petronus to trust him with the graves of Windwir.

Neb

Petronus rode out three days later. Neb watched him and his escort leave the plains of Windwir and slip into the northern forests. There had really been no time for him to adjust to this new responsibility. But whenever he felt the panic rise in his chest, Neb remembered what Petronus had said to him.

"You've watched everything I do here," Petronus told him that first night after Neb had asked him to reconsider his decision to put him in charge. "You won't need to deal with the guard shifts or any other military matters. Just keep the work moving and the workers supported. Anything that can't wait a day or two for a bird, decide by council or ask whoever Rudolfo attaches to you." Then the old man had paused, smiled, and put a hand on Neb's shoulder. "I know this is a lot. But I would not give you more than I thought you could handle." And finally, he'd leaned forward, his voice low. "You of all people understand why we must finish this work."

Neb had nodded, and from then on he'd spent every waking moment with Petronus, following him everywhere he went and asking him every question that he could imagine.

Now, three days later, he felt uncertain all over again. After Petronus vanished, he sent the workers back to their tasks. None of them balked. Then he checked the supply wagon schedule, the artifact wagon and the galley. While at the galley he had the cook pack him a lunch, and he started walking the line, surveying the effort remaining. Having to move the snow first was extending the time, and though the cold wasn't yet unbearable, they'd still had to shorten the shifts considerably. One of Neb's biggest hopes was that Petronus would issue a plea for help with the gravedigging effort.

Neb walked out each direction, trying to keep the hem of his new robes up off the snow as he went. They had carved Windwir into quadrants. The city proper—those parts within the walls—was the inner layer, quartered by north, south, east and west. Most of that section had been taken care of before the snow fell to take advantage of finding any artifacts while the ground was clear. Beyond the city itself, they quartered the outer layer. They'd finished the eastern and southern quadrants, but uncertainty about the Marsh King's intentions—regardless of his words—had kept them from the north, and they were already digging trenches in the western quarter in preparation for the work beginning there.

By the time Neb reached the outer northern quadrant, he was ready to eat. He cleared a small patch of ground beneath a tree and pulled out two pieces of pan-fried bread and a slice of lamb. He ate the sandwich, sipping from his canteen between bites, and wondered for the twentieth time that day what the Marsh girl Winters might be doing right now and whether or not she wondered about him and when he would see her again.

He felt himself blush, and forced his mind back to the plains. She popped into his head more and more and he wasn't sure why. He'd even dreamed about her twice. He was talking to Brother Hebda about the Churning Wastes and he saw her just outside the window, standing beneath a solitary pine tree in a vast wasteland, watching him with a strange smile on her dirty face.

Suddenly, someone sneezed, loudly, and Neb jumped. He looked around and saw no one.

"I know you're there," he said.

Silence.

"You are a Marsher Scout," he said. And suddenly a thought occurred to him. "You are the same Marsher Scout that took me to your king."

Still, no answer. Neb shifted, wondering if he should ask what he wanted to ask next. He tried to push it aside, but couldn't. "Do you know the girl Winters?" he asked, feeling his face and ears go red.

This time, he heard a grunt. Neb decided to assume it was in the affirmative. "Tell her that Nebios ben Hebda saw her beneath the tree in the Churning Wastes."

Another grunt.

Neb drew an apple out of his pouch and munched on it. Then, as if an afterthought, he pulled another. "Here," he said, holding it up. "Catch." He tossed it in the direction of the grunt and watched it melt into nothingness as the scout snatched it from the air.

Silently, they ate their apples. Then Neb stood up and stretched. "I have to get back," he said. But as soon as he said it, he felt awkward. "Give her that message, please."

One last grunt, and Neb turned and left the forest. All the way back, he stopped periodically and scanned the snow for other sets of footprints. There had been enough foot traffic with the fighting and the patrols that he really couldn't tell.

Was it possible that the scout had followed him all morning? Maybe he was still out there, carefully walking in Neb's own footprints, hanging back but never letting the boy leave his sight.

Could it be that the Marsh King had assigned Neb a bodyguard? Unlikely. More likely, he was a scout on patrol or posted on the perimeter.

Still, the thought of that level of attention from a king made him smile. It wasn't so long ago that the only kings he knew were in books.

Neb looked to the sky, saw that it was growing white, and moved eastward toward the river, putting his mind to the work ahead.

Chapter

26

Rudolfo

Spring came early to the Named Lands in rare fashion, and war moved on around it. For Rudolfo, the months had been a blur. He'd divided his time between Windwir and the front as the war moved southwest and Sethbert's allies fell back. He'd lost a good portion of his Wandering Army holding Rachyl's Bridge on the second river, connecting Pylos to the Entrolusian Delta. They'd held their first true parley just after that, though no terms had been reached. And the two Popes were starkly contrasted—Resolute in his fine, white linens and Petronus in his simple brown hermit's robe—as they spoke in voices that were sometimes hushed, sometimes raised.

Now, Rudolfo rode with Petronus from the seventh forest manor to Windwir so they could escort Neb back with that work finished. He'd spent three rather luxurious days with his betrothed, and he found it more satisfying than anything he had ever known. Since Gregoric's death, her strength had become his own. It was a strange sensation. For so long, it had been Gregoric as his right hand and he'd never imagined this level of partnership possible. But there was a reckless joy in this new arrangement. She had the strength and spirit of a Gypsy Scout, the mind and strategy of a general. He admired her skills of statecraft and misdirection. And for all of that, she was a formidable lover as well.

Still, he carried the loss of his friend near at all times. They'd been like brothers for longer than he had memory, and the world did not make sense without him in it. Perhaps because it was combined with the loss of Windwir that this particular death had struck him so hard. Though the Francines would say that all loss connected back to earlier losses, and that Gregoric represented the last vestiges of a time in Rudolfo's life when he was innocent and responsible for nothing.

As he rode, he looked up to the hill above the town. Most of it had been cleared now that the snow was gone, and he expected the workers he'd hired to level it and start digging the basements within the next week. The stones were already being cut in the shallow hills at the base of the Dragon's Spine. He had deferred to Petronus on all matters regarding the library, but the Pope had been more concerned about planning the council of bishops than plodding through the details of the restoration. Isaak continued the work of identifying the resources that hadn't already gone to the Summer Papal Palace. They'd located a small private library on the Emerald Coasts that would now be en route with the passing of the snow.

Rudolfo watched the men moving on the hill and saw the glint of light on steel, the morning sun reflecting off Isaak's metal head. He turned in his saddle to stare at the narrow glass door of his bedchamber's balcony. Wrapped in a red silk sheet, Jin Li Tam stood in the doorway and watched him leave.

He smiled and whistled his horse forward to catch up with Petronus.

The old man had aged in the last handful of months, but it was no wonder. The skill with which he moved across the political landscape impressed Rudolfo, but it had to take a toll. The Named Lands were locked in its fiercest conflict since the settlers had come across the Keeper's Wall.

Rudolfo saw that the Pope was also looking to the hill. "Three years by our best estimates," he said. "But Isaak is confident that we can restore nearly forty percent. He's having the mechanicals double check their inventories."

Petronus nodded. "I'm impressed with his work."

Rudolfo smiled at this. "He is a marvel. They all are."

"Yes," the Pope said, "but Isaak is different from the others. They're more reserved. They don't seem to have the empathetic capacity that he does."

Rudolfo had noticed this as well. The other mechoservitors spoke when spoken to for the most part and kept to themselves. They also hadn't clothed themselves and hadn't taken on names, preferring their numeric designations. Yet oddly enough, they looked to Isaak as their leader.

"I think Windwir changed him as it changed all of us."

Petronus sighed. "More, I would suspect."

Rudolfo agreed. "I tried to convince him again yesterday that he should have one of the other mechoservitors fix his leg. He said he wanted the limp as a reminder of what he had done."

Petronus scowled. "You reminded him, I'm sure, that Sethbert did this?"

"Yes."

Petronus's brows furrowed. "Where is Sethbert these days?"

"He's back in the City States dealing with insurrection. Tam's blockade has sown its discord. Lysias continues to hold their borders up, but between Pylos and the Wandering

Army, it's starting to wear them down." He chuckled, but it was a dark laugh. "Turam's nearly done for; the crown prince has pulled back to reconsider his commitment." Rudolfo had been in communication with the Marsh King, but she had insisted on staying near Windwir until the graves were filled in. He hoped to spend at least some time trying to convince her that now, with that work finished, they could use her military leverage in the southern lands.

He suspected that the Marsh King's forces could end this war and bring about successful parley. But she'd surprised him by her refusal to leave that work. At first, he'd thought it had to do with the gravedigging.

But the last few times he'd visited Neb, the boy had remarked that he thought he was being followed by Marsh Scouts. Rudolfo saw a connection of some kind there. After all, Neb was supposedly the dreaming boy mentioned in the Marsh King's War Sermon.

Still, if it was the boy she was concerned about, he hoped that she would trust him and his Gypsy Scouts to make sure Neb was well cared for.

Rudolfo started, suddenly realizing that Petronus had spoken. He looked up. "I'm sorry?"

"I said: Perhaps this insurrection will do our work for us."

Rudolfo nodded. "I hope so."

But as he rode south, Rudolfo doubted it could be so simple as that.

Jín Li Tam

Jin Li Tam slipped from the manor into the afternoon light. She used one of the many concealed passageways and doors within the large house after telling her escort that she would be bathing. She'd even filled the large marble tub with hot water and perfumed oils. After, she'd taken first one passage, then a ladder down to the basement, its tunnels eventually bringing her to the manor's low stone wall beyond its northern gardens.

Eyes constantly scanning for watchers, she'd slipped out of a hidden gate she found during her winter reconnaissance of the manor.

She wore nondescript robes and sturdy boots to guard against mud and melting snow. She moved quickly over the ground.

When she reached the River Woman's hut beyond the town, she waited in shadows and watched to be sure that the old alchemist was indeed alone with her cats.

Last night, she'd used the last of the powders and so far, she'd not had the result she was looking for. Twice since winter she'd thought perhaps it had taken, but both times came to nothing. Today, she would decide whether or not she should keep trying.

It was the longest winter she'd ever experienced, a cold and white expanse of time largely spent indoors. The only bright patches were the few days Rudolfo managed to spend with her as he moved between Windwir, the front and the work Petronus and Isaak were doing. She wasn't accustomed to a cold so bitter that it could freeze a river in its track. She wasn't accustomed to a house becoming a cage.

Certainly, Rudolfo would not hold her. But where else could she go?

From time to time, the tropic warmth of her father's house sprang to mind but she knew she could not face him. After Gregoric's death, she'd stopped returning House Li Tam messages, even those from her brothers and sisters as they did their part in her father's work. Eventually, the messages stopped coming altogether.

It was a silence she'd never experienced, and a part of her grieved it but another part felt a freedom growing within her beyond anything she had ever known.

She'd always prided herself on being her own woman, a strong woman, self-contained and able to hold her own against any circumstances. But as the time marched on away from the Desolation of Windwir, from her discovery of her father's hand in Rudolfo's life and her realization that she herself was a critical component of that work, she saw clearly now that she had never been her own woman. She'd been her father's daughter and nothing more. All of these events had shown her that this was no longer enough, that there actually could be a higher calling than the Tam matrix.

To her father's credit, he'd not pressed her. But perhaps, she thought, this too is what he wove into the elaborate tapestry that he and all of those other fathers before him had created.

Smoke leaked from the chimney of the small hut, and she saw movement inside. Jin Li Tam broke her cover and walked the muddy path up to the porch, knocking lightly on the door.

The River Woman met her with a smile. "Lady Tam," she said, sounding delighted to see her. "Please come in. I've just put on some tea."

Jin kicked off her boots on the porch, then concealed them behind a chair. "Thank you," she said.

Once inside, she saw that the small cottage and its connected shop was even more full than the usual sacks and jars, overflowing from the counters onto the table and stacked in some instances to half her height.

"War is tragic but good for business," the River Woman said. "Magicks for hooves, magicks for men, magicks for blades and interrogation. Even the physicians have orders in, anticipating their own work ahead." The woman clucked. "Men and their violence," she said. She poured tea into two ceramic cups and placed one in front of Jin Li Tam. "But enough of death," the River Woman said as she sat down across from her. "Let's talk of life."

Jin Li Tam nodded and sipped her tea. It had a strong lemon and honey flavor to it, going down smooth and hot. "I've used the last the powders," she said. "I will need more."

The River Woman smiled. "I can't give you any more," she said.

Jin Li Tam blinked and set down the cup. She felt a moment of panic, and it folded in on itself, reproducing more anxiety as she realized how afraid it made her that she might not be able get more of the powders and continue her attempts with Rudolfo. As much as she hated the deception—and had even convinced herself a dozen times that she would tell him—she'd gotten quite adept at slipping the powders into his drinks in those hours before they were to be together. She knew that telling him about this deception meant leaving footprints that he could follow back to other deceptions, eventually seeing her father's work—and her own work in support of her father—in his life.

She could not bear the way he would look at her once he realized that House Li Tam had murdered his brother, his parents and his closest friend in order to move his life in a direction one man thought it should go in.

All of this flashed across her mind, and she felt something squeezing her heart. "I don't understand," Jin Li Tam finally said. "You have the recipe. I can arrange whatever ingredients you may need delivered."

The River Woman shook her head, still smiling. "It would not be prudent, Lady Tam."

Jin Li Tam felt anger rustling awake within her. She could hear her own voice getting cold as she pushed back the chair from the table. "I need those powders," she said. "If you can't make them for me, I'm sure Caldus Bay's woman can oblige me."

The River Woman's smile continued, broadening as she clucked. "Lady Tam," she said, "please sit down."

Uncertain, Jin paused, then sat. Suddenly, she didn't feel she could meet the River Woman's eyes. She looked around the room instead.

She felt the old, rough hand slide over her own and give it a squeeze. "I can't give you any more," the River Woman said, "because they might harm your baby."

Jin's eyes snapped up. "My what?"

The River Woman nodded. "It's all over you now. The tone of your skin. The brightness in your eyes. It's in the very way that you walk." She stood and walked over to a cabinet, drawing a gold ring with bits of pink and blue ribbon tied to it.

Jin Li Tam felt her heart flutter and expand. "You mean—?"

The River Woman nodded again, picking up a bucket of river water. "You're with child. Recently, too, I'd say." She winked.

Jin Li Tam did not know what to say. Instead, she sat still and watched as the woman clenched the ring and its strings in her closed fist, speaking to them in a mumbled tongue she could not place. The River Woman poured the water into a wooden cup, then dropped in the ring, still mumbling.

"Now," she said, "we see what your water tells the river."

Jin went into a back room, feeling suddenly awkward and exposed. She felt fear and elation arguing within her over whether she should run or dance. Afterward, when she brought the cup back out, the River Woman took it and set it on the table.

"Now finish your tea, dear," the River Woman said. "It will take awhile."

Jin Li Tam looked at the cup and the ring at the bottom of it. The threads were tucked neatly beneath the gold circle, their tips waving slightly in the blended waters. "What if it's wrong?"

The River Woman shook her head. "Forty years and I've yet to not know a woman with child when I saw her walk into this hut—even as soon as the morning after if you get my meaning." She grinned and sipped her tea.

They finished their tea in silence and sat, watching the cup. Finally, the River Woman clapped her hands. "Delightful," she said. The blue thread had become disentangled from the ring and drifted to the top.

Jin Li Tam didn't need to ask what it meant. She fell back into the chair, letting her breath out. She felt tears in the corners of her eyes, and her stomach suddenly felt uncertain. "A boy," she said in quiet voice.

The River Woman nodded. "A strong one, by the looks of it. What will you name him?"

She didn't even think about it. The name leaped to mind immediately even though she'd not thought about it before this very moment. "Jakob," she said. "If Rudolfo concurs."

The River Woman's smile filled the room with light. "A strong name for a strong boy."

Jin Li Tam couldn't take her eyes off the cup now and its blue thread floating in the yellowed river water. "He will need to be," she said. "He is inheriting a tremendous task."

The River Woman nodded. "He will be strong because he has strong parents."

One of the tears broke loose, and Jin Li Tam felt it trace its course down her cheek. "Thank you," she said.

The River Woman leaned in, her voice low. "Lady Tam," she said, "it occurs to me that you are more concerned about how this child came to be than you need be. Lord Rudolfo will be delighted and he will not question this." She paused. "I consider this to be a private matter between you and me."

Jin Li Tam nodded. "Thank you," she said again.

As she left the hut to make her way back to the manor, she found herself wondering what kind of mother she would be. She'd barely known her own mother, spending most of her time with large groups of siblings, taking instruction from her father and his brothers and sisters as they raised her to be a Tam. The idea confounded her. Two parents bringing one child into the world and staying near that child until old age carried the parents away. That child creating children of their own and the turban passing down from father to son in the shadow of a new library in a different world.

It was the most terrifying undertaking Jin Li Tam had ever imagined.

Once inside her room, she reran the bath and stripped down, pausing in front of the full-length mirror to study her stomach.

Easing herself into the hot, sweet-smelling water, Jin Li Tam smiled.

Neb

Neb felt the weariness deep in his bones now that the work was done. He'd walked Windwir twice in the last week to be certain, but despite the winter's storms they'd finished ahead of schedule. And though the sense of accomplishment permeated him, he felt a sadness in the midst of it. Over the months, he'd seen more and more of the Marsh girl, Winters, and they'd fallen into a routine together. At least twice weekly now, she met him out on the northern edges of the camp, when he could discreetly slip into the forest. They walked together, and somehow, somewhere along the way, their hands had touched and then joined so that now, whenever they walked alone, they did so hand in hand. They had not kissed again, but Neb found himself thinking of it all the time, uncertain of how to bring that about again.

He laughed as he walked north across the empty plain. Over the last several months, he'd commanded a camp of gravediggers, presided over discipline, even buried some of their own dead when the war crossed into their work. He knew how to order and inventory the supplies for a camp, and he found himself suddenly understanding and even proposing military strategy. All impressive for a boy of fifteen years.

Sixteen now, he realized suddenly. Sometime in the last few weeks a birthday had slipped past him unawares.

He had learned much and had proven much, but he still did not know how to kiss a girl.

As he approached the line of trees he called out, and she broke from them, running nimbly across the ash and mud.

"Nebios ben Hebda," she said, smiling and out of breath. She looked around the field and looked south to what remained of the gravediggers' camp. The tents were already coming down as the workers began their exodus. A small contingent would be traveling north with Neb to aid the construction of the new library. Most were scattering to what homes they could either find or make or return to. "You really are finished," she said.

Neb nodded. "I am. Petronus and Rudolfo should arrive tomorrow. I'll ride back with them to the Ninefold Forest to see what help I can be with the library."

Winters smiled. "Your work here was impressive. I'm certain you will be an asset to them."

He smiled, feeling the heat rise in his cheeks. Odd how only she could do this to him. "Thank you," he said. "Shall we walk?" He extended his hand to her and she took it.

They walked to the river first, pausing there to watch a deer at the far side. They'd never come so close before, but nature reasserted its rule quickly. Someday, Neb thought, if no one built here, this plain itself might return to the forest it once had been.

As they walked, they didn't speak this time. Before, they'd talked about his dreams and the Marsh King's dreams and where they intersected. He'd always been amazed at her grasp of those—as if she were in them, herself. And she had been on a number of occasions, or at least the image of her.

She'd shown up in other dreams, too, that Neb could never talk about. Just thinking about them made his hands get sweaty and his mouth go dry. In one of those dreams, they lay beneath a clear canopy looking up on a moon far more massive and blue and green and brown than the one that hung in their night sky. They lay there naked in their own sweat, holding one another in their arms. She had rolled into him in that dream, her body sending shivers through him as she whispered in his ear.

"This dream is of our home," she had said, and he'd awakened afraid that she really had been there, not just some image of her conjured out of his imagination and his desire.

As they turned west and walked with the river to their back, they fell into a rhythm. After a while he looked over to her, and saw the sadness on her face.

She looked at him and as if reading his mind, she explained. "We will never have these times again," she said. "I will miss them."

Neb shrugged. "I'm sure we'll see each other again, Winters." He knew he should say something else, thought about it, and hoped they were the right words. "I want to see you again," he said.

She squeezed his hand. "I do, too. But it will be complicated."

He stopped, suddenly knowing what to do, exactly what to do, and the words tumbled out before he could think himself out of them. "Then come with me, Winters. Surely, the Marsh King would understand and grant you this? Perhaps Rudolfo would speak to him on our behalf. Come and help me with the library."

She stopped walking and dropped his hand. A wry smile played on her face, and the beauty of it, despite the smudges of mud and ash on her face, made his heart ache. "An interesting proposal, Nebios ben Hebda."

He blushed at the word "proposal," and started reaching for words to dismiss his outburst. But she continued before he could finish that dismissal. "What would I do in the Ninefold Forest? How could I help with this library?" She took a step closer to him, and his nose was alive with the earthy scent of her. He could feel heat radiating from her, and he willed his feet forward one step.

Just one step. And then the kiss. But he couldn't do it. "I'm sure Petronus would have work you could do," he said.

She chuckled. "I'm sure he would. But I'm less concerned about his plans for me and more interested in *yours*."

Neb's felt his face go red and lost control of his tongue. He opened his mouth, but the words escaped him utterly.

Her eyes were playful now. "Childhood is but a day behind us, and adulthood looms ahead of us the day after tomorrow. Whose house would I share? What family would I have?"

The words came out suddenly before he could stop them. "We'd be together," he said.

She laughed. "Would you take me as your bride, Nebios ben Hebda, and grant me a Gypsy wedding filled with dancing and music? Is that what you would do?" She paused. "I suspect that's *not* something Androfrancines do."

It wasn't; he knew this. Though there had been special dispensations down through the years, strategic alliances and such. And with the Order so completely shriveled now, it wouldn't be out of the question. Still, he'd not considered marriage at all in this. He really hadn't considered anything beyond the fact that he did not want to be away from the Marsh girl.

Her face went serious now, but it remained soft. "I know you've seen my dreams of home."

Neb's mouth dropped open, and he felt panic rising.

She reached out and took both of his hands, holding them loosely in hers. "You have seen my dreams. I have seen yours. We do not need to concern ourselves with matters that the Gods have already spoken to." She leaned in and kissed his cheek. "No matter where we go from each other, we will always come back."

You've seen my dreams of home. The words resonated within him. Not the Marsh King's dreams. *My dreams.*

She stood still before him there, her eyes searching into his own, her lips slightly parted as she watched and waited to see if he would hear the words beneath her words.

"You are . . . ?" His words trailed off as he tried to make sense of it.

She nodded. "Today is the day I have held in my heart with hope and fear. Though the dreams give me great hope, and my fear is only that my deception might somehow hurt your trust in me."

Neb looked into himself. Surprise seemed to overwhelm any hurt he might feel, yet it made sense. Never had he seen the burly, fur-clad Marsh King in his dreams, but she had intersected them again and again. And her deception made sense to him. Just his few months leading, he'd come to realize quickly how carefully a leader had to be with who knew what. It wasn't a matter of trust, he realized, but of practicality. Hers was a secret that could take the teeth out of the Named Lands' carefully sown fear of the Marshers. To find out that a slip of a girl was the power behind that army . . .

Her eyebrows furrowed, and concern washed her face. "Nebios, I—"

Neb didn't wait for her to finish. The moment arrived and he recognized it for what it was. Without thinking, without giving himself even a second to hesitate and change his mind, he stepped forward and wrapped her in his arms. He enfolded her and pressed himself to her, his mouth moving in slowly even as her head came back and her eyes closed.

Then Neb kissed the girl whose dreams shared his own, the girl who was in all actuality the Marsh King that the New World trembled to think of.

He kissed her and kept on kissing her, hoping that the dreams were true and that their paths would cross again.

Vlad Li Tam

Vlad Li Tam waited in an office in the upper room of a squat, square guard tower on the Pylos border. He'd left the preparations at home in the hands of his capable children, steaming for Pylos in one of his iron ships for this clandestine meeting. His fourth son and his thirteenth daughter accompanied him along with two squads of their best trained men and women. Even now, they were magicked and taking up various positions around the guard tower. Vlad sat with his aide and waited.

There was a knock at the door and the aide opened it. A man in Androfrancine robes entered, pushing back his hood. General Lysias looked out of place in those robes, his eyes narrow and looking around the room.

Vlad Li Tam gestured to the chair across from him. The aide quickly refilled the glasses with Firespice, that Gypsy liquor that he'd grown to love. "Please sit, General," he said. "Drink with me."

Lysias held the glass beneath his nose, inhaling the scent of it. Then he took a long drink. "I bring word from Sethbert's nephew," he said. "Erlund is agreeable to the arrangement, though he isn't pleased with it."

Vlad Li Tam shrugged. "Pleasure and displeasure do not enter into it."

Lysias nodded. "I told him I saw no better resolution to this conflict. The City States are nearly in civil war. The blockades—in addition to the loss of Windwir—have crippled the Entrolusian economy."

Vlad Li Tam wondered how it felt to move from being a general of the most powerful nation in the world to a desperate man hoping to save at least some of that nation's pride through last-minute bargaining. "The delta will most likely never recover fully from this," he said in a quiet voice.

Lysias swallowed. "I agree, Lord Tam. But we must save what we can. This entire event has been a great tragedy."

Vlad Li Tam thought about the children he had lost along the way. Most recently, the son who had given himself in the Entrolusian camp and the daughter who no longer spoke to him. And before that, others he did not wish to think about in this moment. "It has been unfortunate," he agreed.

Lysias drew a pouch from beneath his robes and passed it over. "We've drawn up the terms and—"

Vlad Li Tam waved him away. "Burn those, Lysias. There will be no written terms." He looked to his aide, and the aide came forward with a cloth-wrapped object and a sheet of parchment. The aide put the sheet of parchment into Lysias's hands and unwrapped the metal object. It was roughly the length of a forearm, a metal tube ornately decorated and set into a wooden crossbow stock. "This belongs to Resolute," he said. "It's a powerful weapon."

Lysias looked up from the note he read. "And this letter?"

Vlad Li Tam smiled. "It matches Resolute's handwriting. Any scholar who could tell otherwise is long dead."

Lysias looked at the weapon, then returned to the note. "And you think they'll believe this?"

Vlad Li Tam sipped his drink, savoring the burn of it as it traveled down his throat. "They will. The rumors continue to grow. Sethbert wasn't exactly discreet about his role at the beginning of this."

Lysias's jaw tightened. "He claimed he was in the right. He claimed he had evidence that the Androfrancines intended to restore the spell and use it to rule us."

"Ask him," Vlad Li Tam said slowly, "to produce that evidence and I suspect he will be hard-pressed to do so." His eighteenth son had taken care of that for him. "Once word of this next tragedy unfolds, expect a new Papal decree offering terms. Tell Erlund that this will be the final offer and that all he need do is accept the terms and demand the arrest of Sethbert." He leaned forward, his eyes narrowing in the dimly lit room. "And if he thinks to protect his uncle in some way, tell him that what is offered here is a mercy. The boot is firmly on the delta's neck. One twist of it and she is broken."

Lysias nodded. "I will carry your message."

Vlad Li Tam stood. "Very well, I think our work here is done. The letters of credit will arrive quietly once Sethbert is in custody."

Lysias bowed his head. "Thank you, Lord Tam."

Vlad Li Tam returned the bow, careful not to incline his head more than what was proper. After the general left, he sat again and finished his drink.

Later this week, one of the two Popes would be dead. Once the Named Lands heard the details of the note Resolute would leave behind, no one would doubt that Sethbert had brought down the City of Windwir and its Androfrancine Order. Resolute's grief-stricken confession would lay out his shame at having told Sethbert of the spell's existence and speak of the guilt that gnawed at him until he could no longer bear to live with it any longer. It would point to accounts at House Li Tam that even now were being carefully created and funded to point accusing fingers at a man whose paranoia and ambition had nearly cost the world the light of knowledge, and at a cousin who would be his puppet Pope, doling out what little light remained for profit.

After this, Sethbert would lose his following and the war would lose its grounding.

The Overseer would be stripped of his lands and titles, reduced to flight. And that was as much as Vlad Li Tam would do for now. But he was certain that it was enough.

Rudolfo and Petronus would take care of the rest.

Chapter

27

Resolute

A warm spring rain fell beyond the opened windows of Oriv's makeshift office. When the Entrolusian insurrection had started heating up, Sethbert had insisted that his cousin return to the city states with him. He'd told the Pope he thought it would bolster his people's morale and possibly quell the fighting, but Oriv suspected it had more to do with keeping him nearby and easier to watch.

So now Oriv—he no longer thought of himself as Pope Resolute—spent his days working at the small desk or making speeches that he did not believe in.

And drinking too much. He stared at the empty cup and reached for the bottle of brandy. Since that winter day when Petronus declared himself, Oriv had found himself drinking more and more. It was an easy snare to fall into. The warm sweet liquor, in sufficient quantities, promised to blur the edges of his memory and take the teeth out of it.

And there was a lot he wanted to forget, to not feel. First and foremost, there was Windwir. From a distance, he'd seen the gravediggers' camp and the scars in the snow where the filled-in trenches hid the bones of a city. He'd needed to prove to himself that it was really gone. And now, more than that, he wanted to forget it had happened at all.

There was also the war to forget. Because even though on the surface this was called a war between two Popes, at the heart of it he knew it wasn't. There was one Pope—Petronus—and Oriv knew he could bring the violence to an end quickly by simply bending his knee and accepting Petronus's authority over him. And yet he wouldn't. Partially at his cousin's insistence. Mostly, though, because he did not know how to stop.

But there was even more to forget than these things. There was the deeper truth beneath it all.

Oriv could no longer dismiss Rudolfo's charge: His cousin, Sethbert, had destroyed Windwir.

He'd had his suspicions shortly after reaching Sethbert's camp seemingly so long ago. He'd overheard bits of conversation between the Overseer and his general, Lysias. Grymlis and his Gray Guard had also brought him rumors from among the soldiers. And once Petronus left Windwir for the Ninefold Forest Houses, that crafty old fisherman had turned in his shovel for a pen. His tracts and proclamations were riddled with accusations against the Entrolusian Overseer, though always careful not to implicate Oriv.

Those tracts were everywhere in the Named Lands now. Combined with the blockade and the devastated economy, those damning pamphlets fueled the Entrolusian insurrection. Civil war had already swallowed Turam, and even what little remained of the Order was divided. Those of the Androfrancines who had not found their way back to the Papal Summer Palace were now in the Ninefold Forest. And with winter now past, there were rumblings that some of the higher ranking arch-scholars and bishops—men old enough to remember Pope Petronus—were planning a migration eastward.

He filled the cup to the brim, lifted it and tipped it back. It took most of a bottle now for him to forget. Half of another for him to sleep.

Oriv heard a knock at his door, and tried to stand. He swayed on his feet and sat down heavily. "Come in," he said.

Grymlis pushed open the door. "Excellency, may I have a word?"

The old soldier looked more tired than usual. His eyes were red-rimmed in the flickering lamplight, and his shoulders slouched.

Oriv waved him in. "Grymlis. Come. Sit. Have a drink with me."

Grymlis walked into the room, pulling the door closed behind him. He sat in the chair across from Oriv, and their eyes met. Oriv looked away, then pointed to the bottle. "Help yourself."

Grymlis shook his head. "I don't need it."

Oriv thought for a moment that the old soldier would suggest that perhaps Pope Resolute didn't need it, either. He'd certainly been free enough with that opinion in days past. But instead, he watched the old soldier pull a flask from his pocket and pass it across. "Try this," Grymlis said. "It's got more kick."

Oriv accepted it, unscrewed the cap, and sniffed it. "What is it?"

"Firespice—a Gypsy brew. Very potent."

Oriv nodded, took a sip, and felt it burn its way down his throat. He stretched the next sip into a gulp, then screwed the cap back on and held it out to Grymlis.

"Keep it," he said.

Oriv wasn't sure why, but the generosity moved him. "Thank you. You're a good man, Grymlis."

The general shrugged. "I'm not sure about that." He leaned forward. "But I want to be a better man than I am. And I want the same for you as well, Oriv."

He used my given name. Oriv chuckled. "We all could do with being better men," he said.

Grymlis nodded slowly. "We could." He paused and looked

around the room. "Tonight," he said. "We could be better men *tonight*."

Oriv leaned forward. "How?"

"We could leave this city," Grymlis said. "We could flee to Pylos and denounce Sethbert for the traitorous whore-child he is. We could end this war and go help rebuild what can be rebuilt. Keep the light alive."

Even as Grymlis said it, Oriv knew it was true. He'd thought the same thing a dozen times in the last few months. Since winter, the war had spread. Everyone had their side and everyone made their warfare in service to their so-called light. But it didn't take a Pope to figure out that what the New World had fallen into had nothing to do with light and more to do with fear.

He wanted to tell Grymlis that he was right, that they should pack what they could carry and quietly gather the contingent. Sethbert's men were tied up putting down riots and quelling revolution. They could reach the ruins of Rachyl's Bridge easily by dawn and trust the rangers to ferry them across.

But instead, he snorted. "And you think Petronus would have us back after this?"

Grymlis shrugged. "Possibly. He was ever a fair man." He leaned in even closer. "But does it matter? What matters is that we can stop this if we choose to."

Oriv felt his lower lip shaking. "I'm not sure that I can."

Now Grymlis was leaning in close enough that he could smell the wine on the old man's breath. The line of his jaw was strong and his eyes flashed. "Say the word, Excellency, and I will do it for you. I will call my men and we will carry you away from this. You need do nothing but say you wish it."

But Oriv didn't say anything. He blinked back the tears and unscrewed the top of the flask and drained it with one long gulp.

Grymlis's shoulders sagged. He pushed himself up to his feet. "I've a bottle in my room," he said. "I'll fetch it for you."

Oriv nodded. "I'm sure this will all sort itself out, Grymlis."

Grymlis nodded as well. "I'm sure it will, Excellency."

He let himself out, and Oriv watched the door close. Already the Firespice was taking the edge off, and he saw the fuzzy underside of forgetfulness. Maybe tomorrow, if he felt better, he would go to Sethbert and suggest another parley. Perhaps they could end the fighting. Perhaps they could become better men.

When Grymlis returned with the bottle, Oriv quickly unstopped it and poured it into his cup. The old general sat across from him and watched him drain it in a long swallow. Then, Grymlis stood and walked behind Oriv to close the room's open windows one by one.

After, the general went to the door and opened it to let the others in. Oriv looked up at them—four Gray Guard and two Entrolusians he knew he should recognize. They moved into the room quickly as Grymlis shut and locked the door.

"What are you doing?" Oriv demanded, trying to stand but finding that his legs would not carry him. The Gray Guard moved in behind him and held him down in his chair. One of the Entrolusians reached down and took the cup from his hands, placing it on the small table next to the bottle of Firespice. Suddenly, he recognized him. "General Lysias?"

The general said nothing, instead looking to Grymlis. Oriv watched their exchange of glances and tried to stand again. Firm hands held him in place.

"What's this about?" he asked.

Grymlis took a cloth-wrapped bundle from the other Entrolusian and pulled out a long object that Oriv recognized only too well. "What are you doing?"

Grymlis's big hand closed over Oriv's, and now Oriv struggled to keep his white-knuckled grip on the arm of the chair. But the alcohol had numbed him, and Grymlis pried it free easily. Oriv felt the cold wood of the artifact pressed into his hand. He felt the cold iron of the artifact's barrel pressed into the soft tissue between his chin and his throat.

"What are you doing?" he asked again in a voice that sounded more like a whimper than a demand. Only now he knew exactly what Grymlis was doing, and he twisted and turned in the chair in the hopes that it would somehow be enough.

"I'm protecting the light," Grymlis said, his voice heavy and hollow despite the hardness in his eyes.

"But I—"

And in that moment, Oriv found the forgetfulness that no bottle could ever offer him.

Petronus

Petronus crested the last hill and climbed down from his saddle to stretch his legs. Below, the flat, wide river moved sluggishly south, and on its farthest shore the town of tents had shrunk to more of a small village. A few figures moved between the last of the tents and a fleet of wagons. Beyond the tents, the expansive plain that had once been Windwir stretched out, a soup of mud and ash.

Rudolfo dismounted beside him. "It looks quiet," he said.

Of course it *was* quiet. The work had been done for nearly a week. The Entrolusians had been gone for some time now, retreating south to deal with problems within their own borders. Petronus looked at Rudolfo and then back out over the muddy waste. "He's done good work here," he said.

Rudolfo nodded. "He has. There's a captain hidden inside that boy."

Or a Pope, Petronus thought, feeling his stomach sink. The wind stirred, and a few drops of rain spattered on his cheek and hand. "Indeed," he said, glancing again to the Gypsy King.

Behind them, he heard the sound of a small bird rustling as a scout cooed and whispered to it. The brown war-sparrow entered his line of sight with a flutter and shot down the hill to cross the river.

Climbing back into his saddle, Petronus carefully nudged the horse along the muddy track that wound them downhill. When they were halfway to the bottom, Petronus noticed the workers gathering on the far shore. A handful of men boarded the barge they had rigged with ropes and pulleys to serve as a makeshift ferry. Slowly it made its way across the water, and when Petronus and Rudolfo reached the river's edge with their escort, Neb stood waiting.

He's not smiling. This surprised Petronus. The boy—young man now, he realized—seemed taller and more broad-shouldered, but those weren't what caused him to fill out the Androfrancine robes he wore. No, Petronus realized. It was confidence. A quiet confidence, to be sure, but that was the strongest kind.

The boy's face was flat and hard, the jaw set. "Father," Neb said, bowing slightly. "Windwir is laid to rest."

But there is more. Petronus dropped from the horse. "You've done excellent work, Neb."

Neb nodded. "Thank you, Father."

Rudolfo climbed down as well and clapped the young man on the shoulder. "I was telling his Excellency that you have the makings of a fine captain."

"Thank you, Lord Rudolfo," Neb said, inclining his head to the Gypsy King. Then he fixed his stare on Petronus again. "I received a bird for you just before dawn under Androfrancine colors." He extended a scrap of paper. "It's from House Li Tam."

Petronus took the note and scanned it. It was uncoded—a rarity for his old friend—and to the point.

Resolute is dead by his own hand, the note read. *Sethbert is deposed and flees the delta.* Petronus felt his own jaw set, and handed the note to Rudolfo. He knew he should feel some kind of relief, but didn't. With Resolute dead and Sethbert out of power, it was only a matter of time before the war burned itself out. This was good news for Petronus, good news for all of the Named Lands. And yet, it saddened him. One more life snuffed out. And at least a part of him felt suspicion at the convenience of it.

The sober look on Neb's face told Petronus that the young man felt the same way.

Rudolfo looked up from the note, grinning like a wolf. "If this is true, the war is over." He handed the note back to Petronus. Then, he turned and slipped back to confer with his men.

Petronus pulled Neb aside. "Are you ready to fold it up here?"

Neb nodded and glanced north quickly. His face went wistful, and there was hesitation in his voice. "I am."

The girl, Petronus realized. He's seen more of her. Thirty years ago, he'd have insisted that the young man keep himself free from such entanglements. But time and change had softened him, and he couldn't fault the boy for finding something akin to love here in the Desolation of Windwir. He put his hand on Neb's shoulder. "You'll have to tell me about her on the way home."

The beginnings of a smile pulled at Neb's mouth. "I'm not sure I can, Father."

Petronus squeezed the shoulder and dropped his hand to his side. "In your own time, son. Meanwhile, I'm famished. Is the galley tent still up?"

"They're cooking a digger's feast for you," Neb said, gesturing to the barge. "Beans and biscuits with pork gravy. The last of our stores." A line of men stood near it, ready to shove it back into the river and work the ropes that would carry them across.

Petronus led his horse up the low ramp. Rudolfo joined him, his eyes bright. When everyone was aboard, the ferry lurched into the water.

I'll not be accompanying you back, Rudolfo signed.

Petronus nodded. He'd wondered as much after the Gypsy

King's hurried and hushed council with his men. *Riding south?* he signed in reply.

"I've decided to do some hunting," Rudolfo said with a smile and a flourish of his hand. *Sethbert is mine.*

Petronus's fingers moved. *But you'll take him alive?*

Rudolfo blanched. "Of course," he said, his voice low. *My physicians will have their opportunity to redeem him beneath their salted knives.*

He felt himself frown. He did not approve of the Gypsies' adherence to those darker forms and rituals of redemption. It was a barbaric leftover from an age when Wizard Kings doled out justice in white cutting rooms beneath couch-strewn observation decks. Where, sipping their chilled wines and eating their sliced pears, lords and ladies listened to penitent screams beneath a scattering of stars that pulsed like heartbeats in blackened sky.

It flew against everything P'Andro Whym had made.

Still, the Named Lands needed to see some kind of public justice for Sethbert's crimes, and Petronus's own plans served a higher aim than that. Healing would not come from justice alone. There also had to be change.

After all, Petronus thought, change is the path life takes.

He looked at Neb again and felt his heart breaking at what he knew awaited them in the Ninefold Forest.

Sethbert

Sethbert stirred beneath a pile of damp, molding hay and squinted into the shadowed barn. Daylight peeked in through gaps in the roof and walls, and he found he couldn't distinguish between the sounds of dripping water and what he thought could be footfalls in the puddles outside. Either way, he couldn't stay here. He sat up slowly, holding his knife with a white-knuckled hand.

It had all happened so fast. Lysias had come for him with a squad of scouts in the middle of the night, pulling him from a deep sleep. "Resolute is dead," the general had said grimly. "He's left behind a letter that implicates you in the destruction of Windwir and the Androfrancine Order."

Sethbert disentangled himself from the drugged prostitute that lay tangled in his sheets. "Who killed him?"

Lysias looked away. "He killed himself."

He wasn't too surprised by this news. Oriv had been drunk most of the last few months, a weaker man than Sethbert had thought he would be. "Fine," Sethbert said. "Burn the letter. Keep word of his passing quiet. We—"

Lysias shook his head. "It's too late for that, Sethbert. Word is out. Your nephew has the letter."

"Then tell my nephew—"

When the flat of Lysias's hand struck Sethbert's cheek it was a resounding crack in the quiet room. "I don't think you understand why I'm here."

Sethbert's hand went to his face, feeling the heat where Lysias's blow connected. His eyes narrowed. "You're here to arrest me, then?"

Lysias smiled. "I am."

Sethbert's chuckle was a bark. "Then let's go." He scrambled out of the large, round bed and pulled on his trousers. Lysias watched, bemused, as he shrugged into his shirt. "I don't know what game you're playing at, Lysias, but Erlund will see reason through whatever cloud of belly-gas you've squeezed into his lungs." He looked to the portrait of his mother that hung on the far wall. "He'll want the documents, I'm sure."

Lysias nodded. "Yes, by all means."

Sethbert looked around the room. At this point, the scouts had not yet drawn their weapons. They looked uncomfortable, their eyes moving from Lysias to Sethbert.

They're still my men and they know it.

He gestured to one of the men and pointed to the large picture. "Bring down that portrait," he said. He smiled when the scout went right to it without glancing first to Lysias for confirmation.

Behind the portrait, set firmly into the stone wall, was the round, hinged lid of a Rufello lockbox. "May I?"

Lysias shook his head. "What is the box's cipher?"

Sethbert considered his options carefully, and finally recited the words and numbers slow enough for the scout to push the various tiles and knobs into place. With a click, the lid swung open.

The scout peered in, then turned to Lysias, his mouth tight. "Nothing, General."

Sethbert felt his stomach lurch, and saw Lysias reaching for the hilt of his knife. Two of the scouts did the same.

With a howl, Sethbert threw himself toward the window, catching the heavy curtains and pushing the thick cloth ahead of him to shield him as the glass and latticework shattered. Plunging into the midnight rain, he leaped from the small balcony and into the Whymer Maze below.

That had been hours ago. He'd used the passages beneath the maze—the ones his father had shown him when he was a boy—and made his escape. The tunnels dropped him into the more colorful quarter of the city, where he'd rolled a drunk for his tattered clothing and a pair of shoes that were too tight for his feet.

At first he'd thought to stow away on one of the boats in the harbor, but with the blockade he was certain to not get far. And it would not take long for Lysias to spread a net for him, putting guards up at the city gates and along the river bridges.

In the end, he crawled into the sewers and followed them out of the city. Then he worked his way along the coastline until he found the barn.

He stood slowly, mindful of the blisters on his feet and the sharp pain in his ribs and shoulder from last night's hard landing in the garden.

He'd hoped to sleep here, but his mind wouldn't stop racing. Where would he go? What was left for him now? And where had the document pouch gone?

Less than a handful knew about the Rufello box. And its

cipher had been passed from father to son for generations. No one else could've possibly known.

Unless.

It had to be Li Tam's bitch-whore of a daughter. But it made no sense. If she had the cipher, why hadn't she taken the documents months ago? She'd shared his bed enough, the pouch tucked safely away. Why would she wait so long? And certainly, if she'd read those documents, she'd understand full well what kind of hero Sethbert truly was.

She's a thousand leagues away, some saner part of him interjected. She'd been gone for months now, working in the far northeast with that damned fop Rudolfo and his paper Pope.

If not Tam, then another Androfrancine lap-slut. But who it was—and how they broke into the ancient lockbox—mattered little. What counted now was survival. Because with the documents now gone, it was clear to Sethbert that there was no place for him left in the Named Lands. They would hunt him down wherever he fled. The weight of that realization caught in his throat.

The Gulf would be at the mercy of the iron armada, cutting off any escape south to the Isles or west to the Emerald Coasts. But east, Sethbert thought, there was a line of small fishing towns along the forested shores of Caldus Bay. Perhaps from there he could steal a boat far from Li Tam's blockade and follow the ragged edge of the Keeper's Wall south, around the Fargoer's horn and into the Churning Wastes.

Sethbert went to the barn door and looked out. He saw nothing between the field and the river's edge. The sun was bright, and the few rain clouds left in the sky were drifting slowly east.

Stomach gurgling with hunger and fear, Sethbert followed the weather.

Rudolfo

Rudolfo rode south alone over the protests of his men. Had Gregoric been alive, he would have never gotten away with it. He'd have disobeyed directly, or at the very least followed from a distance under magicks. Even Aedric might have intervened in some way, but he was already south. The new first captain was working with the Rangers of Pylos to shore up Meirov's eastern and western borders and keep her neighbors' problems in their own backyards.

So he rode alone, his horse magicked for speed and stamina, and he leaned into the slanting rain. He'd sent word before he'd left, carefully coding notes to Jin Li Tam, his head physician, and Aedric. And Petronus had informed Vlad Li Tam on Rudolfo's behalf, asking him to keep watchful eye on the Delta's waterways for the renegade Overseer, and letting his future father-in-law know that he rode to rendezvous with Aedric. He meant his Wandering Army to hunt Sethbert, and he meant to parade that murderous pig-bugger through the towns of the Named Lands on the long route back to the Ninefold Forest.

He smiled at the thought of it, and whistled his horse faster. If he pushed, he'd only need four days. With the magicks his horse could take that abuse, but no more. Once he reached Aedric and his men, he'd have to trade out for a season. He patted the horse's side. With all he'd been through since Windwir's pyre, this one had earned a break.

We all have.

Hours behind him, the last of the gravediggers' camp was down by now, and the caravan no doubt wound its way northeast. He could have brought some of his men, but he'd not wanted to leave the Pope any more exposed than he already was. Even if the war was all but over, he couldn't afford to take any risks with Petronus's safety.

But deeper than that, something else prompted Rudolfo to solitude. He'd felt a darkness gnawing away inside of him, stirred to life that night he ran with Gregoric on his shoulder. And when that that cloud came over him he found that he couldn't abide anyone's presence.

He was certain it had something to do with the Francine's Fivefold Path of Grief. And he would walk those paths again and again until he finished. It wasn't as if he were a stranger to them. He'd been down these routes before with his brother and with his parents.

But Gregoric. It still stabbed at him.

He shook his head, hoping to clear it. He thought about the work ahead, but found it bored him. He turned his mind instead to Jin Li Tam and their time together, but the memories of that couldn't hold him, either.

But when he thought of Sethbert, he found a white, hot point of light to focus on other than the past.

It was the future. And in it, Sethbert screamed beneath the salted knife.

Chapter

28

Rudolfo

Rudolfo dismounted and handed his reins to a Gypsy Scout. There at the edge of Caldus Bay was the shack with its boathouse, surrounded by soldiers of the Wandering Army, his scouts and a squad of Pylos Border Rangers.

They'd received dozens of birds with dozens of reported sightings. Rudolfo had divided his force and scattered them to follow up on each lead. It had paid off.

When they'd first found Sethbert here, the Rangers had inquired around the town and learned that the boathouse Sethbert hid in was none other than that of a certain fisherman, Petros, who was away on business.

Sethbert hadn't put up a fight, but he had insisted that he would only surrender to Rudolfo. The Rangers had quickly sent word to the Gypsy Scouts with Sethbert's demand.

Rudolfo had left immediately, riding with the wagon that his Physicians of Penitent Torture had driven south. It was a large, enclosed structure with wooden sides that could be dropped to properly display the black iron cage furnished with the various tools of their redemptive work.

Rudolfo approached Aedric, the new first captain of his Gypsy Scouts. He was Gregoric's oldest boy—nearly twenty. He would teach his friend's son how to be a strong first captain, and perhaps, if the Gods did not grant him an heir, he would offer his fatherhood to the boy. He wondered how Jin Li Tam would feel about that. He suspected that she would see the value of it, but he realized suddenly that the days of making decisions of such magnitude without speaking with her were gone now. Not because he worried that she would take issue with his decision—he knew she would not. But rather, because he knew her now, knew that she had eyes that could see around corners he never dreamed of. She was a valuable ally.

"First Captain," Rudolfo said, inclining his head slightly.

"General Rudolfo," Aedric said, bowing. "The fugitive Overseer of the Entrolusian City States awaits you."

Rudolfo nodded. "Is he armed?"

"I'm certain of it."

He stroked his mustache. "And do you think he means to harm me?"

Aedric's eyes narrowed. "He means to try, Lord."

Rudolfo unbuckled his sword belt and handed it to a waiting aide. "Lend me your knives," he said to Aedric.

Aedric handed over the belt of scout's knives, and Rudolfo buckled it around his narrow hips.

Rudolfo waited for Aedric to insist he not go in alone, to tell him it was too dangerous. He smiled inwardly when the young first captain did not. "I will whistle for you when I need you." Then, he looked to the two physicians that had driven down in the wagon. "Salt your knives and ready your chains."

Rudolfo went to the door. "Sethbert," he called out.

He heard scrambling and the sound of things being knocked over. He pulled open the door, and his eyes followed the ray of sunlight as it slanted into the filthy room. The smell overtook him first. Rotten fish and human feces. Rudolfo drew a silk kerchief from his sleeve and held it to his mouth and nose, inhaling the perfumes from it.

"Rudolfo?" The voice was hoarse and far away, laced with something he thought must be madness. More scrambling, and Rudolfo saw a filthy form crawl into the light. Sethbert had already started losing his fat, his clothes hanging off him. He was covered in filth from head to toe, his hair and beard matted with mud, his clothing ripped and gray with grime. His eyes were wide.

"Yes," Rudolfo said. "I am here. This is over now. Come out."

Sethbert smiled, relief washing his face. "I will come out. Soon." He offered an exaggerated wink. "But first, did they not tell you that I intend to hurt you?"

Rudolfo's hands clenched the knife hilt, his eyes on Sethbert's hands, both splayed out on the muddy boathouse floor. "With what do you intend to hurt me?" he asked.

"With knowledge," he said.

Rudolfo waited.

Sethbert continued. "I had the evidence. I saw it. I saw the charts and the maps. They intended to use the spell to enslave us."

Rudolfo laughed. "I thought you were going to hurt me, not amuse me," he said. "What would the Androfrancines gain from enslaving us?"

"I'm a patriot of the light," Sethbert said. The madness crept into his eyes now, too, and his face twitched in the shaft of morning sunlight.

Rudolfo scowled. "Enough of this. You've run out of time, Sethbert."

He stepped back and almost missed the next words because Sethbert whispered them, low and with a sharp clarity.

"Ask the whore who shares your bed who paid for the coups that killed your parents."

Rudolfo spun, the knives coming out. "What did you say?"

Sethbert's eyes met his, but the Overseer did not utter another word.

Later, after the physicians had chained Sethbert into the wagon, Rudolfo rapped on the outside of it with the pommel of his long, narrow sword and ordered the black-robed driver to make the return trip at a leisurely pace, stopping in what towns they could along the way.

He'd hoped he could follow, but he knew now that he could not. Sethbert's words had chewed at him despite the Overseer's obvious madness. He'd actually believed that the Androfrancines meant to harm the people they were sworn to protect. In the end, the paranoia of a madman brought down a city.

But this other—it touched on a suspicion he had harbored for a long while now. Everyone had said that his parents' death was a terrible tragedy, an unseen insurrection that exploded in one night of intense violence that left Rudolfo an orphan. They'd shaken their heads when, even at his young age, Rudolfo suggested an investigation. It had seemed too convenient, and in two thousand years of forest life, there had never been insurrection. The night his parents died, he stayed up past dawn drafting his strategy for investigation. Gregoric's father was supportive, but the pontiff felt the Physicians of Penitent Torture would better serve the occasion. Rudolfo listened to the pontiff. It was the first and last time he did not follow his instincts.

Even now his instincts led him, and he raced his new horse westward.

Ask the whore who shares your bed who paid for the coups that killed your parents.

No, Rudolfo thought, I will not ask her.

Instead, he would ask her father.

Neb

The mechoservitors fascinated Neb.

Certainly, he'd seen them on occasion in the library—though not often. Now, he could walk among them, talk with them and on occasion work with them as they cataloged and inventoried what pieces of the library lived within their memory scrolls.

Today, he worked with Isaak integrating the inventory of the latest caravan from the summer papal palace. After Resolute's unexpected suicide, the Androfrancines at the Palace had quickly accepted Petronus's invitation to return to the fold. But when a certain Captain Grymlis showed up at the gates with a small contingent of Gray Guard, Petronus turned them away.

"The Gypsy Scouts guard the Son of P'Andro Whym now," he told them. "If you would be true to your vows, obey me now. Bury your uniforms and take up new lives far away from here."

Neb had never seen anything like it. To a man, they stripped naked, buried their uniforms in the forest floor and left.

That had been two weeks ago.

Now, the wagons full of books and artifacts had formed a steady stream, two or three per week. Androfrancine refugees and property from the Emerald Coasts, from the Summer Papal Palace and even a few from the City States on the Delta trickled into the Ninefold Forest. Word of the restoration had spread throughout the Named Lands, and a corps of engineers already worked hard at digging its deep basements.

And Neb worked with Isaak to inventory each wagon so that the information would be recorded on the metal man's memory scroll.

He watched the metal man work, his eye shutters opening and closing rapidly as he wrote. "Sethbert will arrive day after tomorrow," Neb said.

Isaak looked up. "What do you think they will do with him?"

Neb shrugged. "Rudolfo means to keep him on Tormentor's Row, to let his physicians do their redemptive work upon him with their knives."

He'd studied those darker aspects of the Whymer cult, and shuddered to think of what that meant. The varying cuts had names, and each of them folded into the others until they formed a vast Whymer's Maze of lacerations.

When Isaak said nothing, Neb continued, "But Petronus wants to try him for the Desolation of . . ." He saw the mechanical flinch and let the words fall off. "I'm sorry, Isaak."

Isaak shook his head. "You've nothing to apologize for, Brother Nebios. A part of me thinks he deserves justice for his crimes."

Neb nodded. "When I met Petronus, I was standing under Sethbert's canopy, studying the position of his guards." He paused. Had it really been so many months ago? "I'd stolen scout magicks from Lady Tam, and intended to use them in order to kill Sethbert."

Isaak's eyes flashed. "You knew what he had done?"

Neb nodded. "I did. But Petronus saw me and stopped me."

Isaak pondered this. "You were a boy who survived the spell. Now you're a hero of the Androfrancine Order. Do you believe your restraint led to these things?"

He chuckled, putting down the book he'd just lifted up from the wagon. "I had no restraint of my own. Petronus restrained me."

Isaak fixed his eyes on him again. "But are you glad for it?"

Neb thought about this. "I think so. Yes," he said.

Isaak looked to a point beyond Neb now and stood. "Lady Tam," he said. "An unexpected delight."

Neb looked up and blushed. Lady Tam still radiated beauty, though now it was clear that she wasn't half as pretty as Winters. Still she was beautiful, and when she smiled at him he felt his face grow red. "Hello, Isaak," she said, inclining her head to each of them. "Nebios." She smiled. "How is the inventory?"

Now Neb stood as well. "We've found three mechanicals. Small ones, to be sure, but two of them are still in good repair."

"I should be able to restore the third," Isaak said. "It appears to have slipped a gear."

Jin Li Tam looked to the wagon, and Neb thought for a second that her face registered surprise. He followed her eyes and saw the golden bird in its golden cage, its wings hanging broken and its neck twitching. "Where did this wagon come from?" she asked.

Neb stared at it. Something about the golden bird nagged at him. He suddenly smelled the sulfur and ozone of Windwir's firestorm, and he flinched.

Isaak looked at the registry. "This one is from the Emerald Coasts," he said. "A private collection."

He saw the bird flying low to the ground, its golden feathers steaming. It was at Windwir, he realized. Neb opened his mouth and a stream of unintelligible words tumbled out, fragments of scripture jumbled together with glossolalia. He closed his mouth quickly and looked at Jin Li Tam.

She stared at him. "Neb?"

He waited for the tension to leave his throat. Finally, he spoke. "I saw this bird at Windwir."

Neb watched her eyes narrow and her jawline tighten. "Really?"

He nodded. "I did."

She nodded, her eyes suddenly far away. "I hope you can fix it," she said. Then, her eyes returned to the present. "Petronus is calling for you both," she said. She paused. "Take him that bird. Tell him I said I will speak to him about it later."

Neb grabbed up his stack of papers. He probably wanted to talk about the council.

The Council of Bishops was just a few weeks away. Many of the gravediggers who had come north with Neb had been put to work building bleachers and crafting the massive tents to contain it. The last birds of invitation were to go out to-morrow.

Neb started toward the manor and the suite of offices they had grown into, then realized he was being rude, and turned to wait for Lady Tam and Isaak.

Isaak held the birdcage in his hands.

Jin Li Tam was staring at it, he realized, and Neb had never seen a more profound look of sadness upon her face.

Petronus

Petronus's office adjoined the converted guest room that Neb and Isaak worked from. The steward had insisted that he have privacy and wouldn't hear of him using his living quarters as his work space. Instead, they moved a small desk, some bookshelves and three chairs into a large walk-in closet. The closet even had a small window that opened out on one of the manor's many gardens. As spring hurried on, Petronus could smell the flowers blooming, though of course he had to stand on his desk to see them.

He looked up the knock on his door. "Come in," he said.

Neb came in first, and Petronus swore that every time he saw the boy he was taller. His shoulders had broadened and he even had the beginnings of a beard, trimmed as neatly as a boy could manage. He wore the robes smartly, though he still walked in them as if they weren't really his, as if he weren't really a member of the Order. "You called for us, Excellency?"

"Come in and sit down," Petronus said.

Isaak limped in behind Neb. He carried a small metal bird in a dented cage. The bird twitched and clicked. They both sat in the waiting chairs.

"What do you have there?" Petronus asked.

Isaak put the cage on the desk. "It is a mechanical. Jin Li Tam said she would speak with you about it later."

Neb spoke up. "I think it was in Windwir when the city fell."

Petronus studied the bird. It looked familiar. Like something he had seen in someone's home. "I'll look forward to Lady Tam's explanation. Meanwhile . . ." Petronus reached beneath his desk and pulled out the cloth-wrapped object that had arrived by rider earlier this morning. He'd recognized it immediately, of course. It was from the Papal Offices in the Summer Palace, one of a few hand cannons that had been restored before the Order decided it dishonored kinclave to make them. He laid it on his desk. "This arrived from the new Overseer, Erlund. It's what Oriv employed to . . . well, to end his life." He unwrapped it and watched Neb's eyes go wide. "It was used during the days of the Younger Gods, long before the Old World and P'Andro Whym." He looked from Neb to Isaak. "This is familiar to you?"

Isaak nodded. "It is, Father." Petronus wasn't sure why the metal man insisted on the ancient title, but it pleased him. It seemed more humble.

"You recognize it from your time in the library?"

The metal man shook his head. "No, Father. I was not permitted to work with any weaponry apart from the spell." Exhaust leaked out from his back and his gears whirred. "Oriv used it when Lord Rudolfo and Lady Tam took me from the Summer Papal Palace. He killed one of the Gypsy Scouts with it. But I thought Lord Rudolfo brought it with us."

"Perhaps this is a different device," Petronus said. But even as he said it, he knew it wasn't likely. There had been less than a half dozen of these in the world, and none of them should have ever left the care of the highest officials of the Order or officers of the Gray Guard. When he was Pope, they kept one in his bedchambers, and one in each of his offices. The others had been locked away in vaults deep beneath the library.

Neb looked at it, and Petronus wondered if he noticed the bloodstains in the stock. They'd wiped it down, but it had sat in the blood long enough for it to stain the light wood stock. "It's fairly simple mechanics," Petronus said. "A spark ignites a wax-paper envelope of powders. The explosion of these powders propels a projectile—or in this case, a handful of iron slivers. It's wildly inaccurate beyond a handful of sword-lengths."

But close enough for Oriv's purpose. If it really *had* been his purpose. Petronus was suspicious, especially now, with Isaak's recollection that the weapon had come into Rudolfo's care once before. He would ask him about it upon his return.

Because if the weapon had been in Rudolfo's care, it had somehow managed to leave it again. And if that were the case, it was possible that Oriv's suicide might not have been exactly that. Not that it mattered at this point.

It was clearly an instance of Oriv's tragic end being in everyone's best interests. Especially Oriv's best interests if the note he left behind spoke any the truth at all, that he had collaborated with his cousin for the Desolation of Windwir. His quick exit, mouth on the muzzle of this restored artifact, saved Oriv facing Androfrancine justice.

Petronus would never let him suffer beneath the knives of Rudolfo's physicians in the way that Sethbert now did on his long journey north. But he'd have still enforced what strong punishment he could, and Oriv's life would have been forfeit.

He looked at the weapon, then looked to Isaak and Neb. "I want this destroyed," he said. "It is a secret we can no longer guard properly."

He watched Neb's eyes widen. "But Excellency," he said, "it could be—"

Petronus did not let him finish. "Brother Nebios," he said in his sternest tone, "it is not to be studied. It is to be destroyed." He leaned in, feeling the anger rise in his cheeks. "I'll not let another weapon fall into the wrong hands."

As soon as he said it, he regretted it. He saw the look of confusion on Neb's face, then saw understanding dawn as the boy went pale. "Another weapon?"

Petronus said nothing, even when Neb repeated his question. Finally, he covered the weapon back up. "Destroy it," he said.

Neb nodded. "Yes, Excellency."

Now Petronus looked to Isaak. "I want you to go over the inventories again. I want to see what war-making magicks and mechanicals still live within the mechoservitor memory scrolls. We will have hard decisions to make in the days ahead about which parts of the light we keep and which we allow to remain aptly extinguished."

Isaak nodded. "Yes, Father."

They stood and left. Neb cast another curious glance at Petronus, but he pretended not to notice. He knew the boy would be curious now. He might even hate him for this.

If not this, Petronus thought, he certainly would hate him for what was coming.

And Petronus would not blame him for that. He hated himself as well.

Jin Li Tam

Jin Li Tam waited until dusk before approaching Petronus's small office. Neb and Isaak had left for the evening, and the suite of rooms that housed the Androfrancine Order's operations was quiet and dark except for the light coming from beneath the Pope's door. The Gypsy Scouts who guarded him announced her arrival and ushered her in.

The old man looked up from a stack of paper and laid down his pen. "Lady Tam," he said, inclining his head slightly.

"Excellency," she answered, returning his nod. Her eyes found the caged bird on the corner of his desk. When she was a girl, she spent hours listening to the bird, teaching it simple phrases, in the moist heat of her father's seaside garden. It seemed smaller now.

And battered, she realized. Its metallic gold feathers were streaked with black burn marks, and the bird's head hung askew along with its entire right side. Bits of copper wire protruded from a charred eye socket. It couldn't even stand properly—it crouched in the corner of the cage and twitched, its one good eye blinking rapidly.

She sat on one of the plain wooden chairs in front of his desk, her eyes never leaving the bird.

Petronus must have followed her gaze. "You recognize this mechanical?" he finally asked.

She broke her stare and looked to Petronus. "I do, Excellency. It was my father's—a gift from the Androfrancines. It arrived with his library today."

Petronus's eyebrows raised. "His library? Why would Vlad Li Tam send his library?"

She had spent the better part of the day wondering the same thing. Her father cherished his books, and she could not imagine what might lead him to relinquish them. "I've been asking myself the same question, Excellency," she said.

"Have you asked him?"

She shook her head and paused to find the right words. "My father and I are not in communication."

Jin Li Tam watched the surprise register on Petronus's face. She met his eyes and saw the questions forming in them, then watched as he forced those questions to the side. "So for some unknown reason, Vlad Li Tam has donated his library to our work here. And he's included this mechanical bird." He paused. "You seem disturbed by this, Lady Tam."

She nodded. "There's more," she said, swallowing. Part of her was afraid to move forward. Over the past months, she'd gone from questioning her father's will to despising his work in the Named Lands.

I hate my own part in it even more, she thought, looking back to the bird again. She realized Petronus was waiting for her to continue. "Neb thinks he saw the bird near Windwir on the day the city fell."

Petronus leaned forward, his eyes narrowing. "Did your father ever use the bird for message transport?"

She shook her head. "He did not. He considered it to be too noticeable."

Petronus nodded slowly, now looking at the bird himself. "I had wondered if he had a hand in this."

Jin Li Tam's stomach sank. She'd not yet said it, but she wondered the same. Certainly, Sethbert had brought down the city. There was no question of that. He'd admitted it to her freely. But she knew Sethbert—given to fits of mood and rage, given to as much slothfulness as ruthlessness. She did not doubt he carried out Windwir's Desolation. But she did not believe for a moment that he wasn't led in that direction. And there was one man in all of the Named Lands whose sole work was bending people to do his will, using his network of children to gather the intelligence and execute his strategy. Finally, she said the words that she'd dreaded saying since the moment she saw the bird. "I fear my father used Sethbert to bring down Windwir."

Petronus nodded. "It must be a hard conclusion for you to arrive at," he said. His voice took on a gentle tone. "It is hard to discover that what we love most is not as it seems."

She nodded. Suddenly, she found herself fighting tears. She forced them back, and thought about this old Pope. His words carried conviction and she found a question forming in her mind. She hesitated, then asked it. "Is that why you left the Papacy?"

Petronus nodded. "It is part of it."

"And now, all these years later, you've come back to it. Do you ever wish you'd just stayed in the first place?"

Petronus sighed. "I wish that every day." When he spoke next, his voice was heavy with grief. "I keep thinking that if I had stayed, perhaps I could have averted this tragedy entirely."

She'd wondered similar things today as she thought about the bird and what it might mean. She'd been with the Overseer for nearly three years, feeding information to her father and leaking information to Sethbert at her father's direction. *I should have seen what was happening, but I was blinded by faith in my father's will.*

Petronus continued. "I wish it every day," he said, "but I

know it's a net with all manner of holes in it." He forced a smile to his lips. "The truth of it is that given what I knew then, I made the best decision I could make. If I had stayed, I'd most likely be buried now with the rest of Windwir. And the work I'm now doing is far more important than any other I've been called to."

Jin Li Tam nodded. "I understand."

Petronus looked at the bird. "I will have Isaak check its memory scrolls and see what can be learned about this matter." He paused, looking uncomfortable. "Your father and I were good friends once," he said. "I would like to think that the boy I knew could not cause such darkness in the world."

Jin Li Tam didn't answer right away. She thought about Rudolfo—about his family and about his friend Gregoric. And she thought about the countless others her father and his father before him had bent like the course of a river to bring about their strategies in the world. She thought about the children—her brothers and sisters—that had been sacrificed along the way, no doubt in higher numbers than she would ever truly know. "My father," she said, "is capable of much darkness."

They sat in silence for a minute.

Finally, she stood. "Thank you for your time, Excellency."

Later, when she was in her room, she sat on her bed and looked out of the window. Flowers were blossoming as spring took hold. The rains were finally letting up. She thought about Petronus's words, and then she thought about the baby growing inside of her.

The work I'm now doing is far more important than any other I've been called to.

Jin Li Tam rubbed her stomach, and hoped that the light from this present work would outshine the darkness of her past.

Chapter

29

Rudolfo

The Li Tam estate was a flurry of activity when Rudolfo reached its unguarded gate. The large building towered above the palm trees, squatting over a green sea and white-ribboned beaches. Half of the iron armada was docked; the other half lay at anchor further out in the bay. Rudolfo saw crates, barrels and boxes stacked along the waterfront as servants loaded the ships.

He'd made the trip in six days—a wonder to be sure—and he'd only stopped when necessary. Riding alone and anonymous had its privileges—one of them was the relative ease of finding accommodations along the way. Rudolfo used that time to plan out the confrontation ahead.

But when he arrived to find the gate unattended, the estate's doors flung open wide and servants and children hauling boxes and crates through the gardens and down to the docks, it gave him pause.

They are preparing to leave. But why? He looked around again. They moved with methodical urgency and occasionally someone would shout out a question or a direction. There was a system, an underlying strategy, to how the work was laid out. And the workers were divided into crews.

Rudolfo singled out a middle-aged man with long red hair. "I am Rudolfo, Lord of the Ninefold Forest Houses and General of the Wandering Army," he said as he bowed slightly. "I would speak with Lord Vlad Li Tam."

The middle-aged man nodded. "He is expecting you." He pointed to the far side of the estate. "Follow the smoke."

Rudolfo sniffed the air, catching the faintest hint of smoke—and he could see it rising beyond the house. He set out across the garden, the smell growing stronger as he went. As he rounded the corner of the estate's north wing, he saw the bonfire.

Vlad Li Tam stood by it, feeding it slender, bound volumes from a wheelbarrow. His back was to him, and Rudolfo thought how easy it would be to kill him.

Still, he could not. Because Vlad Li Tam would only put himself in that position if he had weighed it carefully and seen a favorable outcome.

Perhaps death was the favorable outcome he saw.

Rudolfo closed the distance between them as Vlad Li Tam tossed the last book into the fire and turned to the handles of his wheelbarrow.

He looked up. "Lord Rudolfo," he said. "You'll forgive me if I continue my work while we talk? I have much left to do."

Rudolfo nodded.

"Very good," Vlad Li Tam said. "Follow me then." He pushed the wheelbarrow down a narrow path lined with bright flowers and through the open doors of his estate. Rudolfo followed him through the side entrance, walking just behind him as Li Tam rolled the wheelbarrow across the thickly carpeted hallway. They turned to the right and then to the left past walls that were now bare but still showed the outlines of the art that had recently hung there.

"You are leaving?" Rudolfo asked.

Vlad Li Tam looked over his shoulder. "I am."

They slowed and entered a vast library, its shelves scattered with a few leftovers—common books of little value orphaned on the shelves by hasty hands. "Where will you go?"

Vlad Li Tam shrugged. "I do not know. Away from the

Named Lands." He gave Rudolfo a hard look. "But my personal activities are of no concern to you. The Ninefold Forest Houses has a great deal of work and responsibility ahead."

They moved past the shelves that stretched from the floor to the ceiling, stopping before one massive bookcase that stood slightly askew. Vlad Li Tam took hold of it with both hands and pulled. It swung open to reveal a room within a room—a smaller library decorated with a large rug, a small table and a single armchair. All but one of the shelves was now empty, and Rudolfo tried to calculate how many trips the man had made to the fire outside. All the books were identical—small, black-bound volumes standing neatly in a row. Vlad Li Tam started at one end, lifting a single volume as if weighing it in his hands.

Rudolfo's eyes narrowed. "Regardless," he said, "I am beginning to believe that your personal activities concern me very much." He paused. "What relationship existed between House Li Tam and the heretic Fontayne?"

Vlad Li Tam balanced the book in the palm of his hand and remained silent for a moment. He carefully placed the book in the wheelbarrow. "Very well," he said. Then, he straightened and turned to face Rudolfo, smoothing his silk robes. When he spoke, his words were clear and firm. "I sent him to instigate insurrection in the Ninefold Forest Houses and to murder your parents." Then his voice became quiet. "He was my seventh son."

Rudolfo's hands curled around the hilt of his knife. He felt heat rising in his face. "Your son?"

Vlad Li Tam nodded. "I loved him very much."

The words struck Rudolfo like a blow, and he did not know why. Perhaps it was the way the old man said it. "Why would you do such a thing?"

Vlad Li Tam sighed. "You of all people should understand why. Certainly, you know the First Precept of the Gospel of P'Andro Whym?"

Change is the path life takes. Rudolfo nodded. "Yes."

"And T'Erys Whym's First Assertion?"

It was the credo of his Physicians of Penitent Torture. *Change can be forced by careful design and thoughtful effort.* They carved their Whymer Mazes into the flesh of their patients and hoped, by traveling those labyrinths, to bring about lasting change—true repentance. "You know I am familiar with it."

"A river can be moved," Vlad said, "with enough time and pressure." He turned back to the bookcase and took down another book. "So can a man . . . or a world."

Rudolfo drew his knife halfway from its sheath. "You killed my family to effect some kind of change upon me."

Vlad Li Tam nodded. "I did. But it is about far more than just you. It is about protecting the light." His eyes were suddenly hot with quiet anger. "I've done my part for the light, Rudolfo. I've paid my price to its service. If you need to see some kind of justice to move beyond the injustices done you, you can certainly have that. But after you kill me, go and do your part." He turned back to the bookshelves and pulled down another volume. "I would also appreciate it if you would allow me to finish with these."

Rudolfo released the hilt of his knife, letting the blade slide back into place. How many trips to the bonfire had the old man already made? Twenty? Thirty? It was hard to say, but Rudolfo imagined that the shelves had been full when he started. An ugly realization dawned on him. "These books . . . ?"

Vlad Li Tam answered before he finished asking. "They are the record of House Li Tam's work in the Named Lands, commissioned by T'Erys Whym during the First Papacy."

Rudolfo studied the unmarked spines. The magnitude of it awed him. "They go back that far?"

"Yes. To the Days of Settlement."

Vlad Li Tam pulled down the last volume and passed it over to Rudolfo.

He opened it and saw the script—it was a House language that he was not familiar with, though some of the characters were familiar to him. The words were crowded together, and there were numbers in the margins that he assumed must be dates. This book was only partially finished, and he realized with a start that it must be *his* book, this last volume. He remembered Vlad Li Tam's words.

It is about far more than just you.

He weighed it in his hand, and thought for a moment that perhaps he should keep it. If Jin Li Tam would not translate it, perhaps Isaak or one of the other mechoservitors could, with time. But did he truly want to know? And what would knowing change?

In the end, he handed the book back to Vlad Li Tam.

Now that the wheelbarrow was full and the shelves were empty, they returned to the fire. They didn't speak until they were outside again.

Finally, Vlad Li Tam looked up and met Rudolfo's eyes again. "I was asked by the Order to secure a new location for the Great Library under a strong caretaker." He paused. "You are the new shepherd of the light."

"But why me?" Rudolfo asked.

Vlad Li Tam shrugged. "Why *not* you?" The old man tossed a book into the fire, and Rudolfo watched the flames consume it. Whose lives were those? What deeds had been done, there on those pages? How had that river been moved and at what price?

It was a Whymer Maze that Rudolfo wasn't certain he could navigate. And each question only drove him in deeper. "And what is your forty-second daughter's role in this?"

Vlad Li Tam's face became a mix of sadness and pride. "She's my best and brightest, an arrow that I've sharpened since the day she was born." His voice sounded paternal. "She was made for this time, just as you have been."

One last question called him deeper into the maze. "What of Sethbert? Was Windwir part of your work?"

Vlad Li Tam's eyes narrowed. "Why would I snuff out the light in order to save it? Sethbert's actions are Sethbert's responsibility."

But Rudolfo heard no answer in his reply, and saw the care with which the old man avoided the question. And there was anger in his tone . . . maybe even fear. *He knows more than he tells me.*

"If I am your so-called Shepherd of the Light, perhaps you should be more forthright in your answers," Rudolfo finally said.

But Vlad Li Tam said nothing. Instead, he dropped another book into the fire.

They stood by the fire and said nothing for a time. Vlad Li Tam continued methodically tossing in books, and Rudolfo watched secret history upon secret history go up in flames. All of the work of House Li Tam over the centuries, first under the guise of shipbuilders and later as the greatest bank the Named Lands had known.

Finally, Vlad Li Tam reached the last book. The Book of Rudolfo, Shepherd of the Light. He held the book gently in his hands. "You don't have any children, do you, Rudolfo?"

"You know I do not."

Vlad Li Tam nodded, slowly, staring into the flames. "Our friends in Windwir could've helped you with that," he said.

Could they have? Perhaps, but he doubted it. Rudolfo shook his head. "Androfrancine magicks are often greatly exaggerated."

"Nonetheless," Vlad Li Tam said. Then his voice went quiet. "I have had many children." His eyes shifted from the fire and met Rudolfo's. "I've given sixteen of them to make you the man you are. Seventeen if you count the daughter who denounces me because of her love for you." He looked away. "If you had children," he said, "you would appreciate how seriously I take my appointed work in this world."

Rudolfo nodded, his fingers slipping to the hilt of his scout knife. "I do not have children," he said. "But if I did, I should not treat them as game pieces."

He would have drawn his knife then and killed Tam where he stood, but something stopped him. Something he'd seen a long time ago when he was a boy standing with a very different man by a very different fire. He'd seen it there by his brother Isaak's pyre where he stood with his parents. He saw it now here with Vlad Li Tam.

It was a tear running down the line of a grieving father's face.

Rudolfo watched that tear, his fingers caressing the hilt of the knife. Each question had taken him in deeper, and now, at the heart of this labyrinth, he found himself uncertain of what to do next. And that uncertainty revealed another discovery—that somehow, not being sure-footed was more alarming to Rudolfo than the idea that this old man before him had cut this Whymer Maze into his soul with a physician's salted knife, changing the course of his life by carving away pieces of it at key moments. How far had it gone? A twin, older by mere minutes, dies in childhood of a treatable disease and the youngest becomes heir. Two strong and loving parents are murdered, thrusting that young child into leadership at a fragile age. At a place of intersecting alliances, a close friend—a last anchor to innocence long lost—is murdered, and a strong partnership of marriage becomes rooted in the fertile soil of grief comforted, and blossoms into something like love.

Inquiry had led him into the center of this maze, and from this place, Rudolfo could see clearly now that he could drink an ocean of questions, and find himself adrift in doubt and thirsting for yet more answers.

Vlad Li Tam did not meet his stare. He raised that last book up over the fire, and Rudolfo turned away.

He did not want to see this grieving father burn the book Rudolfo's life had written. "If I see you again, Lord Tam," he said over his shoulder in a tired voice, "I will not hesitate to kill you."

As he mounted his horse, he did not look back.

Behind him, Rudolfo heard the book land in the fire and heard the hiss and crackle as it ate the pages of his life.

Petronus

Petronus looked at the storm of paper that had gathered over the surface of his desk and sighed. Through the open window behind him, a warm breeze carried the smells of the town mingled with the scent of flowers blossoming in Rudolfo's gardens.

He rubbed his temples. His eyes ached from the steady march of cramped script he'd read over the last few months, and in the past week the headaches had started up. His hand hurt, too, and he'd even sent Neb to the River Woman for salts to soak it in. The amount of paper was daunting even when he'd first arrived here, but it had increased steadily from that point and so had the hours he'd needed to put in if he was to untangle the knots and tie off the loose ends before the council. It was dark when he entered his office and started each day, and it was dark when he left.

Today would be no different.

He heard Isaak's approach beyond the partially closed door—the clicking and clanking of his gears and motor, the heavy footfalls and the slight hiss of escaping steam preceding the metal man's tinny voice. He poked his head into the room. "Father?"

"Hello, Isaak," Petronus said. "Come in."

Isaak walked into the room. In one hand he held the cage containing the golden bird that Petronus had asked him to investigate, and in his other he carried a small stack of paper.

"I've finished my work with the mechanical bird," Isaak said. He placed the golden bird on the corner of the desk, and Petronus noted that he set it in exactly the place he had picked it up two or three weeks earlier.

Petronus stared at it. Isaak had wanted to repair it, but Petronus had not wanted to take that step until they knew more about it. The bird lay in the bottom of its cage, its head twitching and its one good eye rolling loosely in its socket. One of its charred wings still lay bent and sparking, and its metal talons opened and closed mechanically. He forced his gaze back to Isaak. "Did you learn anything?"

Isaak's eye shutters flashed. "Its memory and behavior scrolls were significantly damaged by fire. Any more recent instructions are beyond retrieval, but it is indeed the property of House Li Tam. I found an inscription from Pope Intellect VII, gifting it to Xhei Li Tam."

Surprised, Petronus looked from Isaak to the bird. Intellect had been Pope centuries before the Order had begun its research in Old World mechanicals. "It's not Androfrancine work, then?"

"No, Father. It is a restoration, not a reproduction."

Petronus chose his next words carefully; Xhum Y'Zir's spell was a sensitive subject for the metal man. "Is the damage consistent with the . . . *events* . . . at Windwir?"

Isaak's eyes darkened, first one and then the other. He turned away. "Yes, Father." A gout of steam whistled, and his mouth flap opened and closed. Petronus had learned early on how to read these behaviors. Isaak was troubled. Finally, the metal man spoke again. "I do not understand it, though. It is certainly of durable design, and it was significantly damaged."

Petronus nodded. "Yes."

Isaak's voice lowered. "The other mechoservitors and I were on the ground in the midst of the Desolation. Why weren't we damaged?"

The old man shrugged. "Your leg was damaged."

Isaak shook his head. "Sethbert's Delta Scouts damaged my leg. The spell itself did not damage me or the others of my kind. I do not understand this."

Petronus felt his eyebrows raise. He hadn't realized the injury was not a result of the spell, and he wondered why he'd not thought about this sooner. There were fourteen mechoservitors in total, and all but Isaak were in the library when Windwir fell. He'd seen the blackened wreckage, the ruined remains of the few Androfrancine artifacts the gravediggers had collected in the wagons. Very little of it would be salvageable. And yet the metal men had emerged unscathed for the most part. "I do not understand it either."

Isaak placed the stack of paper on the one remaining bare surface of Petronus's desk. "That brings me to the other matter you asked me to investigate, Father."

Petronus rubbed his temples and tried to remember. His head felt full and he could feel the ache behind his eyes. "Which matter?"

"I have reinventoried the Order's holdings regarding magicks and mechanicals adaptable for military use. My process and findings are in this report."

More paper. Petronus looked at it but did not pick it up. "Can you summarize your findings for me?"

Isaak nodded. "Certainly, Father. In short, there are none remaining."

Now Petronus reached for the report and scanned the first page. "None?"

"No, Father. Though it should not be a surprise. Brother Charles was very careful to remove the most sensitive knowledge from his mechoservitors."

Petronus sighed. That part of the light was now lost, but perhaps that was a buried blessing in all of this. If it weren't gone, they would have been forced to make hard choices. After seeing what the worst of that war-making magick could do, he could not bring himself to grieve the loss of that darker light. His stomach sunk, suddenly, and his head snapped up. He fixed Isaak with a hard stare. "What about the Seven Cacophonic Deaths? What has become of it?"

He'd expected a reaction, but when it played out before his eyes, Petronus jerked backward in his chair. Isaak's entire body started shaking, his jeweled eyes rolling as his mouth flap whistled. His long metal fingers opened and closed, and his helmetlike head rolled on his slender neck. A low whine grew in pitch, and a gout of steam shot from his exhaust grate. Water leaked from his eyes and mouth. His chest bellows pumped furiously. "Father, do not ask me—"

Petronus felt a desperation edge into his voice, lending it

an angry tone. "Under Holy Unction, Isaak, I compel you: What has become of the Cacophonic Deaths?"

Suddenly, Isaak stopped shaking and his shoulders went slack. When he spoke, his voice was flat and reedy, as if far way. "That portion of my memory scroll was damaged in the casting of the spell, Father."

Petronus leaned forward, his voice more calm. "Damaged beyond *any* possible recovery?"

Isaak nodded. "Yes, Father."

Petronus nodded, relief flooding him. Still, it broke his heart to bring it up. Over the months he'd worked with Isaak, he saw more and more how that deep wound within shaped the metal man's soul. "I'm sorry to be so forceful, Isaak. But some things should never have come back from the Churning Wastes. Some parts of the so-called light should stay in darkness."

Isaak looked away and said nothing. Petronus couldn't tell if the metal man looked relieved, troubled or both. He decided to change the subject. "So has there been any further news on Lord Rudolfo?"

Isaak shook his head. "No, Father. Lady Tam has heard nothing. First Captain Aedric and the Gypsy Scouts have sent birds back—they've made inquiries along the coastline, but have no news as of yet."

Petronus nodded. The Gypsy King surprised him, abruptly vanishing after Sethbert's capture. Rudolfo was a wily one, but like his father, his sense of duty anchored him. When he concluded with whatever private matter he attended to, Rudolfo would be back to finish the work he'd started here, because like Petronus, he would do what he was made for. "I'm sure he'll turn up," Petronus said.

"Yes, Father." Isaak turned to the door. "If that is all, I have a meeting with the bookbinders to discuss logistics."

Petronus forced a smile. "Thank you, Isaak."

The metal man left, and Petronus relaxed in his chair. Outside he heard a child laughing, and for the briefest moment his nose filled with the smell of salt water and freshly caught fish as the laughter evoked unexpected memory. His feet could nearly feel the warm wood of the boat docks slapping at them as he raced a young Vlad Li Tam for his father's waiting boat.

The sudden image of his friend as a boy flooded Petronus with sadness. Beneath that sadness, he knew, lived a terrible wrath toward someone he once loved as a brother.

"I was made for this," Vlad Li Tam had told him long ago when Petronus had asked him if he ever wondered what his life would've been if he weren't Lord Tam of House Li Tam. Afterward, they'd gone fishing together for the last time, and it had almost touched the magic of earlier days, before destiny had found and chained them.

I should go fishing, he thought. Surely one of the servants or Gypsy Scouts could point him toward rod and tackle. The river that cut through town was not very wide, but he'd seen deep patches of green beneath the shade of the trees that lined its edge, and he knew that trout rose in it, their brown backs rippling the water as they fed.

But in the end, Petronus stayed at his desk and worked until his eyes blurred and his hand ached, unshackling himself from the desk long after the sound of frogs filled the forest-scented night beyond his window.

"What I was made for," he said quietly to that dark.

Jin Li Tam

Jin Li Tam awoke in the middle of the night to commotion in the halls, and crept to the spyhole in her suite's sitting room to look out over the stairwells and landings of the seventh manor. She saw servants and scouts rushing about as quietly as they could up and down the stairs, in and out of the doors.

She'd slept lightly these last two weeks, apprehension growing inside of her. It was unlike Rudolfo to simply vanish without a word. He'd turned Sethbert over to his Physicians of Penitent Torture, then ridden off without escort and without letting anyone know where he went or why.

One of the Gypsy Scouts had brought word back of Seth-bert's capture, and she'd practically interrogated him. The Overseer had surrendered personally to Rudolfo.

Sethbert said something to him. But what? Something about Windwir? Something about the motive for his terrible crime?

Whatever it was, Rudolfo had left without a word and without the Gypsy Scouts whose sworn duty was to protect their king at all times and all costs.

And now, she surmised, he had returned. She slipped into a light silk robe and went to the door that led to the bathing room. She could hear movement in the suites beyond her. Low voices whispered hurried instructions as his room was readied.

He must have caught them unawares. She chuckled. He'd probably used one of the many concealed halls, and now they were scrambling to dress out his room, despite the fact they had done so each and every morning in expectation of his return. Of course, he would've never asked for such a thing. But they knew their king.

The commotion quickly dissipated, and after a few minutes of silence, she heard soft footfalls in the hall. They fell in a measured stride she'd grown to anticipate over the months, and she listened as Rudolfo paused by her door before continuing on down the hall. She heard a door open and close, and she waited another ten minutes.

Quietly, she slipped through the bathing room and into Rudolfo's bedchamber. He wasn't there.

Jin Li Tam moved from room to room, not finding Rudolfo in the den or the sitting room. She went to the main door of his suite and opened it onto the wide hallway that encompassed the row of children's rooms and the main entrance to her own suite.

Of course, she realized. She walked to the door of that first room, the one that had belonged to his brother. She raised her hand to knock and then lowered it. Gently, she turned the knob and pushed the door open.

Rudolfo sat on the small bed. He was wearing nondescript clothing, his curly hair framing his face. He looked younger without the green turban of his office, despite the salt and pepper of his beard. He was holding the small sword in his hands, and he looked up at her.

I will not ask him where he's been. "I'm glad you're home."

His eyes met hers for a split second and then darted away. They had been angry eyes, she saw, and he had not wanted her to see them. "I am glad to be home."

I will not ask him where he's been.

But he started talking as if she had asked him. "I've been to the Emerald Coasts to speak with your father," Rudolfo said. "I've had a lot of time on the way back to think about what I would say to you, the questions I would ask."

More than the words, the very tone of his voice struck her like a fist. It was flat and distant, almost devoid of emotion. She'd heard it before, but only during the worst of his grieving over Gregoric. And those times, it was not so calculated.

He knows now. Some part of her had hoped she was wrong about her father. Some part of her that surprised her, that had never existed before meeting this man.

Before, she would have left no room for flights of fancy. But now she realized how desperately she'd hoped she'd been wrong about what her father had done to Rudolfo to make him the man he was.

She didn't know what else to say. "I'm sorry."

"How long have you known?"

She stepped into the room and pushed the door closed. "I've pieced it together since I've come here."

Rudolfo nodded and stroked his beard, his eyes again meeting hers. "And would you have ever told me?"

She shook her head. "I would not."

"Did you know that your father is leaving the Named Lands?"

"I wondered when I saw his library arrive," she said. "I am no longer in communication with my father."

Rudolfo looked away again. "They are loading the iron

armada with livestock and goods. There is another library—
a secret library—and your father has burned all of its books."
He looked back to her and his eyes narrowed. "You should
know that I have vowed to kill him if I see him again."

Jin Li Tam blinked and nodded. I might help him, she realized. She felt anger and sorrow on Rudolfo's behalf, and
anger and sorrow of her own. She did not see how her father
wasn't involved in the Desolation of Windwir. He had used
Sethbert in the same way that the mad Overseer had used
Isaak—dancing him on a string. She believed it with all her
being.

The flatness in her own voice surprised her when she spoke.
"I think he was behind Sethbert's genocide."

Rudolfo looked up, his eyes slightly wider. "You believe
your father brought down Windwir?"

She nodded slowly. "I do."

The Gypsy King stared at the child's sword in his hands,
then sheathed it and hung the belt back over the peg on the
wall. Finally, he looked up at her. "I do not think he did. But
he has done enough."

Jin Li Tam swallowed. "What does this mean?"

Rudolfo stood. "Nothing. The Androfrancines will hold
their council. We will plan our nuptials. We will rebuild what
we can and we will safeguard it." He touched the small turban, tracing his finger over it. "I have another question," he
said.

"I will answer it if I can." She shifted, her feet suddenly eager to move.

His eyes were hard and his jaw clenched. "Your father
claims you denounced him. He says it is because you have
love for me in your heart. Is this true?"

The directness of his question tangled her tongue. She felt
small and naked suddenly. Finally, she found words that she
had never imagined saying. "It is true," she said in a quiet
voice. "I do love you." His silence told her that he could not
say the same, but she laid that aside. "What my father did to
you is wrong," she continued. "I see this very clearly. But the

man you became—he is formidable and strong. He is able to ruthlessly pursue what is right and appropriate."

He nodded. "What you say is true. But it is a hard truth." He picked up the turban and held it to his nose, inhaling. "You know about my brother, then?"

"I do."

He opened his mouth to ask a question, and she knew what it would be. *Was my brother's death a part of this, too?* But then she saw him change his mind. "This was his room," Rudolfo said. "Tomorrow, I will have it emptied and have his belongings disposed of. I've held on to it for too long."

Tell him. But part of her thought she should wait for a less somber time. Part of her was unsure of how he would react. But tonight was a time for truth. She cleared her voice. "Actually, Lord Rudolfo, I have another idea for this room."

He raised his eyebrows. "Yes?"

She leaned closer to him. "You were wrong about your soldiers."

He looked at her blankly. "My soldiers?"

Jin Li Tam offered a tight-lipped smile. "I've been to the River Woman," she said. She watched as the realization dawned on his face. "It is a boy. I would like to name him Jakob if you will permit it."

Rudolfo opened his mouth and then closed it again. His brow furrowed. "You're certain?"

"I am certain. You are to be a father. We will raise a strong heir to guard the light you rekindle here."

"This," Rudolfo said slowly, "is unexpected and fortuitous news." He looked at her with something like wonder on his face. Gradually, it faded.

He knows it was my father's design.

She wanted to ask him if he thought that he could love her beyond this terrible knowledge. Certainly, he'd felt something then—she'd seen it on his face, heard it in his voice. But it wasn't love. It was need masquerading, based on the careful manipulations of House Li Tam. She wanted to ask, but she would not.

Instead, she would wait and see what honest thing could be built between them without deception. Jin Li Tam realized she knew very little about love.

But this much she knew—those who truly love should not require reciprocity.

Inclining her head toward her betrothed to show her respect, she slipped out of their future nursery and returned to her solitary bed.

Chapter

30

Rudolfo

Rudolfo, Jin Li Tam and Petronus dined together the next night. Rudolfo had arranged it before falling into his bed and sleeping away most of a day. He'd also insisted that Isaak attend, though the metal man did not eat. They started late. Overhead the sky moved from purple to gray, and the moon started its slow, upward crawl.

At Jin's suggestion, the cooks presented grilled venison and forest mushrooms in a garlic sauce, folded into a bed of rice and served with flat, fried bread and steamed vegetables. They drank crisp, cool lemon-beer and ate creamed berries for dessert.

Isaak sat politely at the table from beginning to end, speaking when spoken to but otherwise just listening. Rudolfo made a point of engaging him in the conversation where appropriate.

Rudolfo looked to him now. "How is the restoration going?"

"It's going well, Lord. Construction is so far ahead of schedule that we'll have to start working at night to keep up with them."

Spring was turning to summer now, and the fourteen me-choservitors worked beneath a large silk tent at the base of the hill. They had tables stacked with parchment and quills and bottles of ink, and they reproduced from memory what they could. The completed stacks were bundled, tied with twine and hauled by wheelbarrow to the bindery across the river. Originally, they thought it would take three years to restore what remained of the world's largest receptacle of knowledge.

"That's good news," Petronus said. "And I've received the letter of transfer. More good news."

Isaak nodded. "It is."

Petronus smiled. "Neb informs me that other holdings are finding their way home."

Isaak hummed and clicked. "Two hundred twelve volumes have arrived from various sources, along with diverse Androfrancine artifacts of interest. And we have letters from two universities inviting emissaries to review their holdings for items unaccounted for. We've always anticipated a forty percent restoration when we're finished. More if we reform the Expeditionary Office."

But when Isaak said those words, Rudolfo saw the look on Petronus's face, and knew that the Pope had no plans for a return to the Churning Wastes.

And he never speaks of future work beyond this Council. Rudolfo noted this.

They continued talking in low voices, drinking their wine and discussing the council and the work remaining.

Afterward, they reclined on pillows and listened to the beginning of night.

Isaak stood. "Humble apologies," he said, "but with your leave, I will return to my work." He clicked and clanked, then bowed before Petronus. "Good evening, Father."

Petronus chuckled. "Continue your excellent work. I'm sure we'll talk more tomorrow."

Isaak nodded, looked at Rudolfo and Jin Li Tam. "Thank you for your graciousness."

"You are always most welcome," Rudolfo said.

They listened to his pistons clacking as he exited the garden and took the stairs inside.

Jin's left hand moved quickly, her fingers shifting against the backdrop of her gown and tablecloth as her right hand reached for her napkin. *You should dismiss me and speak with Petronus alone,* she signed.

Rudolfo inclined his head slightly. "Perhaps our guest and I should take our plum brandy privately tonight?"

She smiled at them both. "I think you both have much to discuss." As she stood, her hand moved again, now against her hip and leg. *Be mindful; this old fox is crafty.*

"Not just crafty," Petronus said, "but also fluent in seventeen different nonverbal Court languages." He looked at her, his eyes crinkling with his smile. His own hand moved in the same pattern of language. *You have found a strategic and strong and beautiful woman, Rudolfo.*

Jin Li Tam blushed. "Thank you, Excellency."

She leaned over Rudolfo briefly, squeezing his shoulder before she left. Two Gypsy Scouts followed her as she left the garden.

Rudolfo clapped, and a server appeared with a bottle and two small glasses. He filled their glasses and vanished.

Petronus dug an ivory pipe and a weathered leather pouch from his plain brown robe and held it up. "May I?"

Rudolfo nodded. "Please."

Petronus looked nothing like a king, Rudolfo realized, and certainly acted nothing like any Pope he'd seen. He watched the old man pinch dark, sweet-smelling leaves between his thumb and forefinger, watched him shove the wad down into the pipe's bowl. He struck a match on the table and drew the pipe to life, a cloud of purple smoke collecting and twisting around his head before drifting out over the garden.

Petronus waited until Rudolfo lifted his brandy cup then raised his own. They held their cups up, saying nothing, and then drank.

Rudolfo tasted the sweet fruit, felt the fire as the brandy burned its way into him.

After a minute passed, Rudolfo cleared his voice. The gardens emptied as his Gypsy Scouts and servers shifted to take up positions nearby but out of earshot. "The time to talk plainly is upon us. Vlad Li Tam flees the Named Lands. Sethbert is silent beneath the physicians' knives. What are your intentions for the Order?"

Petronus shook his head. "You can no longer afford to think like that, Rudolfo. The Order is irrelevant. I am irrelevant. What's left of the library is all that matters."

Vlad Li Tam's words came back to him. *A new location for the Great Library. Under a strong caretaker.* "You are the Pope. You have a part to play in this."

Petronus shook his head. "My part in this is nearly finished. I left this behind for a reason. I intend to leave it behind again, Rudolfo."

Rudolfo blinked. "You can't mean that. They need you."

"No," Petronus said, "they truly don't." He sighed. "But *you* do. And I can give you what you need."

Rudolfo felt his eyes narrowing. "What is that?"

Petronus exhaled a cloud of smoke. "I can give you the Great Library."

I could take it. But even as he thought it, Rudolfo knew that he would not. "What do you want?"

"I think you know what I want."

"Continue," Rudolfo said. He suddenly knew what was coming.

"I will make it plain." Petronus looked at him, his eyes suddenly hard and bright. "If your guardianship of Windwir is not sufficient motivation, then by way of the kin-clave between your houses and mine, as King of Windwir and Holy See of the Androfrancine Patriarchy, I require the extradition of Sethbert, former Overseer of the Entrolusian City States. He will be tried for the Desolation of Windwir and for the souls lost in his act of unprovoked warfare."

Rudolfo thought of Sethbert now, in his cell on Tormentor's Row. He'd arrived a few days ahead of Rudolfo, and the Gypsy King was surprised at his reluctance to watch the physicians at their work.

Before Windwir, he often took his lunch on the observation deck when they were in session so he could listen to the physicians' calm exegesis beneath the screams of their patients. But since his trip to the Emerald Coasts, since discovering that he himself—along with the rest of the Named Lands—had languished beneath someone else's salted knife, he could not bring himself to take comfort in that work any longer. And he'd suspected for a time now that Petronus might invoke the Order's rights by kin-clave.

"I will extradite him for trial," Rudolfo said. "But you will give me a Pope if you won't stay yourself."

Petronus smiled and shook his head. "I will give you what you need, but I do not guarantee you a Pope." When Rudolfo opened his mouth to protest, he continued. "The honoring of kin-clave should not be confused with someone else's backward dream."

Rudolfo tilted his head, not sure if he'd heard properly. "Backward dream?"

"The world of P'andro Whym—like the world of Xhum Y'zir and his Age of Laughing Madness—is not the world of today, Rudolfo, and certainly not the world of tomorrow. In the early days, before the Whymer Bible was compiled, before the Androfrancines named themselves and robed themselves and built their Knowledgeable City at the heart of the world, they met a need because it was there at the moment." He held up his empty cup, turning it in the candlelight. "The cornerstone of Androfrancine knowledge is that change is the path life takes, yet we all dream backward to what has been rather than dreaming forward to what *can* be . . . or better yet, to dream in the *now*."

Rudolfo sighed. He could feel the truth of the old man's words in the dull ache of his muscles and soul from his long, contemplative ride. "We love the past because it is familiar to us," he said, "whether that past is light or dark."

"Yes," Petronus answered. "And sometimes, we try to carve the future into an image of the past. When we do so, we dishonor past, present and future."

The words struck Rudolfo, and he understood now at least part of Petronus's strategy. "You do not feel the Androfrancines need a Pope. It is why you left."

Petronus waved his hand. "It was many things. It was also about knowing my own soul. If I had continued, whatever I did would be a lie."

Rudolfo leaned forward. "How did you know? What brought you to that place of knowledge?"

Petronus shrugged, and laughed loudly. "My whole life brought me to that place of knowledge. There was no one thing. I woke up one morning and simply knew." He tapped out his pipe. "You'll understand soon enough."

Rudolfo raised his eyebrows. "What makes you say that?"

The old man smiled. "Your life has changed, Rudolfo. Your Wandering Army will soon wander no more and your Gypsy Scouts will run the forests without their Gypsy King. You will live in one house with one woman. And soon, your library will be the center of the world. This little town will grow beyond its past just as you have grown beyond yours. Add a few children—an heir to nurture, perhaps . . ." Petronus let the words die. "I know you know these things. I know you think about them."

Rudolfo's guard slipped and his thought slipped with it, coming out in a quiet voice. "What if my life becomes a lie?"

"Or what if it's becoming true?" Petronus stood.

Rudolfo shook the sudden doubt away, and stood as well.

"Will you take Sethbert off Tormentor's Row and place him in a simple cell?"

Rudolfo felt a twinge. "I will order it so."

"I will see him tomorrow." Petronus walked to the stairs,

then turned back to Rudolfo. "We will hold the trial at the conclusion of the Council of Bishops."

Rudolfo nodded. "I concur."

Petronus paused at the top of the stairs. "Do you remember what you said of Neb? That he would make a fine captain?"

Rudolfo nodded. The boy was intelligent and capable, a strong leader who influenced others without knowing it. That was a blade that could be sharpened into the fine edge of an intentional strategist. "I do. The Order is fortunate to have him."

A dark look crossed Petronus's face and Rudolfo saw loss there. "Remember those words, Rudolfo."

Rudolfo said nothing. He felt a another twinge, something restless moving beneath the surface of this all. He felt his eyes narrowing, but if Petronus noticed, he did not show it.

"Sleep well," the Pope said as he started his descent back into the manor.

"I will," Rudolfo replied. But he knew that he wouldn't. A gnawing feeling of dread grew in his stomach about the coming council, and at the center of it stood a man with a strategy Rudolfo did not yet fully grasp.

Neb

More and more, Neb found himself feeling at home in the Ninefold Forest. The work satisfied him, and the forest Gypsies fascinated him. And the Northern Marshes were just across the Prairie Sea from him.

As the days slipped past, Neb watched the small town fill to overflowing. The last large caravan arrived from the Summer Papal Palace that morning, and yet more tents went up in the large open meadow where the council pavilion stood.

This is all that is left, he thought as he watched the men in their dark robes walking among the rainbow-clad forest Gypsies. It staggered him, remembering a time when this many black robes would have been a relatively small gathering.

He'd brought the matter of recruitment up to Petronus several times in the last two months, but the Pope had deflected it. At first, Neb thought it was coincidence combined with the distractions of Petronus's office and the exhaustion he must surely feel. After all, the old man rarely slept these days, poring over page after page of parchment in his office late into the night, arriving early in the morning to do the same all over again.

But now, these deflections recurred enough that Neb realized Petronus was avoiding the subject. Still, in itself that may have been no more than a desire to take care of the more pressing issues. The mechoservitors worked day and night now to reproduce the library from their memories, their hands blurring as they moved pen across paper. Rudolfo had recruited a half dozen bookbinders and outfitted them in nearby tents while proper facilities could be built. Already, the manor was filling with stacked volumes, its halls and rooms smelling of new paper and fresh ink.

If that weren't enough to keep Petronus's attention on the here and now, there were vast Androfrancine properties that required difficult decisions. A group of one thousand did not have the same needs as a group one hundred times that size, but which holdings should be kept and which should be abandoned or bartered or sold off? Even if the Order planned for recruitment, it had taken two thousand years to build its power, and Neb doubted it could ever come back in the same strength it had before, even bound to the Ninefold Forest Houses.

And then there was the matter of Sethbert and the trial. The thought of the former Overseer rekindled a rage buried deep in Neb. Since the screaming wagon arrived, Neb had stopped dreaming about Winters and the reunion he longed for. Instead, he dreamed of killing Sethbert.

Isaak found him at the edge of town, watching the Androfrancines move about in their small city of tents. "Pope Petronus is calling for you."

"How is he today?" He'd noticed the dark circles, and had

even heard Petronus snap at one of the servants the day before. He had an edge about him that Neb hadn't seen, even during the worst of their work in Windwir.

Isaak shrugged. "He is exhausted. He seems . . . weighed down."

Neb nodded. He'd never asked Petronus why he'd left so many years ago, but he couldn't imagine that coming back was something he'd wanted to do.

I forced him to it. No, he reminded himself, Sethbert's act of violence had forced Petronus to it. More than that, it was the kind of man that Petronus was.

"We do what we must," Petronus had told him those times Neb had brought it up. "You did what you had to do and so will I."

Still, Neb regretted his part in it. He thanked Isaak and made his way back to the seventh forest manor.

Petronus's door was closed when he reached the office. He knocked at it, and a gruff voice answered.

When he saw the look on Petronus's face, he froze.

He knows about the weapon, he thought. He'd wanted to do what he was told with it. He'd taken it and had gotten halfway to the blacksmith with his fire and hammer, intending to have it broken into pieces and melted down. But he'd ended up in the forest with it, running his hands over it, feeling the history of it. It was probably five hundred years old, rebuilt no doubt from Rufello's Book of Specifications. It represented something—a part of the light, he supposed—and in the end, he could not bring himself to destroy it. In the end, he'd buried it in its oilcloth beneath the massive, mossy stump, marking the place with a few white rocks.

Neb opened his mouth to explain, but Petronus gestured to a chair and spoke first. "Sit down, Neb."

Petronus was distracted, shuffling papers on his desk until he found a neatly folded and sealed note. "I wanted to talk with you before I gave you this."

Neb looked at him, suddenly not so sure it was about the

weapon. He saw deep grief on the man's face, and his eyes were dark. "What is it, Petronus?"

When they were alone, he'd insisted that Neb call him by name, but now Petronus's eyes hardened. "You will address me now as Excellency or Pope," he said.

Neb felt his jaw go slack and his stomach lurch. "How may I serve you, Excellency?"

Petronus nodded slowly, closing his eyes. "*Would* you serve me, then, Nebios?"

Neb swallowed. Suddenly, he felt afraid and alone and uncertain. "You know that I would do anything for you, Father." He wasn't sure why he'd slipped into the older, more familiar term. Perhaps because he'd heard Isaak use the same. Or perhaps because over the last nine months, the man had played the role.

Petronus nodded again. "Very well then." He handed the note over to him. "I am rescinding your status in the Order."

Stunned, Neb took the note but did not open it. "If this is about—"

Petronus shook his head. "It is not about you." Their eyes met. "The assignment in Windwir and your work here were only intended to be . . . *temporary.*"

Neb wasn't sure what he felt. On the surface, shock. Below that, anger and despair and confusion. "I don't understand. There is much work to be done still. I can—"

Petronus's voice rose. "Enough," he said. "You named me your Pope." His eyes narrowed and he leaned forward. "Would you so easily challenge my authority?"

Neb swallowed and shook his head, fighting back the tears that suddenly threatened to ambush him.

Petronus looked away. "Your work has been exemplary, as my letter indicates." Neb stared at him, watching the old man's eyes go everywhere in their avoidance of his own. "You have become a fine young man and a strong leader." He paused. "You will of course be permitted to attend the council and trial if you wish it." But his eyes told Neb that he would rather he did not.

Petronus went back to shuffling the papers on his desk, and Neb sat in silence, staring at the folded note in his hands. He wanted to tear it into pieces and throw it back at the old man, shouting at the top of his lungs that he would not be discarded so easily. He wanted to cry and run to the old man's side and beg him to tell him what this was truly about, because he could see plainly that something dark—something terribly dark—worked at the soul of the man he credited with saving him from the madness of those early days after the Desolation.

No, he realized. Petronus did not save him. Hope did.

The old man continued shuffling through his papers, not speaking.

Because there are no other words left between us, Neb realized.

Finally, he stood and left the office, fleeing the manor for the forest. As his feet slapped at the grass and pine needles, Neb suddenly realized that once again his dreams were true.

"You will stand and proclaim him Pope and King in the Gardens of Coronation and Consecration," Brother Hebda had told him in that first dream of many. "And he will break your heart."

Brokenhearted, Neb sobbed in the forest of a place that no longer felt like home.

Vlad Li Tam

Vlad Li Tam could not abide wool during the summer, and he wondered how it was that anyone else did. The archeologist's robes were rough on his skin, particularly after three days in the saddle.

The iron ship had dropped him with his horse and his small entourage on an isolated portion of the coastline near Caldus Bay. He'd sent the remainder of his armada ahead, intending to catch up to them near the Whispering Isles at the edge of the Named Lands.

He'd intended to be done. He'd planned to send his children for this last bit of the work, but in the end he couldn't, despite Rudolfo's threat. Years of personally delivering his most important messages would not be denied, and finally, at the end of things, he'd come to the Ninefold Forest for the first time since that night long ago to meet with his seventh son and hear his final words.

The Gypsy Scouts had questioned them briefly about where they'd come from. An Androfrancine at a small table, shielded from the sun by a small canopy, recorded their names and positions within the Order. After the brief interview, he directed them to the field of tents outside town.

They added their own tents to that small canvass city, and while his sons put them up, he wandered among the dark robed men, watching and listening for any scrap or tidbit that might help him.

Eventually, he left the Androfrancine sector and wandered across the wide, low bridge into the town itself. He joined himself with others dressed like him, moving strategically through the parts of the town he would need to visit. Finally, he came to Tormentor's Row and the low stone buildings that served as the Ninefold Forest's prison—the one place he knew he would not be able to reach personally and where his coffers were not deep enough to purchase influence. He paused, listening for screams but hearing none. Of course, by now Sethbert would be in a cell. He expected Petronus would have insisted upon that, not wanting to legitimize that particular Whymer interpretation, with its cutting and peeling in the name of redemption.

Those guards would be above reproach, but the cooks would not be. And the message would be easy enough to send through them. A long strand of hair—Sethbert's sister's, in fact—tied to the foot of the game hen he would take for his final meal. The hen would be served whole just as Sethbert preferred. And another strand of hair—this one shorter and taken from his nephew Erlund, tied carefully around the small bird's bill. More threats at the end of a string of threats.

Of course, Vlad Li Tam had no intentions of killing Seth-bert's family. All of his children but those he'd brought with him for this last northward journey—and the daughter who no longer acknowledged him—waited for him on iron ships loaded with all of House Li Tam that they could carry.

But the threat would be clear, and sometimes a threat was enough to move the river. Vlad Li Tam was certain he could count on Sethbert taking the cue and keeping silent. And that silence would let his old friend finish the work he'd been made to do.

Smiling to himself, Vlad Li Tam continued his stroll through the town. He paused again at the gates of the seventh forest manor, studying the windows and doors and compar-ing them to the drawings and specifications he'd memorized so long ago.

There were messages for the manor as well, messages he would deliver personally.

But only after he finished moving the river.

Chapter

31

Rudolfo

Petronus, the King of Windwir and the Holy See of the An-drofrancine Patriarchy, reconvened the council with upraised hands.

Throughout the pavilion, voices went silent. Rudolfo sat

aside from the others not just as their host but also as someone who wanted to see as much as he could.

The first two days of the council had been simple matters of organization. Petronus had first submitted himself for examination— receiving confirmation from at least a dozen gray-headed Androfrancines that they did indeed know him to be who the announcements and letters claimed he was. With that out of the way, he issued and expounded upon encyclicals on everything from property dispersal to the construction and management of the library.

Before adjourning for lunch on the third day, he had elicited gasps of surprise when he gestured to the metal men in their acolyte robes. "These new brethren that we have made will watch over our library, and the Gypsy Scouts shall guard them."

Rudolfo smiled at this.

One of the bishops stood, angry. "They have no souls and you give them the light?"

Petronus had stared at the man and raised one of the new books into the air. "I give them nothing; they earn this. They work night and day to give back what was taken from you." The Pope smiled. "And you who have souls—how many of you have helped them?"

The bishop reseated himself while Rudolfo smiled.

After lunch, after Petronus reconvened them with his silent blessing, he looked at Rudolfo and gave a grim smile. "Soon," he said, "I will close this last council of mine. But first, we have unfortunate business together." He nodded toward the main entrance, and six Gypsy Scouts escorted Sethbert into the tent. They walked slowly to accommodate his shackles.

Rudolfo looked at the man who had once commanded a nation. Despite being fed well under his care, Sethbert had shed most of his fat. His hair had been shorn for the physician's work. His flesh had been cut, forming the holy lattice of a Whymer Maze upon his skin.

Scars of the Whymer knife, Rudolfo thought.

Rudolfo felt a stab of shame, and turned his eyes away.

Petronus

The crowd went to their feet; the thousand indrawn breaths were audible. But Petronus noted that Rudolfo and Jin Li Tam remained seated.

Petronus looked at the broken man before him. "Sethbert, former Overseer of the Entrolusian City States, once kinclave of the Androfrancine Order, do you understand why you are here today?"

Sethbert's lower lip quivered. "I do."

The work of those damnable physicians. Petronus felt a stab of anger, but suppressed it. But in the truest sense this trial was not for Sethbert's benefit, it was for his own and for tomorrow. No more backward dreaming

Petronus looked at Isaak and nodded. The metal man stood as Petronus continued. "Did you, of your own free will and with forethought of malice, order this mechoservitor's script altered in secret?"

Sethbert hung his head. "I did, Father."

"And what was the nature of this alteration?"

Sethbert looked up briefly, his eyes red and hollow. He opened his mouth and closed it. "I . . . I had it altered, yes."

Petronus's jaw went firm. "How did you alter it?"

Rudolfo looked at Isaak, and found himself squeezing Jin's hand harder than he realized. The metal man stood alone among his kind, his eye-shutters flickering and his bellows pumping. A low whine came from his exhaust grate.

Petronus studied the man. Sethbert looked around the room, first glancing at the metal man, then taking in the others. He saw Rudolfo, and their eyes met. He saw Jin Li Tam, and she looked away. Finally Sethbert saw Neb, and Petronus heard him gasp at the look of controlled rage upon the young man's face.

Sethbert's voice shook and for a moment, Petronus thought his eyes offered an imploring look, not for release but for forgiveness. "I altered it so that he would recite Xhum Y'zir's Seven Cacophonic Deaths in the central square of Windwir."

Petronus leaned on his podium. "You did this thing?"

"I paid someone to do it," Sethbert said. "I did it. Yes." And suddenly an odd thing happened. Sethbert's eyes became bright and hard.

"Why?"

Sethbert said nothing.

Petronus scowled. "Surely you had a reason."

Sethbert looked around the room again, possibly for a sympathetic face. There were none. And he had no way of knowing that his own family had been excluded from the proceedings at Petronus's command. The Gypsy King had actually protested this the night before, but had left the matter alone when Petronus raised his voice and reminded Rudolfo that though the trial was held on his soil, it was entirely an Androfrancine affair.

Sethbert drew himself up, broken no more. "My reasons were my own."

Petronus saw the line of his jaw, and realized that Sethbert would never tell. Not even the physicians had broken that part of him. It made him wonder what—other than a profound sense of rightness—could create that kind of resolve. Regardless, this matter was not about Sethbert. It was about a perception of justice and about a better future. He continued. "But you acknowledge guilt?"

"I do."

Petronus looked out over the crowd, scanning the room. Now his own eyes went to Rudolfo and Jin Li Tam, then to Isaak and finally to Neb, though the young man looked away quickly. It broke his heart to see it, but he'd known he had to protect the boy.

Then he saw another familiar face far up and to the right, partially hidden behind the hood of a low-level archeologist's robes.

Vlad Li Tam nodded to Petronus, a grim smile playing at the corners of his mouth.

Petronus forced his eyes away and looked back to Sethbert. "Then as Patriarch and King, I find you guilty." Petronus moved around the platform. "Does any here dispute my finding?"

No one spoke. No one moved.

Petronus continued his slow walk, his eyes narrow and studying the faces around him. He stopped in front of the new bishop who had challenged him on the matter of the mechoservitors. He stared at him and the bishop stared back. "What sentence does this crime merit?"

At first, the bishop didn't answer. Slowly, he worked his mouth open. "He should be put to death, Father."

Petronus nodded. "I agree that he should." He walked slowly to another bishop, one Rudolfo knew to have been an archeologist working in the Churning Waste until recently. "Do you agree?"

The archeologist nodded. "I do, Father."

Petronus whipped a fishing knife from his robes. He held the short blade aloft, watching as Rudolfo signed and gestured his rushing Gypsy Scouts to stand down.

Alarm spread over Rudolfo's face, and his hands moved quickly. *What do you play at, old man?*

Petronus ignored him. "Sethbert dies today. Who will carry out his sentence?"

Someone nodded to the band of Gypsy Scouts. "Have them do it."

Petronus chuckled. "Too long we've invited others to our unpleasant tasks. This one we will do ourselves."

Sethbert now was shaking. His bladder cut loose, wetting the front of his tunic and breeches. But he did not speak.

Now Petronus turned to Isaak. "You. What of you?" Isaak took a tentative step forward. "Of all of us here, he wronged you the most. He bent you against your will and turned you into a weapon beyond our wildest imaginings. He gave you the words to level a city and kill every man, woman, child and beast within."

The metal man took another step forward. "I want to," Isaak said now. "I truly do." He hung his head. "I cannot." When he looked up, his eyes went dark and his voice took on a tone of profound sadness. "Life is sacred."

Petronus nodded. "And that makes taking it so much harder. Any time we do so, we take something from the light." He turned away from the metal man, facing the crowd. "A wise Gray Guard once told me that being willing to die for the light was easy, that being willing to kill for it was a harder matter. Not everyone's shoulders were meant to bear such a burden." He looked at Rudolfo. "It is no secret that I do not wish to be Pope. I made that statement plain enough thirty years ago. You have asked me for a new Pope. I will give you one." He waited, letting the words settle in. "Whichever of you Androfrancines gathered here will come, take this knife and execute this condemned man, may have my Patriarchal blessing and bear the signet of the Gospel of P'Andro Whym. Kill this man and be our Pope."

No one moved. The room became silent.

Then, slowly, Neb stood up.

Vlad Li Tam

Vlad Li Tam watched the fisherman move the pieces on his board and saw his father's handiwork. He had not expected Sethbert's sudden resolve. His threat had been unnecessary. Now he saw the young man standing, and he saw the look of grief flash for just a moment across Petronus's face.

But Petronus would have anticipated this. Because they had taught each other as boys during that summer long ago, he knew how to read him. Petronus had taught him to fish, how to cast the net and pull it and how to cast the rod and drop the hook where trout were rising. In turn, Vlad Li Tam had taught him to play queen's war, and he had been adequate but awkward.

Now, he played this game as a master.

Petronus stared at the boy. Finally, he repeated himself

slowly, intending the words for the one young man in the room who had no hesitation. "Whichever of you *Androfrancines*," he said, "come and take this knife." He broke his gaze with the boy and looked to the mechoservitor who sat listening to the session so that it could later be reproduced on paper. "Let the record show that the young man, Nebios ben Hebda, was removed from the Order by a Writ of Excommunication by Papal Discretion."

Vlad Li Tam smiled. Another of his old laws.

Glaring, Neb sat down.

A voice rang out, and Petronus looked away from the boy. "A Pope would not do such a thing," one of the bishops said. "The Whymer Bible forbids it."

Petronus waited. A murmur rose beneath the tent, and a wind outside whipped through the three entrances, carrying the scent of evergreen and lavender.

Vlad Li Tam watched his old friend's next move and nodded. The brilliance and beauty of his father's work was something to behold. In that moment, he realized his own part in that work, and it awed him.

"Very well," Petronus said. He walked to Sethbert and stood before him. "None of you will kill for the light."

Petronus laid his hand on the side of Sethbert's face, gently as if he were a father comforting a wayward child.

But when the old man brought the knife up with his other hand, he was fast and sure, with the precision of a fisherman.

Petronus dropped the blade. He raised his bloody hands above his head.

"This backward dream is over," Petronus said. "I am the last Androfrancine Pope."

Then he tugged off his ring and dropped it alongside the red-stained knife.

Vlad Li Tam stood and quickly slipped from the pavilion. He moved fast, his escort beside him.

Soon, he thought, I will return to fishing.

Chapter

32

Petronus

Petronus scrubbed the blood from his hands and forearms in the fountain outside the manor. He'd slipped into a plain brown robe in the commotion that ensued just after his last act as Pope, then he'd made his way out the back of the pavilion and cut through the forest to the town.

So far, it had gone exactly as he'd planned, though he despised himself for the pain he'd caused the boy, Neb. He'd already sent out the birds, disposing of the properties and transferring what holdings remained into Rudolfo's name. All that remained was to pack and go home.

He moved past the Gypsy Scouts that guarded the manor without speaking, and slipped into his office, locking the door.

"I know why Sethbert destroyed Windwir."

Petronus looked up to see Vlad Li Tam sitting at his small desk. He had expected him, knowing there would be words between them as soon as he saw him sitting in the crowded tent.

Petronus felt the anger rise in him. "I'm not so sure that Sethbert *did* destroy Windwir. At least not without prompting." He pointed to the golden bird. "We know your bird was in Windwir. Did it bring word back to you?"

Vlad Li Tam's eyes narrowed. "You suspect me. But I had nothing to do with Sethbert. Rudolfo was *my* work. Just as you were my father's."

Petronus felt the words hit him like a fist. "What do you mean?"

Vlad Li Tam shrugged. "You were made for this day, Petronus. Just as Rudolfo was made to guard the light."

"You're lying." But Petronus wasn't sure.

Vlad Li Tam smiled. "Regardless, I have something for you."

He drew out a leather pouch and handed it to Petronus. "You'll find evidence here that there was a secret program in the Order to restore the spell."

Petronus took the pouch and placed it on his desk. "I don't doubt that. But that is hardly damning."

"There is more," he said. "The bird *did* tell me that Windwir had fallen. But I did not send the bird to Windwir. It had been missing from its cage for nearly a year before that."

Petronus looked up, surprised. "Where had it gone?"

Vlad Li Tam stood. "I intend to find out. I am leaving the Named Lands. I will not see you again." When he said it, Petronus heard finality in his former friend's voice.

They did not embrace or shake hands. Petronus simply nodded, and Tam left.

Petronus looked at the pouch. Finally, he picked it up, sat at his desk and unclasped the buckles. He drew two bundles of paper out and started scanning one. The first several pages were bank receipts in Whymer script acknowledging Petronus's closure of Androfrancine accounts. These were followed by Documents of Transfer, moving all remaining holdings to the Ninefold Forest Houses. But the last page stopped his eye. It was a Letter of Contribution addressed to the Order and dated three days before the transfer of holdings occurred.

Vlad Li Tam had found a way to pass his vast wealth on to his daughter through the Androfrancine Order and the Ninefold Forest Houses.

Petronus retied the strings and placed the bank letters on the stack of correspondence that waited for Rudolfo, Isaak and Neb to sort through after he was gone.

He opened the second bundle—meticulous reproductions of Order correspondence and reports. He went through page after page, looking at the drawings and seeing it written plainly in some places, veiled in others. He watched it unfold in front of him, and he couldn't take his eyes away from it. Beyond just the restoration of the spell, they'd made calculations and ciphers on the population impact of the Seven Cacophonic Deaths if used in a limited fashion. They had even developed a delivery system for the spell. A walking, talking and thinking machine brought back from the days of the Younger Gods, resistant to the magicks of such as Xhum Y'Zir.

Petronus felt his heart break for Isaak and the other metal men. These documents had to be forgeries. They simply had to be, because what he read stood in the face of everything he knew about the Order. True, he'd grown to hate it as much as he ever loved it, but he could not believe this. Sethbert's decision to strike first suddenly made sense, and Petronus felt a pang of hot, sharp grief twist in his stomach as what he'd done settled in.

Then he saw Vlad Li Tam's note at the bottom. The ink on it was still wet and smudged.

They meant to protect us.

It made sense now. The Androfrancines had ever considered themselves the shepherds of yesterday, guarding the New World from itself and from a past they feared might be repeated.

They meant to protect us.

He felt the tears now, pushing at his eyes, and his thoughts turned suddenly as that greater strategy took form before his very eyes. Someone out there had penetrated Vlad Li Tam's network of sons and daughters or his closely shielded staff. They had somehow maneuvered the rescripting of the golden bird to implicate Vlad Li Tam in the Desolation of Windwir. A savvy player of queen's war, when the consort was threatened, would have moved him to a point on the board as far removed from that threat as possible. Vlad Li Tam, dismantling his vast network, had done so.

But who was the other player, that Vlad Li Tam would

remove himself utterly from the New World, transferring his wealth to the Androfrancine Order and donating his holdings to the new library, leaving nothing behind but his daughter?

Someone beyond the Named Lands.

Petronus felt his knees go weak.

The Androfrancines had known this, at least some part of them. And they had feared it even to the point of seeking out the terrible song of Xhum Y'Zir to protect the Named Lands from this invisible threat.

In the end, their best intentions for the light had nearly extinguished it.

Perhaps his actions had been justice. Perhaps they had been mercy. Either way, Petronus had done what he had done. Sethbert lay dead and the Order lay dead alongside him. He thought of Grymlis and the Marsher village so long ago.

He put papers in the pouch and put the pouch with the small pile of things he intended to take back with him to Caldus Bay.

By the time he'd finished packing, the tears had already begun.

Jin Li Tam

In the pandemonium that followed Sethbert's execution, Jin Li Tam slipped from the pavilion. She'd seen something unexpected there—one of the younger Androfrancines looked surprisingly like one of her many siblings, and when their eyes met, he had looked away, and then vanished through one of the three wide entrances.

She followed.

She felt no anger over Sethbert's death. He would've died regardless, she realized. And despite the years she spent with him, at no time had she forged any kind of bond with the man. She had no more doubt that he had brought down Windwir than that her father's hand was intricately tied to all of these events, right down to the execution that for all practical purposes ended the Androfrancine Order's legitimacy. Certainly, those few who remained—the Remnant—could try to come back from this, but it would never be successful. And what could they come back to? She had no doubt that Petronus had wrapped the Order's loose strings before disqualifying himself from the Papacy by wetting his hands with Sethbert's blood.

She wondered if that were her father's work as well.

The thought of her father brought her back to the moment, and she pressed her way through the gathering crowd. She caught sight of the young Androfrancine moving quickly ahead of her and she quickened her pace. But when she caught up to him, it wasn't her brother after all.

"I'm sorry," she said, slipping back into the crowd and looking around.

You want to see someone from House Li Tam, she realized. She thought about this. Why? Over the past few months, her anger had ebbed and flowed like the tidewaters of Tam Bay in her home city. When the anger rolled out from her, the sand in her heart filled in with grief to the point that she longed for the anger's return. Inevitably, the wave crashed back to enrage her all over again.

But suddenly, now, at the end of it all, it was as if both her anger and her grief toward her father had vanished beneath the tip of Petronus's knife. Rudolfo had told her once that people spent their lives living with a thousand insignificant injustices, and that sometimes seeing justice served on one great evil could move them forward from the path where they'd been stuck. That sudden death, both of Sethbert and the Androfrancine Order, left her hollow and spent, thinking only of the better world she hoped to give her baby.

She took her time returning to the manor. She knew she should wait for Rudolfo, but she felt a sudden craving for solitude, and knew that his work for the night was just beginning. There would be uproar to quell, fears to assuage and assurances to offer to what little remained of P'Andro Whym's lineage.

It was near dark when she approached the hidden doorway

near the rear garden, and she stopped. The door was open, and a figure stood in the shadows of the concealed passage. She drew closer and stopped again, suddenly afraid and uncertain and alone.

Her father broke from the shadows, dressed in a deep gray archeologist's robe. He said nothing, his face unreadable and hard though his eyes were soft. She said nothing, certain that her own face matched his own and equally certain that her eyes did not. She thought she would feel the anger again at the sight of him, but absolutely nothing stirred inside of her.

Their eyes met, and he nodded once, slowly. Then he moved past her, his shoulder brushing hers as he went. She turned around to watch him go, and she thought he walked more slowly and with less confidence.

She considered calling after him, but she did not know what to say. Instead, she watched him walk away, and after he'd gone, she went into her new home and closed the door. She had a life to build with Rudolfo and their unborn son.

She did not find her father's note until much later. She had not thought to look for it, though she could not remember a time when he'd ever failed to leave word for her. It was simple, scrawled quickly and without code.

For my forty-second daughter, the title read, *upon the celebration of her nuptials and the birth of her son, Jakob.*

It was a poem about a father's love for his daughter. At the end of it, the father sailed into the waiting night and the daughter learned a new way of life.

Neb

The crowd caught Neb up and moved him. By the time he disentangled himself from it, most had left the pavilion to gather in the field outside. Voices buzzed, rising in an ever-growing noise. He stayed by the entrance watching Rudolfo speak with a handful of the Androfrancine bishops, even while his Gypsy Scouts loaded Sethbert's body onto a stretcher to carry it off.

I would have done it for you, he thought. But he knew that Petronus buried his own dead in his own way and that he'd intended better things for Neb. Just as he also knew that the old man had no more wanted to kill Sethbert than he had wanted to take back the ring.

We do what must be done.

Isaak limped out of the pavilion. "Brother Nebios," he said. "Have you seen Father Petronus?"

Petronus no longer wore the title, but Neb didn't have the heart to remind Isaak of that. Instead, he shook his head. "He left quickly."

Isaak's eyes fluttered and flashed. "I am alarmed by the events of this day."

Neb nodded. "I am too, Isaak."

Isaak continued. "I know that what I have seen is wrong. I know that it goes against the teachings of P'Andro Whym. I also know that it must surely mean an end to the Order that brought me into this world. And yet I feel an unexpected satisfaction."

Neb studied him, unsure of what to say. His own satisfaction came from knowing that the man who killed his father would never harm anyone again. But another man—Petronus—had made him an orphan all over again, bringing down what little remained of the only family he had ever known.

You were always an orphan, some voice deep inside of him said. He looked at Isaak again. He was an orphan, too, Neb supposed.

"I will look for him in his office," Isaak said. "I must speak with him about what has transpired here today."

Neb walked with him in silence, certain that they would not find Petronus in his office. He doubted they would find him at all, at least not around here. The old man's work was done now, for better or for ill, and the world must now move forward from it.

They passed the canopy with its long trestle tables and benches, stacks of paper and bottles of ink. Even now, a few of the mechoservitors sat, gears humming and eyes flashing, as they wrote down the events of the council so that it might be preserved in the Great Library.

At Neb's questioning look, Isaak paused. "I sent them out right away to record it all. I thought it could be important someday."

Neb said nothing, and they continued without further words.

The office was dark and the door closed when they approached. The lamp was still warm when Neb relit, it and most of the papers had been neatly arranged on the desk for the next day's filing. He saw an envelope with his name on it, and he took it, breaking the seal.

I'm sorry, it read. *You were made for more than backward dreaming.*

Isaak's eyes dimmed, and his bellows pumped. "What does it mean?"

Neb lay the note back on the desk and leaned over the other pages. Notes and receipts of transfer, letters of credit, disposal of excess properties. All signed and sealed with the papal signet, and waiting for whoever would find them first. "It means the work goes on," he said in a quiet voice. "It means we lament what light is lost and honor what remains."

Leaving Isaak, he wandered the hallways and finally escaped into the gathering darkness. He ran into the woods as far as his feet could carry him, then found a stone and sat on it. He had no tears. He felt no anger. He simply *was.*

"I was always an orphan," he said to that darkness as it drew in close around him.

He remembered Petronus's note. *You were made for more than backward dreaming.*

Perhaps he was. Neb thought about Winters. He thought about the dream where above them, a large brown world filled the sky. *This is our home,* she had said, laying naked beside him, and he believed her. Somewhere beyond this time, a new home arose.

Someday, in the fullness of time, he would help them find it. But until then, he would stay here in the Ninefold Forest. Perhaps Rudolfo would let him serve the library in some fashion.

"Are you still here?" he asked the empty forest.

Nebios ben Hebda heard the soft grunt and the slightest stirring from somewhere nearby, and he smiled.

Rudolfo

Rudolfo caught up with Petronus on the road to Caldus Bay on the evening of the following day. He'd spent most of a night and a day soothing his shaken guests. When he heard that the old man had slipped quietly out of the city the night before, he called for his fastest stallion. He waved off his Gypsy Scouts, and Aedric didn't balk when he saw the anger in Rudolfo's eyes.

He pushed his stallion hard, riding low and feeling the wind tug at his cloak and hair. He inhaled the smell of the forest, the smell of the horse, and the smell of the plains ahead.

When he spotted the old man and his old horse two leagues into the prairie, he felt for the hilt of his narrow sword and clicked his tongue at his steed. He pounded ahead, overtaking Petronus, and spun his horse. He whipped out his blade and pointed its tip at the old man.

Petronus looked up, and Rudolfo lowered his sword when he saw the look of devastation on the old man's face. Those bloodstained eyes, he realized, looked too much like the red sky he'd seen over the smoldering ruins and blackened bones of Windwir.

The old man did not speak.

Rudolfo danced the stallion closer to ask a question that he already knew the answer to. "Why?"

"I did what I must." Petronus's jaw clenched firmly. "Because if I didn't, everything else I did would be a lie."

"We all do what we must." Rudolfo sheathed his sword,

the anger draining out of him. "When did you know? When did you decide to do this?"

Petronus sighed. "Some part of me knew it when I saw the column of smoke. Another part knew it when I saw the field of bones and ash."

Rudolfo pondered this and nodded slowly, searching for the right words to say. When he couldn't find them, he spurred his horse forward and left the old man alone with his tears.

⤺

Rudolfo raced the plains until the moon rose and stars scattered the warm, dark night. At some point, everything fell away but a false sense of freedom that Rudolfo embraced for the moment because he knew it would pass soon. He sped through the darkness, feeling the stallion move beneath him, hearing its hooves on the ground and the snorting of its breath. It was he and his horse and the wide open prairie, with no House Li Tam, no library, no Androfrancines, no nuptials and no heir. And though he knew it was false, Rudolfo honored the lie of it until he saw the forest on his right. Then he slowed the stallion and turned for the trees, eventually slipping from the saddle and leading the horse on foot back in the direction of what was true.

He took the less familiar paths, and thought about his life. He thought about the days before Windwir fell and the days after. He thought of nights spent in the supply wagon because he preferred it to a bed. He thought of days spent in the saddle instead of his study. Beds shared with more women than he could count and the one woman he knew he must have.

My life has changed, he told himself, and he realized that it would not have if he had not wished it so. He had chosen to rebuild the library, to keep something good in the world of its philosophies, art, drama, history, poetry and song. He had also chosen to align himself with Jin Li Tam, a beautiful and formidable woman that today he could respect, and one day he would love. Between them, they would bring forward a life who would also, if Rudolfo had his way, be formidable and beautiful. And he would inherit the light and be a shepherd of it as his father was.

Rudolfo thought of these things, and he thought of the old man making his way towards the coast, tears wetting his white beard. He thought of his friend Isaak limping about on his mangled leg and wearing his Androfrancine robes. He thought of the boy, Neb, who had stood when Petronus bid someone kill for the light. He thought of Vlad Li Tam at his bonfire, burning the record of his family's work.

The Desolation of Windwir has reached us all, he thought.

It no longer mattered why. It mattered that it never happen again. And Rudolfo saw clearly his part in that, and he saw how a lamentation could become a hymn.

The less familiar paths fell away, spilling him onto the road. He crossed it, still leading his horse, and stayed to the forest, though he could see the lights of his sleeping city now. He continued on, approaching the library hill from the southern side.

He would stable his horse. He would let himself into the manor. He would approach Jin Li Tam in her bedchamber, and he would whisper quietly with her into the morning about a forward dream that they could share between them. In the morning he would give the order to dismantle Tormentor's Row, and let go of that backward dream so that his son, Jakob, and his metal friend, Isaak, could build something better. But first, he had to see the small part that he had started for them.

Ahead, he heard soft voices, a low humming, and a whispering sound he could not quite place. Leaving the horse, he stepped forward, silent as one of his own Gypsy Scouts, to pull aside the foliage that blocked his view.

The bookmakers' tent lay open before him, its silk walls rolled up to let in the night. The soft voices were those few of the remnant who had stayed behind to help, moving from table to table, laying out parchment and fresh quills. The metal men worked at those tables, their gears and bellows humming and their jeweled eyes throwing back the lamp-light.

Rudolfo stayed for an hour, sitting in grass that grew damp with dew, soothed by the sound he couldn't place before.

It was the sound of their pens whispering across the pages.

Postlude

It is a bird, and it has been dead for a month but does not know it. Its snapped neck leaves the head hanging limp as its wings pound the sky.

It flies over a hillside beneath a blue-green moon and perches for a moment on a fresh-hewn cornerstone.

It flies over a field of ash beside a river, and it opens its beak to taste the memory of war and bones upon the wind.

It flies over an ocean, an armada of ships gathering at its edge, steam from their engines fogging the bird's dead eyes.

It flies homeward, this dead messenger, at the Watcher's bidding.

The bird enters a small window. It lands upon a scarlet sleeve, and when it opens its beak, a metallic whisper leaks out.

"Thus shall the sins of P'Andro Whym be visited upon his children," the kin-raven tells its master.

Acknowledgments

Writing can be a solitary act but there is certainly a community aspect to it as well.

I would like to thank the following people for their part in bringing *Lamentation* together:

First, my amazing wife and partner, Jen West Scholes, and my great friend Jay Lake, who finally accomplished the seemingly impossible task of getting me to write a novel. Right there beside them, I'd be remiss if I didn't thank John Pitts for his constant support and friendship, and Jerry Jelusich for the same. These four kept me cranking the words out at a breakneck pace, driven by their enthusiasm, and then loaned their keen eyes to the revision process.

Robert Fairbanks introduced me to sword and sorcery as well as Dungeons and Dragons. Your map of the Named Lands, sir, brings back great memories. Thank you for that, and for nearly thirty years of brotherhood.

My father, Standley Scholes, who told me if I wanted it bad enough I'd crawl across broken glass to get it. You were right, Dad, and it wasn't so bad after all.

I'd also like to thank Shawna McCarthy and Doug Cohen at *Realms of Fantasy* —I'm glad you two loved Rudolfo and the gang enough to publish "Of Metal Men and Scarlet Thread and Dancing with the Sunrise" and introduce the short story that stretched into the Psalms of Isaak. (Shawna, that note to go write a novel with these characters was a great boost!) And I'm grateful to all of you out there who read the story and loved it enough to write to me and say so. That's great encouragement.

Allen Douglas: Your artwork for the *Realms* story was so powerful that it showed me how much more there was to what I'd started there and was the diving board into inspiration. It's on my wall now, to remind me.

And then there's my agent, Jennifer Jackson, Thirty-second Daughter of Vlad Li Tam: I'm glad you loved the book, and I'm pleased to be in such great company at the Donald Maass Literary Agency.

To Beth Meacham, Tom Doherty, Jozelle Dyer, and the fine crew at Tor: Thank you for your enthusiasm and support for this project. It is contagious and often fuels my fire. I am grateful for your hard work on this book—and on the ones to follow. I look forward to our work ahead.

There are dozens of other people who helped along the way. Thank you all.

And last but not least, thank *you,* Dear Reader, for giving your time to this book. I hope you'll return to the Named Lands with me soon.

Ken Scholes
Saint Helens, Oregon
March 2008

Turn the page for a preview of

CANTICLE

KEN SCHOLES

Available October 2009
from Tom Doherty Associates

TOR®   A TOR HARDCOVER   ISBN 978-0-7653-2128-2

Prelude

Sunrise on the Churning Wastes was a terrifying glory. Each morning the Gypsy Scouts watched it from their station on the Keeper's Gate.

First, the cold air took on the warm scent of salt and sand. Then the sky was washed in deep purple, shot through with veins of red, twisting and spreading out on a flat horizon that stretched forever past the low hills that marked the Whymer Way leading into the Desolation of the Old World. And in that moment before the sun rose red and angry as a fist, the world went silent and still.

Today, in the heart of that moment, a brown bird dropped into the Watch Captain's net.

He unrolled the tiny scroll it carried and squinted at it in the crimson light from the east. Then he whistled his men to Third Alarm and watched the front guard magick themselves to slip into the morning shadows.

He hastily coded a note to Aedric, the First Captain of Rudolfo's Gypsy Scouts, and passed it to his birder. "See this to Seventh Forest Manor," he said.

Then he climbed down the stairs to the base of the massive, closed gate and stood to the side with his arms crossed.

A metal man in robes approaches from the west. This was most irregular. General Rudolfo's metal men worked at the library. And their leader, Isaak, was the only one of their lot who wore robes. The Watch Captain scanned the road that led down from the jagged stone hills to the west. That winding road came from only one city.

Windwir. Now a Desolation because the Androfrancines couldn't leave well enough alone. They'd brought back Xhum Y'Zir's Seven Cacophonic Deaths, and the spell had been their undoing. An entire city and its Order snuffed out, ending their long guardianship of the light, the knowledge of the Old World that had fallen to the same spell two thousand years before.

And now, it seemed, the metal man who had cast the spell and doomed the Androfrancines approached his post unannounced. "Most irregular," he said out loud.

He watched the road, picking his men out easily despite the magicks that concealed them. Each was a quiet, individual wind that gently moved the blades of grass and the pine boughs as the invisible scouts slipped into position. During the war last year, he'd been a lieutenant and he'd run with his men. Now, the double-edged blade of promotion set him apart from them. And with the promotion came a new assignment here in the mountains that divided the old world from the new.

Birds flitted across the massive stones of the Whymer Way and the wind shifted, carrying the sound of metal footsteps.

A robed figure limped into sight, wheezing and bubbling. One of its jeweled eyes hung by a strand of gold wires and the other rolled listlessly, its shutter bent open. The Watch Captain stepped forward, ready to bark orders. Rudolfo would have the head of any man who failed to help his friend, and the metal man, Isaak, was more kin than friend to the Gypsy King. But he hesitated.

"Brother Isaak?"

The metal man looked up. Its voice burbled as its bellows wheezed. "My name is Charles," the metal man said in a watery voice. "I am the arch-engineer of mechanical science for the Androfrancine Order in Windwir. I bear an urgent message for the Hidden Pope, Petronus. *The Library is fallen by treachery. Sanctorum Lux must be protected.*" With a click and a clack, the mechanical collapsed into a pile of steaming metal, bits of it sparking and popping.

The Watch Captain shouted for another bird and whistled his men in from the forest.

High above, a kin-raven circled.

Chapter

1

Rudolfo

Late-afternoon sun washed the expansive forest in red, and Rudolfo watched it from the highest point of Library Hill. It had been a long day of paperwork amid the pandemonium that gripped his Seventh Forest Manor's staff, and finally Rudolfo had fled under the pretext of an unscheduled inspection of the library construction. He had quietly strolled the basements and subbasements, grateful for the break in routine.

Of course, he couldn't blame the staff for the chaos. It was, after all, *his* Firstborn Feast they were preparing. In mere weeks, Rudolfo would see his first child into the world, and it was the custom of the Forest Gypsies to celebrate that event with great vigor. That it was Rudolfo's firstborn *and* an heir transformed the event into a minor affair of state, with dignitaries expected from a dozen or more houses. Even the Marsh King was attending. Rudolfo smiled at this, knowing that the large hairy man who posed as the Marsh King did so at the command of a fifteen-year-old girl who was the true heir to that Wicker Throne. But tonight, Hanric would play the part of king alongside Rudolfo and the other lords in attendance. Those aspects of tonight's festivities bored Rudolfo. Instead, he thought about the men who were the true hosts of tonight's event—the men who rose to their captain's challenge to honor their Gypsy King and the Gypsy King to Come.

The Gypsy Scouts could be proud of their work. They'd hunted and fished for six weeks to stockpile the game required for the festivities; they'd sent birds and riders all over the Named Lands to gather the finest sampling of wines and spirits. They'd even hired in cooks from the Emerald Coasts to study the best of the Forest recipes and reproduce them with southern augmentations to draw out the flavor.

Rudolfo chuckled. Tonight, the Marsh King would sit to his left and the Entrolusian ambassador would sit to his right. The Entrolusians had sent their ambassador because Erlund was beset by the fires of rebellion on the Delta. When Erlund's uncle, Sethbert, had destroyed Windwir, he'd hoped to shore up the Entrolusian economy by annexing the Ninefold Forest Houses with the help of his puppet Pope. Rudolfo and his kin-clave had pressed them back, and eventually Sethbert's plans were unraveled and the Overseer himself tried and summarily executed for the genocide of the Androfrancine Order and their city.

How long ago had that been? Six months? Seven? It had crawled like years. League upon league of paperwork. Hour upon hour of meetings. Entire days that slipped past him without seeing the sky or feeling the wind on the back of his neck. The last time he'd stood here, the bookmakers' tent was still below in the heat of Second Summer as metal man and Androfrancine and Forester worked together to reproduce what they could of Windwir's Great Library.

Now winter wrapped the forest, and the bookmakers' tent was packed away. Their tables now crowded the basements of Rudolfo's Seventh Forest Manor, and the books they produced filled the hallways and spare rooms to overflowing. Until now, of course, when those spaces were suddenly required.

Rudolfo paused and wondered where they had managed to store all of the books. And how long ago had it happened?

What it pointed to disturbed him. *I didn't even notice.* There was a time when he would have picked up on the slightest difference in the length of any one of his scout's beards. But now mountains of books vanished beneath his very feet and it took him days to realize it.

He heard the clicking and clacking, the slightest wheeze of bellows, and turned to watch his metal friend approach.

"Lord Rudolfo?" a metallic voice asked.

"Isaak," Rudolfo said. "You've found me."

Isaak stepped into view. "Yes, Lord." He paused, smoothing his Androfrancine robes with his metal hands. "I trust you found your inspection satisfactory?"

Rudolfo chuckled. He should've known the metal man would worry. "You are doing wonderful work here, Isaak."

Isaak blinked. "Actually, Lord, there are many more besides myself performing this work. The list is rather extensive, but I have a file of names in my office for your review. Or I could recite them—"

Rudolfo raised a hand. "A compliment to all involved," he said.

Isaak nodded. "Thank you, Lord. We serve the light."

"We do indeed," Rudolfo said. "But truly, Isaak, you are a fine foreman for this work."

Isaak inclined his head slightly. "Thank you, Lord. Might I add that Lieutenant Nebios has been extremely helpful in that respect."

Rudolfo had seen Neb's leadership throughout the gravedigging of Windwir. That was when he'd first recognized that there was a fine captain buried in the lad. And some of Isaak's methods looked surprisingly similar to Neb's. "So he's been advising you?"

Isaak blinked again. "I have been making inquiries and cross-referencing them against library holdings on Francine observations of human leadership dynamics." He paused, releasing steam through the exhaust grate in his back. "Neb is a natural leader."

Rudolfo nodded and stroked his beard. "Yes," he said. "I see that, too." But beyond what Rudolfo saw, the Marshfolk saw Neb as the one who would someday find—and take them to—the new home as promised in their Book of Dreaming Kings.

Rudolfo turned his eyes back to the forest and his home in it.

The sun was nearly down now, and the lights of the manor and the town called to Rudolfo. High above, as the sky went from purple to charcoal, swollen stars pulsed to life and a blue-green sliver of moon danced behind a hazy veil of cloud. Rudolfo drew in a lungful of night air and smelled the roasting meat from the kitchens far below.

"I suppose we should get ready for the feast," he said, clapping Isaak on the shoulder and feeling the cool metal beneath the rough wool robe.

Isaak nodded. "Lady Tam sent a scout for you. I told him I would pass her message along."

Rudolfo chuckled. A few weeks earlier and she'd have come herself, but the River Woman insisted she rest now. She'd balked initially but at the last accepted the midwife's instruction and forced herself to bed. Rudolfo knew better than to taunt the tiger in her cage. "I was finished here," he said, turning to Isaak. "Walk with me."

They walked in silence among the massive, scattered stones that were slowly taking shape. The air was cold on Rudolfo's face and his breath showed. Picking his way carefully through last week's snow, he and Isaak descended the hill that was gradually transforming the Ninefold Forest, turning it into the center of the Named Lands.

It had already started, of course, not long after Petronus had executed Sethbert and transferred the wealth of the Androfrancine Order into Rudolfo's name for the reestablishment of the library. And just yesterday, another university—this one a larger bookhouse out of Turam—brought their petition to establish a presence near the Great Library. Rudolfo had listened to their request, told them he was honored by their interest in the Ninefold Forest, and that he would take the matter under consideration. It was the fourth university to ask in as many months, and he wasn't sure how long he could keep them at bay.

Rudolfo's boot slipped on a patch of snow-crusted ice and

he stumbled. He felt a strong metal hand grip him before he could fall. He glanced over at Isaak. "Thank you."

Isaak nodded and waited until Rudolfo was steady before releasing him. They reached the bottom of the hill and followed the road back into town. Already, the forest between the hill and the town was thinning for new construction. Soon, Rudolfo's Seventh Forest Manor and the small town that surrounded it would grow into a city.

What would my father think of this? Rudolfo paused. Orphaned at twelve, he rarely thought about his father. But he thought about him more now that he stood on the edge of fatherhood.

A handful of Rudolfo's Gypsy Scouts fell in around them as they walked. They hadn't yet changed into their dress uniforms, and their rainbow-colored woolen trousers and shirts were damp from the forest. Uncharacteristically, they grinned at their general.

He smiled back at them. "I hear you've pulled together a Firstborn Feast like no other before it," he said to them.

Their grins widened and then vanished as First Captain Aedric approached from town. His face looked worried and he gripped a note in his hand. For a moment, he seemed to study Isaak and then fixed his eyes on Rudolfo. "I've just had two birds from the Wall."

Rudolfo stopped. They had inherited the watch on the Keeper's Wall when they took on rebuilding the library. The mountain range separated the Named Lands from the Churning Wastes, the ruins of the Old World. The Androfrancines had controlled access to the one pass until Sethbert broke their back and Petronus dissolved the Order, passing its role on to Rudolfo and his Ninefold Forest Houses.

Shepherd of the light, he thought.

"What is happening at the Wall?" He took the notes and read them quickly. Coded into the message was an emphatic urgency. A metal man, clothed in robes, claiming to be an Arch-Engineer of the Order's Office of Mechanical Science in a city that was now desolated. *I bear an urgent message for the hidden Pope, Petronus,* Rudolfo read. *Sanctorum Lux must be protected.*

He looked up from the note and turned to Isaak. "What is the name of the engineer who created you?"

Isaak blinked, his eyes flashing golden in the crisp twilight. "Brother Charles, Lord."

Rudolfo nodded. "Yes. Brother Charles. Arch-Engineer of the Androfrancine Office of Mechanical Science?"

Isaak nodded. "Yes, Lord."

He stroked his beard. "When was the last time you saw him?"

Gears whirred to life inside the metal man and he shuddered, venting steam into the cold night. "I . . ." The mechoservitor paused. "The evening before the city fell. He had given me my assignment and sent me with the Gray Guard escort into the spell vaults."

So it was possible that he could've escaped, Rudolfo thought. And perhaps he knew of Petronus—it certainly wasn't impossible, though the old man had surely kept his secret from most. But it did not explain the metal man.

"And we liberated all of your"—he searched for the proper word—"peers from Sethbert's camp?"

Isaak nodded. "I've accounted for my brothers."

Rudolfo nodded. He looked at Aedric now. "What do you think?"

Aedric's hands moved quickly into the sign language of the Gypsy Scouts. *I don't like it,* he signed. "I think we ride for the Keeper's Wall and see for ourselves what this is about."

Rudolfo looked to his men and then to his first captain. *They would go with me now, Firstborn Feast or not, if I said we must.* The scouts were sons of scouts and had served the general of the Wandering Army and lord of the Ninefold Forest Houses as their fathers before them had, raised on the knives and the powders. And Aedric himself was Rudolfo's best friend's firstborn son. Gregoric and Rudolfo had been close since childhood, and when Lord Jakob and his wife were murdered, Rudolfo had taken the turban and passed the First Captaincy to his friend. They'd fought together in many political skirmishes and helped divert resurging heresies at the Order's behest, equally earning their reputations as fierce leaders and formidable strategists. But Rudolfo knew the truth: A leader is only as capable as the men he commands, and his men were the best in the New World.

Their loyalty is nearly love, he realized. *They learn it from their fathers.* The reality of that gave him pause, and a thought pushed at his mind. He shoved it aside, forcing his attention to the matter at hand. "I concur with you, Aedric." Then he used the hand language of the Gypsy Scouts in such a way that none could possibly miss it: *But tomorrow morning is soon enough. We feast tonight as these men honor my first fatherhood.*

The Gypsy Scouts were silent, but Rudolfo's eyes darted over to see several of them grinning again. He smiled at them and inclined his head.

As they took to the road, making their way through the bustling streets of his growing tribe, Rudolfo brought back the thought he had pushed away. These men, he realized, were yesterday's children, and they would pass their knives to tomorrow's children soon enough. And in that brief time between, the world had changed again—and was still changing—as the Named Lands reeled and floundered from the loss of its Androfrancine shepherds. Still, the Gypsy Scouts would pass their knives onward, sharing what they learned from these precarious times.

And I will pass my knives, now, too, Rudolfo thought. He hoped they would be sharp and balanced for the world they were making.